RACHAEL TREASURE

The Dare

preface
publishing

Published by Preface 2009
First published by Penguin Books Australia 2007
under the title *The Rouseabout*

10 9 8 7 6 5 4 3 2 1

First published in Great Britain in 2009 by Preface Publishing
1 Queen Anne's Gate
London SW1H 9BT

An imprint of The Random House Group

www.rbooks.co.uk
www.prefacepublishing.co.uk

Addresses for companies within The Random House Group Limited
can be found at www.randomhouse.co.uk

The Random House Group Limited Reg. No. 954009

A CIP catalogue record for this book is available from
the British Library

ISBN 978 1 84809 086 6

The Random House Group Limited supports The Forest Stewardship
Council (FSC), the leading international forest certification organisation.
All our titles that are printed on Greenpeace-approved FSC-certified
paper carry the FSC logo. Our paper procurement policy can be found at
www.rbooks.co.uk/environment

Typeset by Palimpsest Book Production Limited
Grangemouth, Stirlingshire
Printed and bound in Great Britain by CPI Bookmarque Ltd,
Croydon CR0 4TD

THE DARE

Rachael Treasure lives on a sheep farm in Tasmania with her husband John and her children Rosie and Charlie. Together they breed and train kelpies, border collies and water stock. ... each year they travel to Gippsland, Victoria to assist with the Treasure family's cattle operations.

Rachael began her working life as a jillaroo (trainee farmhand) before attending Orange Agricultural College in New South Wales. She also has a BA (Communication) from Charles Sturt University, Bathurst. She worked as a rural journalist for *Tasmanian Country*, Rural Press publications, the *Weekly Times* and ABC rural radio, until she quit her day job for an adventure on a cattle station in Queensland and to begin her fiction-writing career.

For more information see Rachael's website at www.rachaeltreasure.com.

FOR MY MOTHER, JENNY SMITH

AND IN MEMORY OF MY GRANDMOTHERS,
EDNA MAY SMITH AND JOAN MARY WISE.

One

Kate Webster hung upside down on the spindly Hills hoist in the backyard of her rented house in Orange. She felt her temples pulse with blood and the bite of the clothesline's metal bars behind her knees. Her long dark hair hung down and brushed the brittle, neglected lawn. From other, leafier gardens, the smell of suburban dinners drifted over the fence into her own barren yard. Swinging gently, Kate raised a tacky plastic sheep trophy to the dusky pink sky. Gold plastic glinted in the evening light.

'Whoo-hoo! Victory is sweet!' she hollered. With her other hand, she lifted a chunky brown stubbie from the ground and clanked it against the bottle of the bloke hanging beside her. He looked cute, Kate thought. Even upside down, with the first-place blue ribbon tied about his head in a big kewpie-doll bow. Christ, she thought, as drunkenness rushed to her head. Did I win him too? What *was* his name again?

Kate thought back over her day. She was *supposed* to have been working, dishing out sound, serious advice to farmers at the Orange Field Day in her shapeless navy polo shirt with the Department of Agriculture logo stamped above her right boob.

Even though it was her first field day, she'd engaged the

1

farmers straightaway. It wasn't just her pretty young face that drew them in. It was also her earthiness, the fact that she was recognisably one of them; the way she casually kicked the dirt with the toe of her unpolished boot as if inspecting the soil and root systems of pastures, her arms folded across her chest. Standing shoulder to shoulder with the men as she talked. Despite her greenness within the department, Kate realised she could do this job on her ear.

So, not long after lunch, she'd done a runner from the department's display and entered herself in a sheep-counting competition. When her turn came, she relished being in the dusty yards with the sheep, instantly judging the sheep's flight zone, summing up how toey they would be. When she had them sussed she swung the gate open a little way, and as the lead sheep darted past she began to flick her hand in the sheep's direction, counting. Just as she did back home on the farm. She quickly tallied the big-framed wethers, scanning them with intense dark eyes. Three. Six. Nine. The sheep rattled past, lifting dust with pointed seashell hooves. When Kate reached one hundred she hooked her index finger into the pocket of her faded jeans. At two hundred, she slipped another finger in. Her other hand hovered above the mob as they rushed through the gate. The tail enders bunched and bustled beneath the fug of dust but Kate instinctively stepped towards them to slow the rush and expertly resumed the steady flow.

Then she was back in the rhythm of the count: 294, 297, 300. Another finger in the pocket, then six final sheep galloped past. The last one baulked before she shut the gate. She turned towards the lanky judge and gave him her tally as the crowd offered up a scattered clap. They watched the strong, curvy girl with the face of a country beauty lob the fence. Then they turned their attention to the next competitor.

At the end of the competition, trophy and blue ribbon in hand, Kate had made a beeline for the makeshift bar that leaned beneath a rusty corrugated-iron roof. She knew she should have headed back to the department's display to help her colleagues pack up. But surely one celebratory beer wouldn't hurt.

At the bar Kate washed the dust from her throat with a swig of ice-cold beer. The thinning crowd straggled past on their way home. Some had cattle canes, or freebies from the fencing companies, others had bags of brochures on pumps and the latest tractors. Tired mums pushed cranky kids in prams, while husbands trailed behind. The men glanced longingly at the bar. Kate turned her back on them and swigged again at her beer.

From the other end of the bar a young guy in a blue stock-and-station agent's shirt had nodded at her. He was wearing a big black cowboy hat, like Tim McGraw on the Country Music Channel. His jaw hadn't seen a razor for days and his already tanned skin was darkened even deeper with dust.

'Congratulations,' the stock agent said, a smile lifting one corner of his sly-dog mouth. 'Most blokes count in twos, but I noticed you can count in threes.'

'Yeah, well, I'm not "most blokes",' Kate said, sending him a cheeky smile that invited him to move over to her. He took up her sheep trophy and ran his fingers across the plastic ridges.

'Pretty rough conformation,' he said. 'You'd cull that one for sure.'

As he sat the trophy back on the bar and fingered the yellow tassels of her blue ribbon, Kate noticed how good his arms looked, strong and tanned, emerging from the casually rolled-up sleeves of his stockie's shirt. Pen and notebook in his shirt pocket. Mobile phone clipped to his plaited belt. A stock-standard stockie, Kate concluded. But a cute one.

'Another beer?' he asked.

'Sure,' said Kate. 'Who's counting?'

* * *

3

God, she thought now, as she looked at his black hat lying on the lawn beneath the Hills hoist. What *was* his name again? Was it Andrew? Mark? She shut her eyes and blood pumped behind them. She'd been upside down too long. When she opened her eyes again she was met with the vision of the stockie's flat, smooth stomach, which revealed itself as his shirt tails drooped towards the crackling dry lawn. Hair on his stomach trailed invitingly towards the silver buckle of his leather belt. He'll do, Kate thought, ramming her own shirt into her jeans so she didn't expose her soft, milky white tummy to him. She swigged on her beer again.

'I am Count Kate and I love to count! Ye-ah-ah-ah!' she sang out. '*Sesame Street*,' she explained. 'One of my regular shows. Love it.'

'You also like paddling pools and trikes, by the looks,' he said, nodding towards the cluster of colourful toys scattered around the yard.

'They belong to my dog, Sheila,' Kate said. 'She's spoilt rotten.'

At the sound of her name, Sheila emerged from her kennel on the back step to lick at Kate's upside-down face.

'And I love you too,' Kate said.

'Your kelpie obviously likes to give you tonguers,' said the stockie flirtily, his face turning slowly redder in the glow of the sinking sun.

'Tonguers and beer. That's what she likes.' Kate tried to prise the dog's liver-coloured lips apart and pour beer into her mouth. But the old dog was wise to the drunken version of Kate. She sighed and padded off to her mat, her long claws clicking on concrete.

'Not up for a beer, eh? More for me then!' Kate said, angling the beer to her upturned mouth. She felt the cool liquid fizz out her nostrils. Laughter spluttered from her lips, together with froth, beer and spit.

'Gawd! I hate bat-skolling,' she said, wiping her mouth with the back of her arm.

4

'You're a crazy girl. But I like it.'

The stockie swung nearer her so the Hills hoist shuddered. As he pressed his stubble-fringed lips to her mouth, Kate couldn't stop laughing. The whole clothesline shook. Suddenly, like a twig, it snapped. Kate's shoulder slammed the solid earth. The stockie fell with her, hitting the dust.

'Ow! I think I broke my bum bone,' he groaned.

Kate lay on her back next to him looking up at the evening sky beyond the garish orange tiles of the roof. She shook with laughter and wondered if she would wet herself. As she snorted with hilarity, the stockie rolled over to her, swiping the blue ribbon from his head before gathering her up. He kissed her hungrily with an open mouth, like he was eating a meat pie. His hands grappled under her shirt for her breasts, and he pressed his fingers on her as if he was fat-scoring the backs of prime lambs. As his hand slid across Kate's midriff, she pulled it away and moved it to her bum. She'd much rather he touch her there. They kissed like that on the suburban lawn in Orange, New South Wales.

Kate felt detached, as if she was watching it happen from outside herself, knowing she shouldn't. But as the stockie persisted and she tasted his beer and sweat, she felt the heat rise between her legs. She wanted to feel someone's skin against hers. Anyone's, really. A man to make her forget. This bloke would do. She pressed hard against him and plunged her hand into the stale warmth of his jeans.

But then the phone started to ring inside. It rang and rang. Kate knew who it was. She pulled back from him guiltily.

'I have to get that. I have to go,' she said.

Kate resisted waking. The pain of her hangover sliced through her scalp. Her guts rumbled and knotted like twisted sheets. She rolled over to blink at the dawn light invading the room through a crack in the blind. She pulled the pillow over her head but she knew there was no escaping it. She could still hear Nell in the next room.

'Mummy! Mummy! Muuuum!'

Nell's voice quavered as her calls turned into cries. Kate rolled onto her back, looked at the fly-spotted ceiling and groaned. The stockie from the field day was still in her bed.

'Oi,' she said, prodding him in the gut so that he grunted. Through clenched teeth she said, 'You have to go. You have to get out of here. I don't want my daughter to see you.'

'Daughter?' he murmured into the pillow. '*Daughter*? You said you had a *dog*, not a daughter.'

Just then, her housemate Tabby began thudding on the door.

'Kate. For God's sake . . . get up! Nell needs you and I'm not doing the rounds this morning!'

Kate didn't need X-ray vision to know that Tabby was standing there outside her bedroom door. She'd be wrapped in her glowing white bathrobe, her blonde hair swept back in a neat ponytail, her face made up and ready for work.

Kate also knew that Nell would be trying to drag furniture over to the door in her room so she could reach the handle and get out. She'd have big fat tears on her red cherub cheeks. Her pull-up night nappy would be sodden with wee and she'd have morning hair. Sticky-up hair, soft-as-fairy hair, Kate thought. A cocktail of love and guilt swamped her. She glanced at the man beside her. The dark hair on his outspread arms suddenly looked coarse and ugly. She wished he would go.

'Hell,' said Kate, jumping, as her clock radio blasted out Lee Kernaghan.

'There ain't nothing like a country crowd, little bit crazy and a little bit loud. We've got our own way of turning things upside down . . .' sang Lee.

With a jolt, the song's lyric reminded Kate of the night before and a sudden vision of the Hills hoist looking like a broken TV antenna with its snapped limb and slack wires made her cringe. Then Kate remembered the call from her

6

aunt Maureen. Her stern voice cutting through Kate's alcohol-addled brain, demanding to know where the hell was she? And why hadn't she come to pick up Nellie? Then, Kate remembered, an hour or so after the call, Maureen had turned up. Her lips were thin with fury as she deposited a ruffled, sleepy Nellie on the doorstep, while Kate tried hard to seem sober and pretended there wasn't a naked stranger passed out in her bed.

Kate pulled back the doona and groaned as she hauled on her grubby dressing-gown. She tossed her hair up into a purple band that had long ago lost its elasticity. Then she threw the bloke's clothes onto his dozing body and shoved his hat over his head.

'Bugger off now please, Tim McGraw,' she said, before stepping painfully on the plastic sheep trophy lying on the floor.

'Ouch!' she said, hopping from the room.

Steam rose from Kate's coffee cup and swirled in a beam of sunlight. Kate slouched with her head in her hands as Nell sat beside her, banging her legs rhythmically against her chair. Nell held up her Vegemite toast and made plane noises before cramming the soggy slice into her mouth.

'Mummy sick! Mummy sick. Bleaaarrrck,' she said, sticking out her brown-smeared tongue. Kate gave her a weak smile.

'Just eat your breakfast, stirrer.'

Nellie grinned so hard that chewed toast tumbled from her mouth and plopped onto the tiled floor. Behind the sliding glass door, through cloudy pupils, Sheila eyed the crumbs, drooling. Kate sighed. She hadn't fed the poor dog last night and she was out of dog food again. Tabby strode in, snatching up her keys from the kitchen bench.

'Shall I cook again tonight?' she said. 'I've got netball though, so dinner won't be until 7.30.'

'Sure,' said Kate queasily.

Tabby glanced at the clock, picked up her sleek black briefcase and arched an eyebrow at Kate.

'You'll be late for work,' Tabby said. She headed out the door to her sweet-smelling banker's car, where Kate pictured her sliding her tiny, neat bottom onto the clean upholstery. Kate jumped at the slam of the car door. It said it all. She swallowed down a wave of nausea as she gulped her coffee.

'I want a drink too, Mummy! Drink! Drink!' said Nell, holding out her grubby little hands.

'All right.' Kate sighed, pushing herself up from the table. 'A "please" would be nice.'

Sheila whined at the door and gave two quick scratches on the glass. Kate let out a noise of frustration and flung the door open. She threw a piece of cold toast, margarine congealing in dobs on the crusts, and Sheila caught it with a crocodile snap.

'I'll take you for a walk tonight,' she said, slamming the door.

'Must be hard keeping a working dog in town,' said a voice from the doorway. Kate turned to see the Hills-hoist man standing in his boxer shorts. She leapt across the cool kitchen lino and pushed him out of Nell's view.

'Shower's that way,' she said, pointing down the hall. Behind the grimy glass, Sheila began to bark loudly, her hackles raised.

'Siddown, Sheila!' growled Kate.

'Who's that, Mummy?' Nellie asked. When Kate ignored her question, Nellie thudded her juice on the table. Orange liquid splattered across the floor and up the wall.

'The plumber, Nell,' Kate said. 'It's the plumber. Come to fix the shower.' Nell rubbed her little hands through her hair and frowned.

'I need toilet, Mummy.'

'But the plumber's using the bathroom.'

'*Toilet!*' Kate watched Nell's cheeks turn pink and her jaw jut out.

8

'Oh, *Nell!*'

Leaning both elbows on the kitchen bench, Kate covered her face with her hands. God, she thought. How did life get so crazy?

Two

Kate flung a browning apple core from the twin-cab ute and hastily brushed yesterday's sandwich crumbs from Nell's booster seat. She stood back and watched her little girl clamber up and wait to be strapped in.

As Kate turned the engine over, she looked at Nell in the rear-vision mirror, noting her unbrushed hair and mismatching clothes. Vegemite already stained her shirt front. Kate sighed. What sort of a mother was she? It looked like Nell was coming home from day care, not going to it. She pulled out into the suburban street and memories of her journey from Tasmania to the mainland three years earlier swelled in her. Her unplanned journey to motherhood. It had been just weeks after the Rouseabout B&S Ball. She was on her way to agricultural college, travelling to the mainland for the first time in her scrappy little Subaru ute. There'd been no need for childseats and dual-cab utes back then.

On a dozey summer evening Kate had driven her ute into the open mouth of the ship's hull. On the wet gleaming deck, Kate had looked up to the cherry-red towers that belched diesel fumes into the crisp air. Two blasts of the horn, the glug and shudder of reverse-thrust engines and the town of Devonport slid away into the distance. People waving from the rocky groyne became tiny specks. She felt the pinch of sadness that none of her family were there, waving. None of what was left of her family.

She recalled the 'too cool for school' way she'd slung herself onto the thick upholstered couches in the ship's bar and sipped at a Bundy, hating the aftertaste left by the town-water ice.

Here she was, a fresh-faced Tasmanian country girl, raised on the windswept east coast. A girl who wore Blundstone boots for work and cowgirl boots for play. A girl with an old kelpie curled up on a blanket in the ship's dog trailer, below in the hold. Parked near the dogs was 'Thelma', Kate's bomby old Subaru, its mottled paintwork covered with B&S stickers across the tailgate. It was all she'd needed then. A half-reliable ute with a tattered front seat for Sheila to sit on and a torn tarp to keep most of the rain off her bags in the back. And one functioning wiper that scraped haphazardly across the driver's windscreen.

Back then, she had been off on an adventure. She'd buried the memory of her mother's death, turned her back on her father and screamed at her father's new woman before she'd gone. She'd only paused momentarily to kiss her brother Will and hug her horse Matilda goodbye, and take one last look at the farm. Bronty. Her home.

Australia's mainland was hers to explore. There would be B&Ss and boys and wild, crazy nights with new friends. Along with that, she was hungry to learn. She would soak up all the agricultural knowledge they could give her at college, so she could grow to be like her mother – a woman with a vision for the future of farming.

Kate vowed to take over where Laney had left off, to make a deep and stubborn furrow in the agricultural industry – the industry that *should* be recognised by everyone as the heart-beat of the country. Kate swigged on her rum and cast her eyes about the ship's crowd. She heard her mother's voice in her head. 'It'll be your children, Kate, the farmers of the future, who will rescue all of these people. They don't know it, but food is the most important thing. Farmers are the key to the future. And you can be part of it if you choose.'

That night on the ship there was only one thing that drowned out Laney's voice in Kate's head. It was a niggling suspicion, deep within her body, that she had made a huge mistake. She thought of the box that she'd tucked in the side pocket of her backpack. The pregnancy-test kit.

Kate had finished her drink, then shouldered her pack and gone out onto the deck to watch the mutton-birds skitter above the thick dark swell of Bass Strait. When her fingers were numbed from the icy wind, she pulled open the heavy door and made her way unsteadily along the rolling ship's corridor. Then she locked herself in a swaying toilet cubicle that held the faint stench of vomit and unpacked the kit to find out if what she feared was true.

She remembered the asphyxiating feeling of the ship's toilet cubicle and the roll and slam of the hull on the unrelenting swell. Her shaking hands had ripped at the foil packet and taken out the plastic stick. When she saw two blue lines screaming 'positive', her whole world had rolled too. She was pregnant. Alone and pregnant, wishing like hell she'd never gone to the Rouseabout B&S ball and done what she had done.

Early the next morning, when the impatient queue of cars, caravans and trucks clattered out from the ship's belly and into Melbourne's crowded centre, Kate had pulled over at a phonebox on the Esplanade that ran parallel to the brown, newly combed beach. Her mind scrambled in panic. She'd automatically dialled her father's number, hoping to reach Will. Instead, her stepmother Annabelle had answered.

'Is Will there?' Kate said.

'He's out and about.'

'Oh. Is Dad there?'

'I'll put him on.' Kate heard the phone clunk down. 'Henry!' she heard Annabelle call. A moment later, her father's voice.

'You're on the other side then?'

'Yes.' Kate struggled to hold back her tears. She couldn't say any more.

'Kate? What's going on?' Her father's voice sounded annoyed. Kate imagined his cooling coffee sitting beside his congealing porridge.

She blurted it out. 'I'm pregnant.'

There was silence. For a long time, she could hear the clicks over the optic fibres that lay beneath the seabed. A painful silence stretched across the water from Melbourne to Tasmania, right to her father's ear. Kate was sure he hadn't said it out loud, but in her head he shouted, 'Silly girl! I knew you'd do something like this to me! Stupid bloody girl!'

When he at last did speak he quietly said, 'What are you going to do?'

'I don't know.' She desperately wanted him to say come home. But instead, across the coldness of the line, with a southerly wind at her back, Kate heard his words.

'Better keep on going to your Auntie Maureen's. She can sort you out better than I can.'

Kate knew deep down he didn't mean it that way. Like a slap of rejection. But it was what she had been looking for from him back then, wasn't it? That last severance between father and daughter.

She slammed the phone back in its cradle and ran to her ute. Holding Sheila's head in her lap, Kate bunkered down in her ute between Port Phillip Bay and the steep cliff of the city's skyscrapers, not knowing what to do. Wishing like hell she had her mother with her, here on this earth.

For an hour she sat stroking Sheila's silky ears and thinking of the tiny cluster of cells dividing inside her. She could book herself into a clinic. Have a termination and then be on her way to college. Life would go on as normal. But then, she thought of her mother. She thought of the seeds in the attic at home on Bronty that Laney used to cup in the palm of her hand and move about with her fingertips.

'The life in these seeds,' Laney would say, looking wide-eyed at her children, 'is a miracle beyond comprehension.'

The seeds had been collected by Henry's mother and his grandmother and great-grandmother before that. Each generation of women had carefully catalogued and stored them in beautifully crafted wooden drawers beneath the sloping roof of the attic. Seeds from healthy vegetables that had been grown and collected since settlement. Seeds deposited carefully in browning paper envelopes decorated with tiny trails of hungry silverfish that mingled with the swirl of three generations of Webster women's handwriting. There were tiny black pinpricks or smoother round orbs, all kinds of shapes and sizes of seed from Bronty's extensive colonial garden.

One day, when Kate was about ten years old, her mother told her a story as she gazed at the tiny black seeds, some no bigger than fly spots.

'Your gran so desperately wanted a brother or sister for your dad,' Laney said. 'But babies sometimes don't come when we plan them. Life's all about healthy seeds, and having healthy soil to grow them in. And babies are the same – you can't have a baby without a healthy seed and a healthy womb. That's why you've got no uncles or aunts. God only gave your gran one healthy and precious seed, and that seed was your dad. And look what a bloody good tree he's grown into.'

Kate remembered her mother in the Bronty vegetable garden, stooping to point out the curl and twitch of a runner-bean vine that had clambered its way over Kate and Will's lopsided scarecrow. How she encouraged her children to crunch their white teeth through snowpeas and gorge themselves on strawberries until Will's already pink shining cheeks broke out in hives.

Kate knew in her heart what her mother would say about the baby. She would tell Kate to let this seed grow, and make a life, in case there were no more seeds within her. This might be the only one.

14

She sat up straight, resolved. She put her hand on her flat tummy, feeling as if part of her mother was now embedded in this baby. Kate fired up the engine of her old ute and drove on to New South Wales.

Three

It had started to drizzle. Kate sat at the wheel of the ute, the windscreen wipers sighing across glass. Nell imitated their screech-swipe repetitions with the sway of her head. Annoyed, Kate swore at the traffic lights winking red. She cursed herself for having such a shocking hangover and for once again picking up an anonymous bloke so publicly. Her housemate, Tabby, was right, as usual. She would be late for work. Horribly late.

'Sssshit, shit,' mimicked Nell in the back. Kate gave her a stern glance.

Outside the day-care centre in Orange's leafy city street, Kate hoisted Nell onto her hip and slung a dusty nappy bag over her shoulder. She reached to open the high child-proof gate, fingers grappling with the stubborn plastic catch. At last it opened with a whine. Buggered if she could get the hang of those things. Before she went in, Kate panted a few breaths into her palm then inhaled deeply through her nose. Did she still smell of grog from the night before? On the drive over she'd been having flashbacks of Clothes-line Man and his stupefied face when she'd given him his marching orders. Now she was burping up after-rum bile. Fiona the childcarer would surely notice.

The shouts of children grew louder as Kate made her way

inside, ducking under wonky colourful fishes that swam on nylon threads from the ceiling, as if fishermen lurked in the rafters.

'I see you're admiring our fish theme,' sang Fiona brightly. 'Oh, look. You've done Nellie's hair with gel. Very pretty,' she said, taking the bag from Kate's shoulder.

'Ah. No. I think you'll find that's orange juice and Vegemite toast,' Kate said.

'Isn't Mummy a trick?' Fiona said as Kate picked a glob of chewed-up bread from Nell's curly almost-white hair. 'What time will you collect her tonight?'

But Kate knew what she meant. *Don't be late again.*

'Same time as usual,' Kate said.

As Fiona reached for Nell, Nell's rose-pink bottom lip began to pout and she turned her head away. Wrapping her arms around Kate, she kicked her little legs and screamed.

'Nooooo! Don't want to!'

'Come on, Nell. Mummy's got to go to work.'

'Nooo!'

'Remember what Mummy told you? Mum has to work to pay the rent. And to buy clothes and things. And food . . . so you can throw it on the floor. I'll be back soon. I promise.'

Prising Nell's arms from around her neck, Kate passed the sobbing child to Fiona. God, why wasn't it getting any easier, Kate wondered?

'Look over here, Nell. We've got a new birdie. Do you want to see his pretty yellow feathers?'

Fiona winked at Kate and began to walk away. Kate tried to shut out Nell's sobs that came in jagged gasping breaths. A lump rose to her throat. She wanted to hug and kiss Nell and hold her, and never let her go. She wanted to fall down on the floor, right here, right now, and sob into her little girl's hair.

I'm still a child too, Kate wanted to scream. *And I want my mummy! Where's my mummy?* But instead, she turned and quickly walked away.

As she sat outside the day-care centre in the ute, trying to settle herself, Kate remembered the blustery bitter spring days on her Aunt Maureen's farm on the outskirts of Orange. She had just turned twenty and her stomach was leading the way wherever she walked. She felt like the round dome of skin on the front of her body belonged to someone else. She was seven months pregnant and five months into her first-year studies at the agricultural college. And she was missing her mother every single day.

She seemed to spend most of her time at Aunt Maureen's kitchen table with her university texts spread out before her and her hand absently roving in circles over the mound of her unborn child. But when she wasn't bowing her head over an assignment or hiding her pregnant body behind the desk in the university library, Kate was out on the farm, trying hard to conjure the paddocks of home from her memory. She'd offered to check the ewes and lambs for Aunt Maureen and Uncle Tony every morning and evening, just to get away.

As she eased her body awkwardly through the taut fence-wires Kate found her centre of gravity shifting each day. Despite her strong legs, she'd tackle the hills only to find her energy draw away from her. She'd feel her breath catch in the claws of her rib cage, not sure if it was the growing baby or panic that made it so hard to draw air into her lungs.

One very bleak day, when the clouds seemed to hug the neat grapevine-streaks on the hillside, Kate sank onto the cold pasture and put her head in her hands. Pregnant. At twenty. In this strange countryside. Longing for home. Her mother. Her life. Her island. This was not how it was supposed to turn out.

Here on the Tablelands of New South Wales, there was no outlook across the tumblesome grey water of Bass Strait. No sea breeze to bring her the salty freshness of home. Just rolling, naked hills and bedraggled clusters of bushland, sedated with heat in the summer and sulking beneath fog in the winter. She found herself constantly comparing it to the wildness of the angled coastal scrub that clung to the wind-bashed hills of her father's east-coast farm.

From where she sat, Kate spotted a grey blob in the distance, much like a stump or a boulder on a sloping hillside. She knew it was one of her uncle's ewes and that the old girl was down, cast on her round-bellied side with her hooves stuck in the air. Straining and straining to push the lamb from her soft pink folds. Kate gagged at the thought. As she hauled herself up and trudged over to the sheep, morning sickness washed through her like a wave. Morning sickness that the doctor had said would go at thirteen weeks. A queasiness she endured along with the reflux, the rashes, the aches in her joints and the intense itchiness of her skin. But even the sheep-dogs having a crap on the tussocks still made her gag . . . just the thought of their slimy turds.

Kneeling awkwardly at the rear end of the ewe, she slid her hand in, hoping to find hooves. Not a head, nor a tail, but hooves. Once she had the tiny bony black ankles in her grasp she muttered something comforting to the ewe, then pulled. The ewe let out a strangled baritone bleat as pain ripped through her body and her legs jerked straight. As Kate pulled, she watched the lamb's head and shoulders slip through, wet in its sac, so large it seemed to split the ewe's pelvis and vagina in half.

God, this will be me soon, Kate thought as she heaved again. She listened to the ewe grunt and saw the glazed look of shock pass over her yellow-grass eyes. The lamb slid out, dead, its head elongated and grotesque inside the translucent birth sac. Its tongue poking out, blue. Its body still wet and warm, streaked with globs of yellow membrane and blood. Steam rose from its side into the clear morning air, and with it the smell of rotting meat. It had died inside the ewe days ago.

Kate wiped her slimy hands on the ewe's flanks and thought about the baby fluttering with life inside her. She grabbed the ewe's wool above her bony hips and hauled her hind legs up.

'C'mon, girl. Try to stand.'

Kate watched the ewe totter off, dark crimson placenta trailing from her, her head down, giddy with pain, legs shaking. The dead lamb forgotten for the moment, from shock.

Kate picked the lamb up by the back legs and began to carry it home to throw in the incinerator. As she walked, its head bumped along the ground. It was a big ram lamb.

Kate thought of her mother, and she thought again of death. The way death had taken years to steal Laney. Cancer stripping the flesh slowly from her mother's bones and sucking the colour from her skin. Skin that became so dry and brittle it rustled like rice paper when Kate gently rolled Laney over in the bed to wash her back or change the sheets. Towards the end, the only place Kate found light and life had been in Laney's eyes. Only there could she recognise the mother she had known.

After a while, the hocks of the heavy lamb bit into Kate's knuckles. She couldn't just sling it in the bush like she would at home. There were no Tassie devils in this countryside to crunch through the bones of the dead, leaving just a scattering of lamb's teeth or a tiny ivory hoof in the bracken ferns. She looked down at the speckled little lamb and wondered why she didn't feel sad for it. She imagined having her own stillborn baby out there in the paddock. How would she feel to lose it?

Kate's shoulder was aching now from carrying the lamb and her breath was coming quickly. Breathing for two. She thought about the way her mother had heaved for air when she last climbed the stairs to the attic at Bronty. She'd wanted to see it one final time. To feel it. Kate now worried what her father's new wife might do to it. Had Annabelle been up there, hauling down the old hinged stairs with the hand-worn rope? Had the attic whispered its secrets to Annabelle? Secrets that it had held for four generations of Bronty women. Surely, Kate thought, that woman from Sydney wouldn't dare touch what was kept there. Would she?

20

She pictured Annabelle, with her whitened teeth, enamel nails and chemical-blonde hair. Kate wished that she'd got a ladder and with her pocketknife cut the rope short so the ceiling door remained shut and out of reach to Annabelle. That way her father's new wife might forget the room that sat above the house and it could remain cut off, like an island. Perhaps she would ask Will, the next time she phoned him, if he had ever thought to do the same.

Back at Maureen and Tony's farmyard, Kate flung the lamb into the whispering ash that lay swirling at the bottom of the 44 in the spring winds. She'd burn it later. As she stomped back to the warmth of her aunt's kitchen she picked at the crusted afterbirth on her reddened hands before plunging them under a hot tap.

At the table, she tried to force down Weet-Bix with warm milk. She had an hour before she had to be at uni, where she would waddle into the austere lecture theatre. As she sat in the front row, not game to make a show of hauling her large body up the stairs, she'd feel the eyes of the other students clamp on her and she'd feel herself almost die inside from shame.

She'd worn her Wrangler jeans as long as she could, until her leather belt had run out of holes. The fabric of her RM Williams T-shirts had stretched out in front of her, making the horns on the Long Horn logo extra long. And when, finally, she'd given in and bought maternity clothes, she still wouldn't abandon her Canadian cowgirl boots even though she struggled to shove her swollen feet inside their leather confines. A pregnant girl in cowgirl boots. She'd laugh at her image in the mirror. She recalled how she'd stood drunk at the bar in her new maternity clothes, making fun of herself, showing off the wide stretch of elastic that rose up and over her entire bulging gut. Boasting it was all beer in there, not a baby.

The boys had looked on incredulously while the girls laughed. Yet she could tell they were shocked. Shocked that she was drinking. Swigging on cans as if she didn't care.

Shocked that she was their age and pregnant in their midst. Shocked that she thought she belonged.

Now, Kate looked sadly at the cheery yellow and blue flowers painted on the bricks outside the day-care centre. She sighed. She knew she didn't belong to the world in there either. She fired up the ute's engine and floored it, revving away down the street.

Four

Kate sat at her desk clutching a box of KFC. The partitions in the Department of Agriculture's open-plan office did little to hide her hung-over state. Dimity from accounts, with her up-turned nose and round glasses, soon ferreted her out.

'Heard you were a bit of a *Tassie devil* at the field day,' she teased.

Kate shrugged and offered her a chip. When Dimity shook her mousy head, Kate crammed a chip into her own mouth. She was halfway through chewing it into a potatoey pulp when Buzz Thompson appeared beside her desk. She looked up at him.

'In my office. Now.' As Buzz walked off, Kate noted his bull-like neck and the cauliflower ears that gave away his passion for playing front-row rugby union.

In Buzz's office Kate threw herself down in a chair and began to swivel from side to side, as if trying to dodge his steady gaze.

'What was yesterday about?'

'What do you mean?' Kate asked.

'You know what I mean.'

'Oh! The sheep counting. Yes. I won it. Great PR for the department, huh? Show the cockies that some of us bureaucrats have practical know-how.'

'That's not what I'm talking about.'

Flashing to Kate's mind came the picture of herself with the stockie in the field-day car park. She was pressed up against a mud-splattered Hilux ute, too drunk to care about passers-by as he groped her breasts beneath her Department of Ag. uniform shirt. The taste of beer and the tangy smell of stale manly sweat.

Kate cast her eyes down to her lap.

'You've already had two warnings,' Buzz said and all Kate could do was nod.

'We took you on because you were bright. Very bright. But it isn't working out for you here. I think you're aware that your three-month review is due?'

Kate had a sense of what was coming. She looked at Buzz's ruddy face and his tousled sandy hair.

'I just can't keep you on,' he said. Kate was about to speak, but he held up his hand to silence her. 'I know your personal situation. That's why I've made some enquiries and I've recommended a transfer to Tasmania.'

Kate couldn't help herself.

'Transfer to Tasmania!' she cried. Laughter spluttered up. 'You make me sound like a convict!'

'I'm serious, Kate. You're not cut out to be in an office every day. You know that. And with your little girl, you need more flexibility. They're crying out for departmental field agronomists and rural advisors in your district in Tasmania. Because of the politics down there, there's been a big injection of funding into that area. You've got enough experience under your belt now for them to be really keen on you. You'll be able to work the hours that suit you. Maybe even work from your family farm.'

'*Family*,' Kate said incredulously. 'The only family I have is here.' An image of her father came to her, sitting rigid at the helm of his tractor, harrowing the black loamy soil in lines straighter and neater than a pinstriped suit. The way he seemed to scrutinise her face, searching out her mother in her looks. Yet

24

he seemed always stung when he found Laney's image there because she, Kate, never quite measured up. She'd see him flinching from her over-loud laugh, a replica of her mother's. Even here, sitting in Buzz's office, Kate felt the sting of her father's disappointed gaze. Panic gripped her at the thought of going back to Tasmania with Nell. She couldn't go. Even though Will was there to prop her up, she couldn't go.

Back in Tasmania, people would take note of the dark-haired mother and the fair-haired child and they'd work it out sooner or later, how Nell had come to be. They'd look at the girl and nod knowingly about the father. Sweat trickled down the small of Kate's back.

'Look,' Buzz continued. 'I'm doing you a favour. *Another* favour. Either you apply for the position or I'll terminate your work within the department with no reference from me. I'm sure I've only heard half the things you've got up to in the past few months.'

Kate blinked, her eyes sliding away from him. Since she'd moved into town from Maureen's farm, her private life had spun out of control and she knew Nell was bearing the brunt of it. Kate was bright enough to wing her way through work, good enough with clients to satisfy their needs, arsey enough to toss together a farm-funding application so that it shone out above all others. But with Nell she couldn't wing it. Kate knew that to be a mother, to be there for her little girl, she couldn't just fake it. If she lost her job, she could risk losing herself, and then maybe even her child. Kate bit her lower lip. Buzz stood up and put a comforting hand on her shoulder.

'Dimity has the details about the job in Tasmania and I expect you to apply today,' he said sternly, but with kindness in his eyes. 'And there'll be no farewell parties either.'

As Kate walked back to her desk, her first reaction was one of dismay. But it was quickly followed by a sense of excitement. She was free. She could bundle up Nell and hit the road. Travel across Australia. Work up north at anything. Fruit picking. Burger making. Rouseabouting. Drive until they found themselves. But then the reality set in. Travelling across remote Australia was no place for Nell, especially now she was not far away from starting school.

Kate slumped at her desk and thought for a moment. She pictured her freckle-faced friend Janie, back in Tassie with her chubby baby twins and her rock-solid farmer husband, Dave.

Janie diligently sent over birthday presents for Nell and Kate. She regularly emailed photos of the twins and news of their milestones . . . when they had first smiled, first rolled over, first eaten solids. She signed off her emails with 'Miss you', and umpteen hugs and kisses. Kate had written back, but more briefly and never honestly about her life with Nell.

Janie seemed absorbed in motherhood, and thriving within it. Compared to Janie, Kate felt like a failure. But perhaps, Kate thought, if she went back, Janie could help her become the mother she should be for Nell.

She clicked on her email program. She would write to Janie and ask her what to do. But as she started to type, emotions welled up in her and the words got tangled on screen. She wrote about how lost she felt. That she was a negligent mother. That she was a slack friend. That she was out of control with men, searching for something in them yet not knowing what that something was. A page in, re-reading her melodramatic words, Kate scoffed at herself before hitting the delete button. Janie didn't need to know all that.

Kate thought back to the time when she and Janie had first become friends. Janie had just ditched school and was working at her parents' garage, opening up shop when her mother was too drunk or stoned to get out of bed. Wishing her dad would get back from his interstate trucking haul to help tally the accounts, but dreading his return in case he took to her mother again with his angry fists.

Sitting behind the messy counter stacked with chocolates, oil filters, fuses, fanbelts and past-their-use-by chips with a blow heater roasting her feet, Janie would pore over the frothy dresses of Hollywood brides in the latest *Who* magazine, all the while sucking on a red lolly-snake.

Kate, on her L's, would drive into the tiny servo with her dad, the wheels of their ute making the bell ring *cha-ching*. As her dad glugged diesel into the ute, Kate would amble in and buy a roll of barley sugars for her mother. Glucose to keep her body going just that bit longer.

'How's your mum?' Janie would ask.

'Still crook,' Kate would say. 'How's yours?'

'Still useless,' Janie would say.

'I wish mine would get better.'

'I wish mine would get dead.'.

And then they'd both laugh, feeling a friendship growing between them. They were both living grown-up lives, both isolated from their peers, who were worrying about pimples and pubes and schoolwork. But Janie and Kate were tangled in tragedy that made them older than their years. And that's how their friendship had formed; two girls who relied on each other. Inspired each other. Two girls who would never normally have mixed.

Kate loved Janie's directness and the bitter humour she dealt out about her family, yet she also saw and appreciated Janie's kindness. And Janie loved the way Kate could take her out of her bleak petrol-drenched world and into the rolling landscape of Bronty on horseback. They'd ride through she-oaks and Oyster Bay pines and stands of ironbarks clinging to stony outcrops, then down onto the flats, and on towards the sea, the soil turning from rich red to sandy. Kate could see them now, on the Bronty beach, at sixteen, swigging on cans of warm illicit rum that they'd stashed in their back-packs, sitting bareback on the horses. Janie's brown legs against the chestnut belly of the horse, her long, curly blonde hair, darkened by saltwater, and her freckled face turned upwards, laughing, in the direction of the sun.

Staring at the blank screen Kate began to type. Short and sweet, she told herself, like Janie herself. Short and sweet.

'G'day Janie. Been given the arse at work. Should Nell and I come home? Whaddyareckon?' Then she hit the send button.

Next, she rang Will's mobile number. Silence on the line and then the robotic sound of ringing. Would it go straight to message bank? Hearing Will's friendly voice on the recording always brought his image to life and Kate could clearly picture her big, burly brother's shining black eyes and messy black hair set off by his ruddy farm-boy cheeks. Will's earthy charm reached everyone, including the farm animals, who followed him with their eyes. Pure adoration from his dogs, devotion from his horses. Trust from the sheep and cattle that moved around quietly in the presence of his steady ways.

Will could turn his hand to anything. His welds were perfection, his fencing stays were square, his fertiliser mixes and seed ratios were measured to exacting specifications. And he always had energy for everyone. Energy for the farm. For his father. For Kate and her drunken midnight phonecalls. Even for Annabelle when she needed cajoling. He seemed to ignore the bumps and furrows of their fractured family life by burying himself in the work of Bronty. He and Kate rarely spoke of their mother.

Kate wondered now how he'd take the news that she'd been sacked. When at last he answered the phone he sounded breathless, clearly busy at something on the farm.

'You're not a recording? It is the real Will I'm speaking to?'

'Live and larger than life,' he said. 'How's my sis and her little Smellie?'

'Good. I'm good. She's good. We're good.'

'And . . . ?'

Kate glanced about the office. Dimity ducked her head and resumed her work. Kate swivelled her chair so her back was to her and lowered her voice.

'Buzz has just sacked me.' As she spoke, she felt the prickle of tears surprise her.

'Ah, *Kate*.' She could hear it in Will's voice, his deep concern, his frustration at her. But she could also hear his love.

'Well, not exactly the sack . . . but close enough. He's lined up a transfer to Tassie. There's even a chance to set up a home office. What should I do?'

'You know what I think. It's simple.'

'But I can't come home, Will.'

'You can, Kate. You *can* come home.'

'But . . .'

'There's no buts. It's time. I'll look after you both, I promise. And Dad'll be fine. I'll sort him.'

'And Annabelle?'

'Leave her to me. I'll fix her.'

'But—'

'Kate,' Will's voice cut firmly across hers, 'a good job is being handed to you on a plate. You'd be stupid not to take it.'

'But—'

'*Kate*, Mum would want Nell and you home, here, at Bronty, no matter what. You know that.'

Kate fell silent. Will had played his best hand and she felt her bravado melt away. She was scared of being alone in the world with a small child and no job. She was tired of always wondering what life would be like if she moved back home.

She sighed.

'I need you down here, Kate,' Will said. 'It's time we got this seed idea off the ground. I need you to start that. So come home, please.' He paused. 'I'd like to share Nell's life too. You hog her all the time over there! Come home.'

'I'll think about it,' was all she could give him before hanging up. As the rumour of her 'transfer' spread through the office like wildfire, Kate dropped her face into her hands. Could she really do it? Could she go home?

She recalled the last time she'd seen Will, when he'd gingerly ducked his head around the maternity-ward door. He was carrying a silver and blue balloon that announced, 'It's a boy!'

'Sorry,' he said, nodding towards a pink-swaddled Nell,

who was sleeping in the perspex crib beside the bed. He handed Kate the balloon. 'Only one left in the hospital shop. Seems there's been a run on girls in here.' Then he spoke with less bravado. 'Aunt Maureen phoned to tell me you'd had her. How are you, Sis?'

Kate started to cry. Will was in some ways like their father; so cautious, so measured. Yet here he was. He'd dropped everything and flown from Hobart to Sydney, then taken a train all the way out to Orange just to see her. He brought with him all the memories of home. As she hugged him she could smell the sea air on his jacket and the faint earthy scent of the old split-timber shearing shed. Kate shut her eyes. If Will knew about the arrival of the baby then her dad must know too. Why, then, hadn't he come? Or even called? Will sensed her hurt.

'Dad had to stay to look after the farm. He said to say congratulations.'

Still traumatised by the birth, her hormones running riot, Kate cried even harder. Had her father really said that? She felt so ashamed. The shame of Will seeing her with a baby. The shame that her father knew she now had a child.

'Hey,' Will soothed as he held her close. 'She's a beautiful baby. There's nothing to cry about.'

But there was, Kate thought. She was just twenty and she had a baby! And her mother wasn't here. What would life be like now? Will held her at arm's length.

'Did it hurt?' he asked shyly. Kate rolled her eyes.

'*Hurt? Hurt!* The whole baby thing is a bloody conspiracy. Women who've had kids lie to you. When I was pregnant, they said, "You'll forget all about the pain once the baby arrives." Crap! I'll never forget that pain. Never. Just be thankful you're male.'

When she'd first arrived at the hospital with every muscle tensed, Kate tried hard to listen to the gentle commands of the midwives, who helped her move about on the big double bed. It was a bed designed for women and their partners to share in the 'joy' of the birth. As the labour pains worsened, the room closed in, so all Kate knew was that bed. The taut blue sheets getting more and more scrunched and the plump pillows becoming grimier with sweat as the pain ripped through her in waves, hour after hour. The bed became both her haven and an island of horror all at once.

'Breathe through it, Kate. You're doing well,' the midwife soothed.

'I can't do it!' Kate screamed after the hours ran into one blinding stretch of time. 'I can't! It hurts too much.' Pain hijacked her mind and she felt she would go mad, or die. 'I'm scared,' she sobbed as sweat trickled from her brow, sticking strands of black hair to her scalp. Another contraction. She clutched the pillow, knuckles white, teeth clenched.

'What are you scared of?' the midwife asked calmly.

Kate wanted to say she was scared of dying, like the ewes, or of giving birth to a perfect, but dead, little lamb. But another contraction hit her and all she could do was crouch on all fours and grunt through it. The next thing she knew, Aunt Maureen was by her side, looking ruffled from discovering late in the day that Kate had gone into labour at college that morning. She felt Maureen rubbing her back and heard her soothing voice.

It felt like her mother was there now. Kate calmed a little. The midwife was handing her a corrugated plastic pipe with a blue mouthpiece on the end.

'Suck it in, Kate. It'll help. Trust me on this one,' she urged.

And it did. Kate felt herself float up with the ether. But the gas wore off and the pain would come again. The guttural sounds from Kate's throat seemed to come from someone else. She felt all animal as a deep moan rose within her.

'Blow out the pain, blow out the pain, Kate,' a frizzy, red-haired midwife said. 'It won't be long and we'll tell you to push.'

She couldn't speak. Her pupils dilated with fear like those of a trapped animal; she didn't understand what was happening. Then she was on all fours again with the midwives urging her to push. She felt her joints in her sockets being ripped apart as if two tractors were having a slow, excruciating tug-of-war on either side of her pelvis. She imagined the heavy hooks of the tractor chains tearing apart red muscle, creamy ligaments and the white of the bones. Just when she thought she would die, she felt the head of the baby pass over the solid cup of her bones. Then the shoulders and with a final push the baby slithered out in a pool of liquid. And Kate felt what the women had talked about. The amazement. The joy that rose up, beyond all that pain, shock and fear. Tears streamed down her flushed cheeks as she gazed at the gasping, glistening baby.

'Hello,' she said to the tiny blinking being, who looked more alien than human.

'Well done, Kate,' the midwife said. 'You've got yourself a beautiful little girl.'

Four days later, Kate was in a cycle of sleeplessness and pain. Hospital hell. She fed Nell from cracked and bleeding nipples. She became quite used to the midwives grabbing hold of her lumpy, bursting boobs and bossing her baby's lips to them.

There was the endless clatter from the corridor; the ceaseless hospital traffic of cleaners, nurses and kitchen staff. They all swept in and out of her room, pushing trolleys, mop buckets or medical machines, the wheels clacking and rattling over the floor. Night and day blurred into one behind the venetian blinds. She tried to read her university textbooks but the words swam and blurred on the page. And in between the snuffling, squeaking and crying from Nell, Kate was trying to get her busted body to work again.

'Do you need more Voltaren?' the nurses asked. Kate giggled at the name despite her pain. Each time they said 'Voltaren' she pictured a bronzed, topless beefcake with long blond hair from a romance novel cover. She imagined 'Voltaren' sweeping into her room to rescue her. He'd pull back the curtain dramatically, swipe away her packets of Ural, haemorrhoid cream and maternity pads and take her up into his arms.

'Yes, I'd love Voltaren,' she'd say, keen for the fogginess that the drug brought to her. Strong painkillers didn't just help the sting from the raw wound where the baby had torn her. They helped her block out what her life might be beyond the hospital walls. A life with this tiny delicate little creature in it. Her daughter, Nell.

As Will stooped over the swaddled, doll-like baby Kate knew what he was thinking. Nell was the image of her father with her cute little ski-slope nose, bright blue eyes and fair hair. The paperwork for Nell's birth certificate lay on the shelf beside the bed. Kate had tried to fill it in but she got stuck at the part that asked for the name of the father. She wanted to ask Will if she should just lie and write 'unknown', when a cluster of college students burst into the room.

'Hey!' Kate said, propping herself gingerly up on a pillow to avoid knocking her stitches. She could still see the doctor bent over her spread legs with the light gleaming down on her. Despite his private-school manner, he had felt as rough as a shearer tugging dental floss through the bright, bloodied cut of a half-shorn sheep. Kate hoped her visitors wouldn't notice the meaty smell of warm blood that was still seeping out of her. She pulled the hospital blanket over her legs up to her waist.

'Congratulations,' Bindy said, rushing forward to hug Kate and gush over the baby.

'Bindy, everyone, this is my brother Will.' Kate gestured in his direction. 'Will, these are some of my mates from college. But don't mind them.'

'G'day.' Will nodded at them and stepped back to let them gather around the crib.

'Where's her second head?' quipped a red-faced Bilzo.

'And her webbed feet and hands so she can get back across Bass Strait?' said Freshie.

'If he was a boy were you gunna ringbark him?' asked Bilzo cheekily. 'We know what you Tasmanians are like on tree trunks.'

'Shut up,' Bindy said, slapping them both on the shoulder. 'Lucky they didn't circumcise *you*, Bilzo, or you'd have nothing left to wee out of.'

'Ooo!' chorused the boys. Kate looked at them and smiled. They had gradually become her mates at college, despite her pregnant state. They weren't from the coolest crowd and Kate loved them for that. They began to bring her into their world by teasing her good-naturedly. Calling her the 'breeder'. Buying her milkshakes from the college canteen to 'fill up her milkers' and making jokes about her growing 'beer gut' and about her sharing the genetics of stumpy, rotund Tasmanian cricketer David Boon. But now, on the other side of childbirth, Kate felt so removed from them.

'Speaking of wee,' Bilzo said to Kate, 'mind if I use your loo, Boonie? We had a few roadies on the way here. Gotta go have a chat with the unemployed. Might drop a coupla friends off at the pool while I'm there.'

'Sure, Bilzo. Go for your life,' Kate said. 'Don't slip on the afterbirth,' she called as he shut the door.

'I thought motherhood would civilise you! Still as gross as ever, eh?' Bindy said, then she stooped over the crib and said gently, 'Oh, Kate, she's just *gorgeous*.'

Bindy looked up from the baby with an expression that was more sad than joyful. It was as if to say she was sorry Kate had stuffed her life up so early. But then she brightened as she moved over and sat a heavy shopping bag on the bed.

'Sorry it's not wrapped.'

Peering into the bag, Kate let out a cry of delight.

'Bloody fantastic,' she said as she pulled out a blocky six-pack of Bundy and cola onto the bed. 'I'll have to hide it from the midwives. Thank you *so* much.' At the bottom of the bag was a Bundy rum bar mat with a polar bear on it and black and yellow lettering.

'The boys pinched it from the pub. Thought you could use it as a baby vomit cloth or something.'

'We washed it,' said Freshie, stepping forward. 'And we brought you this.'

He thrust forward a *Utes Annual* magazine with a muscly looking girl wearing a cap and a Deniliquin Ute Muster blue singlet on the cover.

'Thanks, Freshie,' Kate said, taking it from him. 'I'll treasure it.'

'Sorry it's creased, but I already read it.' As the boys picked up the book to argue over the Ford and Holden utes, Bindy perched her backside on the bed while Will sat in a chair.

'How *are* you?' she asked in a quieter voice.

'Fine,' Kate lied. 'When I look in the mirror I scare myself though. Imagine waking up to discover your body looks like Pammy Anderson on the top half and Humphrey B. Bear on the bottom half. That's me nude at the moment. Bloody scary, I can tell you!'

Kate wondered if she would ever be brave enough to let a male touch her again. In the harsh lighting of the hospital bathroom she had picked up her flaccid belly in both hands and jiggled it. It was like someone had let the air out of a tyre. She'd also been shocked to see the glaring red stretch marks that ran over her skin, like tropical-fish stripes. Kate hadn't known how much her body would change. She didn't know then that the marks would eventually fade, but her hips would widen and her tummy would always remain softer. It felt like she'd left her teenage body behind somewhere. She hated the body she had now.

Bindy was about to reassure her when Bilzo emerged from the toilet. He was snapping on a pair of the latex gloves that were shelved on the wall.

'Look what I found,' he said, waggling his fingers in the air. Then he reached around the corner of the bathroom door, pulled a maternity pad from its packet and held it aloft. 'Check out the size of these, boys!'

As the boys whooped Bilzo started dancing around the room with the chunky pad singing a Beach Boys surfing song.

'For God's sake, Bilzo, settle down,' Bindy said crisply. 'You'll wake the baby.'

Kate glanced at Will and smiled apologetically. He had shuffled to her bedside and whispered, 'I'll come back later.' Before she could protest, he'd gone.

That night, with the bundle of Nell asleep beside her bed, Kate let the illicit taste of rum tingle on her tastebuds. She propped herself up on a fat hospital pillow and flicked through the ute magazine. Her eyes fell on a photo of a group of smiling girls, their arms around each other as they sat on the back of a ute, holding stubbies. They wore hospital bands on their wrists, signifying that they had not only paid to get into the ute muster, they belonged. They belonged to the crazy, piss-drinking crowd that was getting dusty, loud and dirty. Kate stared at the picture and fingered her own hospital tag, thinking of Janie, thinking of the last time she'd worn a tag like this one. The time she went to the Rouseabout B&S Ball.

My God, she thought. She felt so old and damaged she couldn't imagine going to a B&S ever again.

'Should you be drinking that?' came a voice from the doorway. It was Will. 'I know it's past visiting hours, but the nurse let me in.'

Kate smiled, feeling a rush of warmth that he was there. Now, sitting at her work station with Buzz's words running round her head, Kate smiled. After all this time, she was going home. Home to Will.

Two weeks later, Kate found herself outside her low-slung brick house with Aunt Maureen. Her aunt reached out and smoothed down Nell's hair, fighting back tears. Kate sensed her aunt's tension. She waved the lunch box that she held in her direction.

'Thanks for the tucker, Auntie Maureen.'

'Much better for you both than truck-stop food.'

Kate heard the quaver in her aunt's voice. They both knew what Kate was going back to in Tasmania . . . or rather, what she wasn't going back to. Laney wasn't there anymore. She no longer lived on that sometimes bleak but sometimes glorious island. The old stone and weatherboard house by the sea would seem hollow, like a shell. But Kate recalled the excitement in Will's voice when she had told him she was coming back. She held onto his love and faith in her as if it was a safety rope pulling her back to shore.

Maureen stepped forward and gathered Kate up in a hug. They held each other tight for a moment. Then they stepped apart. Maureen helped Nell clamber up into the back of the twin-cab and pressed a kiss to her brow before clicking her seatbelt in.

On the front seat of the ute, crammed between bags and boxes, Sheila panted slowly, licking her lips and looking worried. Kate slammed the ute door shut and turned the engine over.

'Drive safely,' Maureen called out.

Kate nodded. She wanted to say thank you, Maureen, for helping her with everything. Everything. The pregnancy. The birth. Getting her through college. Everything. But she pressed her lips tight together and grimaced more than smiled. Then she drove away from her life in Orange. Forward to her past.

Five

Melbourne's jagged gunmetal skyline was ringed with silt-filled air. As Kate drove towards the city, she wound up the ute window to block out the smell of car fumes. She checked Nell in the rear-vision mirror. Her cheeks slack with sleep, her delicate dark eyelashes resting on pale skin. A halo of white-blonde curls surrounded her little face. Kate glanced in the mirror at her own dark eyes, the eyes of her Irish ancestors. Unlike Nell, she had tanned olive skin and long black hair with a glossy sheen, like a gypsy. It was good she was no longer wandering. She was going home, taking Nell back to where she belonged.

Kate looked ahead. She was getting close to the slate-grey sea and the ship that would take her home. As she gingerly merged with the stream of traffic onto the ring road, Kate pushed in an Adam Brand cassette. The thudding music helped shut out the aggressiveness of her surroundings. The in-your-face billboards, the grotty industrial sprawl, the roaring B-double trucks flying past in the outside lanes. She turned Adam Brand up. His deep cheeky voice made her feel like she was set apart from the city and all that it stood for. She felt country blood in her veins and the energy of her youth. But at the same time she felt old, so much older than the last time she had hurtled along this freeway in the opposite direction . . . running away from her family. Turning her back on her island home. Trying to escape herself and the tiny speck of life that was growing within her.

As the ship pulled away from the city, the clouds parted for the late-afternoon sun and the bay sparkled bright. Kate squinted to the horizon as gulls hovered overhead. In front of her, Nell clung to the railing, her small head bowed over the drop below, both fearful and exhilarated to see the chop of white water thrown up from the blue-green and to feel the cold sea air on her face. For Kate, the sea smelt of home, and of comfort.

'The water here's not as blue as at Bronty, though. Nowhere near as blue,' Kate explained to Nell.

She conjured up the white crescent bay that fringed her family farm and buried her face in Nell's soft neck, breathing in her sweet smell. She pictured the house, a hotchpotch construction of white weatherboard and whitewashed stone. At one end of the house the dark-grey roof rose to an angular point, like a capital A. Within this point sat the square eye of the attic window, which looked out over the paddocks and across to the sea. An old-fashioned rose had rambled on the walls for so many years that the house sat half-cloaked in greenery in the summer. Kate wondered how it was going to be, returning to the house that Annabelle had now claimed.

Kate was still reeling from the sudden introduction of Annabelle into their lives after her mother had died. It had happened without consultation. Without consent. Without warning.

But it was all Kate's own fault. She was the one who'd suggested, six months after her mother's death, that she and Will should send their father on a cruise. Kate had searched the Net, ordered the brochures. A sharp white ship rising as high as a casino, floating on sparkling blue seas, cruising to a happy land. Kate wanted her father to sail away to that land, and to come home healed. Instead, he'd found Annabelle.

During her mother's long illness, Kate had watched her father recede from her like a slow tide. As a child, she had run to him with outstretched arms, knowing she would be lifted high with a smile and spun so that the world blurred to the colour of gum trees and dry grass. He'd squeeze the laughter from her and plant kisses on her cheeks. But when her mother's illness came, and the more Kate grew into a woman, the more Henry pushed his daughter away. He tried to insist she return to boarding school, even though her mother's prognosis wasn't good. Kate refused to go. She was staying for Laney, despite what her father said.

Kate took on the roles of nursemaid and cook, and there were days when she felt older than the hills around her. In between changing saline bags that trailed plastic tubes into her mother's failing veins and washing her mother's sunken body, Kate would drift back into the kitchen to her Year 11 schoolbooks.

'Do you have to clutter up the place in here?' her father would bark at her, hating the way her long dark hair fell so much like her mother's over her shoulders. Kate would scowl at him, swiping the books from the table and stalk off to her room. Only Will, with his jovial face and great galumphing humour, could coax her out again.

In the years her mother battled, Kate and her father did the same, fighting different demons, hissing behind clenched teeth at each other so Laney couldn't hear. Will always trying to placate them both in his gentle, kindly way.

It took Kate three years to pass her HSC and it took her mother three years to die. When Kate finished school, a year later than her former classmates, there was no celebratory dinner, no parties, no boys, only a funeral. And then, not long after, the invasion of Annabelle.

Across the water, Annabelle stood on a chair in the kitchen at Bronty, pulling down faded green-checked curtains. The kitchen window looked out over the roadside paddocks of the farm and away to the bleached stretch of sand beyond the dunes. Beyond that lay the sea. Today it was turquoise melding into a deeper blue. Annabelle squinted against the bright beauty of the beach, looking up to grapple with the wooden curtain hooks.

'These things are so dusty!' she said to Henry, who stood patiently, holding the chair. He was trying to catch snatches of the stock report that muttered from a radio on the kitchen dresser.

He looked through the half-fallen curtains to the two gnarled old pines that flanked the gateway. Even though he knew Kate was on the boat tonight, he half-expected to see her driving through them any minute. The thought made Henry anxious. And now, knowing he would soon glimpse his granddaughter for the very first time, Henry was feeling even more unsettled. He stared out at the pines, which had been planted by Kate and Will's great-grandfather, pressed ceremoniously into the earth on the day his first son was born. Their thick, old-man limbs shaded a rusted sign that read *Bronty*. It was the second generation, Henry's father, who had hung the sign there, all new and painted white. He'd hung it on the day he brought his bride home. Two years later, their only son arrived in a howling gale so fierce the sign blew down.

'The first job you did on this place, son,' Henry's father used to say, 'was to re-hang that sign. Your mother said you were too young to go out in the wind, but you were all right tucked up in your pram. Just a couple of days old you were. Out there working with me.'

Henry wondered if he should ask Annabelle to cancel her order for a new sign. He liked the old one. Still, he thought, it was good she was sprucing the place up with new things and new projects. Time never stood still with Annabelle. He couldn't dwell on the past with her in the house.

Henry, who'd never been on a cruise in his life, first met Annabelle in the long empty corridor of the ship Kate had booked for him. He was searching for his cabin when he saw her. Annabelle had a glossy perfection to her that only city women could achieve. Her long pink nails had tapped the cabin number printed on his boarding ticket, and then she'd extended her delicate finger to indicate the sign on the wall. Her wrists tinkled with tiny sparkling gold charms and pale blue eyeshadow highlighted her large, innocent eyes. She smiled warmly, with pretty painted lips, and the neckline of her soft white shirt revealed a hint of white lace beneath. He'd never met a woman so polished. Her perfume lingered long after she had gone. When Henry had unpacked his things and stepped from his cabin again, he didn't go out on deck in search of sea air. He went searching for Annabelle, intrigued.

Annabelle looked down at him now from where she stood, barefoot, on the chair and shook her head.

'I don't know where Kate thinks we'll find room for them in this house.'

'We'll have to make do. Besides, I think it's only temporary,' Henry said soothingly. 'She told Will she's thinking of renting office space in town. Though he suggested Kate could eventually set up an office in the attic.'

'The *attic*! Oh, Henry, he can't be serious.'

Henry had been just as unimpressed with the suggestion. He hadn't visited the loft since before Laney died. There was no way he wanted to stir up his memories again.

He could just hear on the radio that cattle prices were rising and it was getting dry. Perhaps he should sell the steers. Lighten the load before winter. Annabelle tugged at the curtains and cursed. Henry glanced up at her.

He remembered Laney sewing the curtains in this very same kitchen. Her head bent, her long dark hair falling away to expose her pale, smooth-skinned neck. He had touched her there and she'd looked at him and smiled.

Henry watched as Annabelle tossed the curtains to the ground. Then she reached for the ready-to-hang lace curtains that she had just ripped from a plastic packet. She shook them out and they fell like froth.

'Amy has exams soon and she *must* study, so she *can't* move out of Kate's old room. And now with Aden home between jobs, we'll be bursting at the seams!'

Henry, his head inclined to one side to indicate his interest, nodded and frowned. The long-range weather forecast would be on next and Will would be in for lunch soon. He'd make a decision about selling the steers then. They'd have to have a talk about what they should do with the extra people in the house . . . Kate and her child. Annabelle was right. They couldn't all pile in on top of each other like this for more than a few nights. Part of him felt an uneasy warmth in knowing he would see his daughter again; another part just felt that old bitterness. A simmering fury that had kept him distant from her these past few years. It was a fury stoked to hide the guilt within him. It was easier for him to block Kate out with simple justifications that he played in his head like a tape on loop. She didn't want him in her life. She was a grown woman. She'd chosen to go away. She'd deliberately kept the child from him.

Annabelle waved the lace curtain in his direction.

'And it's not as if this house is childproof. How am I supposed to provide for a three-year-old? I shouldn't be expected to look after other people's children! I've done my child rearing.'

'I'm sure she won't expect you to look after the child,' Henry said.

Annabelle forged on. 'What if she doesn't find a place to rent in town? William already sprawls his papers all over the place! Oh, Henry! It seems to be endless . . . trying to get this house in order.'

Henry noticed her voice winding up – like a plane engine about to take off. He reached over and turned off the radio. Then he ran his hand up her slim, tanned leg that was encased in apricot Capri pants, taking in her painted pink toenails.

'It'll be fine,' he said quietly to her. 'There's always the old whalers' cottages. We could fix one of them up for Kate. Get a stone-mason in for a quote.'

Annabelle's cheeks flushed red. 'They've had hay in them for the past thirty years, Henry! You told me that when I suggested them for B&B's. Besides, I thought renovating *here* was a priority.'

His daughter had done it again, Henry thought. Turned everything upside down. Upset Annabelle. And she hadn't even arrived back home yet.

'Things will sort themselves out,' he said. 'We'll get used to having them about, I'm sure. It'll just take a bit of time,' he said, wrapping his arms about her legs and lifting her into the air. 'Now stop waggling that peachy backside in my face or I'll have to bite it.'

Annabelle laughed. 'Stop it, Henry!'

He set her down on the floor and looked at her, forced good-humour crinkling the corners of his eyes.

'I'd sell a paddock off for you . . . just so you can have your extensions, and we can fit us all in.'

She reached up and kissed him on his clean-shaven cheek.

'I know you would. My handsome man from the land.'

As Henry stooped to kiss her, Will sauntered in and cleared his throat. Henry let Annabelle go. Will reached for the kettle and shuffled past them, glancing only briefly at the newly hung curtains.

'How's things looking over the back?' Henry asked.

Will shook his head.

'Bloody dry. Have to shift the cows in a day or so, start feeding them.'

'You could get Kate to help,' Annabelle said.

'I was thinking Aden could do it. Kate and I will have our work cut out for us here getting the attic sorted out for her office. If we fit it out properly there may even be room for them both to sleep up there.'

'A three-year-old negotiating that ladder? I don't think so,' said Annabelle.

44

Will looked down to the floor and momentarily shut his eyes. When he looked up, he was smiling broadly at her.

'This is Kate's home too. We'll find a way, won't we?' His question was delivered in the lightest of voices, and with the cheeriest of faces. Yet his words sat heavily between them. He saw his dad prickle. Will knew that guilt was eating away inside his dad. Guilt for not helping his daughter when she had most needed it. Shame for sticking his head in the sand over her pregnancy and not going over to the mainland to bring her and the baby home. Will knew his father held all those things within him, yet the truth of them would never be uttered.

'Who's for a cuppa?' he said, reaching for mugs that hung from silver hooks beneath the cupboard. As he did, Amy stalked into the room. Two cords trailed from her ears and into her pocket. The iPod's silver discs beat out tinny music. She looked sullenly from behind her black square-framed glasses at the drying sandwiches on the table. A burst of late-afternoon sunlight lit up her short spiky hair, tinged with crimson and orange streaks.

'Hello, darling,' said Annabelle. 'How's the study going?'

Amy pulled a 'so-so' face.

'Hot drink, Amy?' Will said, waving a cup in her direction.

She shook her head, grabbed an apple and retreated from the kitchen. Will watched her go, then tossed coffee into a cup.

'Might need a hand later, Dad,' he said. 'Need to shift some of the heavier things about in the attic.'

'Trolley's in the shed. You could use that,' Henry said.

'Fine,' Will said. Cup in hand, he sat heavily at the kitchen table, and stirred his coffee for some time. He couldn't wait to walk the coastal paddocks with Kate again and talk about their plans for the place. Plans that had once been talked about by his mother and father, until Laney got sick. Blueprints for a future that were now frozen in time in the attic. Will had just come down from there. The attic ran the entire length of the original section of the homestead and seemed to have a personality all its own. It grumbled its moods when the sun shone too hot, or cracked angrily when frost stung the tin roof. Sometimes, in windy weather, the attic was a loud and boisterous place. On other days it had a stillness, as if it were contemplating the possibility of what it contained – the seeds of their mother's dreams.

Laney had often taken Kate and Will to play up there, and to share her farming visions with them. She wanted them to learn the family past that was catalogued and contained there. The past that could show them the way ahead. Sometimes Laney would simply take them up on rainy days to listen to the thrashing wetness on the roof, and she would tell them the rain sounded like God was hurling nails down from heaven. They'd lie on the old Persian rug and look up to the naked bulb that dangled from a plastic-coated wire and barely be able to hear their own laughter above the din. The three of them relishing the warm dry attic as the rain teemed down outside, laughing at the most mundane things, like Will's wiggling socked feet. Above the stacks of clutter was a small window made up of squares of thick uneven glass that blurred the view to the sea. The heavy wooden seed cabinets, their faces labelled in their great-grandmother's neat hand, watched and seemed to smile at them. These were memories Will carried with him always. He wanted Kate back to share those memories, and to build the future at Bronty. He swigged down his coffee and went outside in search of the trolley.

Six

At the crest of the hill, Kate slowed and pulled the ute over to the tangled grassy verge. The highway stretched along the coastline before her like a winding black snake. Today the sea was choppy. A brisk wind shunted clouds across a pale nursery-blue sky. The sight of the dark pines around the Bronty homestead filled Kate with mixed emotions. It was home. So familiar. Yet it felt so strange, knowing Annabelle was entrenched there now.

'Look, Nell. That's Bronty,' she said to comfort herself, 'the place I told you about. Mummy's old home. Our new home.'

But Nell was too busy tangling her Wiggles shoelaces together to look up. Kate sighed. She pulled onto the highway and drove down the hill towards Bronty. As the ute juddered over the grid Kate took in the vista of several tree-lined creeks that tumbled down from the mountains to merge with the coastal lagoon, a still pond of tidal water dotted with water-fowl and flanked by tawny grasses.

Kate smiled to see Matilda in the sloping horse paddock, lying flat on the ground, the filtered autumn sunlight warming her round bay sides. Beside the mare, Will's chestnut gelding, Paterson, stood with his head hanging low, bottom lip drooping.

On the other side of the drive, hoggets grazed white in the

47

mottled grey-green turnip crop. Freshly wigged and crutched, they turned their snowy faces towards her. They must be Will's replacement Merino ewe lambs, Kate deduced, please to see the evenness in their line. The smell of sheep drifted into the ute and Sheila sat up from where she was curled on the front passenger seat. She peered at them through her foggy old eyes and licked her lips.

'We're home, Sheils,' Kate said, scratching the dog behind the ears. But when she saw the house, Kate felt tension rise. She couldn't bring herself to go up there yet.

Instead she steered the ute over the short pasture towards the horse paddock. The grumbling sound of the diesel engine caused Matilda to lift her head. Paterson pricked his ears.

When the ute neared, Matilda hauled herself up, shook lazily and ambled towards the fence. Kate smiled. She hadn't seen her horse for all those years. The sun-sheen on her coat and the way her belly sprang out round told Kate she was well. Will had kept her hooves trimmed and her mane and tail groomed.

'Look, Nell! It's Mum's old horse.'

Nell's face lit up as Kate let her down from the ute and led her by the hand to the fence. She lifted her so Nell could rest her hand on Matilda's forehead.

'Horsey!'

'This is Matilda . . . and the other one is Patto. He's your uncle Will's horse. They're both Walers. The old war style of horse. Dinkydi, digger, good-on-ya-mate, Aussie horses!' Kate set Nell down.

'Digger-di,' Nell repeated as she clasped the wire and looked up at the horses with one eye closed in a squint against the sun. Kate slipped through the fence, put her arm around Matilda's chunky neck and breathed in her sweet musky horse smell.

Visions of her mother flashed in her mind. Laney, in gumboots, clumping both horses up into the float in the dark. Driving the winding coastal highway to town so that Will and

Kate could ride their Walers at the local dawn service. Chilled air and the sound of 'The Last Post' raising goosebumps on their skin on frosty Anzac Day mornings. And later, her mother treating them to hot chocolate at the tiny bakery that was filled with the sweet smell of dough and air so warm it hugged them. As Kate and Will swirled marshmallows through their drinks, war veterans patted them on the back and thanked them for bringing the horses all the way in for the service. Laney always had time – time for the old townies, for the horses, for her kids. Back then, none of them had known there was hardly any time left at all.

Kate slipped back through the fence and gathered Nell up in a hug. Perhaps here, back on Bronty, she could make more time for Nell. She could buy her a little pony, and take her to the bakery for treats. It was all there before them. A new life.

She turned to look at the house. It was shaded by leafy oaks and poplars, which were mottled yellow and green. She glanced up at the attic window, a black square, yearning to see her mother standing there waving to her. But the window was empty, the roof above it peeling grey. Clearly, Annabelle hadn't got that far with her 'improvements'.

Kate was about to load Nell into the car seat when she heard the tinny hum of a postie bike approaching. A smile lit her face. Will!

He tooted the clownish-sounding horn of the little faded red Honda, swerved and skidded to a comical stop. His dog Grumpy, a thickset tri-colour border collie with a ruff like a lion's mane, and a young dog Kate didn't recognise spilled from the back of the bike and Grumpy busied himself by pissing on Kate's tyres. The young dog danced in front of Nell, wiggling its whole body. Sheila watched their carry-on sedately from her place on the front seat.

'Big bro!' Kate said, taking in how much weight he'd put on since she'd last seen him at the hospital. She stretched her arms out wide.

'They let you back into the state!' he said, hugging her and putting his cold cheek against hers.

'Only just.'

'Annabelle's been trying to tell the whole district you got the sack from the Department of Constant Name Change and that you'd be home soon.'

Laughing, Kate shoved him a little as she let him go.

'*Transfer*! It was a transfer!'

'Whatever you'd like to call it, the word's out. Janie's been ringing me every half hour to see if you're back. And how's my little niece?' Will asked, crouching to Nell's eye level. 'Good? Did you like going on the big ship?'

Nell backed away behind Kate's leg, clutching her mum's jeans.

'Say g'day to Uncle Will, Nell.' Kate looked up at Will. 'A bit shy, but she always comes round.' She was waiting for Will to say something like, 'Geez, she's like her father.' But he didn't. Instead he ruffled Nell's curly blonde hair.

'Very cute.'

'Horses look well,' Kate said quickly, steering the focus away from Nell.

'Bit fat. Like me.' Will patted his belly, then the tinny petrol tank of his bike. 'I've been taking the steel horse lately. Annabelle's allergic to horse hair, so she won't have me in the house if I've been near them.'

Kate pulled a face. 'How is she?'

'Crapped off.'

'So she hasn't changed then.'

'She's feeling a bit crowded out.'

'Right,' Kate said flatly.

'Gotta have room for Amy and Aden.'

'Amy *and* Aden? The whole A-team is here together?'

'Yep, the A-holes are alive and well. Aden came home last week. He's not sure he wants to be a city boy anymore so he's pulled out of Sydney and come home to Mummy. She's decked him out in moleskins and he's trying out the position of Man from Snowy River, without the horse. Useless as.'

'And Amy?'

'Amy's home bludging from uni again.'

'How's Dad handling having the big A and the two little a's about?'

'You know Dad. Doesn't say much. Just works.'

'Gawd, Will. How awful.'

Will shook his head.

'Bloody glad you're home.'

They fell silent for a time. Kate could see the strain on Will's face. He looked older. Kate was shocked to see grey flecks in his hair. He was only in his mid-twenties, yet frown lines slashed deeply across his brow.

'You look like you've been working too hard.'

'Me? Nah.'

'Come on. You need a lift. There's more to life,' she said, grabbing his elbow and opening the ute door.

'What? Where? Up to the house?'

'Nah, bugger that! Let's go to the pub.'

'The pub! But what about . . . ?' he nodded towards Nell. Kate waved her hand in the air.

'She'll be right. Nell loves going out.'

'But I've got sheep to shift. You've got cows to move.'

'I do? Ah well, there's always tomorrow. I'll help. I promise. We'll take the nags. Get Annabelle sneezing. She can look after Nell for me.'

'Kate,' cautioned Will.

'C'mon, Will. Live a little! Surely we can have one welcome-home drink. My shout.'

Will shook his head, but Kate had already buckled Nell into the car seat and plonked a packet of Tiny Teddies in her lap. Then she whistled Will's dogs up onto the ute. They scrabbled over the lumpy tarp that covered Kate and Nell's bags and she clipped them onto short chains.

'You'll have to nurse Sheils,' Kate said as she swept aside

the rubble of takeaway papers, cassettes and drink bottles in the front cab.

Will frowned but clambered in anyway, wrestling an overweight Sheila onto his lap.

'Some things never change,' he muttered.

'What do you mean?' Kate asked, revving the ute.

'Kate Webster and responsibility. Never the twain shall meet.'

Ignoring him, Kate spun the wheels of the ute.

'Mind the soil compaction, please! That's my new pasture you're working up. It's been air-seeded!'

'Some things never change,' Kate quipped.

'What do you mean?'

'William Webster and anal retentiveness.'

'Get a grip.'

Kate glanced over at Will, her eyes bright.

'Let's get Janie to come to the pub too. Dave could mind Nell. You've got your phone? Call her.' She turned up Adam Brand's 'Get Loud' full blast and revved over the grid onto the highway.

'Welcome home, little sis,' muttered Will. 'Welcome home.' But he couldn't help his smile.

Seven

Janie tossed Thomas the Tank Engine melamine plates onto the kitchen bench and spooned tinned spaghetti onto cold toast. She hooked a strand of her blonde wavy hair behind her ear before hastily unwrapping sliced cheese to throw onto the steaming orange mush.

'Tea's ready!' she yelled. She could hear squeals in the bathroom and Dave's deep voice cutting over the top. They weren't getting out of the bath again. Little buggers.

'Brendan! Jasmine! Do what Daddy says!' she yelled over her shoulder. She was about to fill a couple of sipper-cups from the tap when she heard the dogs bark and the slow idle of a diesel engine outside. Peering through the grime-fogged window above the sink, she saw a red twin-cab ute roll to a stop.

'Yes!' she said. It would be Kate. She looked again to make sure it wasn't just someone calling in to tell them one of the obnoxious bulls was on the road again. Or some townie with a gun licence and no idea, wanting a shot. 'Dave. I think they're here!' She stopped talking when she saw Kate get out of the driver's side.

'Oh my God,' Janie whispered to herself. Kate was as pretty as ever, but curvier than Janie remembered. The sight of her old friend brought back a rush of memories. Suddenly Janie was transported back to those dark adolescent years when she had first met Kate. The filthy house she'd grown up in, at the back of the servo. Her mother's Winfield Blue breath, laced with whisky. Off milk in the fridge and nothing in the cupboard for breakfast save a stale pack of Crunchy Nut Cornflakes, surrounded by small black pellets of mouse dirt.

Kate had come into her life and made her aware that she deserved better. And as Janie began to pick herself up and out of the hovel that was her home, she discovered she had talents, whatever her mother might say to the contrary. She had the talent to comfort, and make the people who drove into the servo feel special. She could mother and fuss and humour. It was such a joy to discover that she had the power to give to others what she herself had never received. And Kate was at the heart of it. Janie had enfolded her in her warmth and nurtured her through the darkest days of Laney's illness, knowing she had needed Kate as much as Kate needed her. Now here Kate was, back home with her child in tow, and all the feelings from those years stirred and swirled around them.

'*What*?' yelled Dave from the bathroom above the din of the twins crying. Janie didn't answer. She ran from the house, not pausing to put on her boots, hopping over the gravel in her holey socks.

'Ahhh! It's *you*!' she said, bear-hugging Kate.

'Ahhh! And it's *you*!'

Laughing, tears springing unexpectedly from the corner of their eyes.

'Look at you!' Janie said, holding Kate at arm's length.

'Look at *you*!'

'Yes, yes, housewife, mother, farmer. Glam as ever.' Janie smoothed down her rumpled flannelette shirt and Kate noticed how tired she looked and how she had put on weight since the birth of the twins.

'You haven't changed!' Janie said.

'Neither have you!'

54

But they both knew nothing was the same. Since they had last seen each other, everything had changed. Everything.

'Just dished up a shocker of a tea for the kids, I've gotta get changed and then we're all set for the pub. Dave's on the bath and bed shift now,' Janie said, punching Will lightly on the upper arm as a greeting.

'Good on him,' Will said. 'So you're up for the pub then?'

'You bet. But first things first! I want to meet Nell! Where is she? Let me see.' Janie dived for the ute door and jerked it open.

'Oh! *Look at her*. She's gorgeous!'

Nell grinned back at Janie's friendly round face.

'But she's so sweet and innocent-looking,' Janie said turning to Kate. 'Not a bit like her mum.'

'Ha. Very funny,' Kate said.

'Hello, Nell. I'm Janie, your mum's friend from way back.'

Nell blinked at her, then her grin grew wider, revealing rows of dainty white teeth.

'She sent you prezzies in the mail. And photos of her baby twins. Remember?'

Nell nodded.

'Want to get out and stretch?' Janie unclipped the seatbelt. 'C'mon inside the house and meet Brendan and Jasmine. They're littler than you, but you'll like them.' She turned to Kate. 'I normally feed them better but you sprung this on me, so I hope Nell doesn't mind tinned stuff.'

Kate shook her head, thinking guiltily of all the slapdash meals she'd thrown in front of Nell.

Janie talked on. 'They can play for a while then into bed if we're a bit late. You got a cot or something for Nell?'

'Swag in the back of the ute. I'll bring it in,' said Kate, unflipping the tarp. 'She'll sleep anywhere and eat anything. Won't you, darling? We won't be long. Just the one drink.'

Janie looked from Kate to Will, her frown deepening on her freckled face.

'You! Have just *one*? I don't reckon.'

'Course it'll just be one.'

'Sure,' said Janie. 'Will, back me up here.'

'Don't look at me, Janie . . . you and I both know what she's like.'

Yes, Janie did know what Kate was like. She grimaced.

'I haven't set foot inside the pub since the twins were born. Kate shows up and five minutes later I'm back in like Flynn! But why stop at one?'

As they walked towards the weatherboard house Kate punched the air.

'I *knew* you'd come good for me, Janie. Go, you good thing!'

'I do have time for a shower first, don't I?'

'Sure,' said Kate, feeling impatient to go already.

As they walked towards the house, small resentments ran inside their heads, niggles of annoyance like nibbles on a fishing line, despite their joy in seeing each other again. Janie, still slightly sour at Kate for not coming back to Tasmania for her wedding. Kate, still a bit miffed that Janie had never got over to the mainland to see Nell. Then there was the big niggle. The unmentioned night of the Rouseabout Ball, still drifting between them like a fog.

A low mist dimmed the moon's shine as it slid upward, full-bellied, behind the gums on the hillside. The street outside the pub was dark and empty except for Kate's ute and a boxy, rusted Land Cruiser. The store across the road was shut and the petrol bowsers were locked. It was a township on hold until morning.

Curled up, with her nose in her tail, Sheila slept on the front seat of the cab, while Will's dogs dozed on top of the beaten old tarp in the back. Their ears moved when sounds drifted from the low-slung hotel.

The Millbrook Hotel was built from hand-chipped convict sandstone that had been slathered thickly with white paint over the years. Tonight the white pub with the steep iron-black roof glowed in the moonlight. Its small windows, like cat's eyes, shone with yellow light. When Kate saw the pub again she ran her hands over the smooth upright wooden post of the verandah and laughed.

'Huh! This place hasn't changed.'

'Yes it has.' Janie rolled her eyes. 'Dave reckons it's got worse.'

'*Worse!* How could it?'

'Old Boggy Jocks carked it last year. The Halfwit and the Whore run it now.'

'The halfwit and the who?'

'Boggy's daughter, Bev, and her toy boy, Jason. Bev's old enough to be Jason's mum. But she's in lerve with him. L.E.R.V.E. lerve!'

Toy boy. The phrase jolted Kate. It was a term she sometimes thought of, remembering that night. But he hadn't been a toy boy. Had he? He'd been seventeen, only two years younger than her. Over the legal age. Then Kate shut her eyes for a moment and thought to herself for the millionth time, *How stupid. How could I have been so stupid?*

'C'mon,' she said, forcing herself to think of something, anything, else. 'It's Will's shout.' She dragged a protesting Will by the sleeve towards the pub door, hauled it open and stepped inside.

'God, just look at the talent in this place!' Kate said, putting her hands on her hips and surveying the row of empty stools that lined the bar.

'Yep, it's always crawling with hot men,' Janie said.

The three of them moved towards the vacant bar. Kate's eyes scanned the wall above it, which was plastered with photos. No new ones since she'd last been here four years earlier. There was the snap of old Boggy-big-gut, the past publican, with the fish he'd caught one lazy summer day before his overworked heart gave out. His nephew's log truck after he'd rolled the jinker near Lake Leake. The big nights where some clown put on a chick's bra and his mate wore his undies on his head. A snapshot of old Clarry taken the night he rode his horse right in to the bar and ordered them both a beer . . . a light one for the horse, because he was the one driving home. Pool comps, cricket finals, footy nights, darts tournaments, all clustered together in a fading dog-eared collage of days long gone. On the wall next to the potbelly stove was a beer ticket machine, and on the muttering telly above it, footballers scrambled for the ball.

Kate squinted at the small TV and tried to read the score. As she did, a stick-thin woman with long jet-black hair and eyes rimmed with too much mascara emerged from out the back. She rushed towards the bar, putting on a show of urgency. Kate noticed the woman's breasts were plumped up with a lacy crimson bra that emerged from a low-cut black top.

'Thought I heard customers,' she said, laying her silver-ringed fingers flat on the bar. 'What can I get yez?'

Will ordered three beers.

'How about a Slippery Nipple as a chaser?' Kate suggested. 'Might as well get stuck into it. No time to muck about.'

'Sorry, love, we don't do Slippery Nipples here. But I can get you a Mudslide from the fridge. If yez like?' Kate nodded. The woman inclined her head and bellowed, 'Jason! This girl here wants a Mudslide.'

'Three,' corrected Kate.

The woman tucked her chin in and looked cynically at Kate as she yelled, 'Make that *three* bottles, Jason. *Perlease!*'

'Cascades and Mudslides . . . how wet can you get?' Kate said, taking a gulp from her beer glass. A young man with spiked hair and a chunky silver necklace rushed the Mudslides out to the bar. He set them down and smiled vacantly at them. The gaze of one eye wandered out to his left.

'You're a darlin',' the woman said as she draped herself over him.

'Cheers,' said Kate. She picked up the bottles and moved away to sit at a sticky table, grained with plastic faux-wood. As she turned her back, she was sure she heard the woman muttering 'Bloody mainlander' under her breath. Kate whispered to Janie, 'The halfwit must be a quarter-wit if he's going out with her. She's a shocker.' She pulled out a moulded plastic chair.

'Shh!' said Janie. 'The whore's been very delicate since Boggy Jocks died. She's likely to slag in your beer if she thinks you're taking the mickey out of her. Dave reckons they really are nice. She just takes a while to warm to strangers . . . especially people from the mainland.'

'I am not a mainlander,' Kate shot back.

Janie pulled a face at her.

'Just, whatever you do, don't order a meal here.'

Once settled at the table Janie glanced at Will, then moved her focus to Kate.

'So, when are you going to see him?' She fingered a torn cardboard beer coaster. Thylacines with smiles that snarled.

'See who?' Kate said, knowing full well who she meant.

'You know you should see him.'

'Why?'

'You know why. He needs to know.'

'No, he doesn't.' Kate could feel the anger rising in a hot red flush on her cheeks. How dare Janie bring this up now? She noticed Will shift uncomfortably in his chair.

'He's just got engaged. I saw it in Sat'day's paper. Did you know?'

'Bit young, isn't he?' Kate swigged her beer.

'He's twenty-one,' Janie said. 'That only seems young to you tertiary-educated types. Round here, in these parts, it's not. He's a good bloke.'

Kate felt the jab from Janie, a defensiveness that stemmed from the fact they came from such different worlds. Kate felt herself prickle.

'So what if he *is* engaged? What's it got to do with me?' she asked.

'He should know before he gets married. It's not fair on him and—'

'Not fair? He doesn't have to know. What difference does it make? Can we not talk about this please, Janie? We're here to have fun.'

'But—'

'Look. I'm not discussing bloody . . . bloody Virgin Boy, okay? It's the past. All over.'

'Virgin Boy? Not after you'd finished with him,' Janie said dryly.

Kate glared at her, but Janie persisted.

'He needs to know he has a daughter, Kate. You have to talk.'

Kate rolled her eyes.

'Janie's right,' said Will. 'You should tell him about Nell.'

'Why?' Kate, under pressure now, could feel a nerve in her temple flicker and jump. Will grabbed her hand as she went to lift her beer to her mouth. He forced her to meet his eyes.

'Because you know very well that it's the right thing to do. Plus, his dad had a car accident that's buggered him for life,' Will said. 'He's virtually stuffed. So it might be nice for Nell to meet her grandfather before it's too late. It's for Nell's sake too, Kate. It's not always just about you.'

Kate looked down at her lap.

'Nell has a right to know who her father is, too,' Janie said.

Kate looked up at them and nodded. She downed the last of her beer and cranked the top off the Mudslide, feeling defeated.

'Okay. Okay. I'll deal with it. Trust me. Just give me time.'

Pushing back the chair, she swigged on the bottle and skulked away towards the jukebox. After making her selection, she turned and gave Will and Janie a grin. They rolled their eyes as Madonna's 'Like a Virgin' blared out through the drab pub. Kate danced towards them, swivelling her hips.

'Very funny,' Janie said, but Kate couldn't hear her over the pumping music.

*   *   *

Nearly two hours later at the Millbrook Hotel, all three dogs were perched on the bar stools, their ears pricked towards Kate. Sheila squatted matronly on tubby haunches. Will's dog, Grumpy, looked serious and king-like on his seat. His impish red and tan kelpie pup, Bra, wobbled nervously on the vinyl stool top, her coat and eyes gleaming beneath the bar lights.

'Why's she called Bra?' Jason asked.

'Because she rounds them up and points them in the right direction,' Will said.

Bev threw back her head and hacked up a smoker's laugh, while Jason looked blankly at the kelpie.

All canine eyes were on Kate as she held a packet of Twisties between stained yellow fingers. She commanded the dogs once more to 'stay'. Janie held a camera up. She, like Kate, swaggered from too much booze and her words ran together.

'Okay, Jason, get posing,' Janie said. The halfwit put his arm around Bev and smiled a gappy-toothed smile.

'In a bit closer to the dogs, Bev-ly,' Janie said.

'Have you got everyone in?' asked Kate.

'Yes.'

'And are you getting enough cleavage in?'

'Yep. They're both in. Bigger than Texas, eh, Bev?'

'They sure are,' Bev said with another husky laugh, hoicking her bosom up further.

'Now say lesbians,' Janie said.

'Lesbians?' the halfwit queried.

'It's an alternative to saying cheese. Now say lesbians . . .'

'Lesbians!' they yelled, except for the halfwit, who said 'What?' After the flash went off, they all whooped and the dogs leapt down from the stools, young Bra barking and bounding in front of Will. Only Sheila remained at the bar waiting expectantly for her Twistie reward.

'What would the health inspector say if he came in right now?' Will shook his head and called Bra away from an upturned peanut bowl. Her thick pink tongue busily in search of salt.

'Bugger the health inspectors,' Kate said. 'This place is all right.'

'You reckon? You ain't seen out the back,' snorted Bev.

Janie set the camera down.

'C'mon, Webster, you've got me totally blotto and I've got friggin' playgroup in the morning! I'm supposed to have made the bloody playdough. Let's go.'

'Ah, playdough-schmaydough,' Kate said, clicking her fingers. 'More vodka please, Jason!'

'But . . .' Janie watched as Jason leapt into action, pressing the lips of glasses to the spirit measures that hung like big black spiders above the bar.

'Not for me, Jase. I'll be over the limit if I have any more,' Will said.

'We can ring Dave. He'll pick us up,' Kate said.

'And leave the kids alone in the house while he comes to town?' said Janie.

'They'll be right. They're asleep.'

'Oh, Kate, that poor child of yours,' Will sighed. 'How has she survived?'

Kate squinted at them both.

'Who are you? The mother police?'

With Vodka shooters lined up like glass soldiers, Kate hustled Will and Janie into position. She tipped back her head and slung a glassful into her opened mouth, then reached over the bar and re-filled it with water from a tap. 'There you go, Will. Happy now? You can play pretend pisspot.'

'Gee, thanks,' said Will, taking hold of the tiny glass between thumb and forefinger.

'Wait!' Kate said. 'There's one more thing I have to do . . .'

Will and Janie groaned as Kate went over to the jukebox and put 'Like a Virgin' on again. She writhed her way back to them, mouthing the lyrics in a pouting parody of Madonna. Just as Kate ran her fingers through Janie's hair and thrust her pelvis against her leg, the door opened behind her. Kate failed to notice the look on Janie's face for a while as she waggled, humped and 'hey!'d in true Madonna style.

'What?' she eventually asked. Janie swallowed and flicked her eyes towards the door. Turning, Kate saw three people watching her floorshow.

Kate instantly recognised her stepbrother Aden, his city-slick buzz cut propped up with product and a wicked grin on his angular handsome face. Next to him was a slim girl in a pretty pale-blue dress and navy coat, looking like an out-of-place princess. She didn't look amused. And behind them stood a man.

Kate blinked as she stared in a drunken squint. She took in the young man's six-foot-plus confident stance. The way he filled out his navy and red rugby jumper, his broad axeman's shoulders tapering to a slim waist, his hips made even more lethally sexy by his thick, brown leather belt. His fair hair was cropped navy short and his cheekbones were more glorious than Michelangelo's David. And then, Kate saw his eyes. The same saltwater-blue eyes the boy had had. The seventeen-year-old boy from the B&S. Kate felt the breath pulled from her lungs.

'My God,' she mouthed before looking away. *It was Nick.* An older, filled-out, mature version. But it was Nick nonetheless. He was unmistakable. Kate bit her bottom lip until it hurt. Nick bloody McDonnell.

Will stepped through the rabble of dogs that enthusiastically welcomed the newcomers, his tubby hand outstretched in welcome.

'Nick McDonnell. How would you be?'

'Great, thanks, Will.' He took Will's hand warmly. 'And Janie, how are you?'

Kate didn't recall his voice from that night, but it was deeper now, of that she was sure.

'Bit blotto,' Janie said. 'Kid-free time for a change. Dave's got 'em.'

Nick nodded and smiled. 'Good for you.'

Kate took in the way his firm mouth turned up at the corners.

'You remember my sister Kate?' Will asked, pushing her forward.

Kate stood looking at the toes of Nick's shiny RM Williams boots. Then she glanced up, her dark eyes flashing nerves, and muttered, 'G'day.'

Aden emerged from behind them, grabbing Kate in a jovial headlock.

'You're in deep shit, Kate Webster.'

'Get off, Aden!' She tried to wrestle free, her heart skipping like pelted stones on a river.

'We *were* going to welcome you home, except you cleared out before you'd even set foot in the place. Mum's freaking out. She cooked lunch and then dinner for you.'

'Ah, how sweet of her. Heartfelt, I'm sure,' Kate muttered.

Will quickly stepped in.

'Aren't you rude buggers going to introduce us?' He indicated the girl who stood a little way off from their cluster, red-cheeked from trying to prevent Grumpy's wet-black nose from prying into her crotch.

'Yes. Sorry,' said Nick, turning to her.

'Allow me,' said Aden. 'We just met outside. This is Nick's fiancée, the lovely Felicity. Green, wasn't it? Felicity Green?'

'You got it,' she said.

'Felicity, I think you already know Will and Janie. This is my wicked stepsister Kate.'

'Nice to meet you.' Kate held out her hand. Felicity took it, her head inclined to one side, smiling serenely. As she held Felicity's delicate fingers, Kate felt her own hand was coarse and large. She couldn't help herself.

'Teacher or nurse?' she asked pointedly.

Felicity opened her mouth as if to say, 'How did you know?' then realised Kate's question was a jibe.

'Um . . . nurse.' She withdrew her hand and flicked her hair away from her perfect heart-shaped face with a toss of her head.

'Nice to meet you, *Nick* and *Flick*. And let me tell you, you two *click*,' Kate said with a cheeky wink.

'Good one, Wordsworth,' Will said. 'Here's a dollar, you juvenile. Go and put some decent music on.'

Kate pulled a face at Will, but moved away, cheeks burning red, calling the dogs to her, painfully conscious that 'Like a Virgin' was still throbbing through the tiny bar. Nick looked down towards the grotty brown lino floor, trying to stifle a smirk.

'No one's ever noticed that before. Nick and Flick,' Nick said. 'Pretty funny when you think about it.'

'She's had a few,' said Will by way of an apology.

'We all have,' chipped in Janie.

'We're only having one. Aren't we, Nick?' Felicity said.

'Yes.' His eyes settled on Kate, who was crouching, stroking her old red kelpie.

Kate was cringing at what she'd just said, feeling guilty, rude and stupid all at once. She wanted to crawl under the dark cave of the pool table and hide from the glamorous (and probably very nice) couple she'd just snubbed. Aden moved over to her and slid his hands about her waist from behind. He lifted her up and swung her around.

'You're in big trouble,' Aden sang like a primary-school kid.

Kate wrestled away from him.

'I know I'm back in Tasmania when my stepbrother starts groping me like that.'

'Oh, come on. Bit of brudderly-love.' He came at her again with outstretched arms.

'Crap,' she said, pushing him away.

'I've been instructed to take you home.'

'Bugger off. I'd already *be* home if all your lot weren't there.' She turned to face him, glancing self-consciously at Nick before lowering her eyes.

'Get over yourself, Kate,' Will said, stepping in. 'Aden's right. It's time we went home. It isn't fair on Annabelle and Dad. They've been looking forward to seeing you . . . and Nell.'

At the mention of Nell, Kate glanced nervously towards Nick, but he was leaning on the bar now, talking to Felicity.

'I think I'll stay with Janie tonight,' Kate said, wanting to be out of the pub.

'Wouldn't it be better if you just came home?' Will urged.

'If I stay at Janie's I won't have to disturb Nell.'

'Fine. Your choice. I'll drop you off,' Will said shortly. 'Aden, could you please let Dad and Annabelle know Kate's sorry she didn't make it for dinner and she'll be out in the morning. Right, Kate?'

Kate shrugged.

They left in a flurry of drunkenness and dogs, shouting their thanks to Jase and Bev as they went. Nick stood at the empty bar with Felicity. The halfwit and the whore, too drunk to care about serving their new customers, pashed together on a wooden bench beside the fire.

'Can I get you a drink, Flick?' Nick asked uncertainly.

'Please don't call me Flick.'

A little later, outside the pub, Felicity's voice echoed in the empty street. 'Who was she?' she asked as she pulled her coat around her thin body and shivered.

'Who?' Nick opened the door of the ute and waited for her to get in.

'You know. That girl.' Nick winced as he slammed the door and walked around to the driver's side. Felicity turned to seek out his face in the darkness. 'Aren't you going to tell me?'

Reaching for his seatbelt, Nick felt trapped in the small cab. He could feel Felicity's intense pale eyes locked on him.

'Which girl?'

'You know.'

Nick shut his eyes. 'No one. She's no one.'

'Nick . . .' Felicity placed her slim hand on his knee. It wasn't a tender touch. It was a warning.

'She's just some friend of my brother's. Haven't seen her for years.'

'A friend of your brother's?' Felicity said. 'Since when has Angus ever had a *friend* who was female?'

Nick didn't want to talk about it. Not now. He was still reeling from seeing Kate again. He planted his foot on the accelerator and the V8 Holden ute lunged out onto the highway. A dark-blue blur in the black night. As he stared at the road ahead his mind turned back to Kate, despite Felicity's seething presence beside him.

From what he could tell, Kate hadn't changed much. She still wore her dark hair long and filled out her jeans to perfection. He loved her curves. She reminded him of those Rubenesque women reclining on soft satiny pillows and swathed half-naked in sheets. The sort of paintings he'd almost fallen into during art classes at school after the B&S. He'd trace his finger over the long flowing hair of the women and relive his night with Kate. Her face was just as he remembered . . . stunningly, heartstoppingly pretty, her skin smooth as caramel cream. She'd hardly changed at all. Maybe the rumour wasn't true, Nick thought. Maybe she didn't have a kid to some college bloke on the mainland, after all.

He pulled up outside the nurses' quarters in the next town, beneath the gleam of a solitary street light. Felicity looked sulkily at him. 'She's quite attractive, I suppose, that Kate Webster. Don't you think she's attractive? A bit plump, but still really pretty.'

'No. Yes. I mean I've never noticed. You're the attractive one. You looked gorgeous at dinner tonight.'

He reached out and ran his hand over her long straight blonde hair.

'Don't,' she snapped, shrugging off his touch and straightening the engagement ring on her bony finger.

Nick sighed. 'So, are you coming out to the farm after your

shift?' He turned to her and began toying with the buttons on her coat.

'Maybe. I need to clean the saddles for Saturday.'

'Oh. Okay.'

'Well, I'll see you then.' She reached for her handbag.

'Don't I get a kiss?' he asked.

Felicity undid her seatbelt and got out of the car.

'Not tonight you don't. There's something you're not telling me, I just know it. No talk, no kiss.' She slammed the door and her heels clicked up the path towards her little brick nurse's house.

Nick watched her shut the front door without a wave. He sighed again as he drove away and looked up at the moon. It was high in the sky now, hanging above the white mist like a giant yellow egg yolk. He clenched the steering wheel. She was back. Kate Webster was back.

Eight

Janie bustled in clutching a Mickey Mouse pillow and doona and shoved them at Kate.

'It was either Mickey or the Wiggles and I thought all those sexy Wiggles-butts would get you too excited.' When she saw Kate rocking back and forth, Janie plonked into a chair. Kate clutched her arms around her knees and stared into space. 'Kate? What's wrong?'

'I can't believe I was playing *that* song when he walked in. How embarrassing! Oh my God, Janie, it was him! Nick friggin McDonnell! Arrrghh!'

'Shhh. You'll wake the kids.' Janie threw a cushion at her and Kate covered her mouth and snorted laughter through her nose. 'This is all a big joke to you, isn't it?'

Kate smothered a smile. 'No, it's not. I'm deadly serious.'

'Yeah, right. Sometimes I wish you'd just grow up!' Janie tried to say it lightly but Kate heard the anger in her tone.

'*Grow up*?' Kate repeated. 'God, Janie, you of all people know that I *had* to grow up. I've never been anything *but* grown-up. Surely now's my time to have a bit of fun?'

Janie sat down on the arm of the chair next to Kate. She sighed.

'You can still have fun *and* be responsible, Kate. It doesn't have to be one or the other.'

'Yes, Mum,' Kate said sarcastically.

'There's no need to gripe.' Janie dropped down on her knees and sat in front of Kate, searching for her eyes. 'From what I can gather you're not giving Nell much sense of being grown-up.'

Kate crossed her arms. 'Just because you *chose* to marry Big Dave and have kids at a stupid age and trap yourself doesn't mean you can cast judgement on me! I didn't have a choice, did I?' Kate tugged the doona over herself.

'Trap myself! You know as well as me I was trapped *before* I met Dave, not after! At least you got to finish school! And yes, the study was hard for you, I know it was. But you had a mum who let you know you were smart. *I* barely knew what a book was. So don't give me lectures about choices. We both took up the dare that night, remember?'

'Remember?' Kate almost spat. 'How could I forget?' She pulled the doona up over her head. Janie stood, looking down at the shape of her friend.

'Good night, Kate,' she said eventually, flicking the light off and stalking out.

As Kate's eyes adjusted to the dark, she noticed moonlight seeping in under the doona. She could just make out the maniacally grinning face of Mickey Mouse on the pillow. Suddenly she wished Janie had chosen the Wiggles sheets. Peeling back the doona, she looked up at the moon framed in the top left-hand corner of the window. It had been a full moon on the night of the Rouseabout B&S. The night she had first seen Nick, and first worn that dress.

Kate smoothed the cherry-red silk dress over her hips and twisted around to do up the zip. Her mother would have zipped the dress up and laughingly complained that it was too short and the neckline too low. But then she would've kissed her and told her to go out and have fun anyway. Kate sighed, wishing her mother was there to call out, 'If you can't be good, be careful.' But her mother wasn't there to shut the zip's tiny silver teeth that ran along Kate's spine. Her mother was dead. Kate thought of her mother lying in the dark coffin beneath the black clay soil of the local cemetery. Raw grief ripped through her again, and she had to clutch the edge of the sink. Looking up, she took in her reflection in the bathroom mirror. A young version of her mother.

'You scrub up well, Webster,' she said sarcastically to her reflection, knowing that her glossy, glowing appearance hid the turmoil within her. The B&S ball tonight was a chance to get so blind she could escape the pain of the last few weeks. The Rouseabout! A Bachelor and Spinsters Ball. A weekend ticket to oblivion.

Will had smuggled Kate into her first ball when she was just sixteen. Her mum didn't try to stop them from going. She had just quietly warned Will to keep his sister safe and not to tell their father. She'd cover for them. She was like that, Laney; willing to trust them both with enough rope. In her eyes, life was not only to live . . . it was to be tasted and drunk in and challenged and seized.

Turning away from the mirror, Kate steeled herself before she walked into the lounge room to face her father. He was slumped in an over-stuffed lounge chair with his feet up on an old, cracked leather footstool. His face was obscured by the *Tasmanian Country*, which he held in front of him.

'Bye then,' Kate said, hoping he would speak. Instead, he lowered the paper, took in the sight of her short red dress, shook his head slowly and raised the newspaper again.

'Dad,' she said, reaching out to touch him. Angrily he jerked his arm from beneath her fingertips, the paper rustling noisily. 'Bloody hell, Dad, can't you say something nice? She'd be pleased we're going out to have some fun.'

Her father twisted his body away from her and turned his head so that he now seemed to be staring at the stock report. She knew he wasn't reading though. His eyes were clenched shut. Spinning around, Kate strode over to the mantelpiece where sympathy cards and dying flowers clustered together. She grabbed at the cards and tugged the flowers from the vases. Reeking green droplets splattered the floorboards.

'Mum would *hate* all this,' she said, throwing the crumpled cards and wilted flowers into the unlit fire. 'How can you think it's too soon to be going out? It was too soon for her to die! Don't you get it?' Kate was shouting now. 'How else am I supposed to go on from here?'

Henry scrunched the paper in his fists.

'Go!' he said. 'Just get out!'

Kate was about to scream that she bloody well would go and never come back when Will walked into the room in his op-shop blue velvet dinner suit and ruffled pink shirt. He took in the tangled mess in the fireplace, Kate's flushed face and her father's mournful look.

'Come on, Kate,' he said in a gentle voice. Then he turned to Henry and crouched down beside him.

'The stock are all checked. Just the dogs need a feed tomorrow. I've left some wallaby in the meat shed. See you Sunday night. Okay, Dad?'

Henry didn't answer. He didn't look at them as they turned and walked from the room.

The Rutherglen homestead, washed in moonlight, looked beautiful but eerily cold as Nick drove towards it. The lights were all out, except for a dim gleam that shone from the side of the homestead. His father was still awake and probably shuffling about the kitchen. Should he mention to him that he'd seen Kate Webster at the pub tonight? But what would his father care?

Nick found his father, Lance, in the laundry. He was bending over a basket trying to tug a shemozzle of sheets into the washing machine. Nick could tell by the way his father fumbled that he was embarrassed. He'd wet the bed again, too sore and slow to get to the toilet. Or too bombed out on painkillers to realise.

'Your mother's got enough to do,' Lance said. 'Save her doing them in the morning.'

'Here.' Nick took the sheets from his father, but avoided looking him in the eye. It was hard to look at him these days. His grey eyes, filled with pain, were sunken in his sallow face. Nick also avoided looking in the direction of the bag that always hung beneath his father's clothes. A bag that slowly filled with his father's excrement. Tonight, under the harsh light of the unshaded globe, Lance looked like the walking dead. 'I'll do it. You go back to bed, Dad.'

'Night then,' Lance said, shuffling out feeling both grateful and humiliated.

Nick peered into the washing machine and groaned when he saw a mass of wet clothes plastered to the sides of the tub. He grabbed another clothesbasket and started heaving the washing out.

At the clothesline, strung between two old apple trees, Nick flung a sheet over the wire. The whiteness of the moon on the flapping sheet prompted Felicity's toey show horses to snort nervously and trot about.

'Settle down,' Nick growled at them from over the fence. As he angrily pegged underpants, socks and old work shirts in a row he looked up at the moon again. It hung so near he could see swirls on its face. He remembered the night, years ago, when the moon had hung that close.

He'd been peering at it from under the dark covers of a ute tarp that had smelt of diesel and fly oil. His brother, Angus, had flipped the tarp away, and helped Nick out from the ute's tray that was stuffed with eskies and swags.

'Now remember, Nick, tonight you're eighteen, okay? If any of those blokes behind the bar look at you funny, just disappear into the crowd and lay low for a bit. You'll be right.'

Nick stood on the short pasture where scatterings of super-phosphate fertiliser glowed beneath the moonlight like unmelted hailstones. He tugged at the drooping dinner suit that hung from his skinny frame as the pounding music from the shearing shed thudded through his body. The inviting tang of mutton and pork spit roasts drifted in the air. Rows of cars and utes gleamed in the moonlight and beyond them figures like ghouls moved about the paddocks. Drunk buggers listing sideways, like they were navigating the deck of a storm-held ship.

'Now, my little brother, the rules,' Angus said, laying a dinnerplate-sized hand on Nick's shoulder and stooping down to look into his excited eyes.

'Rule one: if you get pissed and you're gunna chuck, steer clear of my ute and my swag. Got it? Rule two: if you pick up, and you can get it up, use one of these.' Angus pressed a crumpled condom into Nick's palm. 'Rule three: eating's cheating.' And he thrust a can of Bundy into Nick's hand. The cold aluminium felt good against Nick's palm.

Angus gestured towards the glow of the shearing shed. 'Welcome to B&S land, little brother!'

Nick looked heavenward to the massive white disc of the moon as he swigged on the rum. He felt the harshness of the full-strength Bundy drag like gravel over the back of his throat. His first B&S and his heart was racing. Tugging on his over-sized jacket, he shuffled off in his older brother's wake towards the glowing bonfire and the shearing shed.

Kate leant on the bullbar of Will's Subaru ute in her red silk dress and pulled off her high-heeled shoes. She hung them on the rear-vision mirror and tugged on a pair of hockey socks and scuffed Blundstone boots. She waited impatiently for her brother to finish pissing and tug his fly closed.

'*Now* are you ready?' she asked.

'Revved and ready,' Will said, snatching up his beer from where he'd left it on the bonnet. They walked side by side over the bumpy paddock, past the rows of cars towards the thumping roar coming from the shearing shed.

On her right, a blue marquee begged or borrowed from

the livestock company sheltered trestle tables laden with food. Buttered white bread stacked in tall columns, massive bowls of spud salad and chunky, mucky coleslaws were laid out. Piles of meat on silver throwaway trays. Some girls sat legs crossed, eating from plates, while the drunker ones held food in their fists and tore meat from bones with their teeth like Vikings. As Kate and Will passed, the queue of hungry diners dispersed momentarily as a young gun slung an entire bowl of coleslaw over his mate's head. Kate smiled at the sight of the boy blinking mayonnaise from his eyes and slinging fistfuls of grated carrot and cabbage into the crowd. It was only eight o'clock and they were already running amok.

'Let's find the bar first and come back for tucker after,' Will suggested. Kate nodded and they strode on. A massive bonfire sprayed up dancing sparks into the night sky. Clusters of people stood about, drinking and talking. Some sat on hay bales. Kate noticed a couple lying in the paddock, rolling in a kiss. The girl's dress was pushed up high and everyone could see her pink undies – one bum cheek in, one out – and the dimples of her upper thighs, like the moon's own pale surface. With a whoop, a group of boys busted open a hay bale and covered the couple in itchy-as-hell hay. They barely responded, simply kept on kissing, a slow wave and a sly smile from the boy the only acknowledgement of what they'd done. Kate walked on towards the bar. She was at The Rouseabout, Tassie's rural big-bang annual event, and her heart was racing.

In the shearing shed, the smell of rum awash on the lanolin-and dung-soaked grating had revved the crowd into a frenzy. Like most seasoned B&S-goers, the mere whiff of rum and dung catapulted Kate into a kind of trance. Her only mission tonight was to get totally and utterly drunk. She wanted to go wild, like an animal. To tear away social boundaries and cleanse herself of all the niceties she had endured during her mum's funeral and wake. Tonight she would strip away all pretence and let the rum shut out everything else in her life. She felt the crowd surge around her as people rushed to watch the riders of a mechanical bull.

'Smell that, Janie?' she called, breathing in hard as she slipped and slid over the shearing board. 'Who needs to pop tablets when you can get high on sheep shit mixed with rum? The city kids just don't get it.'

But Janie couldn't hear her. She was too busy pushing her way through the crowd, looking pretty in her homemade, strapless peacock-blue dress. Her curly fair hair, piled atop her head in loosely entwined ringlets, framed her angelic freckled face.

By the time Kate got through the crush of black suits, Janie was standing beneath a banner that read *The Rouseabout Bachelor and Spinster's Ball* with a cartoon of the Footrot Flats dog getting sozzled on grog. The DJ was tucked safely near the wool bins. In his shiny puffy tracksuit, baseball cap turned backwards, and reflector sandshoes, he was the only person who didn't seem to fit. At least he knew how to please the crowd. He put on Adam Brand's 'Dirt Track Cowboy' and a chorus of whoops rang out and rattled off the corrugated-iron rooftop. Adam's sexy voice, as smooth as bitumen, revved the crowd up more.

Intoxicated by her surroundings, Kate nudged Janie with her shoulder.

'Go on. Dare you!' she said as she shoved Janie forward towards the mechanical bull. Janie turned to her and beamed. She was up for anything too, set loose from the sadness of both Kate's loss and her own troubled home.

She stumbled towards the matting, hoisted her satin dress over her stocky thighs, kicked off her work boots and clambered on. Her golden hair tumbled over her pretty, plump shoulders as the bull began to slowly rock and spin. Then faster and faster, winding up. Janie flung one arm into the air and leant back into the movement.

'Spur him, Janie!' Kate yelled. 'Ride that bugger! C'mon!'

Rocking and rollicking, Janie whiplashed back and forth as the crowd buzzed. A fast sharp buck finally tipped her onto the matting. The crowd clapped and roared at the gutsy, busty girl! She crawled, laughing, over to Kate and Will.

'Eight seconds just isn't a long enough ride for me!'

As she stood catching her breath, a young boy was pushed into the centre of the arena to ride the bull. His curly blond hair was wet from rum. He staggered slightly and grinned from ear to ear. Kate took in his angelic smile, and the way his baggy dinner-suit trousers were hitched up around his skinny frame with orange bale twine.

'Check out that little spring chicken,' Kate said.

'An underager for sure. He's bound to get busted,' Will said.

'Depends what you mean by underage, Will,' Janie said. 'Isn't that Angus McDonnell's little brother, Nick? He'd be seventeen now, wouldn't he? That puts him as illegal for grog and illegal for being at a B&S . . . but definitely legal for sex.'

'Oh, you're feral,' said Will.

'He sure has turned into a cute little puppy though,' Kate said, taking in his curly gold locks and smooth golden skin.

Nick McDonnell clambered onto the bull with its kitsch acrylic red and white hide. The crowd cheered and clapped. He rode with style, despite the clothes he was wearing. His shirt came undone as the bull bucked harder, his bare chest exposed to the crowd.

'That is one cute McDonnell,' Kate shouted over the ruckus.

'Yep. Sure is. You should tell him to ring you in a year when his hormones have finished him off. He's bloody cute,' said Janie.

Kate laughed. There was something so compelling about him. He had a presence. His looks were one thing, but he seemed to shine with confidence and vitality despite his tender age. She laughed again as another huge buck from the bull sent him flying off. He landed lightly and tumbled twice, like

Jackie Chan, then rolled to his feet. Nick held his hands in the air as he acknowledged the cheering crowd.

Next, a bloke as big and square as a giant hay bale ambled forward, grinning.

'Now there's a hunk and a half,' Janie yelled to Kate above the noise. 'Dave Shaw. Jackaroo from Woodsden. He's cutting his teeth there before he goes back to his dad's country not far from you. You know the Shaws?'

'You're talking like a land-grabber,' Kate joked.

Janie eyed the big man on the bucking bull.

'Land ain't what I'm thinking of grabbing tonight,' she said.

Kate turned to Janie with a grin.

'Dare you to kiss him!'

'Get serious!' Janie said. 'I'm on a mission to snare Johnno.'

She looked over to a square-jawed dark-haired boy, who was trying to balance a stack of plastic cups on his head. His mates egged him on.

'Oh, come off it. Will you look at him? You'll never drag him away from Simmo and Blue. Plus, they're bloody mainlanders. No future there.'

Janie took in tubby Simmo, skolling beer, and Blue, a true carrot-top with the freckles to match, dancing about like an idiot. Both were in awe of Johnno and the three came very much as a party package, spending all they earned as Deniliquin jackaroos on going from one B&S to the next.

'Mmmm, good point,' she said.

'Dave's a much better bet. Once you show him those big bazoongas of yours, you'll be in. I dare you. I dare you to crack onto him . . . and . . .' Kate thought for a moment. 'And give him the old blowjob in the back of the ute trick. He'll love you for life.'

Janie threw back her head and laughed.

'You're *off*, Webster!'

'I dare you!' Kate persisted.

'All right then, Maggot-features . . . you're on. But it's my turn to dare *you* something.'

'Go on then. What?'

'I dare you to . . .' Janie paused and looked around the crowd. Then her face lit up. 'I dare you to scalp that little toy boy over there.' She pointed to Nick McDonnell.

'Scalp him?'

'Yeah,' said Janie. 'You know? Take his virginity as your prize!'

'He's hardly a toy boy, Janie. He's only two years younger than us!'

'Yeah, but he's definitely a virgin. You can just tell. I dare you.'

Kate smiled, feeling the tingle of desire and possibility flow through her. Nick was very cute. But still she shook her head.

'Huh! You're full of it, Webster,' Janie said, shoving her a little. 'You say you're having a wild night tonight, but you're all talk.'

Kate felt her skin prickle. The glow of the night suddenly faded. She felt the coldness of her mother's death creeping up on her again and she shivered. She grabbed a rum from Will's clutch of cups and slung it back.

'All right then,' she said. 'I'll take on your challenge, you monstrous wench! I will take on Virgin Boy. I could do with some young blood! Teach him a trick or two!'

Both girls threw back their heads and laughed. Then they clashed plastic cups together as if they were chalices.

'I'll have my conquest by sun-up!' Kate tossed her dark hair dramatically and turned on her heel to make a beeline for Nick.

'Katie,' Will said, gently holding her back. 'Just go easy, hey?'

'What are you?' she spat at him, shrugging off his hand. 'My mother?'

Nick looked up at the pressed-tin ceiling of his bedroom. The moon cast shadows across the ornate designs of leaves and lines. He thought about Felicity, and the way she'd made him feel tonight in the pub. Pressured. It was the way he felt a lot, ever since his dad's accident. He stood up, unfolding his strong legs from the bed, and trod over the cold floorboards to the window. Standing in just his boxer shorts, he wrapped his arms about his broad chest. He felt trapped here in this bedroom. Like he was too big for it. Footy pennants and pony-club ribbons, faded and gathering dust, hung down from the window's pelmet. Model tractors and farm machinery cluttered there too, like a ramshackle miniature clearing sale. The weight of the low ceiling seemed to press down on him. He felt stooped over in here, like he was not allowed to be a man in this room. Not fully grown.

Down the hall he heard his father cough and his mother murmur. Nick wondered how Alice found the energy to console her husband even in her sleep.

He'd got used to the fact his parents now slept in separate beds. Two singles jammed up against the walls of their bedroom, with a roomy chasm in between. A change from the one big soft island of comfort he had clambered into as a child. In between the beds now was a white melamine cabinet filled with all the medical equipment needed to keep his dad's body ticking over: colostomy bags, tablets, rolls of cotton wool, bandages and tape to hold tubes in place, painkillers and tranquillisers. Paperwork from the specialists, X-rays in giant folders, half-empty glasses of water, kidney dishes filled with syringes, fat and thin. The presence of the cabinet and the single beds had stripped Nick of his childhood memories of that room. But the room wasn't the only thing that had changed.

Since the night they'd got the call to say his dad's ute had hit the big old pine out on the Tin Pot Marsh Road, *everything* had changed. For Nick, life seemed to stall. It felt like he was wading through mud. He was numb to the world outside. He'd become old overnight.

In his head he battled fear, in his heart he grieved for his father, and his anger towards their situation now resulted in long silences that sometimes stretched for days between them. Nick felt the stab of guilt as he repeated a silent chant in his mind, 'Why didn't you die that night, Dad?' If his dad had been an animal, he would've been put down; a gun barrel to the head and a single shot between the eyes. Nick wondered why humans focused so totally on preserving life, even though that life might not be worth living. This new life of his father's was far too hard, a long, drawn-out 'recovery' that Nick now knew would never happen. His father would never get better. Only worse.

One corner, one tree and some loose gravel and all their lives had been smashed beyond recognition. Lance McDonnell, driving too fast because he was late for beers at the fire shed.

Nick sighed as he stood at the window. Once he married Felicity he could take it all on. The farm. The fathering. A husband to both his mother and Felicity. He could start looking after it all. Get married and grow up quick. Start moving forward. A future beyond simply living each awkward day with his broken father. Nick would be the responsible one. He had to be. Surely his father could see that.

He and his parents knew they couldn't rely on his brother Angus. Absent Angus – always had been, always would be. Adventures on pearlers in Broome. Skippering yachts in the Caribbean. Running ski tows in Switzerland. Jetting to Dubai to look after an oil baron's racehorses. Nick knew that Angus wouldn't come home for the wedding. Angus who scoffed at family traditions. Ridiculed monogamy. Niggled at niceties.

'Frigid Felicity' Angus had dubbed her, and Nick had almost thrown a punch.

Angus had last visited a few months after their father's accident. Like a gangster, he had swaggered into Nick's room dressed in his European tailored clothes and thrown a wad of cash onto the bed.

'You can have your farm, Nick. I don't need it. Look what

a bit of entrepreneurial initiative can generate.' He'd fished more money from his pocket and waved the cash in front of Nick's face.

'Earned cleverly, but always honestly. There's nothing clever about being a farmer, Nick. Nothing. Look at old Misery Guts in there . . . he was half-dead before he hit that tree. When did he ever stop to truly enjoy life? Now he's stuffed. It's too late. Live for now, I say.'

Nick had wanted to slam his shoulder into his brother's beefcake body and pin him to the wall. But he hadn't. He'd just slunk out of his room, like a dog kicked in the guts.

Nick looked down at his body in the moonlight. His white torso and dark tanned arms. He was fit and strong from his work. He loved farming. It was his life. But now, with no rain throughout the autumn and no clear direction for the future, he felt broken inside. He looked out onto the barren paddocks. The moon cast eerie shadows from the trees. Sheep that would normally be camped at this time of night ambled hopelessly about looking for food. Others stood in clusters with their heads hanging. The deep black shadow of the skillion shed reminding Nick that there was no hay left.

He was committed to this farm, no matter the weather – and committed to Felicity, too, no matter how many sparks had flown the moment he'd seen Kate Webster again. It was Felicity who'd seen his parents through the worst of the accident. She was now his future.

At that moment a cloud pulled away from the face of the moon, which shone so brightly Nick had to squint. Angrily he pulled the curtains shut and clambered back into his tumbled bed. But still the moon persisted, painting a bright stripe across the bedhead. As he lay awake he began to remember.

She was standing in front of him in her red dress and long dark hair. She'd grabbed hold of his hands and dragged him onto the dance floor. He was only just taller than her and couldn't take his eyes from the swell of her plump pale breasts rising from the tight swathe of red fabric that could barely be called a dress. Even in rumpled hockey socks and work boots, her strong legs looked good. Of course he knew her name. Everyone in the district knew Kate Webster. She was the prettiest, funniest girl around. In town, the older boys at boarding school always had her at the top of their 'wank' list. And here she was dancing with him at the Rouseabout B&S. He was seventeen. And Kate Webster was dancing with him.

His cheeks flushed as he wondered if he looked cool or not. The beat of the Violent Femmes' song was tricky to dance to. He wished it was another song. He felt her hands all over his body. His back. His buttocks. Inside his shirt. She swivelled her hips. Pouted her lips. Leaned towards him, dragged his head down with interlocked fingers behind his neck, so his nose nearly touched her cleavage. As he reached out and tentatively placed his hands on her hips, Nick McDonnell was too drunk to notice Kate turn her head and deliver a sly wink. And the group of girls who were watching and laughing at them winked back.

He couldn't recall clearly how it happened. She first kissed him beside the ute, her mouth hot and sweet with rum. Her body pressed against his. He must've eagerly dragged his swag from Angus's ute and carted it to the fenceline with the beat of the music far off in the distance. He did remember the smell of young wattle already wet with heavy dew as it brushed his face. He'd tried to roll the swag out under the trees so no one would see. He wasn't sure why she was keen on him but he was going with it.

When he'd flung back the swag she'd laughed at the rumple of sheets inside. Thomas the Tank Engine.

'Geez. What am I doing?' he heard her whisper to herself. Then she'd giggled.

'I think I can. I think I can,' she chugged and dragged him

down onto the swag. She lay on top of him and he felt her tug at the bale twine that held up his pants.

'I need my bloody pocketknife for this,' Kate said. Instead, she tackled the knot with her teeth. Perfect white teeth and red, red lips, lit softly by faraway floodlights from the B&S. Her dark hair fell on his chest so that he writhed with desire and, at the same time, terror. She ran her fingers over his bare belly and down his skinny white legs.

'It's okay, Tom Tank Engine. You'll love it. Trust me,' she breathed as she kissed him along his neck and ran her fingers through his curls. He felt her wiggle beside him, lifting her brown legs out of her knickers. Then she straddled him.

'Oh God,' he moaned. He'd lost his jacket, he remembered thinking. He'd lost his jacket and in it was the condom.

'Oh God,' he moaned again . . .

Kate's eyes snapped open at the sound of curtains being whipped across the rail. She blinked and saw the silhouette of a large man in front of the window. Early dawn light flooded the room.

'Still dreaming, Kate?'

'Dave?' she said in a croaky voice. 'Where's Janie?'

She propped herself on her elbows and took in the sight of Dave Shaw. Shoulders broad as a butcher's chopping block, hands like meat cleavers. A square-chiselled face that could have belonged to a first-grade rugby league player, framed by a mop of brown hair, and small hazel eyes that exuded kindness. There was an air of simplicity about him, matched by his slow drawling voice. One thing Kate had learnt about Dave, though, was that despite his appearance and the way he spoke, he was as sharp as a tack.

'Janie's sick as a dog in bed. Thanks to you.' He threw a towel at her. 'Better get moving, Webster. The kids'll be up soon and you're fair game down there.'

Kate groaned as she stood up, dragging the doona cover

around her. She smiled crookedly at Dave, who was now in the kitchen crumbling Weet-Bix into bowls.

'Did Nell go to bed okay?' she called as she wiggled back into her jeans.

'Good as gold. And still out to it now. I just looked in on them all. Snoring their heads off.'

Once dressed, Kate wandered into the kitchen and slumped at the kitchen table.

'White with three, thanks,' she said. Dave raised two thick fingers at her and in his deep voice grumbled like a giant, 'Get your own, Webster.'

'It was a big, big night.'

'Yeah. From the way Janie jumped me, it must've been. Women who have twin toddlers don't jump men like that normally.'

'You should be *thanking* me for getting her blind.'

'Yeah, yeah,' he said, tossing a piece of toast in Kate's direction. 'She babbled on about you seeing Nick McDonnell again last night. How's he look to you now the hormones have kicked in?'

'Funny bastard, aren't you?' she said, narrowing her eyes at him.

'You gunna sort all that out? You know. Tell him he's got a kid and everything?' Dave asked.

'God! Don't you start!'

'We know you too well, Webster. That poor bugger will be on his deathbed before he even knows he's got a little heifer trotting about with his genes in her.'

'Shut it,' Kate said, trying to keep the defensiveness out of her tone.

'Well, look bloody useful and go get the kids up for me. I'm going to take them to their gran's. Get them out of Janie's hung-over hair. It's time you took Nell home to meet her own step-gran.'

Kate rolled her eyes. 'Huh. Don't remind me.'

'Kate,' Dave said as he waved a spoon at her, 'it's about

85

time you stopped your disappearing tricks. Will needs all the help he can get out there. Believe me.'

'Will? Huh! He's a big boy. He can look after himself.' But as she said it, Kate felt a wave of guilt. He did need her. Not just to help with the farm. He was outnumbered on Bronty now Annabelle's kids were there. She and Nell should help even the score.

Nine

E arly-morning mist hung in the gullies. From his seat on the tractor, Will looked out across the farm, away to the sea. Not a cloud in sight. If only an easterly would roll in, bringing with it heavy curtains of grey to soak into the parched, icy soil. As the tractor wheels sliced over the ground, Will looked down to the crumbling bare earth. The grubs were doing damage on the hillside where the stock camped. If only he'd had time to spray them. Perhaps if Kate stuck at being home he could get her on the tractor. But then there was the issue of Nell. He couldn't see Annabelle babysitting. Will sighed. His little sister. Still so angry about losing their mother. And here she was, now a mother herself. A mother to the cutest little girl he'd ever seen. Excitement ran through Will at the thought of having Nell in his life. But he had already sensed a wariness behind the little girl's ready smile. He knew she hadn't had much stability in her life so far.

Will dropped the tractor back a gear as he drove down the hill. He vowed he'd make Kate feel safe to be back at Bronty, and to be a person Nell could always rely on.

Ahead on the fenceline, the cattle mooed impatiently at the gateway. They could see the big round bale of hay speared on the tractor's two front forks. The sweet smell of it carried to them on the breeze. They bustled next to one another like

All Blacks in a rugby line-out. The bullies put their heads down to bunt their mates out of the way. Hunger made them stirry.

The giant bale bounced, leaving trails like tinsel in the morning light. The frame of the silver Weldmesh gate glistened with dew and cobwebs as pretty as lace. The gate needed re-swinging, Will noted, annoyed at the endless jobs there were to do on Bronty. He tried not to focus on the niggling feeling of always being behind in his work. Stressed. Never catching up.

He needed to look outwards. He knew how farmers got when all they had was their work. Same paddock, different day. Shitty seasons running into one another. Then when a break came and the grass grew, the workload didn't lessen. It just changed.

But Will kept at it, because of his love for the place and the view that spread out before him. He made himself take note of the sea vista each day. Out there was his mother. Out there was his future. One that was broader and happier than the life he found himself in now. Dodging the bitter comments from Annabelle, trying hopelessly to rise above the hollow left by his father's distance and longing for his little sister to come home so she and Nell could fill the huge gap his mother had left. Perhaps, now Kate was here, things would get better. They could talk their father round. Get started on a seed-cropping business. Create a new family life, the old bitterness buried once and for all. He imagined spending summer days out fishing in the old boat with Nellie. Hauling in glistening flatheads on hand lines. Better days to come.

The morning sun rose over the bay, bringing to life the soft silhouette of Schouten Island. The sun lit up a brown tinge in the cows' black coats. Will wasn't sure how he'd get the heifers through the winter. The shed was half-empty already and the hay wasn't that good anyway. At least it'd fill their bellies, he thought as he looked at them. Drool dangled from their mouths as they ran their rough grey tongues over their wet black noses. Their bellies were beginning to pot-up as the calves inside them grew. But to Will, the flush of spring seemed so far away.

Will shoved the tractor into neutral, ripped on the hand-brake and leapt down, slipping on the damp ground. As he walked to the gate, he heard above the idle of the tractor engine the high-pitched sound of an ag bike. Aden was roaring through a mob of ewes and lambs on the valley flats.

'Dickhead,' Will muttered. He felt his blood pressure rise as he watched the ewes slip and scatter, their lambs tottering about, confused and frightened. Will shook his head and swore again. He'd have to stop him before the whole lot mis-mothered. The maiden ewes were weak enough. This was the last thing they needed.

The only reason the ewes were in lamb in the first place was because Aden hadn't shut the ram paddock gate six months ago. The Merino and the White Suffolk rams partied hard for three days before Will spotted them in with the young ewes. And now the lambs were out of step with Mother Nature, born into a barren world.

Will jogged back to the tractor, reached up and gave three massive revs of the engine in the hope Aden would hear. It startled the heifers and they leapt away from the fence. Black diesel fumes poured from the stack, lifting the circular disc that covered it. At the sound, Aden looked up and waved. But still he continued to rev his way in and out of the shallow drains on the flats that Will had so carefully carved out the year before. The wheels of Aden's new bright-green bike gripped and spat dirt out in a spray of grass and soil.

'Aden! You wanker!' Will yelled, though he knew Aden couldn't hear him. As Will walked away from the tractor he felt his jacket catch on something. Angrily he tugged his coat free and went to open the gate. He gritted his teeth, his shoulders tense. He wished Aden would just leave. Just go away, back to the city.

Will didn't see the tractor inching forward as he fumbled

with the too-tight gate latch. The big black wheels rolled slowly. The round bale looming nearer and nearer, like a monster. Too late, Will sensed something and tried to spin around but he couldn't move. The hay bale pressed against his back. The metal bar of the gate dug painfully into his chest. The weight of the thing was incredible. It crushed the air from his lungs. Panic raced in Will's mind, but he could do nothing. When would the gate give? Bloody old thing. Surely it'd give soon. The chain was fully stretched. But the hinges still held. Pain began to flood his whole being. His eyes popped wide. Above the idle of the tractor, Will could hear the slow creaking of metal stretching and wood moaning. He began to hear gurgling guttural sounds. Then he realised they were coming from him. Air. He needed air. And the pain. It was sending him mad. He was mad with it. He had to scream. Then Aden would come. But Will couldn't cry out. He felt the weight settling down on him. The low growl of the tractor like an animal, crushing his bones. Veins popped in his skull. His eyes bulged. His feet and arms jerked wildly about.

Then a calmness settled on him. His unseeing eyes looked out to the water. His mother was there.

'Mum!' he thought he called out. But there was no longer breath in him. No longer life. Will was travelling towards the water, where his mother was. Back on the land, a crow, black as night, cried out. Aden's bike could be heard revving away and the tractor idled on. Gingerly the cattle stepped forward to sniff at Will's downturned head and tug at the hay. Blood dripped from his lips and seeped, blackening, into the soil. One by one, the cattle drifted away, wanting to be fed, but wary of the smell of death that mingled with the smell of hay.

Nell was sound asleep again by the time Kate pulled off the road into Bronty. Kate sang along loudly to the radio in the hope of staving off the dark feeling that had settled in her about coming back, now Annabelle was permanently installed. She forced a smile on her face. She could handle this. She

90

would kiss her dad hello, give Annabelle a hug and get on with it. This was Nell's home now. It was a fresh start. And she had Will on her side. Will would help her make it right.

But as she drove towards the house and yards the smile fell from her face. A gathering of locals in their State Emergency Service uniforms were watching one of their team drive the Deutz tractor into the yard. An ambulance followed, obviously in no hurry. At the gateway to the garden a policeman was ushering Henry along the path. A blanket shrouded Henry's shoulders, and she couldn't see his face. He got as far as the back step, then spun around and slumped on his backside, lurching sideways for a moment as if he were drunk. Kate could tell now, she could see on his face that something worse than horrible had happened.

Kate jumped out of the ute and looked around desperately for Will. Aden was leaning on a motorbike in the yard talking quietly to a policeman. Amy stood on the porch, her pale face even whiter than normal. Annabelle emerged from the house and began to walk towards Kate, her arms outstretched, a torn look of grief on her face. But Kate walked straight past her and stood before her father, her eyes searching his face.

'Will?'

The expression on her father's face answered for him and Kate felt her legs giving way.

'Oh no. Not Will. Not him. No, no, no!'

Her father pulled her to him and held her. She smelt his familiar smell, a mix of diesel and Pears soap. She wanted to punch him, not hug him. A guttural scream rose out of her, like the one she'd given the day she pushed a baby into the world. A sound so animal and raw. Inside the ute, Nell woke, looked out at the ambulance and police cars, saw her mother and began to scream too.

Ten

A week later, Kate stood next to her horse Matilda in the tumble-down yards, where the post and rail sagged beside Bronty's stone stables. She and Will had dreamed of fixing the yards so they could keep a glossy black Waler stallion and breed stock and polocrosse horses. Shutting her eyes, Kate let go of another memory, let it float away into the ether.

Today they had buried Will. Kate couldn't quite grasp the reality of what was happening. Her vision had blurred, as if her world was ringed with fog. Everything felt surreal. Even here in the yards, near the comforting presence of her horse, Kate's body shook from shock. She felt so washed out it was difficult to pull the girth straps tight. Looking over the small brown hillock of the horse's withers back towards the house, Kate could see the post-funeral crowd gathering in the garden. She could see Nell, the blonde halo of her hair weaving in and out of the dark trouser-legs of the men. Annabelle fussed around them, imploring them with a bright smile to make their way inside. She looked like she was inviting them to a birthday party, not a wake. Just the sight of her made Kate writhe. She couldn't go back into the house. Not yet. She couldn't face what that woman had done to her mother's memory. Nor could she face the funeral crowd, with both Nell and Nick moving within it, so close to one another. And she couldn't face being over there without Will. Without his big bright beautiful face to coax her back into that world.

Kate tugged the stirrup leathers down on Matilda's stock saddle, looking up in time to see Dave scoop Nell up under his arm. He carried the cackling little child like a sack of spuds up the verandah steps and inside. Thank God he and Janie had said they would watch her for a while, Kate thought. Kate could see Nick on the fringes of the crowd. Felicity was standing demurely by his side, her feet together like Dorothy's in *The Wizard of Oz*. Nick had his hand in the small of her back as if he was trying to gently push her inside the house. Kate turned away from them. She was sure Nick had noticed Nell in the church. Everyone must have. Had he recognised that look in Nell's eyes? Eyes that smiled. Metallic-blue, fringed with dark lashes. Had he noticed that they shared the same honey-coloured skin and fair curls? Had everyone seen? But did she even care, now Will was gone? She wondered if she'd ever care about anything or anyone, beyond Nell, again.

She led Matilda out into the driveway paddock, leaving Will's horse, Paterson, walking the fence anxiously. Ramming her boot into the stirrup, Kate swung up into the saddle. She felt odd riding in the thin, slippery pants she'd worn to the funeral. The stirrup leathers dug into her calves and the cold wind flapped soft black fabric about her ankles. As soon as she'd arrived at Bronty she'd ripped off her shoes and pulled on her boots at the ute, avoiding eye contact with the other mourners, who were getting out of their vehicles. She'd tugged on her old polar fleece over the top of her clothes and jogged straight over to catch the horse.

Kate had spent the days since Will's death bunkered down at Janie's, staring numbly at the wall as the twins and Nell played noisily around her. Building blocks scattered about her while the lolly-sweet members of Hi-5 pranced on the TV screen. Grief immobilised her. Henry had called a few times, but when Janie held the phone her way, Kate just shook her head violently, her lips tight shut, unshed tears stinging her eyes.

'Talk to him,' insisted Janie, and Kate would storm from the room.

Now, trotting down the drive on Matilda with the sea breeze racing in to greet her, Kate felt grief surge through her like the swell of the ocean. She and Will had ridden this driveway countless times and always they'd fought about who'd get off to open the gate beside the grid onto the highway. She wished she'd let him win the argument more often.

She slid from the horse and hauled the old wooden gate open. Pine needles caught in Matilda's mane and Kate had to duck her head to pass beneath the low-slung branches. Matilda's unshod hooves clopped over the bitumen of the highway, then fell silent as she ambled onto the soft sandy soil, through silver tussocks bent and wavering. A blustery wind raced in from the bay as they walked down a track, past low-slung boobyalla trees and a few scraggly casuarinas. Up and over a dune and they arrived on the bright white sands of the beach.

The mare lifted her head and pricked her ears as she looked around. Her mane, forelock and tail whipped about wildly as she danced towards the white mare's tails that skipped further out on the grey choppy sea. The wind skimmed over the wave tops, picking up seawater. Kate tasted salt as it landed in minuscule droplets on her lips and caught in Matilda's mane. On the harder sand that shone grey like wet cement, she gently pushed the mare to a trot and then a canter. Hoofprints fell away behind them. Gentle waves washed over the sand like a sigh, blurring the marks Matilda made. Eventually the endless slide of waves erased them from the sand altogether.

Kate wanted to ride out to sea and never come back. It felt

like her mum and Will were out there waiting for her, in the green-blue underwater world. She could just push the mare on, make her swim out over the breakers towards the island until they were both swallowed by the sea. Swimming down and down, Matilda a seahorse, and she a mermaid. She turned the mare to face the water and walked her in chest deep. The breaking waves struck Matilda's broad front like a thunder-clap and sprayed up and over Kate's legs. The salt of her tears mingled with the salt of the sea. She could slide from the horse now and swim. Swim until she sank. Wails began to rise from her chest but were instantly ripped away by the wind. She felt the coldness of the water rise up her legs and splash on her hands and arms. She wanted to die out there in the bay.

But always she could feel it. The pull of Nell. She felt her love for her daughter pulling her back. That sunny little face and fairy-like smile drawing her up and out of the grey. Nell had come back a stranger to Bronty, and without Kate she would have nothing. Kate knew what it was to lose a mother. She swung the mare about and faced the homestead. It sat snugly on the hillside, buffered from the sea breeze by the old garden. From there, between the branches, the attic watched her. Kate resolved to reclaim Bronty as her home, for Nell. Nell could come to know her uncle and her grandmother not in life, but through the landscape that held their memories and their wisdom.

Kate replayed the images in her head of the sunny days she and Will had ridden here on the beach. When the water was as still and blue as in the tropics, but with that cold Tasmanian bite. The exposed shore and colder currents kept the tourists away, so the beach, even in mid-summer, was mostly their own. Her mum larked with them on her chunky Waler cob. They rode bareback, shimmering with seawater, suntans and laughter. Her dad would drive down later with the picnic esky and water for the horses bouncing and sloshing on the ute tray amidst the grease gun, tractor

95

chains and shifters. He would stretch out on the sand next to his wife, grinning, his white feet crossed at the ankles, trailing sand through his fingertips as he watched his children play.

Now, on this wintry beach, Kate vowed Nell would have that upbringing too. She would experience the deliciousness of a Bronty summer. There would be no more running away from home for Kate. She would stay so that Nell could learn to love the farm. Will was here forever now, and her mother too. Kate felt a passion surge in her. So long as she was here, so long as she was home, they would always be together. Nell and her mum and her brother.

She swung Matilda towards the far reaches of the crescent bay and the horse leapt into a gallop. The mare's ears pricked, Kate's teeth gritted. Tears streamed across her cheeks and seeped into her ears like raindrops in a seashell. The rhythm, the life of the horse, thundered on the sand. Ahead of them, a tiny pied oystercatcher scuttled away on spindle legs, while a southern black-backed gull surfed the crest of the wind above. They galloped on. Past seaweed and shells that blemished the sand's perfect sheen. Kate took it in, everything from the minuscule sprinklings of sand in Matilda's mane to the grand bush-covered mountains fringing the shore. She refused to let herself look to the place where Will had died. It was too hard yet to imagine his fear, his pain, as his soul left this earth and flew out to sea.

Even though Matilda was blowing hard, Kate kicked her on faster and the gutsy little mare responded, pounding her hooves harder over the sand. Miles and miles of beach behind them and the crumble of rocks ahead.

When they at last reached the sheltered beach's end, Kate eased Matilda back to a walk. She could feel the mare's sides heaving beneath her legs. Kate dropped the reins and fell forward in the saddle, pressing her cold cheek onto Matilda's hot neck. Frothy sweat like sea foam gathered on her chest. Kate inhaled the smell and listened to the mare's breathing.

A crow called from a bone-grey dead gum high above the shore, but Kate didn't hear. She only heard the wind, the waves and the call of the gulls as they hung like ghosts in the misty grey.

Eleven

Kate's leather Blunnies had dried saltwater stiff, leaving tiny tide marks around their edges. She grimaced as she heaved them off her wrinkled feet and drew off her sodden sandy socks. Then Kate stepped into the Bronty homestead for the first time in over three years. As she did, she was assailed by a décor that reeked of excessive femininity. Laces and frills, peaches and pinks. Gilded frames and porcelain.

'Oh. My. God,' Kate said as she lifted up a china figurine of a girl mournfully selling violets. Grains of sand fell from Kate's damp trousers onto the plush cream carpet. She walked past prints of rose bouquets hung on freshly painted peach-coloured walls and fine, shiny furniture with wood-turned legs as delicate as fawns. Where was the giant old hallstand that tumbled with beanies, umbrellas and caps? Where was the big old clock with the yellowing face, as faithful as a blood-hound? Where had the old Stubbs prints of dozing chestnut mares and foals gone? She hoped Annabelle's home renovations hadn't made it to the attic yet. She was certain Will would have steered her well clear of the precious seeds that were stored there, pressed together in their browning envelopes.

The old hall-runner, the colour of summer elms, no longer led Kate along the polished wooden floor to the kitchen.

Instead, her feet now sank into carpet like she was walking on white marshmallows. Everywhere she looked, she searched for traces of Will and their old life. But she could find none. Panic made her giddy, so she had to stop for a time and breathe deeply, pressing her fingertips to the walls.

She heard noise coming from the kitchen at the end of the hall. The clatter of cups and cutlery. Voices rising above the constant hum of Nell's truck noises.

'Brrrrr, brrrrr, brrrrum.'

Kate stood in the doorway observing the seeming normality of the scene despite the extraordinary circumstances. Annabelle was at the sink, rinsing a glass platter. Janie was stooped at the dishwasher, carefully cataloguing spoons and knives together and china cups in a row, at Annabelle's instruction, Kate guessed. Nell lay under the kitchen table amongst a forest of chair legs, tiredly pushing her toy livestock truck back and forth, her plastic baby loaded in the back as if it were making its final journey to some kind of weird abattoir.

Dave was nestled down in a beanbag in the TV room beyond the kitchen, one twin asleep under each arm, as if sheltering a clutch of baby birds in a giant nest. A quiz show babbled on in the background.

'She's a sweet little thing. Quite polite,' Annabelle said, nodding at Nell, unaware Kate was behind her. 'Surprising under the circumstances.'

'Yes,' said Janie noncommittally.

'Did Kate say when she'd be back? Surely she'd be worrying about Nell by now.'

'No. She didn't,' Janie said as she pushed the dishwasher rack into place.

'Any idea where she intends to stay tonight? I'm about to get dinner under way. And I'll have to re-think the bed situation.'

'Um, I've no idea. But I expect she'll be back soon. Certainly once it's dark.' Janie held up a rose-print teapot. 'Where does this live?'

'Sideboard in the TV room, thanks, Jane.' Kate watched as Janie carried the pot carefully into the TV room. She stooped before the sideboard where two photos, foggy at the edges, showed Amy in braces and Aden with longer, slicked-down wavy hair, like an American teenager on his way to a prom.

'And thanks for staying on to help, Jane,' Annabelle called from the kitchen.

'No trouble,' Janie said. As she turned, she saw Kate in the doorway of the kitchen. Meekly she waved. Annabelle followed Janie's gaze and pulled off her washing-up gloves.

'Ah, Kate, *there* you are! We were worried about you. Nellie darling, your mummy's home at last. Welcome, Kate. Welcome. Come in, darling.' Nell's truck noises stopped momentarily as she quietly said hello and then continued revving.

'She's very tired,' Janie said. 'One too many Wiggle Safari dances with Dave, I think.'

Kate, not sure what to do, got down on her hands and knees and crawled under the table to kiss Nell on the forehead and press her cheek to her soft warm head.

'Hello, darling,' she said, a fresh wave of emotion surging inside her.

Kate's mind flashed back to when Nell was just a few weeks old. It was the first time Kate had felt a love so powerful – joy and fear all rolled into one for the baby she held in her arms. It was three in the morning and Nell was making little snuffling noises as she drank from Kate's breast. Kate had looked down at Nell's perfect little face. Her doll-like hands, curling and uncurling blissfully like a kitten kneading its paws. Kate wondered at the feeling of that all-powerful love. A mother's love.

Now all she wanted to do was hold Nell like that again. She smiled at her daughter, gathering all her internal strength so the smile didn't turn to tears.

'You okay, little Nellsie?' she whispered.

'Can we go home now, Mummy?'

Kate ran her hands over Nell's hair. Home? Kate no longer knew where that was. She wondered if Bronty could ever feel like home again.

'Sure we can. Just as soon as Mummy works out where that is.' She kissed Nell again on her crown and emerged from beneath the table.

'Thanks for looking after her,' Kate said to Janie, giving her a squeeze on her arm.

'It's fine. She's easy. Such a sweetie.'

Kate turned to look at Annabelle.

'Where's Dad?'

'In the office, I suspect. He's still got to organise shearing in the middle of all this, poor man. But that's farming for you, as I've come to learn.' Annabelle flashed a tight smile.

Kate felt anger rise again as she took her in. Annabelle stood in the exact spot where her mother used to. Her slim figure was framed by lace curtains that hung behind her. She wore a candy-striped apron and Martha Stewart-style house slippers.

Kate tried to picture her mum standing on the worn floor-boards beside the sink. Her mum, who used to muddle about the house in cut-off jeans and Henry's workshirts, knotted at her navel, with the sleeves rolled up, her dark hair tumbling every which way. Will dancing about her, flicking her with rolled tea-towels, laughing.

Annabelle raised a tea-towel up, scrunched her face and sneezed loudly into it.

'Oh! Horse hair.' She covered her mouth delicately with her hand. 'Would you mind, Kate? I'm terribly allergic.' Annabelle waved in the direction of the outside shower. 'If you're staying for any length, you can have a shower and leave your clothes in the outer laundry to do yourself later.'

Kate's eyes narrowed. It was as if nothing had happened. It was as if Will wasn't even dead. She felt like hurling insults at the insensitive woman who stood before her. Instead, Kate shut her eyes for a moment and calmed herself. For Nell's sake, she needed to be civil.

'Thanks. I will,' she said. 'But I'm just going to speak to Dad first. I won't be long.'

Janie stepped forward and cleared her throat. 'Kate, if you don't mind, it's really getting on. I'd better get the kids home. I'll see you later, yes? You're welcome to stay on at our place if you like. If not, Dave can drop the rest of your things out in the morning. Okay?'

Kate looked at the half-moon marks of tiredness below Janie's eyes. Gratitude and guilt again stirred in her.

'Oh, God, Janie. I'm sorry. Thanks, you know, *thanks*. I'm not thinking straight.'

Janie stepped forward and as she hugged Kate, whispered in her ear.

'I'm so sorry for you. Again. I'm so sorry. You know I love you very much.' Kate hugged her friend back. 'Give it a go here, Kate,' Janie whispered. 'For Nell. And for Will. Please.'

Kate didn't find her father in the office, as she had expected. The scratched leather chair faced away from the old roll-top desk. The room was empty. Kate pulled the office door shut and turned to look down another hallway of the rambling old house. Then she saw that the ladder-stairs to the attic were down and light was spilling from the oblong hole in the ceiling. Kate blinked, swallowed, then walked towards the light. Slowly she climbed the stairs to the attic.

Henry was sitting at the big old desk, still in his funeral shirt and suit-trousers, his tie slack about his neck. His sleeves were rolled up exposing strong, tanned farmer's arms. He clutched a glass of whisky in his work-worn hand.

The creak of the ladder and the wheeze of the attic floorboards announced Kate's arrival. Henry looked up, his face expressionless. Kate stood beneath the low, slanting roof, taking in the room. Breathing the musty smell of memories. Her mother's hug. Will's laughter.

The attic looked almost the same, Kate thought with enormous relief. She could feel the room filled with the energies of the past . . . that gentle tenacious strength of the Webster women who had been there before them. In here, at last, Kate felt at home.

Even though the attic was full of old furniture, Laney had been clever at making clutter look good. And the attic was just that: organised, artful clutter. The only thing that had changed was the position of the desk, where Henry was sitting. It was clear of boxes and no longer covered in dust drapes and it now faced the window to the sea. Beside it was a wooden filing cabinet. On the desk sat a framed recent photograph of Matilda, with Will's dogs lying across her wide back, their tongues out and ears pricked. Next to that, a selection of new pens were arranged neatly in an old cigar box.

'Hi,' Kate said quietly.

Henry ran his fingertips across the edge of the desk. 'He set this up for you,' he said.

Kate took in what her father meant. This desk, the small touches, had been Will. For her. To make her feel welcome. To give her back a space in this house. Kate's face crumpled. She drifted towards the desk, laid her hand on its polished wooden surface. At the sight of the misery on her face, Henry stood and pulled her to him.

She felt his large palm on the back of her head holding her cheek hard against his chest. She scrunched her eyes shut, not wanting to hear the grief that caught in his chest. Tiny clutching sounds of air. His muscles taut. Shaking. He held her so tightly he began to hurt her neck. The button of his shirt bit into her cheek. He was thudding his hand against her back now. Rhythmic slaps of his flattened hand. Like you'd slap a steer on the haunches to get it up a race. Anger and love all at once in his touch. Pulling her in, aggressively, passionately, hurtfully, lovingly.

'I'm so sorry,' she managed to say. Sorry for being angry with him. Sorry for leaving him. Sorry for getting pregnant and sorry for Will. Sorry for always letting him down. Sorry that he couldn't love her better. Because of her mother, he couldn't love her better.

She clutched him angrily back. The white sliver of her fingernails pinched his skin. Then, at last, she heard him mutter he was sorry too.

But their closeness began to weigh on them too much. When they pulled apart neither father nor daughter could look the other in the eye. Henry pulled off his wire-framed glasses and swiped tears from his eyes.

'He was going to get power points up here for you. So you could have your computer. And then a bed, maybe. If you'd wanted.'

Kate felt the words sting. She nodded. She couldn't shape her voice into words. Her mouth felt slack. Her mind, her body, everything was in shock. Shut down with despair.

Henry sat again in the chair, gnawing his bottom lip. He looked suddenly like an old man. Snowy flecks in his hair beginning to outnumber the black. Eyes as grey as the sea, brimming with all the pain that life could bring. The pain of losing his wife. The pain of losing his only son. The memory of Will that would cause an ache in his chest for the rest of his life. Kate glanced at him.

'Maybe I should go,' she said at last. 'Stay at Janie's.'

He shook his head quickly, side to side.

'No. Please. Stay.'

Kate nodded, tears sliding down her cheeks again. The pain was so great she thought she might collapse. The pain of knowing her father would have had her back under this roof if only she'd been humble enough to ask. Those wasted years away, Nell growing from a baby to a child without Will. And now it was too late. She looked down at the familiar pattern of the old Persian rug.

'He'd insist that I stay, wouldn't he?' Kate said.

'Yes,' said her father. 'He would.'

'Okay then. We'll stay.'

Her father nodded gently.

Kate smiled sadly at him before turning to climb back downstairs into Annabelle's world.

Later that evening, after dinner in the Bronty kitchen, Henry shrugged on his thick woollen coat.

'Just going out to shift the irrigator,' he said. It was after ten and Annabelle was packing away the last of the dinner dishes. Amy had already retreated to the beanbag. The television screen flashed with golden flames and purple swirls as Amy's computer-generated Princess Warrior slayed dragons and vaporised lumbering ogres. With her iPod on her ears, Amy grunted with effort as she pointed the controller at the black box. Somewhere else in the house, Kate could hear the pulse of Aden's 'doof-doof' music muffled away behind a closed door.

Tonight during the meal, Kate had tried to revive the feeling of having Will and her mother at the table, angry at the intrusion of the television, which muttered in the background. She knew her father kept it on to distract himself from the awkward, painful silences between them. The oddness of having Nell sitting on a booster seat at the table, babbling away, shovelling mashed potato haphazardly into her mouth. Annabelle gently but meticulously correcting her manners and making small talk. Kate felt grief swirling in her, killing her appetite. She noticed Annabelle had put Nell in Will's place. Kate watched her father's eyes slide from Nell to the comfort of the television news, the sudden adjustment of circumstances – Will gone and a grandchild at his table – too great for him.

Kate recalled her own childhood at that very same table. Watching television during meals was not an option when Laney was alive. Kate's mother and father had set the rules about mealtimes and television early.

'People who say they're bored are boring people to be around,' her mother's voice said in Kate's head. Laney had always taught Will and Kate to entertain themselves. There was little time in their lives for TV anyway. They were always outside. Playtime in the creekbeds as they gushed and frothed with freshly fallen rain. Little leaf boats slipping over stones while Will and Kate followed them along the creek's edge, leaping sags and tussocks, cheering, sliding and laughing.

And when it was dry, they spent hours with their dinted sun-faded Tonka trucks, digging up the creekbed's silty soil and piling it into mini-dam walls, longing for rain. Rain to make their father happy and their mother whistle and warble like Fred Astaire.

Kate never remembered sitting inside much. There was always work to be done before playtime. The slice of her tomahawk through splintery kindling with a crack and thud, chooks diving for crusts that toppled from the kitchen scrap-bucket. Daily runs for the sheepdogs, let off the chain to gallivant around, while Will and Kate tossed hay to whickering horses. There was washing to get in, lawns to control before they turned into paddock, drench guns to rinse and Dad's boots to clean. Mum's vegetable garden to hoe, seeds to spread, rattled on drying racks and then funnelled into envelopes and recorded. Jobs to do, always together. Kate and Will.

When they were inside, the television lay dormant most nights. A sleeping black square in the corner of the room.

The life in the house came from music and meals. Food and music was to be shared. Fresh food from the garden, her mother delighting in the imperfections and personalities her homegrown vegetables and fruits revealed. The comedy of a carrot with a twisted old man's nose, a lazy potato with a belly and a head, brown slugs in the broccoli and green grubs in apricots, spiders in stems. Life from the garden, making its way to the table and into their bellies. An experience Nell had never had, Kate realised. She'd grown up with supermarket produce; perfectly shaped and sized, yet tasteless and blasted with enough chemicals to kill the spiders, slugs and grubs. With a rush, Kate suddenly longed for those times again – a life with homegrown food, fun and music. To revive her mother's Irish ancestry and pass it on to Nell.

At Bronty homestead, as a teenager, there had never been any reason to shut herself away in her room and blow her skull off with techno noise. Kate's family had danced and sung and shouted to the backdrop of a mishmash of songs. Old LPs, dusty tapes and CDs. The Beatles, Elvis, Slim, Vivaldi, thrown in with Madonna, Rolf Harris, The Pogues and Johnny Cash. She wanted those songs now for Nell. That kind of life for Nell. Nell, who had already been babysat far too often by the TV. Now Kate felt she had a chance to make amends.

'You're watering the lucerne?' Kate asked Henry as brightly as she could. 'I'll come. Help you shift a few pipes if you like.'

Annabelle turned to face her.

'Don't you think we should settle you in for the night? It's very late. Perhaps you could do the morning shift for your father?'

Kate looked at Henry. He nodded.

'A hand in the morning'd be good.' He turned and walked out of the kitchen.

'Come on,' Annabelle said, 'I'll get you a towel.'

Kate followed her along the hall; Annabelle's small designer-tracksuited-bottom wavered like a Siamese cat. From the linen cupboard, she pulled out a set of neatly matching towels, placing a face washer on top. Kate was shocked that the sheets and towels were catalogued in colours and flattened like stacks of cardboard.

Last time Kate had seen in the cupboard, it had been a rumble of sheets tumbled in with tattered, patched-up board games. Monopoly, Twister and Squatter, all mixed in with face washers, hand towels and mop-up towels for orphan lambs or puppy wee.

Annabelle smiled from over her shoulder as she made her way to the bedrooms.

'Amy hasn't had a moment to move her things out of your room. Exams. So you and Nell will just have to make do with the office for now, if you don't mind.'

Just before she went, Annabelle paused gently and said, 'Perhaps we could think about using the space in Will's room?' And then she was gone, pulling the door shut and leaving Kate clutching the towels.

Gingerly, Kate opened the door and stepped across the passage to Will's room. Inside, it was as she remembered. He had a small desk, crammed with books on farming. His single bed and wardrobe meant there was not much room for anything else. She slumped on the bed and stared at the photo on the wall. A young Will in shorts, all smiles as he cuddled a pup and a lamb. Beside him, Kate, holding a bottle of milk with a black rubber teat. She was pulling a stupid face.

Kate stared at the photo, trying hard to conjure the smells, sounds and details of that day when their mother had taken the picture. She pulled Will's pillow out from his roughly made bed and breathed in his smell, her tears pooling darkly on the fabric.

When she looked up she was startled by the sight of Aden standing above her. She turned her head away and swiped tears from her eyes. She felt the bed subside a little as Aden sat beside her. Then she felt an arm around her shoulders, pulling her in.

'Shhh. Shhhh . . . it's okay,' he whispered. Kate let Aden cradle her body and she leaned her head onto his chest. As she cried into his shirt, she realised she had lost the faint earthy smell of Will that had lingered on the sheets. Instead, her senses were assaulted by Aden's aerosol deodorant. She pulled away.

'Katie, c'mon.' He reached out and brushed the sheen of dark hair that had fallen over her face. He hooked the strands of her hair over her ear and Kate felt suddenly exposed. 'We'll get through this.'

She pushed him away from her.

'Leave me alone!' Then she stumbled from the room. In the darkness of the office, she climbed into the narrow trundle bed, fully clothed, shivering. She pulled Nellie's warm, sleepy body to her and cried silently, listening to her little girl's gentle breath.

Twelve

Kate could see the ewes, one thousand of them, dotting the hill. Grey blobs of woolly sheep, grazing every which way. The bluster of the sea breeze stole the sound of the ute's diesel engine, so the ewes only lifted their heads when Kate was nearly upon them. Clipped up in the ute's tray was Will's border collie, Grumpy. He pricked up his ears, only to have them blasted down again by a sudden gust that tore in from the sea. Bunkered down beside him was Sheila. In her state of self-imposed retirement, she had made a nest in the shreds of hay and tangle of ropes that littered the ute. The old dog barely twitched awake as the scent of sheep swept past her nostrils.

The ewes mobbed a bit, but stood, turning their faces towards the vehicle. Will had them quiet, Kate noted. He'd been such a brilliant, natural stockman. Just two weeks had passed since his death and the pain was still so raw. In the house the grief felt worse. A culmination of loss; her mother and Will, replaced by a family of strangers. But out on Bronty, Kate felt her mum and Will with her in the landscape. She was home.

Kate reefed on the handbrake, switched off the engine and checked the ute was in gear. She turned to look at Nell, who was strapped into her booster seat.

'I'm not sure how Uncle Will's dog is going to work today – he doesn't really know me and I don't know him – so I'm going to walk for a bit, to help him get started. You want to come or do you want to wait here? It's a bit yucky out there.'

Nell looked out at the blustery paddocks.

'Wait here,' she said and smiled eagerly as Kate passed her a box of sultanas.

Out in the wind, Kate tugged her cap down hard, her pony-tail only just keeping it anchored. She unclipped Grumpy. He leapt from the ute and bolted in the direction of the sheep. But Kate's piercing whistle called him back.

'Come behind,' she ordered. Reluctantly he trotted behind her heels as she stood, looking up the hill, taking in which way she should send him. With this wind, the sheep would be flighty and the dog would have a battle to hear her. She wasn't sure if she could trust him on a long cast.

Instead, she decided to mob the sheep up a bit more herself. There could be some weak ones and she didn't want to have to lug any up onto the ute by herself. Since she'd given birth to Nell, she hadn't trusted herself with physical work. Her confidence in her body and her own strength had somehow eroded after having the baby. Her hours deskbound in the Orange office hadn't helped, either.

Time, she thought, would bring back her faith in her body – and walking the sloping pitch and roll of Bronty's hills. Kate's thigh muscles flexed with effort as she began to stride uphill.

When her father asked her to muster the ewes for pre-lamb shearing, Kate was keen to gather them on horseback. Riding Matilda, she would have a lot more control of Grumpy. But asking Annabelle to babysit hadn't been easy. Since the funeral, Kate and Annabelle had both been careful to avoid laying bare the underlying bitterness between them that was always there.

This morning, when Kate asked Annabelle if she could mind Nell for a couple of hours, Annabelle flapped about the kitchen.

Her monologue of duties was like a mantra; there was washing to do, beds to make, and meals . . . so many meals with all these people staying . . . Annabelle resembled a robotic Stepford wife on overload.

Kate struggled as the reality of life at Bronty without Will began to sink in. She was lonely without him. And her step-family hadn't yet warmed to Nell as she'd hoped they might. Amy and Aden, uninterested in little children, kept their distance. Annabelle was blatantly bossy around Nell, telling her not to open cupboards or put feet on furniture, treating her like she was always in the way or making a mess. Kate had thought about asking her father to mind Nell, but the concept was so foreign that she couldn't bring herself to ask.

In the days following the funeral, Kate caught Henry looking at Nell with a glimmer of fascination in his eye – even, she imagined, a hint of the first blossoming of love for his little granddaughter. When Nell had first called Henry Grandpa, Kate noticed the way he started at the term. Then, stooping down to look her in the eye, Henry had winked at her and given her a tickle in the ribs. She had giggled and tickled him back. Nell began to gravitate towards Henry. With the unselfconsciousness of a child, she would clamber onto his knee to show him something or chatter on about the discoveries in her world. But even though she was claiming him as her grandpa, Henry was still struggling with claiming her. Kate knew he would baulk at being asked to spend one-on-one time with her. So this morning Kate had no option but to take Nell with her in the ute. There would be no horse riding today.

As she circled the sheep, she could see Nell eating sultanas one by one and watching the stock. Nell was used to waiting in paddocks. At Auntie Maureen's farm, Kate would strap the tiny bundle of Nell into the car capsule while Kate fed out hay bales to the sheep. Sometimes she'd breastfeed Nell sitting cross-legged in the paddock, amongst the scattering of sheep ballbearings, as a line of ewes guzzled down hay in messy mouthfuls. Kate would tug up her top and as she unclipped her maternity bra, the dried grass of last summer would fall onto her baby's face. Little seeds stubbornly stuck to Nell's perfect skin. With grubby, dirt-grained fingers Kate gently wiped them away in case they made their way into Nell's eyes.

Now, in the blast of the wind, Kate was glad to be outside on Bronty, with Nell nearby, free from Annabelle and the homestead. She powered up the hill with Grumpy at her heels.

When she did at last send the dog around the sheep, he skittered out wide in a textbook collie cast and held them calmly. She knew in an instant she could rely on him to hold them while she went back for the ute. She should've trusted him in the first place. She should've known Will's dog would be as gentle and kind as his owner had been. At the ute, she smiled as she tapped on the window and waved at Nell. Nell laughed back, sultanas falling from her mouth.

Kate drove the ute over the hill's rocky outcrop, flanking the sheep, while Grumpy took control at the back of the mob. The dog ran in perfect half-arcs as if he were tracing the invisible outline of a crescent moon on the grass, over and over.

As they neared the fenceline on the lee side of the hill she saw the gateway. Muscles tensed in her neck and shoulders. The stretch of choppy sea beyond blended with dark rain-laden clouds, the sky and sea merging in one churning tempest of grey.

At the gate, Kate got out of the ute and held up her hand to Grumpy. He sat, eyeing the leaders of the mob, hovering, should one break. Kate then went to open the gate. She tried not to look, but she couldn't help it. There was the bent frame, the warped hinges where the bolts had only just held in the strainer post, the scuff marks on the ground, still visible. Spray paint from the police investigations and the tattered remains of fluttering yellow plastic tape. There it all was. The horror of it. Kate broke down, her sobs torn from her mouth by the wind. She kept her back to Nell, so her daughter couldn't see.

Teeth gritted, she shook the gate angrily. Her temples throbbed. Ripping off her cap, she sank her forehead onto the cold metal frame and banged her head lightly until her skin reddened and she began to feel the pain.

'Will. Mum. Will. Mum,' she chanted quietly over and over.

Behind her, the sheep began to wander so Grumpy cast himself out to block the lead. Kate breathed in deeply to gain control, swiped her face, then unhooked the stubborn chain. She dragged the gate open, hating it. Wanting to rip it out with the ute.

She stood back and faced the view as the ewes trickled past, taking it all in. Will's last vision. The sea. That magnificent stretch of coastline. That crescent-moon bay. A living heaven. A haven.

Kate watched as the ewes picked up the sheep tracks and drifted off towards the direction of the shearing shed far below. Then she got back into the ute and sat with Nell, stroking her hair.

'Mummy loves you, you know,' she said. 'So, so much.'

'Bird!' said Nell, pointing to a sea eagle riding high on the wind.

'Yes, darling, there's two out there. See? A mummy bird . . .'

'. . . and baby bird!'

'Yes, Nellie. And her baby bird.'

'Where's the daddy bird?'

'Sometimes the daddy bird isn't around.'

'Why?' asked Nell.

'Coz.'

'Coz why?'

'Just coz.'

Thirteen

The first of the shearers arrived early the next day. The sun was only just dragging itself above the water and sea mist still hovered in the gullies. The men stood in front of the shearing shed, trying to shake the morning chill from their bones. They pulled their coats tightly about them, then ambled to the boot of their mud-splattered, low-slung car. From there they gathered up their thermoses, toolboxes, lunch containers, shearers' slings, ragged sweat towels and shearing moccasins. Stomping up the steps in tired-looking Blundstone boots, the men entered the shed.

Inside, Kate was setting up an area between the wool press and the bins. On a colourful rug, she placed snacks in plastic containers, toys, blankets, pillows and books. Nell was at the end of the board dragging the wool paddle noisily across the floorboards and barking orders at the young dog, Bra, who was tied up in one of the pens. Nell looked like an inflatable dolly in her red padded coat and waterproof trousers. She glanced up when she heard the men come in.

'Got school *and* shearing in here this mornin'?' said one of the men.

'G'day, Razor!' Kate said, her face lighting up with recognition. 'Been a while.' She took in his familiar face that sagged a little at the cheeks, like the jowls of an old sheep.

'You didn't see me a couple of weeks back? In the crowd at your brother's . . . do?' Razor said, clearly not able to utter the word funeral.

'Sorry, no I didn't. I was . . . you know.'

He waved Kate's apology away with an air of understanding. 'Got your little 'un helping us today?'

'That's my Nell. Hope it doesn't bother you having her in the shed.'

'Her ladyship at the house not up for mindin' her then?'

Kate saw the glimmer in Razor's eye, which was punctuated with a wink and a wry smile. Suddenly she knew she had an ally and the coming week of shearing all the ewe mobs on the property seemed less daunting.

Razor stooped down to Nell's level.

'You'll be right, won't you, Gert?' Razor smiled. Nell grinned back. Kate indicated the other man standing near them.

'Who's your mate, Razor? Aren't you going to introduce us?' The younger man looked up from where he was hooking his cutters on a nail above his stand. They dangled on a piece of looped wire like rows of silver shark's teeth.

'Oh, I've met Kate Webster before,' the man said. 'It's just she don't remember me.'

Kate took in his short stature, the beginnings of a beer belly and slightly beaky nose, not recalling him at all.

'Seen you round at a B&S or two in my time,' he said, as if that would trigger something. When Kate still looked blank, he went on. 'Jonesy. Jack Jones. From Campbell Town way.'

He held out his hand and Kate shook it, still staring at his face as if her lapsed memory of him was written there in tiny print.

'Well, c'mon! *Jones*! With a name like that you could be any number of blokes I've met,' she teased, laughing to mask her panic. Was he there the night she tackled Nick McDonnell? Would he recognise something in Nell?

'I don't mind a B&S or three,' she barrelled on. 'Must've

killed off the brain cell that remembered meeting you though. Sorry.'

He smiled at her, a crooked, friendly smile, and shrugged. Then he hung his towel, hitched up his shearer's dungers, tightening his striped cloth belt and went to cast his eyes over the ewes in the catching pens, in a shearer's summation of what sort of work he'd have on today.

Outside the shed, the dogs barked suddenly as a dark twin-cab ute drove in. From it emerged two more shearers and the wool roller. They ambled into the shed and nodded greetings to Kate. Like Razor, they were the regulars, Rocker, B.D., and the slow-moving Trev, ready to take his spot on the table.

'Got some cheap labour there. Under-18 award?' said B.D., indicating Nell on the board.

The men smiled, but there was a melancholy that enveloped them all in the cold shed. The death of Will was still raw in the air. Already they missed his welcome. Will, who was the boss of the shed as the wool classer, would draw the men in with his friendly banter in the smoko room, sparking conversation with his easy nature. But at this year's pre-lamb shearing, the sadness amongst the men was tangible. There was hesitancy in them and a self-consciousness that came with Will's absence.

'So, you the boss classer today?' Razor asked, breaking the silence that was filled only with the pattering of sheep's hooves on grating. Kate shook her head. In the lead-up to shearing Henry had insisted he would step in to oversee the wool table and class the fleeces.

'Nah. I'm just the dogsbody – in and out of the shed for the week. Aden should be here any minute to rousie.' Kate glanced at the clock on the wall ticking towards the 7.30 mark.

'Better hurry up if he is,' said Rocker, stooping to pull on his grey shearer's moccasins.

'He'll be here,' Kate said uncertainly. As she spoke, Henry stepped into the shed and cleared his throat, mumbling a greeting to the men. In his navy woollen work jumper and blue checked shirt that poked two triangles out at the collar, he looked every part the cockie. He removed his hat and hung it on the same nail he hung it on every year. Striding to the wool table, he raised an eyebrow at the collection of child's things in the corner.

'That's normally where the cotted and coloured fleeces go,' he said critically.

Kate felt her face redden. She knew, as the day wore on, once the fleeces began to pile up, space in the shed was a precious commodity. When she had claimed that area for Nell, she'd known she was testing the traditional system – a system Will had fine-tuned since gaining his professional classer's stencil.

'I know, Dad, but can't we put a fleece line straight in the press? Save a bit of space?'

Her father shrugged, displeased, and moved off to shake out one of the stiff woolpacks and place it in a boxy metal frame for the briskets.

Kate glanced again at the clock, wishing Aden would get here soon. She called Nell over to her and crouched down, holding her by the hands.

'Mum's got to work at the shed today and for the next few days. She needs you to stay in here and help too, so Grandpa doesn't get cross. Okay? Now see this line?' Kate grabbed a piece of chalk from the tally board and drew it across the floorboards.

'You don't go across this line, or you'll get in the way of the shearers, right? No little girls past this line. Yes?' She drew a stick figure of a girl, with a circle around her and a cross through it.

Nell nodded. She knew shearing was serious business. She'd been in Maureen's shed each crutching and shearing since she was born. She was used to the noisy rattle of the tin walls, the whine of a wool press under full pressure and the sudden crack of a broom if one fell to the board. She knew to steer clear of the running rouseabouts and the men bent

118

over the sheep. Even at three, Nell was an old hand in the shed. But how could Henry know that? Kate stiffened, realising how much she had to prove to her father today.

'Now, Nellie, later when we start shearing, you can help Grandpa sort the locks and the bellies. Okay?'

'Yes, Mummy, I'll help Grandpa.'

'Great stuff, Nell. Good on you.'

On the stroke of 7.30, just as the men hitched up their dungers to make a start on the first sheep, Aden arrived. He brought with him a waft of deodorant, his hair, still wet from the shower, spiking upwards. His smooth face and fair skin a sharp contrast to the tanned, lined faces of the shearers. Kate handed him a paddle.

"Bout time,' she said, wanting to tear strips off him for being so late. Instead she decided to keep the peace. She surveyed his trendy hair. 'Nice do, mate.'

'Thanks,' he said, patting his peroxide spikes, playing along with her sarcasm.

'You worked in sheds before?' she asked.

'Nope. Only swept up for crutching last time I was here.'

'Great,' she said blandly. 'You'll be flat knacker with four shearers, so you gotta sprint. Okay? I'll help for the first run, but after that you'll be on your own.'

He nodded, a committed expression on his narrow face.

As the men started on their first sheep for the day, Aden leant on the paddle and watched, transfixed, as the men began to push their handpieces through the belly wool.

'Rule one,' Kate said, kicking the base of the paddle out from under him. 'Never lean on a broom or a paddle. A good rouseabout never stops still.'

Shocked, Aden pulled his body to attention, realising the day spelt more work than he had bargained for. Briskly Kate showed him how to skirt the belly wool, flicking the soft grey and white discs over and back. Her hands moved expertly. Swiftly and purposefully she darted about the shed, talking as she went. She explained how to take the short wool from the leg as the shearer made a blow down the hocks.

'If you take the back leg off now on the board, then there's less work for the classer on the table. Quick, grab the next fella's.' She indicated B.D., who was flicking the leg wool over, ready to pivot his sheep onto its side.

Aden struggled to follow the flurry of activity, amazed at the precision and pace with which Kate worked. Hypnotised by the verve of Razor, B.D., Rocker and Jonesy as they stripped the wool from the ewes with maximum efficiency and, seemingly, minimum effort.

'You gotta always be on the ball,' Kate said to Aden, as she stooped and removed dags from a fleece.

'You gotta constantly look out for stain, like this.' She held up the green balls of dried manure and put them in a bin. 'If you see any stain whatsoever – take it out. Poop, pee, blood – all out. And make sure the men have everything they need. A clean space when they bring their next sheep out. Got it? Do as they say. Keep 'em happy,' she said, talking loudly over the buzz and hum of the machines.

Squatting down, Kate showed Aden how to prepare the fleece on the board ready for a pick-up, while Razor finished off the back haunches of the sheep. She showed Aden how to gather the fleece up and throw it on the table. And how to dash back to sweep away the short locks just in the nick of time as the shearer dragged the next ewe into place. She pointed out bins and baskets and gave him tips and techniques, working and moving all the while. She showed him the sheep in the pens and which way they flowed the best, and where the raddles sat on a beam, should there be a wether or a dry ewe in the mob that needed a quick stripe on the nose.

By smoko, two hours later, Aden was sweating as much as the shearers and Kate was nearly at the end of her tether. Aden was needier than her three-year-old, Kate concluded. All the while Nell had been happily drawing chalk on the upright posts of the shed. As the machines fell silent for smoko, Kate noticed Razor, still standing on his place on the board, watching Aden sweep the locks away at a snail's pace. Razor gave Kate a quick conspiratorial wink, in recognition of Aden's uselessness. Then he stood straight, stretching his back, pushing his round belly out even further.

'Ah, I'm gettin' too old for this.'

'You're gettin' too fat for it, more like,' said Jonesy, flicking Razor's rotund gut with the back of his hand.

'Looks like you're in training behind me,' Razor said, tapping Jonesy's belly back.

'Yeah? When was the last time you seen your willy without using a mirror?' Jonesy asked. Everyone laughed.

Razor shook his head.

'Cocky little bugger. If shed staff weren't so hard to find you'd be out on your ear, Jonesy. I've been comfort eating so's I can put up with you.'

Kate smiled at Razor, taking in the sheen on his bald head and the way the coarse black hairs covering his shoulders lay flat on his skin with sweat. He looked tough, but beneath his formidable appearance she knew he was a soft touch. He leant towards her, ushering her away down the board, out of earshot. His serious demeanour back in place as he stepped into his role of lead shearer.

'You sure Aden'll keep up once you're outside? He's not much of a rousie. Suffers from narcolepsy if you ask me. He's even slower than Trev.'

'Couldn't you bring another rouseabout with your team for the rest of the week, if you think we'll fall short?' Kate asked.

'It's your old man's clip. It's his call on how many staff he wants. But good rouseabouts are hard to come by. I've a job to get them meself. He'll probably find no bloody bugger wants to work,' Razor said.

'More like no bugger wants to stand next to your bent-over fartin' arse all day,' Jonesy chipped in.

'Ah, sunshine, you're just jealous of the *"Eeee-lectric Razor"*,' Razor said, swivelling his hips in a twist.

Jonesy turned to Kate and pretended to whisper. 'He thinks the fellas call him Razor coz he's a fast shearer. Really it's coz he needs a back, sack and crack wax. Check out his wombat arse next time he bends over. Hairiest bastard I've ever seen.'

Kate laughed and rolled her eyes.

'Nice,' she said.

'Stick a sock in it, Jonesy. At least Nell's me mate,' he said, sauntering over to her. 'How are you getting on, Gertie?'

Nell was sitting in a wool bin on a pile of AAM, talking to her dolly.

'She's doing all right,' Henry said, looking up from where he skirted the last fleece for the early-morning run. 'She's my little offsider, aren't you?'

Nell looked up at Henry and smiled. Kate took in the way Henry bent his head to the side when he spoke to Nell and the way the corners of his serious mouth turned up in a rare smile. Instantly she felt relief flooding through her.

During her time on the board, Kate had felt the pressure of needing to be ever-vigilant about Nell. Between that and Aden's incompetence, she felt worn down and it was only day one, run one! Now she realised that Henry had been watching Nell too, all the while he worked.

Before she had come to the shed, Kate had planned every diversion strategy possible, to keep Nell quiet. To prove to her father that she could work the shed *and* be a mother. Kate had the inventory etched in her over-busy mind: Nell's little blue and yellow drink bottle had to be handy. A biscuit or three in her red lunch-box. A piece of fruit. A book . . . not just any book, but the ones she loved. A coat, spare trousers for accidents, an extra hat, sun-screen, tissues, wipes, T-shirts for unexpected hot weather, gloves for unexpected cold weather. And for when the wheels really fell off, there was Nell's blood-warm bottle of milk, her baby bunny blanket and her soft, squashy pillow for a special snuggly treat. All the diversions and comforts were tucked away, not just in Kate's head, but also in a big blue bag of tricks that Aunt Maureen had made.

But now, with her father there, working on the table and stopping every now and then to engage in Nell's play, Kate felt the pressure on her easing a little.

As Razor, Trev and Jonesy disappeared into the crib room for their smoko, Kate hoisted the blue bag up onto the greasy slats of the wool table next to Henry and began to rummage through it. She turned to her father. 'I'm going out now to bring more sheep up from under the shed. Do you mind helping Nell to some smoko?'

Henry didn't look at Kate. Instead he looked to Nell.

'Want to eat some cake with Pa?' he asked, holding out his hand to her. Nell leapt up and skipped to him, her arms outstretched in her child's request to be picked up. Kate smiled and handed Henry a drink cup as he swung Nell up onto his hip.

'Thanks, Dad,' she said, then she turned and left the shed. From the smoko room, she could hear Razor's nasal twang rise up in excruciating song and the sound of a spoon rhythmically hitting the lids of the coffee tins.

'Geez! Is someone castrating a cat in there?' Kate heard Rocker call from the back pens as he relieved himself over the grating. She smiled. Despite Will's absence, here in the Bronty shed with the fellas was where Kate belonged. It was where she found life again.

Outside in the bright sunlight that had chased the frost away, Kate began to count the sheep from the pens. As she swung the gates shut, she pulled a notebook from her jeans pocket and wrote down the tallies, eyeing the blows the men had made that striped over the ewes' backs. From her count, Razor was still the gun and, she observed, the neatest shearer.

She whistled Grumpy. He bounded to her as she looked

up across the paddocks to where, yesterday, her father had lumbered over the ground with the tractor and disc plough. The dark red soil marked a big rectangle on the hillside of dull green. Just the thought of the tractor prompted a wave of gut-wrenching grief. Turning away, she stooped and undid the gate under the shearing shed, wishing Will alive again.

As the ewes emerged from the musky darkness under the shed, Kate wondered how the rest of the day would unfold. She had outside work to do now: sheep to backline and drench, dry sheep to draft off, more mobs to get in. But Aden was proving to be slower than a wet week as a rousie, and even though Nell and her father were doing well, what would happen once Nell got tired of being in the shed? Again, she felt the fierce ache of Will's absence.

Later, her outside work done for the moment, Kate rolled back the massive corrugated-iron door so it rumbled like thunder. She stepped inside the shed, bringing with her feeble sunshine that draped itself, gold, over the grating and backs of the woolly ewes. As she rolled the door shut, closing out the sun, she noticed the shearing machines were idle. She could hear Aden swearing and the panicked rappel of hooves as the mob ran like a river in flood, banking up against the fences. She checked her watch. Twenty minutes before lunch. Why had they stopped shearing?

The shearers were standing with their backs to the catching pens. They bowed their heads in silence while they changed their cutters, clutching round-handled screwdrivers and tinkering with their handpieces. Their lanolin-covered thumbs slid cutters back and forth, against the long teeth of the combs. The sound of metal sliding over metal.

Once satisfied that the fresh cutters and clean combs would get them through the next lot of gritty-woolled coastal sheep, the men bent the steely elbows of the down tubes and reconnected their handpieces. With a thud they set them on the floor, in position. They hoisted up their trousers, ready to start. But the catching pens were still empty. Glancing at each other,

Razor and Jonesy swung the doors and moved towards Aden and the sheep.

'We'll give you a hand,' Razor said.

'I'm right,' Aden puffed. 'I don't need your help.'

Henry glanced up from where he and Trev were trying to sort through a tumble of fleece wool on the table. Kate saw that the board was strewn with locks, scattered about and banking up against the walls like snowdrifts. Unskirted fleeces were jumbled in piles at the end of the slatted wool table like towering cumulus clouds before a storm.

Razor fixed his gaze on the puffing young man who'd just rejected their offer for help.

'Suit yourself,' he said, before he ambled off to perch on the wool table and talk footy finals with Jonesy. Rocker and B.D. gave each other a look, then reached for their water bottles and joined the other men.

In the pens, Aden hurled a ewe at the gateway. The sharp angle of her jaw collected the corner of the wooden upright and the whole shed rattled. Aden picked her up again and was about to throw her towards the catching pen when Kate shouted out.

'Oi!'

She pushed her way through the mob towards him.

'The old bitches won't run,' he said, gritting his teeth. As the ewe made a dash past him, she saw him raise his fist.

'Aden! Don't!'

His knuckles connected with the bony face of the ewe. The sheep's frightened eyes rolled back in her head and she sank down on her front knees. Heavy in wool and carrying a lamb, her back legs buckled beneath her.

'Stop it!' Kate yelled. Blood trickled from the ewe's nose and into the soft crevice of her mouth. At the sound of Kate's voice, the bulk of Razor's body hit the catching-pen doors and left them swinging wildly like saloon doors in a fistfight. He scruffed Aden, wedged a big grizzly-bear arm against his neck, and pinned him to a post.

'I had an inkling this mornin' you were a fuckwit, mate. Now you've confirmed it,' he said, clutching Aden's shirt-front and giving him a shake for good measure.

'Get off me!' Aden clasped his hands over Razor's gorilla arm. But as he looked into Razor's eyes, Aden's anger withered. Razor was all muscle, sinew, rough stubble and bad manners when he wanted to be. His yellow-toothed snarl, his pungent male odour and the pulse of the veins on his sweat-smeared temples set him up easily as alpha male. Aden, in his ironed shirt, freshly tipped hair and new boots, looked like he was on the set of a TV show.

Aden again kicked and struggled, but the hands that clutched him had had thirty years of holding the weight of full-wool rams while driving a hot and lively handpiece through their fleece. The hands that held him weren't going anywhere.

'Bashin' up pregnant women ain't on, mate,' Razor said. 'I don't care whether they're a sheep or a dog or a friggin' frog. *It's. Not. On.*'

'Let him go.' The voice of Henry Webster cut through the melee.

Razor turned to face the boss.

'Sorry, Henry, but I won't have any of the shed staff bashin' the sheep.' Razor slowly removed his grip from the red-faced Aden. 'And I won't have my men shearing knee-deep in fleece wool like we've had to since Kate left the shed. It's not on. He's slowing us up. Little Nell there would do a better job of it!' Knowing Will's absence was the reason behind the stressful chaotic morning, Razor softened his voice and looked Henry in the eye.

'If it's okay with you, we'll have an early lunch, mate. Give you time to find an extra rouseabout. All right?'

Henry Webster sighed.

'Fair enough,' he said, knowing Razor was right.

With a tilt of his head, Henry indicated to Aden that he should come with him. Aden tugged down his shirt, stood up straight, and with cheeks flushed crimson followed Henry from the shed, leaving the men to tidy their gear before lunch in silence. Kate moved to gather Nell up, knowing her little girl was perplexed by the scene. She sat her on her hip, gave her a comforting kiss and brushed a few curls from her eyes. When Kate turned towards the men, Jonesy was shaking with laughter.

'Geez, mate, you're a dipstick.' He gave Razor a shove.

'What?' Razor said.

'It's tadpoles,' Jonesy said.

'Tadpoles?'

'Yeah,' Jonesy explained. 'You told him frogs get pregnant. Friggin' frogs don't get pregnant, mate. They lay them goobelly eggs in the dams after they've had a bit of frog sprog and then they have tadpoles. You ever seen a pregnant frog?'

Everyone burst out laughing, Razor stifling a smile and shaking his head.

'He knew what I meant. Anyway, I wasn't giving him a bloody biological lecture.'

'He needs a bloody lecture though,' Kate said. 'Sheep psychology level one, perhaps?'

'Level one'd be too hard for a dickhead like him,' Jonesy said. 'Gave me the irrits as soon as I seen him, he did.'

Rocker added in agreement. 'Sooner we get another rouseabout the better.'

'Problem is,' Kate said, 'who?'

Fourteen

Kate was in the catching pens, stripped down to her T-shirt, a sheen of sweat covering her brow, when Nick McDonnell walked into the shed. Shocked, she swiped away strands of hair that had escaped her ponytail, her eyes glued to him. God, she thought, her dad had asked *him* to be the new rouseabout!

She glanced at Nell, lying near the wool table on her blankets, a book still open, her eyes shut, sound asleep. Her relaxed face revealing so many similarities to the man who stood above her. Kate watched in horror as Nick looked down at her and smiled. He gingerly stepped over the sleeping child and went to shake Henry's hand in greeting.

Oh. My. God. Nick McDonnell is here, thought Kate.

At Nick's arrival, Rocker looked up from his sheep and let out a whoop.

'You bloody bewdy! G'day Nickel-arse!'

Nick waved a greeting.

Razor reached behind for the cord and pulled his machine out of gear. He gently stood the ewe up, letting the old girl find her way down the small drop to the count-out pen. He greeted Nick with a handshake and a grin as wide as his combs. Nick clearly belonged as one of them, Kate thought. He was welcome and well liked.

Aden glanced up from where he was sorting wool and nodded a sulky hello. In the back pens Kate dropped the well-worn wooden latch into position, but didn't let go of the rail, her mouth still open. As she continued to stare at Nick from the darkened back of the shed, she was startled by Jonesy's voice.

'Close your mouth, Kate,' he said as he gently tipped over another ewe. 'He's not *that* handsome.' He gathered the ewe up by the front legs and dragged her out of the catching pen, giving Kate a wink.

For the next few minutes as she moved mobs about in the back pens, Kate watched Nick through the maze of shed uprights, her heart racing. She took in his square-set shoulders and his face, more handsome than her memory of the night at the pub had allowed. His firm jaw, set serious as he concentrated on his work. Yet despite his sombre expression he was undisputedly delicious and downright sexy. But then with a jolt she recalled she was staring at the father of her child. She sucked in a nervous breath. At that moment, Nick spotted her. His face lit up. A sunshine smile. He raised a hand. Kate waved back and swung her leg over the fence, Grumpy leaping over beside her. As she stepped out onto the board she smoothed her palms over her thighs nervously.

'Hi,' she said.

'Hi, Kate.'

She shoved her hands in her back pockets and looked down at her boots. Then, horrified that the position made her breasts stick out, she whipped her hands out again and folded them across her chest.

'Thanks for dropping everything and coming over,' she said.

'No problem. We got plenty of help when Dad had his accident. It's the least I can do for Will.'

Kate was thrown by the sudden mention of Will's name, her self-consciousness instantly quashed as grief rose up again. She felt tears well at the tenderness she saw in Nick's gentle, sympathetic expression. Nick rested his hand on her upper arm.

'I'm sorry. Eh?'

Then his hand was gone and Kate was left feeling as if he'd imprinted his warm, calm energy within her. She nodded, taking in his earnest way. Then suddenly he smiled brightly at her, a crinkle appeared beside his eyes, a dimple on one side of his mouth.

'Better get to work, or they'll sack me before I've even begun.'

'Yep. Leave you to it. You seem to know how the shed runs, right?' Kate said.

Nick nodded, smiled again and was off with the broom. Kate watched him jog to the end of the board. He stooped and grabbed up a fleece, delivering a friendly comment that made Rocker laugh, then made his way to the table, brushing past her, and floated the white AAA wool through the air so it landed perfectly on the wool table slats. Henry nodded at him gratefully, took up the wool and began to skirt the fleece. In a flash, Nick was back at the far end of the board to drag the locks away before Jonesy returned with another sheep. Flicking a belly in Aden's direction for him to skirt, Nick swept his way back down the board towards Kate. She stood at the table opposite her father, clutching wool between thumb and forefinger, skirting the frib quickly from the fleece towards Trev. She watched the flex of Nick's forearms as he quickly swept up the entire shed, then made his way towards the table. Quick broom flicks, clearing the way for Henry and Kate's feet on the well-trodden path around the wool table.

'Excuse me,' he said. He moved past Kate, catching her eye again with a smile as he swept on.

Henry glanced up.

'Good rousie,' he said.

'He seems to be,' Kate said, feeling blood rush to her cheeks.

'Now Nick's here and Nell's asleep, how 'bout you get the

maiden mob in? Best take a horse. Save time on coming over the big hill, rather than take 'em along the creek track.'

'Okay, Dad. No problem.'

She stooped to draw a blanket further over Nell's shoulders and, reluctant to leave the shed now, sneaked one more glance at Nick as he whipped along the board as if he were dancing on air.

Outside, Kate leant against the shed wall for a moment sucking in air and banging the back of her head gently against the tin. It was ridiculous to think of Nick that way. He was engaged, in love with someone else, and he didn't even *know* his connection with Nell. There was no way he'd be interested in Kate now. But she couldn't believe how gorgeous she found him. How she felt electric currents when he came near. How everything in the shed seemed different now he was there. The droning sound of the shearing machines became intoxicating. The smell of sheep manure, lanolin and sweat, mixed with the atmosphere of hard work, framed Nick in a world that Kate adored. She felt breathless in his presence. But at the same time a fear beat in her heart. Had he looked at Nell and seen the likeness?

Will's words echoed in her head. 'You should tell him about Nell.' Kate shut her eyes, and gently shook her head, but still Will's voice persisted. 'It's for Nell's sake too, Kate. It's not always just about you.'

In the horse yard, Kate stepped into the stirrup and swung up onto her horse.

From inside the shed, Nick watched her through a cobweb-framed window. There she was on her horse in a red T-shirt, her dark hair falling down her back in a ponytail from beneath her cap. A collie dog at the heels of her sturdy bay mare. He watched as she tightened the jumper that was tied around her waist. Then she urged the horse into a trot. Nick had had this girl in his dreams since he was a teenager, yet she seemed different in real life. She was a grown-up version of his fantasy-woman, but just as beautiful. She was everything he'd imagined, except for the fact that she had a child. Somehow that just didn't fit with his memory of her.

Nick sensed someone standing close by. Jonesy rubbed a grimy brush over his cutter in a slow circular action, his tongue playing wet on his top lip. He followed Nick's gaze, then turned and smiled wickedly at Nick.

'Ah no, mate,' Nick said, shaking his head. 'Not me.'

Jonesy laughed as he slapped Nick on the back. 'Never thought of riding one and leading one at the same time?'

Nick laughed along with him, but he felt the jolt of being engaged to Felicity, yet looking at Kate with longing. As Jonesy went back to his stand, Nick couldn't help staring at the girl on the horse, cantering further and further along the face of the big dome-shaped hill. Kate Webster. His first love.

Fifteen

Time moves differently in shearing sheds, Kate knew. The week-long shearing seemed to roll like a movie, played on a loop over and over for what seemed like months. Kate was in heaven. Long days in the shed with Nick and Nell. Short nights in the house with Annabelle and her family. Despite her tiredness, Kate would bound out of bed in the darkness of early morning, keen to get Nell ready for the shed. Knowing her day would be spent in close contact with the new rouseabout. She began to see Nick whenever she shut her eyes. The way he bent his head to sort the wool, and how his thigh muscles flexed beneath his denim jeans when he tramped down the pieces in the wool bin. His muscular arms as he lifted himself out of wool packs from the beams of the shed and dashed away to tend to a shearer. He was there in her head night and day.

In dawn light in the old lean-to garage, Nell would sit on Henry's knee waiting for the diesel glow light to click off in the cold farm ute. Her eyes shining, her fair curls escaping her little pink beanie. Kate in the passenger seat beside them, the smoko basket on her lap, the dogs breathing steam and dancing about on the back of the ute. The absence of Will tangible but no longer unbearable.

In the shed, as she set the wool bins up for the day and

penned the sheep, she'd look from the wide loading-bay door for Nick's dark ute to arrive on the crest of the highway, lights still on in the early morning. The sun just giving a glimmer to the surface of the darkened bay.

Later, amongst the flurry of the shed, Nick and Kate skylarked with each other and the shearers. Telling jokes, recounting funny stories, yarning. They shared conversations on the run, in between stooping for fleeces and running for the broom. The pain of Will's death at those times laid aside. At other times, when the men fell quiet on the board, Kate simply soaked up Nick's presence, using it as a tonic to heal her grief. As she tended to backlining and drenching outside, she would come and go from the shed, thoughts about Nick and Henry, and above all about Nick and Nell jumbled in her head.

Sometimes, loading the sheep up the sloping ramp into the shed, she caught glimpses of Nick lifting Nell high up so she could swing from the rough-cut rafters. Other times, from the back pens, Kate would see Henry laying his granddaughter down with a warmed cup of milk, soothing her into sleep, Nick watching him, before both men went back to work.

When Kate came inside and switched on the wool press, Nick would come to help shove armfuls of fleeces into the groaning press. She felt goosebumps rise on her forearms when their skin made contact. Facing each other as they bear-hugged large armfuls of fleece together, Kate wished the wool wasn't in between them. She'd catch his eye and they'd smile at each other.

Five days rambled on to feel like five months. When the last sheep was shorn Kate felt a great sadness. The rhythmic sweeping of the broom as Nick washed the board with hot water and the empty spaces that were left on the board after the men packed away all their gear made her feel lost and lonely. Now she must face normal life again, away from the sense of belonging in the shearing shed. And now, Nick would be gone.

Her banter with the men, egging them on for a big cut-out party, hadn't prompted a result. It was Friday evening. The men were keen to get home to families or to the Community Club for the footy tipping. They only drank one beer each as they hung about for their cheques from Henry. Their departure was punctuated by car doors slamming and engines revving. In the silence after they'd gone, Kate looked over to Nick.

'Staying on for another beer?' she asked.

He ran a black ink roller over the boxy face of a wool bale and the straight-edged lettering of a stencil before he answered.

'Sorry. Can't. Felicity has a nurses' dinner on in town tonight.'

At the mention of Felicity's name Kate felt her heart sink.

'Just as well,' came Henry's voice from where he was perched on the wool table, his briefcase open, a calculator and tally book in hand. 'You've got sheep to take away, Kate.'

Trying not to look downcast, Kate put on her brightest smile.

'Might as well have one for the road anyway,' she said, grabbing a stubby and jamming it into a holder. She turned to Nell. 'You coming to ride the horse with Mum?'

'Yes, please!' Nell got off her little plastic bike and followed her.

'I'll see you later,' Nick said. 'I'll just finish up here and be off.'

'Yep. Cheers,' said Kate, keeping her disappointment well hidden. 'Thanks again, mate.'

She knew it was stupid to think of him the way she had been in the past few days. She felt guilty over Felicity, and consumed with uncertainty about whether she should tell Nick about Nell.

Outside Kate sat in the saddle, her arms looped around Nell. They ambled behind the mob of freshly shorn ewes that hungrily picked at grass as they walked. Grumpy trotted behind them, his tongue pale pink and hanging.

Long shadows of the fence posts stretched out across the Bronty drive like railway tracks. The setting sun felt warm on Kate's back, and Nell leant against her chest. A pair of robin red breasts dipped and darted in front of them, creating fleeting dots of iridescent red on the post tops.

Kate bent and kissed the crown of Nell's head. She felt the joy of being home and a gratitude for the week she had just had. It was moments like this, away from the drudgery of sheet changing, clothes washing, food wiping and trying to reason with a toddler, that Kate could feel the delicious pleasure of being a mother. She realised she wouldn't change her situation for the world. She could feel herself surrendering, giving in to having Nell in her life. Kate knew she could give away the drinking and the man chasing now. She and Nell were back on Bronty and that was all that mattered. Here, Kate felt strong enough to protect herself and Nell from what the world might throw at them.

Will's death had shocked her into a new awareness of the preciousness of life. The preciousness of Nell. And now, knowing Nick was such a wonderful person, and that half of Nell was made up of parts of him, her little girl seemed all the more remarkable. Her easy temperament explained; the reason for her gentleness illuminated. Kate could now recognise traits from two people in Nell. She no longer had to half-guess what her father's genes may have brought to her world.

Kate wished she could undo the mistakes she'd made in the past. Perhaps she should have included Nick from the start and come home to tell him? There'd been times in the early days when she'd felt completely alone. She'd screamed at Nell to shut up during her endless, hysterical crying as a baby. She remembered crouching in a corner on the nursery floor and wailing alongside her baby, wondering why her life had ended up like this. Nell in her cot, pink face puckered and tears pooling in her ears and soaking into the Bunnykins sheets. Her little rose-petal tongue vibrating with screams and her gummy mouth cast open in the black shape of an O. Kate, on the floor tugging her hair with hands that ached from stress and sleeplessness, wishing to God she'd had an abortion. But then Kate had risen to her feet. She'd picked Nell up and held her baby to her, instantly remorseful. The exhaustion, and the fear of failing such a tiny being almost sent Kate mad on the days when she was all alone. In the first year or so of Nell's life, Kate felt like she was groping her way through a fog. But now she could see what a remarkable little girl she had in her daughter. Nell hadn't been an ending in Kate's life – she was her beginning. She was her everything. Kate felt she could now make up for their shaky start together.

But sitting astride Matilda with Nell in her arms, Kate suddenly realised just one thing stood in the way of moving on. She had to tell Nick he was Nell's father. But how?

Behind her she heard a vehicle approaching. Kate knew it would be Nick in his sleek Holden ute with the gleaming silver roll bars. She didn't turn around. Nervously she sat straighter in the saddle, imagining how the conversation might go.

Hey, Nick, you know that night at the B&S when I jumped you? Well, Nell's the result. Kate sighed and tried again in her imagination. *So, what are you doing for Father's Day this year?* God, it was hopeless! *You looked so young, I didn't think your tadpoles would swim . . . but I guess one must've made it.* She imagined sounding flippant about it – as if it were no big deal. But during their time in the shed neither of them had mentioned that night at the Rouseabout. For whatever reasons, their memories had sat, unspoken, between them.

Kate gathered the reins up shorter as Nick's ute arrived beside her. He switched off the engine, and they both moved slowly in silence as the ute's tyres crunched over the gravel, rolling down the slope towards the bay.

It was Nell who spoke first.

'Hurry up, sheep,' she said, smiling at Nick.

'Yeah, sheep! You slowcoaches,' he said, smiling back at her.

'Yeah . . . slowcouches,' said Nell, mimicking him. Nick's face lit up with another smile and Kate felt breathless.

'It's *coaches*, Nell, not couches,' she said, like a school-marm. 'The sheep are slow*coaches*.'

'You're a funny bunny, you are,' Nick said to Nell, before falling silent to watch the white, freshly shorn ewes ahead of him.

'I can send the dog if you like. Move them over faster, so you can get home. You'll be wanting to get to that dinner,' Kate offered.

'Nah, I'm in no hurry,' Nick said.

He rested his arm on the ute's windowframe as if to prove it. He rolled on in silence, Matilda keeping pace with the ute. Kate took in the strong, lean shape of his forearm. Muscular and tanned to the elbow. Muscles that hadn't been there the night she'd run her fingers over his arms. She tried to shut out the memory of the drunken encounter with the skinny lad. Outside the shearing shed she felt exposed again. Uncomfortable.

'Thanks for your help,' Kate said eventually. 'I know it was a big ask, you leaving your farm for so long.'

'Any time. Not much happening there till it rains. Just feeding stock like you wouldn't believe.'

'It's a bugger.'

'Sure is.'

Silence again.

'I really am so sorry about Will,' Nick said. 'You've been a champion these last few days.'

They were nearing the paddock where the mob belonged, the gate resting open against a stick. She could put the sheep away now and tell him. She whistled Grumpy and cast him along the laneway to turn the lead sheep.

'Sit,' she called to the dog. The ewes stopped, looked at

Grumpy, then swung their heads in the direction of the gate. The leaders moved through. The rest of them followed, eagerly trotting onto fresh pasture. Soon the road cleared enough for Nick's ute to pass.

'Well,' he said, turning on the engine, 'see you later.'

'Yeah. See you round. And thanks again,' Kate said.

'No problems. Bye, Nellie-phant,' he said with a wink.

'Bye, Nick Knack,' Nell said, waving her small hand at him.

Kate watched, her heart aching as Nell's father drove out onto the highway and out of sight, still oblivious to the fact that the little golden-haired girl was his.

With the dogs fed in their pens and Matilda munching happily on hay, Kate reached out for Nell's hand and together they ambled over the uneven drive towards the garden gate.

'Come on, let's go get some tea. You've been such a good helper today.'

'Can we go to the garden first, Mummy?' Nell asked.

'But we're *in* the garden.'

'No. Not this garden. The other one. The special one.'

Kate looked down at Nell. She realised Nell was talking about Laney's vegetable garden. In the past, when Nell refused to eat her vegetables, Kate would describe the old garden Laney had cultivated. She'd tell her about pumpkins the size of cars and tomatoes as big as beach balls. The Bronty women who were convinced magic grew there too. She described those women from a different era, who gardened in gloves and long dresses and large straw hats. At the time, Nell had seemed to ignore the stories, so Kate was surprised when she now begged to see the garden.

Since returning to Bronty, Kate had deliberately avoided Laney's garden. No matter how curious she was, the place, like the attic, was a strong reminder of the dreams that had died with her mother and Will.

'But it's nearly dark, sweetie,' Kate said.

'Pleeeease!' Nell bounced up and down on her toes and

139

tugged Kate's hand. Kate looked down at her daughter's open, hopeful face.

'Okay.' She relented. 'This way.'

They rounded the side of the house and followed the gravel path that wove its way past an old elm and an elaborate garden seat. There, at the edge of the lawn, was an archway of jasmine over a peeling white picket gate. Kate could feel her mother and Will out here with them. She touched the place on the gate where their hands would've touched. Unlooping the wire, she pushed it open. The gate creaked. A sound that was so familiar, catapulting her back to her childhood.

When she and Nell stepped into the garden, Kate felt her heart sink. What had once been an Eden now lay like a wasteland, a tussle of weeds and vegetables gone to seed and rotting tumbled over the ground before them. The high picket fence that had sheltered the magical world was also now in disrepair. The far fence had been removed altogether and stacked in piles ready for burning.

'This isn't the garden,' Nell said, confusion and disappointment in her voice.

'It was, darling. It once was.'

'But you said it had magic.'

Kate gripped Nell's hand firmly.

'It can grow magic again. It's up to us. Once the days get a bit longer, after winter, we can come out here and dig it up after Mummy's finished her work. We can make this our own magical patch. You could even build a cubby in the corner over there.' She pointed to a sheltered nook that was fringed with large poplar trees.

Kate imagined them together in summer plucking red tomatoes from a haven of green and snapping the thick stalks of summer marrows. Parsley, chives, silverbeet and beetroot lining neat gravel pathways, with a bench seat beneath an arbour. Food for life. A lush garden to grow their memories of childhood, one past, one present.

If she couldn't reclaim Bronty homestead to keep alive the

memories of her mother and Will, then she and Nell could at least remake this garden as their own tribute. Then, maybe, with time, her father might consider again Laney's plans for the seed business. Kate squeezed Nell's hand in the half-darkness.

'C'mon,' she said. Looking up towards the attic, Kate led Nell back along the path to the house. There, they kicked off boots, peeled away coats and hats and stepped into Annabelle's cream and peach home.

Annabelle was at the sink, fiercely peeling potatoes. Henry was standing at the end of the kitchen table, a weary expression on his face. His hair, normally neat, was standing up in patches where his lanolin-coated fingers had run through it during his day in the shearing shed. Kate could tell instantly that things were more than a little tense between them. Still she pushed.

'Nell and I just took a walk over to the veggie garden and there's no back fence anymore. What happened to it? Did it fall down?'

Annabelle turned towards her and Nell. Kate caught the bitterness of her expression, before she smothered it with a calculated smile.

'Fall down? No. We pulled it down.'

'Why would you do that?'

'Well,' Annabelle began softly, 'no one uses the garden anymore.' She pulled off her washing-up gloves, moved over to the dresser and opened a drawer. 'Your father and I have better plans for that space. Nell will love it. Look.'

She took out a folder and laid it on the table. She hooked a long fingernail under the cover and opened it, folding out a page of sketches. Tapping the designs she said, 'Here you go. Our new plans. Swimming pool here, tennis court there and paved patio cum entertainment area in between. What do you think? Such a great idea. Of course, it'll be done in stages. We have to level it first. And the pool will be last, just so we don't spend too much all at once. I now know what this farming business is like.'

141

Kate couldn't believe what she was hearing. Beyond them, in the darkened TV room, Amy provided a backdrop of indifference. She was oblivious to Henry and Annabelle's previous spat and the bomb Annabelle had just dropped for Kate. She bobbed her head to her music and blew more dragons into dust on the TV screen. The light from the TV crawled in sinister flickers over the walls and furniture and escaped into the brightly lit kitchen.

Henry looked at Kate. She saw the flash of guilt on his face. Kate could feel herself about to erupt. Keeping calm for Nell, she spoke very softly as she reached for a banana from the fruit bowl.

'Here, Nell. You go sit in Grandpa's big chair in with Amy. You can eat this narnie before your bath.' She led Nell by the hand, sat her up in the chair and came back to the kitchen, shutting the folding door behind her. She just needed a few minutes to get this straight with Annabelle. She stood over the plans, looking at the neat lines and sketched-in ornamental garden beds and octagonal pergola. Then she looked up at Annabelle.

'Why the frig would you need a pool when there's a whole bloody beach to swim at?' She swung her arm in the direction of the bay.

'Kate,' warned her father.

'But you can't let her do this to the garden,' Kate said, her eyes flashing anger. Henry turned his back, reaching up to the cupboard for a glass. Moving over to the sink he reefed on the tap, the pipes clunked. 'Dad?'

'Henry and I have already discussed it,' Annabelle said. 'It hasn't been a garden in a long while now, Kate. You've been gone a long time.'

Suddenly Kate felt a thread snap in her. Fury rose up so strongly, she thought it would consume her.

'I've only been gone *a long time* because of *you*!' she yelled. 'You've no right to go anywhere *near* Mum's garden!'

Annabelle clutched her hand to her throat, eyes wide.

'Kate!' her father snapped. 'Settle down.'

'But Dad, you *can't* let her bulldoze Mum's garden! You can't.'

'This is not about letting *her* do anything, Kate. Annabelle is my wife now. It was our decision to renovate the garden.'

'Renovate!' Kate repeated incredulously. 'Since when have you *ever* been interested in garden *renovations*! I can't believe you! Did Will know about this? *Did he*?'

Henry clenched his eyes shut in frustration.

'But what about the seed business? What about our ideas? Didn't he tell you we needed the garden for that?'

Kate saw her father's face morph from frustrated to angry. Colour rose above his collar, spreading from his neck, over his strong jawline to his cheeks, his eyes narrowed and darkened.

'What flamin' ideas, Kate? Up until the past few weeks you've had nothing to do with this place for years. You've had nothing to do with us! What gives you the right to come back here and start telling me *and my wife* what we can and can't do!'

Annabelle stood at the sink, a chastened look on her face, not uttering a sound.

'What gives me the *right*? Dad, it was my *home*! This place was my home!'

'Well, maybe things have changed.'

'Are you saying it's not my home now? That Nell and I aren't welcome here? That I can't run my new job from here?'

Henry didn't respond.

'Are you? 'Cause if you are, maybe I should just leave again? Is that what you want?' She glared at her father. 'Is it? I sure as hell know it's what *she* wants!' Kate pointed accusingly at Annabelle.

Henry didn't react. Kate waited for him to smooth it all over. To beg her to stay. To prove his love for her in front of Annabelle. But he calmly lifted the glass of water to his mouth and began to drink. His Adam's apple sliding beneath the skin of his neck, his eyes looking down over the glass at her, cold, arrogant.

She could feel it happening all over again. That rash anger taking hold, like when she was a teenager. She couldn't stop herself. She let the words fly – her anger wiping away any sense.

'You've never wanted me here!' she screamed at him. 'And even if you did, there's no room for me and Nell anyway – her and her shitty kids have seen to that! I'll start my new job somewhere else. I don't need you! Or your new brood of A-holes!'

'That's enough!' roared Henry, but Kate wasn't backing down.

'You go ahead and let her trash this place, and Mum's memory with it. She'll have Bronty carved up into seaside blocks before you know it to pay for all this *renovation*.'

'Kate!' Henry looked at her with cold steel eyes. *'That's enough!'*

'Yes. It is enough!' Kate said, crying now. 'You have no idea what you're doing to Mum – or to me! And to Will. You never deserved us. You don't deserve Nell!' She turned and flung open the TV-room doors, startling Amy. She gathered Nell up from the chair and pushed past Henry to storm out the door. At the back porch she angrily tugged on her boots and grabbed Nell's little yellow gumboots, sobbing as she did. She carted Nell to the ute.

'Mummy, where are we—'

'Get in,' Kate said fiercely through her tears.

'Mummy?'

'Just get in and sit there!'

Nell's bottom lip dropped and soon she was sobbing too.

Breathing fast, Kate ran to the dog kennels to let out Sheila and Will's dogs. Then, revving her ute, she drove round to the shed, the dogs following, and spun the tyres as she hauled on the steering wheel. Grating the gears, she reversed towards the horse float.

144

If that's what he wants, Kate thought as she wound the jockey wheel around savagely, that's what he'll get. She'd get out of his life and she'd take Nell and all Will's and her animals with her. Henry Webster could go to hell.

Sixteen

'What the . . . ?' Janie pulled back the kitchen curtain and watched Kate's ute and float roll to a halt outside. The headlights lit up a cluster of moths that battered themselves against the big glass eyes.

'I asked her round for dinner sometime this week, not to a twilight pony club get-together,' Janie said.

Dave set down his knife and fork and looked out the window into the darkness. He watched Kate slam the ute's door and stomp round to help Nellie from her seat. On the tray, Sheila, Bra and Grumpy sat sniffing the air at their new surroundings. They pricked their ears in the direction of Dave's sheepdogs, who barked from their pens. Inside the float, two horses tugged hay from a net.

'Things must have gone belly-up at Bronty,' he said, slumping down on his seat. 'Just what we need, eh? We finally get the twins down, I get to eat before midnight and *she* turns up.'

Janie ignored him, continuing to wipe mashed carrot and parsnip from a highchair tray.

'Hope you're up for some counselling. I reckon she'll need it, if she's done what I think she's done,' he said, looking at his wife.

'She needs help, okay?' Janie snapped. 'What is it with you?

Don't be so stingy. She's got no mum and her brother's just died. Give a little, Dave.'

'I know. I'm sorry,' Dave said genuinely. 'I'm just trying to look out for you. She may be your best mate, but you don't have endless energy to give. Do you?' He took in how tired Janie looked. Her blonde hair all awry, bags under her soft blue eyes. She wiped her wet hands on her stained windcheater, rolled her eyes and shrugged.

'No rest for the Mother Teresas of this world,' he said, smiling at her and grabbing her hand, kissing it, drawing her over to his large lap. Janie smiled back, but Dave could feel her weariness long after he'd let go of her reddened hand and she'd hauled herself up to answer the door.

'You could go back,' Janie said a little later, sitting next to Kate. Dave hovered nearby with a box of tissues. Kate shook her head. 'You could get in your rig tonight, drive back over there, walk in and say "sorry". Say you lost your temper. Again. Then you'd still be on Bronty. It's what you want, isn't it?'

Kate frowned, rolling a tissue between thumb and forefinger.

'I don't know anymore.' A vision of her father flashed in her mind. The way he'd coldly gulped down the glass of water. The words she wanted to hear, never uttered.

'Maybe I'm right. He doesn't want me there. It's better if I forget the place.'

'Oh, Kate,' soothed Janie again, touching her hand and motioning Dave to pass another tissue. 'It was bound to happen. You think about it. He's caught between a rock and a hard place with you and Annabelle.'

'Couldn't be that hard, could it?' Kate said. 'Letting his own daughter back to have a go?'

'Yes, but without Will there to throw a bucket of water on you when you lose it, you're pushing it uphill, Kate. *Plus*, she's yap, yap, yap in your dad's ear the whole time about having no space there with you and Nell. Don't forget that woman's got him by the short and curlies. You know how lonely men can be led along. These things always overrule that thing.' She pointed from her crotch to her head. Kate huffed. 'Look at Dave here,' Janie said, motioning to him. 'He's butter in my hands once I've got hold of that thing.' Janie pointed again to her crotch. Dave cast Janie an amused but insulted look.

'Sorry, darling. Joke,' she said to him before continuing on. 'Think about it, Kate. You come back looking just like your mum, plus with a cute-as-pie kid in tow to divert his attention away from her. It's going to implode. Just you being there is rubbing it in for Annabelle – so of course she's going to create a situation where you can't win. And of course your dad's gunna just stand there. Poor bugger wouldn't know which way to jump. She'd have his balls if he stood up for you.'

'Poor bugger nothing. He just wanted a steady stab, so he picked the first floozy that came along. Why did it have to be *her* though? She's started on the house, now the garden. Next it'll be the farm. She's got that mainland way about her – she's seeing the place as waterfront real estate, not our home. I know it.'

Janie sat back on her seat.

'Noooo,' she sang.

'Nooo,' echoed Dave, who now sat at the table with the tissues ever at the ready. 'She wouldn't go that far,' he added. 'She loves Bronty. Doesn't she?'

With the question hanging in the air, Kate heard Nell cry out from the spare bed in the twins' bedroom. She leapt up to settle her before she woke Jasmine and Brendan.

'Poor Nellie,' Kate said, ashamed. 'I shouldn't have lost it in front of her.'

In the darkened bedroom, Kate lay down next to Nell, listening to the soft sounds of the twins breathing from their cots on the other side of the room.

She stroked her hair and Nell snuggled her face into the warm space between her mother's chin and her chest. Kate kissed her head.

'Mummy's so sorry, Nell. I'm so sorry.'

Later, Janie brought Kate a mug of hot chocolate as she slumped on the couch. Kate stared at the steam that rose from the cup. Like her dreams of Bronty, rising, and then gone.

'Thanks,' she said to Janie. 'I'm really sorry to do this to you.'

'Hey,' Janie said, 'it gives me the chance to make up for my mum. Dave reckons I'd mother the whole bloody world if I could. Should see me with the poddy lambs. It's pathetic.'

'Well, I really appreciate it, Janie, I do.' Kate toasted her cup. 'Warm milk all round, you really are wonderful.'

Janie gave a self-deprecating smile back. They sat for a time in silence as Kate sipped her drink.

'Have you thought about asking Maureen to fly down to talk to him?' Janie suggested. 'She could act as a peace broker. Work out a way to get you all on the same page with the farm and the family. Remind him a little of the past.'

Kate bit her lip. 'I reckon I've put Maureen through enough these last few years. She doesn't need more upset. She's barely got over losing Mum as it is. Plus, she's been crook as a dog, couldn't even make it to Will's funeral. It would break her heart anyway, to see what that woman's done to Bronty.'

'Well, Dave and I are here for you. You know that. Eh?'

Kate glanced at her and nodded. 'Thank you,' she said, setting down her hot chocolate and drawing Janie up in a hug. 'You're my bestest friend.'

'Yeah,' Janie said, hugging her back. 'Likewise.'

Janie tucked her bare feet under her backside. As she did, Kate noticed the pale skin of Janie's knee showing through a small hole in her tracksuit pants. Janie shoved her finger through the hole and ran her finger around.

'I'm due for another op-shop hunt. Want to come with me some time this week?'

Kate sensed Janie's tiredness. The hard work with the twins and life on the farm left little time just for her. Guilt again assailed her for turning up on Janie's doorstep. She knew she'd been wrong to storm away from her father. *Again,* she thought angrily at herself. When would she ever learn? But there was no going back now.

Kate looked about the living room. Even though the carpet was threadbare in the doorways and toys clustered untidily in baskets in every corner, the house had a warmth that the love of a family can generate. A humble home with homemade green floral curtains, bomby hand-me-down furniture, covered again with pretty touches thanks to Janie's knack for sewing. There were photos of their babies all around in cheap frames and shots of their wedding day. The backs of the shabby-chic covered couch and chair had soft angora rugs folded over them. It gave the place a cosiness and it amplified the air of caring Janie instantly generated.

As she realised how settled Janie was, Kate started to feel the same panic she'd felt two years ago, when she received Janie and Dave's wedding invitation in the mail. It had come a week after the invitation to her own father's wedding. She'd stared at the stiff, gold-rimmed card and ran her fingers over Dave and Janie's names, wondering if she would ever find someone to be happy with. Here she was, a single mum, struggling from one sloppy day to the next to manage a baby alone, yet there was Janie happily marrying the man she'd met at the Rouseabout, and setting up house with him. Kate couldn't believe Janie was *keen* to have children and settle down. Back then, Kate envied Janie, thinking she was choosing the easy option. But how wrong had she been to judge Janie? Taking on a husband and a farm, let alone kids, was a brave move. Kate looked down at her lap.

'I know you're doing it tough at the moment, Janie, what

with the twins and such a bugger of a season. I won't impose for long, I promise. I just need a night or two to figure out what I'm doing, where I'm going. I'm s'posed to start my new job next month, Janie. A new bloody job and I don't even have a home, let alone an office now! But I'll be right. Won't I?'

'Well,' Janie said, her eyes glinting, 'Dave and I had a little chat at the sink tonight while you were in with Nell. We came up with a cunning plan. We have a suggestion for you.'

'A suggestion? What?'

'Finish your drink and then get your coat.'

'*What?*'

'Patience, Grasshopper, patience.'

'Where are we going?'

'Not far. Certainly not as far as the pub. The kids'll be right for a bit. Come on, woman, drink your drink and get your bum off my lounge.'

And before Kate knew it Janie was dragging her to the back door.

There was no moon, so the night was pitch black. All Kate could see was the soft blue hue from Dave's spotlight. They trudged in silence along the gravel road, Dave occasionally flicking onto long beam so a shaft of light speared the darkness, picking up the yellow-white gleam of sheep eyes in the distance and the occasional red dots of possum eyes on the paddocks. Behind them the lights of the low farmhouse cast a halo out into the night. Inside the house, the children slept.

Mist closed in around the spotlight, stifling the beam. Tiny pinpricks of moisture settled on Kate's jacket.

'Where are you taking me?' she asked.

'To our leader,' said Dave in a robotic voice as he pressed the blue light up under his chin, ghoulishly darkening the shadows of his eye sockets.

'Shut up, you knob,' Janie said, thwacking him on the

151

shoulder. 'Not far now, Webster. Not far.' They trudged on past a row of old pines, giant looming shadows in the dark.

Eventually, three horizontal planks of a peeling white fence caught the shine from Dave's light. Kate's eyes followed the line of the wood and there in front of them stood a squat white cottage. Two windows at the front, door in the middle and shallow verandah framing it.

'After you, ladies,' Dave said as he swung the creaking mesh gate open. He kicked away balls of sheep poo from the path. 'Fence needs doing. But easy fixed.'

Inserting an old key into the lock, he shouldered the sagging door open and flicked on the light. A naked globe above the door illuminated the verandah and a slanting hallway.

'Ta-da!' Dave said.

'Ta-da, what?' Kate asked, frowning.

'Welcome to your new rural financial counsellor's home and office.'

Kate stepped inside. The air smelled rank and stale. She looked at the hall's leaning yellow walls. Even the spiders had moved out, leaving just their webs. Bird shit was spattered on one wall and in the corner a pile of feathers and a skull was all that was left.

'Are you serious?'

'Lick of paint,' Janie said, leading Kate further into the cottage. Kate peered into a bedroom where the floorboards were splintered with dry rot. She moved on into a chilly lounge room. An ancient heater hunched in the corner. Dismally, she looked up at the ceiling that sagged with the weight of a leaky roof.

'A lick of paint *and* some elbow grease,' Dave added. 'But it's a renovator's dream. I've been keen to get stuck into this old joint since we moved here, I just never had an excuse to do it.' He tousled Kate's hair and she batted his hand away, still frowning.

'Dream? You've got a great imagination, Dave.'

'She's not convinced,' Janie said.

'Anyway, what about your extensions?' Kate said. 'Don't you want to get started on your own house?'

'I need practice. Dog kennels first, this place next, then on to the real thing.' Dave stooped and ripped up a corner of the gritty carpet. 'Look. Wooden floorboards all ready for polishing. And . . .' He raised his hands. The ceiling was so low, Dave barely had to bend his elbows. He hooked a finger in a mould-spotted gap of the ceiling and pulled. The sheet of ceiling fell away, showering Kate and Janie in dust and the dried grass from a rat's nest.

'Geez, Dave! What are you doing?' Janie protested.

'Look!' he said with glee. 'Pressed tin. Original. Bloody beaudiful!'

'Mmm . . . very historic,' Kate said, brushing straw from her jacket and shaking white paint flecks from her black hair. 'And an office? Has it got a cupboard I can convert?' she teased, looking into the squashy, gloomy kitchen with the brown and yellow cupboards.

'Follow me,' Dave said gallantly. He swung open a door and there on the western side of the house was a glassed-in verandah. Blowflies were sprinkled across the dusty floor and the tattered remains of lace curtains hung from fencing wire over the grubby windowpanes. Another dead bird and its droppings were the only other things in the room.

'What do you think?' Janie said. She looked at Kate's blank face. 'Do you need to sleep on it?'

Kate looked around the room, then back to the hopeful faces of Dave and Janie.

'Awww! You guys!' She stretched her arms out and pulled them both into a rough hug. 'You sure you want to do this for me?'

As they left the little cottage, sadness and fear tumbled within Kate. She had to let go of her dream of living on Bronty. At least for now. The cottage was an answer.

Walking back towards Janie and Dave's house, she said, 'Of course, I'll pay rent.'

'Just peppercorn,' Dave said. 'You can be my builder's labourer.'

'And I'll pay you for babysitting, Janie,' Kate said.

'No. Don't worry about it.'

'Yes. I insist. No more op-shop tracky daks. I'm paying you to mind Nell while I work. No argument. I'll be able to afford it.'

In the darkness she could feel Janie smiling.

'It'll be perfect,' said Janie. 'You'll see. I'll be able to take Nell to playgroup with my two.'

Dave added more incentives, which they'd rehearsed earlier at the kitchen sink.

'It'll set you up to save your butt off to challenge whatever that woman throws at you. By biding your time here, you can think about finding a way back to Bronty. And you can keep my poor lonely wife company!'

'And it'll stop Dave's mum nagging us for more grand-kids! She'd be up for having Nell over with the twins. Perfect,' Janie said.

Kate stopped and looked up at the ink-black sky. She sighed and swallowed down tears.

'We'll get there,' she said. 'Thanks to you guys, we'll get there.'

Janie pulled her up in another hug.

'Don't you even think about crying. You're my bestest, oldest friend. I'd do anything for you, you know that.'

'But your wedding . . . I didn't even get to it. I'm so sorry.'

'Glad you didn't come,' Dave said. 'You would've drunk all the grog on us.'

'Well, I never made it over to see you when Nell was born,' Janie cut in. 'I've just told you I'd do anything for you, but we both know that's crud. I couldn't even get myself on a plane to go see you and newborn Nellie. So I guess we're even.'

'The air's cleared then?' Kate asked.

'I reckon it is.'

'Well I reckon the air's not just cleared, it's bloody freezing,' shivered Dave. 'Cold enough to freeze the man-boobs off Kim Beazley. Let's go inside and have a nightcap.' And they all laughed.

Seventeen

In the short-cropped house paddock at Rutherglen, beneath the wintry elms, Felicity aimed her showjumper at the red and white striped rails. Her horse, Calvin, threw his head a little against the pressure of the bit, but cleared the poles with the slightest nick of his neatly shod hind hooves. Felicity, with her gloved hand, slapped him heartily on his glossy bay neck. She urged him forward towards the next jump with a click of her tongue and the flex of her thigh muscles beneath beige jodhpurs.

In the machinery shed nearby, Nick swore at the tractor. He swiped his hands over his threadbare jeans and again took up a shifter, wishing the shearing at Bronty had gone on for longer. Beside him his dog, Tuff, lay licking his balls and eyeing a lone, unseasonal blowfly.

'Good boy,' Felicity cooed. Nick didn't glance up. He knew she wasn't talking to him. It was the voice she reserved exclusively for her horses.

The tractor's innards were spread across the concrete floor. From the glass-box cab, the radio played quietly to itself. As Nick bent towards the engine, he caught the familiar tune. Using his boot, he gently nudged aside the tools, bolts and bits on the tractor's step. He lifted himself up into the cab and listened. It was *that* song. From *that* night. 'Blister in the

Sun', by the Violent Femmes. With grease-stained fingers he reached over to turn the volume up. An involuntary smile came to his face. The sound of electric guitar and drums filled the shed and filled his body. His memory of Kate Webster was now fresh in his mind. This time she wasn't wearing a red dress. Now, he pictured her rouseabouting in the Bronty shearing shed, wisps of black hair falling around her heart-shaped face, her smooth strong arms scooping up fleeces. The buzz he felt when she looked his way.

Nick leapt down from the tractor and lifted Tuff by his front paws. Tuff looked up at him with a resigned and embarrassed expression as Nick danced him round the shed. When Nick let go of Tuff's tan paws, the black dog bounded around his master's legs, barking as Nick moved like a Bruce Springsteen clone in his blue sleeveless flannelette shirt and denim jeans. Singing into the silver shifter he clutched in his hands, Nick imagined dancing with Kate down the Bronty board. The muscles on Nick's arms flexed as he thrusted the shifter in his back pocket and picked up his oxy-welder, strumming wildly like an air-guitarist with attitude. How long had it been since he'd felt like this? For a moment he shut out his father's sickness, his mother's unhappiness and the shadow of his absent impossible brother. He forgot the pressure of Felicity's high expectations . . . and Nick was back there, in his youth. Dancing without the weight of them all. Simply dancing with Kate.

Hearing the throb of music coming from the shed, Felicity slid from the towering back of her thoroughbred. The smooth soles of her knee-high boots landed solidly on the ground. She led Calvin into the yard, slipped the bridle from his long bony brown face and patted him again on his white star for good measure. Then she walked towards the shed.

Nick didn't hear her come in, but Tuff did. He bounded to her and sideswiped his body against her legs in an expression of canine joy.

157

'Get out, dog!' Felicity growled. She stood and watched Nick with her head tipped to one side, her blue velvet riding helmet sitting in the crook of her arm as she put both hands to her slim hips.

'Nick?'

Caught, Nick immediately stopped dancing. A look of embarrassment swept across his face. He leapt up into the cab and turned the music down.

'What are you doing?' she asked.

'Breakdown,' he said, picking up a greasy spare part from a box and waving it at her.

'Oh,' she said. Then she turned and walked from the shed, still simmering that Nick had chosen to cast aside a week of his own farm work to help out on Kate Webster's property.

'I can see you'd rather dance with your dog than me,' she muttered as she went to hose her horse down.

The clatter of cutlery and the chink of china plates filled the Rutherglen kitchen as Felicity and Alice, Nick's mother, set the table for lunch. Lance winced as he sat down at the head of the table. He began to straighten the floral placemat with his large fingers and watched as the women worked. Alice sliced quiche while Felicity set a salad bowl on the table.

'Ah! Here he is,' Felicity said brightly as Nick entered the room. 'Just in time.'

Nick gave her a half-hearted smile and almost threw himself into his seat at the table.

'Tractor's still buggered,' he said. 'I'll have to bloody well feed out by hand.'

Lance made a humphing noise. Nick glanced at his father's downturned mouth and pasty jowls, which were covered in black and silver stubble. Nick knew he'd taken his comment as an insult. His father twisted everything Nick said into an accusation that he wasn't helping on the farm – that he wasn't getting better. More useless than a crippled sheepdog. Ought to be shot, his dad would sometimes say.

'I'm not hungry,' Lance grumbled as Alice set a slice of quiche down in front of him.

'Eat just a little, dear,' Alice coached.

'It'll do you good,' chipped in Felicity. Both women turned their backs and went to the bench where the other plates were set out.

'It looks warm out there,' Alice said as she peered through the kitchen window onto the garden. 'Be nice to think we're getting a short winter. I don't think I could face a long one.'

'Be nicer if it rained,' Lance added as he reluctantly picked up his fork.

'The Websters got a shower didn't you say?' Alice asked, setting a plate down in front of Nick. He reached for the tomato sauce.

'Twelve mil,' Nick said. 'Not enough to hold the shearing up. We had a day's worth shedded.'

'At least the rain's something,' Alice said. 'After what's happened to them.'

'They were lucky to get you for the week,' Felicity said, 'seeing as the season's just as tough here and you can never get away from the place.'

Felicity's words hung in the air. Everyone felt the weight of them.

'Will was the first to help us,' Nick said, thinking back a year to their own family misfortunes when Will had set time aside, unasked, to help get the ploughing done. Nick glanced at Felicity, who busily set out cups and flicked the kettle on. She was the only bright spark in this house for his mother and father, Nick realised. They were well used to his own withdrawn ways. Was he only including Felicity in his life because it somehow made his mum and dad's lives easier? Nick sighed loudly. Felicity cast him a glance.

'What will happen to that beautiful farm now that Will's gone?' Alice asked. 'Henry can't manage alone. Do you think Kate will take it on?'

Nick knew his mother was only trying to stir some

conversation along between her husband and her son, but he wished she would stop mentioning Kate in front of Felicity. He chewed quickly, in a hurry to get away. He could sense Felicity had stiffened. Her movement about the kitchen was less fluid, less happy.

'She seemed more interested in pub crawling than farming, the night we met her,' Felicity said, smiling at Alice. 'Of course, you'd know more now, Nick, since you've just spent the week with her. Does she fit the stereotype of the run-around-town single mother like she did that night in the pub?'

'I think she's a very brave person,' Nick said, annoyed. 'She's had it tough.'

Felicity turned her back.

'Makes you think about your own situation,' Alice said. 'About what would happen to your own place. If there was . . .'

'An accident?' Lance spat. He threw down his fork with a clatter.

'You know what I mean,' Alice said. 'We need to discuss these things. About the business and the future. Since Felicity will formally be part of our family in a few months.'

Felicity sat down next to Nick and slid her hand across to his as a peace offering.

'Alice is right,' she said gently. 'We really ought to talk about the future.'

Nick shot her a glance, but she continued talking in her cool confident way.

'I love nursing, but perhaps, if we were to have children, I could work at something from home. Perhaps with the horses.'

Nick glanced warily at his father.

'Let's not get ahead of ourselves here,' he said.

'Well, we have to talk about it,' Felicity said with a smile, but Nick saw the emotions that lay behind it. 'Don't we?' She looked at Lance, who looked at his plate.

Alice sighed and stood up from the table. She pulled a clipping down from a pile of documents on the fridge.

'I saw this the other day. I think we should ring.'

Alice slid the paper across the surface of the table so it lay between Lance and Nick. The ad had a Tasmanian tiger logo on the top left corner. Bold print read: *'Is your farm business ready for a makeover? Rural Consultancy Solutions is offering a partially government funded service to farmers needing assistance with environmental conservation, drought-proofing, succession planning, re-financing, business restructuring and any other areas of concern. Phone now to meet with your new local* RCS *facilitator.'* Alice had circled the phone number in red biro.

'Apparently they've appointed an advisor for this district. He can help us with the business structure now you're getting married.' She turned to Lance and leant over him, her flushed cheeks looking redder against her pale blonde hair. 'They can even help draft a will for us all, which I know is something we've never really considered, now the boys are grown up. And especially before the wedding. Felicity needs to know where she stands in all this.'

'She's got me dead and buried already,' Lance grumbled as he hauled himself up from his chair and skulked from the room. Nick watched his father lurch away. A farm advisor? Wasn't that the job Kate had said she was starting in a fortnight's time? No matter what the situation, his thoughts always seemed to lead back to her. Annoyed, he stood up abruptly.

'I'll be in the shed,' he said.

The two women were left with the half-eaten lunch on the table as they watched Nick's head duck down beneath the window as he stooped to drag on his boots.

'So,' said Alice wearily, wiping her hands on a tea-towel, 'that little suggestion about succession planning went down well.'

Felicity laid a comforting hand on Alice's forearm.

'Don't worry, Alice, I'll talk to both of them.'

Eighteen

The sawdust had been swept up into tiny pale hillocks. Angular offcuts were gathered into a pile on the verandah. On an old table, crusted rollers and paintbrushes sat in paint-splattered buckets. On the uneven verandah boards, Sheila lay sleeping and twitching in a patch of sunlight.

Inside the newly painted weatherboard house, perched on a chair, Kate reached up and threaded another curtain ring on the rail.

'You were always good at sewing,' she said to Janie. 'Mum was going to teach me, but you know the story.'

'Yeah,' Janie said. 'At least she taught you the good things first though. Like encouraging you to go out and get down and dirty on the farm with the animals and in the garden.' Janie knelt on the newly polished floorboards, shaking out the thick folds of curtains.

'She did?'

'Yeah. She taught you the important stuff. Not like my mum. All she ever taught me was to not like yourself and to eat, drink and smoke yourself silly, until you look like Shrek.'

'I don't see much Shrek in you. You've got a good head on you and there's a tonne of domestic goddess naturally in you. You've done all right for yourself,' Kate said, fingering the neat seams of the curtains.

'Must be a throwback,' Janie said.

Kate leapt down from the chair and flung the cream curtains open and shut, then open again, looking outside to a bright blue late-winter sky, dabbed with cotton-ball clouds. Beyond the fence was Dave and Janie's house.

'Hey, I can nearly see into your bedroom from here,' Kate said.

'Well, you won't be seeing much then. Three years of marriage loaded up with twins on top doesn't make for interesting viewing really,' Janie said.

'Wait till the babysitting money comes rolling in, Janie. You can save up for a dirty-Dave weekend and I'll mind the kids for you.'

'All I'll want to do is sleep.'

At that moment Nell, Jasmine and Brendan came thudding in from the bedroom giggling and laughing.

'What have you lot been up to?' asked Kate.

'Mummy!' cried Nell. 'I seen a kitten at window! Out there!'

'Saw, Nell. You *saw* a kitten, *from* the window.'

'He's a wild one,' Janie said, 'and I explained to you about feral cats, didn't I?' Nell nodded solemnly. 'He'll always have a wild streak so Dave'll have to shoot him so he doesn't eat the native birds. Remember?'

Kate knelt down to Nell's level. 'Once we're all settled in, we'll find you a fat fluffy cat who sits inside all day and doesn't chase birds. Okay? A kitty of your very own.'

Nell nodded brightly. 'Yay! A pussycat! Now?'

'No, not now. But later. I promise.' Kate felt Nell slip her little hand into hers. It was warm and soft. Kate squeezed it gently.

'Come on, you lot, it's drink time,' Janie said. 'Who wants one?'

'Me! Me!' cried Nell. Jasmine and Brendan followed suit, waggling their limbs with excitement. They toddled into the next room in Janie's wake, like ducklings following their mother. From the fresh white cupboard Janie pulled out three plastic cups.

'Duice?' begged Jasmine.

'No, darling. No juice. Just water.'

Behind them at the front door, they heard a grunt and a thud. Then a bark from Sheila, startled awake and on her feet in a flash. On the porch, Dave was struggling with a large wooden desk. His sleeves, rolled up along his big arms, his hat pushed back revealing his high smooth brow.

'Here is madam rural advisor's desk . . . now, I expect a year's free advice for this.'

'Where'd you find it?' said Kate, rounding the doorway and marvelling at the size of it.

'Contacts, Kate. Contacts.'

Gripping the edge of the large desk, Kate and Dave shuffled it into place in the sunroom. Kate lifted the telephone from where it sat on the floor and set it on the desk. She picked up the handpiece and listened for the dial tone – the sound of a cricket in her ear. Before she knew it, Dave was wheeling an office chair along the hallway. He hit her with it in the back of her knees. She fell, her backside meeting the seat of the chair solidly. Roughly, Dave shoved her against the desk.

'There! You are now officially open for business.'

'RCS were going to supply me with everything.'

'I've just saved them some money. Filing cabinets, though, I can't do. But my mate has contacts. These things are on permanent loan. Now I'd better get back to it. Happy advising, advisor Kate.'

'Thanks,' Kate called over her shoulder as Dave sauntered out along the hall and into the sunshine. Kate sat at the desk, spreading her fingers over the smooth wooden surface. She felt so lucky to have friends like him and Janie.

From the small square windows of the sunroom Kate could see cattle chewing on their ration of hay. They bunched together on the short green pasture that lay in wait for spring sunshine and rains. Beyond the cattle, a dam like liquid silver sat amongst dark pin rushes. Beyond that, the bush-covered hills rose up from pastures. A good view to have. But not a

Bronty view, Kate sighed. Behind her Janie and the children tumbled into the sunroom, refreshed from their drinks and a thick wedge of sliced apple each.

'Wow. The desk looks great,' Janie said.

'That bloke of yours is a champ.'

'Yeah, I think he's pretty good. So does he – he tells me all the time.'

Suddenly the phone rang, its tone loud and invasive in the small cottage. They all looked at the flat white phone and its rows of grey buttons, stunned that it was ringing, like it was somehow alive.

'My God! That was *quick*. Someone must be desperate for advice,' Janie said.

'I told head office to check the number today. It'll be them.'

'Well, aren't you going to answer it?'

Kate sat up straight, pushed her dark hair back behind her ears and swallowed.

'Hello,' she said in a deep professional voice, 'Rural Consultancy Solutions, Kate speaking.'

'Err . . . Hello?' came a voice. 'Is that that farm couns'lin' service?'

'Yes it is,' Kate said pulling a face at Janie. 'How can I help you?'

'Eh? Ah, yeah. It's Mark Calves here. I need some help with me new compooter. I can't seem to find where to hook the danged thang up to the PTO on me tractor.'

The penny dropped for Kate.

'Dave, you *idiot*.' She slammed the phone down just as Dave appeared behind her with his mobile phone in his hand.

Sticking with his 'Mark Calves' twang he sidled up to her. 'Aww. Gee, Kate. I've got somethin' here that might make it up to yer.' He slid the bottom drawer open in the desk and pulled out a brown paper bag. He opened the bag, proudly proffering a bottle of Bundy rum and a few cans of cola.

'You legend!' Kate said, grabbing the bottle and kissing the label. 'Just what we need for an opening ceremony.'

'I'll get some glasses.' Dave left the room again and went out into the kitchen. A moment later the phone rang.

'Bloody Dave,' Kate said, laughing. She picked up the phone. 'Huwo. Chinese Lestalant and Take Way . . . today special is Cumov-sum-yung-guy soup. Velly, velly nice. You want to make order? Yes?'

Dave reappeared, his large hands full with three glasses. His mobile phone was clipped to his pocket. Janie looked at Kate, horrified, and motioned to her to hang up.

'Velly solly. Velly solly. Long number. Long number,' Kate said quickly before slamming the phone down. 'Oh my God! I thought it was bloody you!' she said, her brown eyes wide and cheeks rising to pink. 'When am I going to learn? What a start! I was going to be so *good* this time round. So professional. But I've buggered it up!'

Janie giggled.

'Who was it?'

'No idea!' They all dissolved into splutters, the children picking up on their mirth and joining in. But soon the phone was ringing again.

'Shh!' said Janie. 'Kids! Quiet.' She led them out of the room. Kate composed herself before picking the phone up.

'RCS. Kate speaking.' Deadpan voice. Professional to the core.

'Yes,' she said, clicking her fingers at Dave and pointing to her bag on the floor. Grabbing it from him, she pulled out her diary and a pen. With her teeth she yanked off the pen lid and began to flip through the diary. She spat the lid out.

'Head office probably told you I'm only just setting up. I don't officially start until after I've been into Hobart again to collect some paperwork, then I'll be taking appointments for next month.'

There was a pause. Kate bit her lip as she listened.

'An appointment? Yes. It usually takes about three hours to start with. Okay, I'll pencil you in for 10 a.m. on the third. It's a Wednesday.'

Kate listened and nodded. 'I'll post you some information about what you'll need for the meeting – a questionnaire – that kind of thing. You can have it ready for me when I come. Okay. Thanks. Bye then.'

She hung up the phone, rose to her feet, grabbed her drink from Dave and took a large swig.

'Who was it?' Janie said, poking her head around the door.

Kate perched her bottom on the edge of the desk, colour drained from her face.

'Kate? Who was it?'

'Alice McDonnell.'

'What! Nick's mum?' Janie screeched.

Kate clamped a hand over her own mouth. 'Gawd! My clients are supposed to be confidential. When am I ever going to learn! You didn't hear that from me, okay?'

'Don't panic,' Janie said. 'We won't say anything. Mum's the word.' She gave Kate a pointed look.

'Give me another drink.' Kate held her glass towards Dave.

'I guess we can officially toast the opening of your service,' Dave said.

'Off to a bloody shaky start if you ask me,' Janie said.

'Anyone but them,' Kate muttered. 'Any bloody one but them!'

As they raised their glasses and toasted the business a loud bang came from the kitchen, followed by crying.

'Jeez! Now what are they into?' said Dave as they all trudged out to round up the children.

'I'm not sure this is going to work. I'm not sure at all,' Kate said as she followed them. But Dave and Janie were too busy untangling Brendan from a chair to reply.

Nineteen

A few weeks later, Kate stood by her ute at the Campbell Town showgrounds and watched the men at the gates huddle next to a glowing 44. The drum smoked and shot out orange sparks into the white mist. The men shoved their hands under their armpits for warmth, and waited for the sun to break through the early-morning fog.

Below Kate, on the lower oval, four-wheel drives towing horse floats rolled in and competitors clattered rugged and bandaged horses down heavy float ramps. She thought of Matilda and Paterson back at Janie's. Unrugged, unbrushed, lazing and grazing in the short paddocks.

While she'd never been into showing, Kate loved the gloss of the pampered horses, the way they cruised the ring with their curved shining necks and flowing tails. She longed to do something with her own horses, like join a polocrosse team. But for now any sort of horse sports would have to wait. Her new job was eating up all her time. It was similar to the one she'd had in Orange, so she slotted into it easily, feeling comfortable in her role as a rural advisor. Even though she was not at Bronty, she was still home, here in her island state, and Nell was by her side. Janie would pick Nell up in the mornings and slot her into the twins' routine. Kate would work until about five then go up to the main house to collect

Nell. She would find Nell happily playing with the twins, pushing strollers, riding bikes, reading books. Kate noticed Janie looking less frazzled.

'She's so good with them,' Janie enthused after the first week of minding Nell. 'I'm not continually having to break up fights anymore. She'll entertain them for hours. When I have to tend to one twin, Nell distracts the other. Plus, I'm not so lonely anymore. I know I've got you to gasbag with. I think I really should be paying you and Nell!'

'I'm so glad it's a two-way thing,' Kate said to her friend.

Now, at the Campbell Town show, Kate turned her attention to the main showground where one-tonne utes with stock crates pulled up outside the giant corrugated-iron sheep pavilion. The men flipped back tarps to reveal spiral-horned Merino rams, trimmed and tarted-up for the show. Inside, the pavilion was coming to life with the clang of gates and the deep bleats of sheep as they were penned on thick beds of golden straw. Next door to the sheep pavilion, the coffee caravan had a queue of still-sleepy exhibitors hoping to warm their fingers around cardboard cups of latte. Near the inviting drift of fresh roasted coffee, ladies in the home industry pavilion were already engaged in frosty spats over whose handiwork should be displayed where.

Kate took in the scene, all the while running her hands over the warm back of Will's young kelpie, Bra. The dog leaned into the pressure of Kate's hand, arching her back like a cat. It was nice to take the young dog out on her own, Kate thought, without old Sheila and Grumpy to divert Bra's attention.

In the past weeks, at Dave and Janie's, Kate had been getting to know Bra, helping out with the stock work when she had time. Bra was a nimble little red and tan bitch, with bright button eyes and a willing mind. Although she hadn't done much work with her, Kate was determined to run her in the trials today as Will had planned. That was if her boss would give her some time off the stand today.

Kate watched as a white stationwagon pulled to a halt at the gate. As the window slid down, Kate saw it was Lisa, her new boss. Kate stepped out from behind her ute.

'Here she is,' she said to Bra. 'Now you sit and stay. And be a good dog.' Bra thumped her tail loudly against the tray of the ute in response. 'Morning!' Kate called as Lisa drove towards her. 'Good trip up from Hobart?'

Lisa extracted herself from behind the wheel, her navy pants creased at the top of her chubby thighs.

'Bit frosty,' she said, reaching for her dark green polarfleece with a Tassie tiger logo emblazoned on the chest. Kate had only met Lisa in person for the first time a few weeks ago, when she'd gone to Hobart to meet her rural advisor team and pick up all her paperwork.

In Hobart, as the glass-panelled doors slid open, Kate felt smothered by the plushness of the RCS office. But her scepticism dissolved when she met the bunch of agronomists, soil scientists and ag. finance experts who worked there. Their scuffed Blundstone boots and unpretentiousness defied their surroundings. They all had agricultural credentials a mile long but were still totally down to earth. And there was Lisa, swamped by her big important desk. She was the cheeriest and friendliest of the lot. A dairy-farmer's daughter, Lisa had glowing white teeth and solid bones to prove it. Short in stature but big on energy, Lisa was just the person to keep Kate keen on the job. She was informal to the point of seeming like a bushie rather than a qualified agricultural scientist and business manager.

She looked very much at home out here at the country show, Kate thought. So thick were her little legs, Lisa almost waddled to the rear door of the stationwagon. Heaving it open she said, 'Come on, slacker, we'd better get set up.' But as Kate helped her drag the large display boards from the back, she couldn't help feeling her heart sink a little, despite Lisa's bubbly presence.

Here she was at a show, again, with sheep judging and

yard dog trials going all day, but she'd miss most of it. Instead of being a farmer and attending shows for the pleasure of it and for the information they provided, Kate was again working on other people's dreams for their own farms. Plus, there'd be no time for pet parades with Nell or face painting or fairy floss. Janie was baby-sitting Nell with the twins at the show today.

Nor, tonight, would there be any drunken predatory adventures at the bar. She was home now, in Tassie's small pond. She had to behave. She *wanted* to behave. There could be no more running away. And if she couldn't go home to Bronty, or make a play for Nick, all she had was this job.

Kate sighed. She'd spend today inside the pavilion at the RCS display trying to seem revved about the meet-and-greet sessions with her potential farmer clients. But she felt the clouds of her past gathering around her. She knew the local people trickling by would see her and take note. Then there was Nell, the little blonde daughter, who seemed to have appeared from nowhere. People would talk today. Kate knew it. Summing up how she looked. How she behaved. They would look at her and label her as the one who had lost her mother and her brother. She would be the girl who had 'got into trouble' after her mother died and went away to have the baby. She was the daughter Henry Webster had kicked out after he married that dolly bird from the cruise ship: the fancy woman who had brought her kids over from the mainland to sponge off him. Kate could almost hear the words that would run around their heads as they looked at her. She felt trapped.

'It'll be a bit strange at first,' Lisa said, sensing Kate's nerves. 'It can be hard coming back to Tassie from the mainland and flexing your university muscle for the first time here. I know it was for me. Everyone still saw me as a kid. It takes a while for them to realise you've got knowledge to offer them.'

Kate smiled and nodded, grateful for Lisa's sensitivity.

As they carted another display board past Kate's ute, Lisa

nodded in Bra's direction. 'I see you've got your pooch with you. Were you thinking of doing a runner from the stand at some stage today to work her?'

Kate shrugged as best she could while carrying a steel-framed, carpeted display panel.

'She was my brother's dog. He was training her up for trialling. He'd mentioned that he had her entered in the novice for this show.'

Lisa cast Kate a caring look.

'I know what it's like at these gigs,' she said, walking backwards as she lugged the panel. 'It's tough talking shop all day. I'm sure you'll find time to work her. I can cover for you when you're up.'

'Really?' Kate said, her face brightening. 'I didn't like to ask, being so new to the job. I just thought I'd bring her in case. Do her good to see a bit more of the world anyway, even if it is from the back of a ute.'

'Go for it. I'm glad you did bring her along. I've heard how great you are with departmental PR at shows. You get very close to the clientele, I hear.'

Lisa shot her a meaningful glance and Kate's mouth dropped open as she recalled her drunken behaviour at the Orange Show and her snog with Clothesline Man. Her reputation had made it over the water.

'What do you mean?' she asked, trying to sound innocent.

'Half your luck,' Lisa went on, laughing. 'I've never pulled a fella at a show. Not once. Not for lack of trying.'

Kate's face shone with the widest grin. Working with Lisa was set to be more than just fun. She was a crack-up. 'Huh! I'll have you know, I'm a changed woman!'

'Yeah? I'd like to see that.' Then the two girls disappeared into the darkness of the shed, their laughter drifting out from the pavilion door.

Mid-morning, before the crowd thickened, Kate stole away from the stand to get Lisa a cup of coffee and to search for

172

Janie and the kids. It was a good chance to get signed in at the dog trials and give Bra a walk.

At the tent the yard-dog secretary slid the entry form and a pen in front of Kate, while Bra stood at her feet sniffing in the direction of the sheep.

'He'd be bloody proud of you having a go with his pup, Will would,' the secretary said, looking out from behind a long blonde fringe. 'We all miss him, you know. He was a bloody nice bloke.'

'Thanks,' said Kate. She paused. 'I'm supposed to be working here with my boss today too, so I can't hang around to watch at all. Would it be okay if . . .'

'Don't worry,' the young woman said. 'One of the boys will come and get you when you're up in the draw.' Her pretty round face opened up with a genuine smile.

'I'm Katrina, by the way. Will often talked about you, when he wasn't pooping himself with nerves before his trial runs.'

'Nice to meet you, Katrina,' Kate said. 'I don't expect to do any good with her but I thought I'd get her out . . . for Will.'

'She'll be fine,' Katrina said. Then she cocked her head to one side. 'The association was going to call to see if we could do anything to help on the farm, but we weren't sure how you'd take it . . . if we could do anything.'

Kate smiled gratefully.

'I'm not out at Bronty anymore. But thanks anyway . . .'

As they chatted, Kate felt the lead jerking in her hand as Bra danced about and tugged on the other end. Kate looked down to see why the dog was uncharacteristically bounding about. There, biting her in a friendly way on the scruff of her neck, was a big black and tan kelpie. Kate's gaze followed the dog's blue stretch of nylon leash to see Nick on the other end. His shoulders looked massive in a bulky dark coat and a big black hat. His face was serious. Deadpan.

'I think your bitch is trying to crack onto my dog,' he said. Then the light of his smile radiated out from under the dark brim of his hat. Straight white teeth framed by full lips, smile

173

lines and that dimple. Kate noticed dark-brown stubble on his square jaw, but couldn't lift her eyes to meet his.

'She's no floozy,' Kate said. 'She's just a pup, that's all. She's not old enough to be into that kind of caper.'

'Isn't she now?'

Kate glanced up and caught the glint in Nick's blue eyes. He was flirting with her. Panicked, but thrilled, she looked beyond him.

'Where's Felicity?'

Nick nodded in the direction of the horse arena, where black, chestnut and bay horses with bright white bandaged legs circled on collected reins, warming up before their classes.

'She's over there. Playing Saddle Club.'

'Oh,' said Kate vaguely.

'You're not riding? Not into showing horses?'

'No. Not horses that you shampoo, anyway,' Kate said. 'Besides, I'm working.'

'Working, eh? Working a dog or *working* working?' he said, nodding at her polarfleece vest with the logo.

'Bit of both,' Kate said.

'Every time I see you lately, you're working. Do you get *any* time off for play? We could play together today, like our dogs.'

Kate felt fear and delight rumble again in her stomach. He *was* flirting. In the shearing shed, he'd been frustratingly matey with her. Under the shelter of that roof, she'd felt comfortable with him. Now, in public, as Nick larked about with her, Kate felt wide open and vulnerable. She *couldn't* flirt with him. The more she saw of him, the sooner she'd have to tell him about Nell. But she couldn't do it yet. She was set to counsel his family soon. It was scheduled in her diary. She was meant to be a third party, objective and removed from their situation. Someone to assist without the baggage of emotion. Plus, there was Felicity. At that moment, standing before Nick, Kate panicked.

'If I did get time off,' she said, 'I wouldn't play with you.

You seem to forget, your plaything's over there in the horse arena.' She said it almost nastily, then instantly regretted it.

Nick opened his mouth, then shut it. She could see him trying to figure out why she'd snapped at him. There had been none of this feeling in the Bronty shed. She tried to think of something to say to soften her rude comment, but she felt the weight of a man's hand on her shoulder. She glanced over and noticed the bandy-legged bloke was doing the same to Nick. The man stood, the narrow slits of his eyes filled with amusement. Katrina looked up from her bookwork and laughed too.

'Can I put in an order for a pup?' the man said in a smoky voice. 'They'd make a terrific cross.' Kate noticed the black gap in the man's smile. She frowned, wondering what he was talking about. Then she looked down at the end of the lead.

Nick's dog, Tuff, and Bra were knotted in lovers' bliss, doggy style. Tuff's tongue lolled to one side, his eyes gleamed with pride and excitement as his body lay draped across Bra. Bra looked nervous but exhilarated, her eyes bright.

'Oh my God,' Kate said, horrified.

'Thought you said she was too young,' Nick said. A wicked smile on his face.

'She is too young to have pups!' Kate squealed. Then embarrassment burned on her cheeks. As the dogs stood locked together panting, like some grotesque two-headed vision from Hades, the dog triallers and the people wandering about the showgrounds began to point and laugh. Kate shut her eyes, wishing like hell the dogs would hurry up and untwine themselves.

'When you're ready, Tuff,' Nick said to his dog. 'When you're ready. Just make sure you get her phone number so she can't do a runner on you.'

Kate searched his face. Was he referring to her in some way?

*   *   *

175

Hours later in the pavilion, Kate lifted her tired feet up and down and looked about.

'Crowd's starting to thin,' she said.

Lisa flicked her head to one side.

'Go on with you, then. Git.'

It had been a busy day. Kate had withdrawn from the trials because of a rule that stated bitches on heat couldn't compete. Instead she'd spent the entire day working. She'd buried her embarrassment about the dogs by talking earnestly with farmers who inquired about the consultancy service.

Janie had appeared around lunchtime with the twins and Nell. Nell had a painted kelpie dog face with thick black whiskers. In her grubby hands she held a fat red balloon, and a ring of tomato sauce rimmed her lips.

Kate picked her up and hugged her. 'What's on your mouth, you grub?'

'Hot chips,' Nell said.

Janie screeched with laughter when Kate told her the knotted dog story and doubled over wheezing so that people stopped and stared.

'You two just can't stop breeding,' she whispered, before ushering Nell away alongside the double pram that was loaded up with the twins and an assortment of lairy looking showbags.

Bra was locked in the cab of Kate's ute, curled up asleep after her very public liaison, the seeds of Tuff's wild oats sown. At the end of the day, Kate had a long list of names, addresses and phone numbers ready for the RCS mailing list, and she had a secret thrill at the thought that her bitch might now be in pup to Nick McDonnell's dog. She tried to concentrate on her work. Looking down at her clipboard, she noted that ten people had booked for home appointments already, a good number, according to Lisa, who knew how long it took for people to realise the benefits of the service and to trust the people running it.

Kate put down her list and bit the end of her pen. She sighed loudly.

'If you're quick you'll probably be able to catch the last run of the dog trials,' Lisa said. 'Just don't do a runner to the bar before coming back to help me lug this stuff out.'

'You sure?'

Lisa nodded.

'Thanks!' Kate pulled on her jacket, flicked her ponytail out from under it and was about to go when Lisa spoke again.

'But no more sexual acts in public,' she cautioned with a grin.

'Who? Me or the dog?'

'Both of you!'

'Thanks. I'll try,' Kate said, pulling a face before jogging outside.

At the rail, Kate watched Matthew Johnson finish up with his muscular dog Modra with a handy score of 85, shooting him to the lead of the Open. As she joined the crowd in clapping Matthew and his dog from the ground, she felt someone tug her ponytail. She spun round.

'Jonesy!' she said.

'Heard your dog's got fleas,' he said.

'Fleas? What are you on about?' Kate asked.

'Yeah. It had an itch to scratch and was scratched.'

'Hah. Very funny. I didn't know Bra was on heat and I'd have to pull her from the comp.'

'Sounds like she pulled something else from all accounts,' came another voice. It was Razor.

Kate grimaced. 'If I get one more ribbing about my rooting bitch I'll—'

But before she could finish speaking the PA system crackled to life.

'Our next competitor is Nick McDonnell and his dog Tuff. He had a first-round score of 83 this morning and is in contention for second place. But seeing as his dog already scored earlier in the morning, by getting into Kate Webster's

Bra, it'll be interesting to see if old Tuff's still got the energy to get round the course this afternoon.'

A ripple of knowing laughter travelled through the crowd and Kate felt their eyes falling on her. Nick doffed his hat, smiled widely and shook his head, before taking his place in the big yard ready for the cast.

With Nick's concentration squarely on the sheep and his dog, Kate took the opportunity to drink him in. She recognised the little mannerisms she knew so well from watching Nell. The crease in his brow, the way he held his mouth slightly to the side as he concentrated on counting the sheep through the draft. The lift of his eyebrow. But she soon got lost in thoughts that had nothing to do with Nell. As Nick bent over to loop the chain on the gate, she took in his perfectly filled jeans. She watched the flex of his forearm muscles and his strong, sure hands. Beneath his hat, his cheeks were smooth and perfect, as was his square-set jaw. His voice was deep and soothing as he worked quietly and calmly with his dog to get the sheep rattling through the porta-yards.

When Nick shut the gate, the crowd clapped lightly. He'd finished his round in good time, but not good enough to beat Modra, Tassie's top dog.

Nick stooped to pat his dog, then climbed from the yards. Kate almost melted with desire as he came towards her with that smile on his face and his dog at his heels. She watched as men stepped forward to shake his hand. Kate turned and began to walk away. She couldn't let herself think about him like that. She would help Lisa pack up and get home to Nell. She'd leave Nick to receive his congratulations from Felicity. That's how it should be. Kate was almost to the pavilion when she heard his voice.

'Better luck next time, Kate,' Nick said, falling easily into step beside her with his long legs. 'And I'm really sorry about your bitch.'

Kate shook her head, not looking at him. 'Don't worry about it.'

'No, I mean it. I'm sorry. *Really*. I'll help you with the pups, I promise. I'll pay vet costs and bring you some tucker for them and help you find buyers. I've already had a few people here today say they're keen . . .'

Kate kept walking. She didn't speak. If only he knew, she kept thinking, if only he knew about Nell.

A bit put out by her behaviour, but amused at her mood, Nick gave up. He stopped and called after her, 'Well, if I knew you were going to be like this, I would've charged you a bloody service fee!'

Twenty

Morning light spilled through the small squares of the cottage window and landed on the kitchen table like spilled honey. With her back to the sun, Nell sat spooning porridge dotted with sultanas into her mouth. Her small fist gripped a plastic yellow spoon with Pooh Bear printed on its end. In the living room off from the kitchen, Sheila lay flat on her side on a sheepskin, dozing by the remnants of last night's fire, her breath soft and steady. In the background ABC radio burbled.

Kate quickly checked on Nell, then ducked into the office, which was full of work to be done. Kate was dressed in her uniform of tidy navy jeans and a blue-striped ironed shirt. Only the thick plaited leather belt with intricate patterns cinched tightly around her waist gave away the cowgirl in her.

She'd dressed carefully. It wasn't just another day at work. Today she was visiting the McDonnell family. As she'd looked at her reflection in the mirror and brushed blusher onto her cheekbones, she told herself she wasn't putting on make-up for Nick. She told herself it was for protection – so he couldn't read her face. But too much make-up and she'd look . . . over-done. Felicity might be there, scrutinising her. She rubbed the blusher off and reached for clear lip balm instead of red.

Kate glanced at her watch. It was hours before she had to clock on for her job. She'd woken up extra early this morning, even before Nell, and now she felt like she'd put in a full day's work already. She was chronically sleep-deprived, running on anxiety.

It had taken Kate weeks to get used to the night noises the cottage had revealed when winter winds shook the roof and floorboards to life. She'd had to leave the hall light on at first so she didn't have to grapple in the dark for unfamiliar switches or doorknobs.

Now winter was winding into spring and sunshine burst into her office, making it invitingly bright and warm. The client folders were building up in neat rows on the shelves. Her living room felt cosy, too, with the small couch, squat wooden coffee table and Nell's beanbag and a big cane basket of toys on the cheery colourful rug. Janie's choice of florals, checks and lolly-stripe fabrics covered the furniture and gave the place a homey feel.

Back in the office, Kate flopped down at the desk and picked up the photo of her mother she kept there, along with one of Will. She needed Laney's advice. She wanted her mother to speak to her. She wanted her to say, 'Tell Nick about Nell today. And take Nell home. Take her back to Bronty where she belongs.' But of course, her mother said nothing. Her gaze spoke only sadness and loss.

'Mum,' Kate said aloud and felt hurt by the silence that the word left behind. During sleepless nights in the cottage she'd searched the shadows that had played on the ceiling of her bedroom as the night stretched on, waiting for her mother. Then, as the darkness dissolved into the wispy grey clouds that lurk before sunrise and unseen birds began to trill, Kate started to think clearly. As if her mother had been whispering in her ear all along.

Gradually she realised that if she could put all her skills, all her energy into a proposal for Bronty, a proposal like the ones she did for her farming clients, then present it to her father, then he might come to see that there was room for them all. If she took on the consultancy advice that she dispensed to clients about 'family relations' she could manage a truce between herself and Annabelle and her children. They could all work together for one farm business – plus an old-style seed business as part of the package. The ideas she and Will had sketched out for the seed venture began to take shape in a proper structure. During each sleepless night, Kate tried to imagine herself counselling the Webster family professionally. All the advice and knowledge she'd gathered at university and at Maureen and Tony's, then in her job, began to bubble up. As the strategies unfolded in her head, she'd leap out of bed and dash to the office, grabbing her laptop and then diving back to the warmth of her bed. With the blue glow of her computer illuminating her face, she downloaded the ideas into a document. As the days passed, a folder of plans, maps and budgets was coming together.

This morning she punched holes into a freshly printed sheet with the heading *Bronty: A Whole Family and Farm Plan* and slipped it onto the metal spikes of the folder. She smiled and smoothed her hand over the paper. Surely her father couldn't ignore what was in this growing, almost living document. It held Will within it. It held his future. She could still make it happen for him, and for her mother. She prickled at the excitement and possibility of it.

'Mum!' Nell's voice bowled in from the kitchen.

'You all right, darling? Mum's coming.' Reluctantly, Kate stood up from the desk. The rest of the plans would have to wait until tomorrow. She still had to get Nell to Janie's before she set off for the McDonnells'. The elation she'd felt from working on the Bronty plans dissipated when the thought of seeing Nick flooded back into her. She was going to tell him today – she would tell him about Nell.

On the way to Rutherglen, Kate slowed down as she drove over the familiar rise. There stretching out before her was a

Wedgwood-blue sea, and the drought-green pastures of Bronty waiting thirstily for spring rains.

Glancing at the first boundary paddock, Kate noticed the slow green crawl of capeweed taking over the sheep camps. She felt frustration rumble in her. If only she had been strong enough to still be on Bronty. She'd be doing something about that. She began to see the patchy nature of the fencing. Some brand new, other sections leaning, wires slack. She noticed how the bush on the hill had only been partially fenced off from the stock – another unfinished environmental project by her over-stretched brother. She saw how sections of the creekbed would only sink deeper each year if plants weren't encouraged to bind the crumbling soil. She knew now what Will had felt. His frustration that such environmental problems could not be addressed head-on. There were never enough hours in the day for a father and son to fix it all. Not without the support of the whole family.

Lately, any extra money that might have been spent on the farm had been siphoned off for the house. Will had stood on the fringes, watching it all grind to a halt. Kate felt sick with guilt that she'd never properly listened to Will or come home to help him. Nausea swelled within her as she glanced at the sea surging behind the dunes.

As she neared Bronty's gateway, she pressed the accelerator down. She couldn't bring herself to look at the house. She'd head straight on up the coastline and into the bush-covered hills towards the McDonnell farm. But then something caught her eye. A man. On a bike. Motoring over the pasture. It was him. The vision of Will. Kate felt hope leap within her. But as she slowed the car, she realised it was Aden. Only Aden.

Kate held back the tears as she sped by. She vowed she'd travel back to Janie's a different way. She would drive the back roads, along the logging tracks over the steep mountains, scudding over corrugation, through dark gloomy tunnels created by plantation timber, anything rather than feel that kind of pain again.

'How dare you organise this behind my back!'

Lance McDonnell leaned on the kitchen table, his large hands clenched into fists. His once strong shoulders were hunched over and his face was a strange mix of blotchy yellow, red and grey. He glared at his wife. Alice ignored him, stooping to pull an orange cake from the oven.

'I'm bloody well leaving and you can tell that departmental scone-gobbler that his meeting is cancelled.'

Alice set the cake down on the stovetop with a bang.

'*Calm down*,' she said through clenched teeth.

Lance shuffled over to the phone on the kitchen wall. He picked up the receiver and held it towards Alice.

'Call him.' His eyes boring into his wife's as though they were in a gunfight.

'I can't,' she said, holding his gaze without flinching.

'Why not?'

'Because I burnt the number in the stove.' Alice reached over and pulled the newspaper clipping violently from the fridge. Magnets from the rural merchandise store clattered to the ground. Still glaring at her husband, she balled the paper up between her palms, opened the old woodstove and threw it into the dark sooty depths.

Lance hadn't seen his wife this fired up since his accident. He shut his eyes and breathed out strongly through his nostrils.

'The doctor said you shouldn't get stressed,' she said. 'And seeing as you're always stressed about this bloody place, what have you bloody well got to lose?' Alice thrust her hands, encased in oven mitts, on her hips. 'I'll tell you what you've got to lose,' she continued, 'because no one else will say it. You'll lose your son. You're going to lose him if we don't do something to change how things are around here!'

'He's not like Angus. He'll never leave this place. Hasn't got it in him.'

'I'm not talking about him leaving physically,' she said, her voice rising. 'You're going to lose him *emotionally*, Lance. You'll lose his love if you push him any harder.'

Alice stopped, waiting for a reaction, but he gave nothing. He'd held himself in so close since the accident. The focus had always been on the physical ... when to change wound dressings, when to take painkillers, was his diet aggravating things? Did he need to go to the doctor again? How soon until the next round of surgery? Appointments, practicalities, surface talk – it was never about the emotional. Lance sank down into a chair.

'And when does this bloody department bloke get here?'

'He's not a department bloke. It's only partly government funded. They're a private group. And he's not a bloke.'

'What?'

'She's a she. Not a he,' Alice said, violently shaking the cake from the tin onto a cooling rack.

'Well, it gets better and better,' Lance said flatly.

In the office, Nick stacked up piles of unopened mail on his father's desk. As he flicked through the endless window-faced bills he noticed a bright yellow envelope with his name printed on the front. He slid his finger under the envelope lip, still stewing over the way his mother had dropped this meeting on him at such short notice. Why hadn't she said anything before? Nick pulled out the stiff yellow cardboard and unfolded it. It was an invitation to this year's Rouseabout Ball.

'Great,' he said dully. Another reminder of Kate. Something he didn't need right now. He tossed the invitation aside, turned on the computer and waited for it to chatter itself to life. Leaning over the desk, he clicked the cursor onto the financial management program.

'Shit,' he said when he saw that his father hadn't made a single entry for the past four months. He cast his eye around the office at the overflowing rubbish tin, the stacks of yellowing newspapers and the tumble of folders and files. As he did he heard Tuff barking. Nick pulled back the old dusty curtain to see Kate Webster getting out of a white anonymous-looking work car.

'Shit, shit, double shit! Triple shit! Anyone but her!' He knew she'd got a job advising farmers, but he hadn't known that she would be the one on *this* job. *This* job, that would allow her to see all his family, exposed. How could his mother do this? And what would Felicity think? Kate Webster, here in this house.

The smell of fresh-baked cake led Kate along the dark old hallway as she followed Alice inside. From the outside the homestead looked so grand and impressive, but inside, Kate thought, it just looked tired. She took in how small Alice was against the vastness of the high-ceilinged house. She was a neat little woman with a halo of blonde hair. Nell's hair. Kate swallowed.

When she followed Alice into the kitchen it took a while for Kate to notice Mr McDonnell on a chair in the corner of the cluttered kitchen. She nearly jumped in fright. The sunken man was sitting dead still. It was like he was part of the house. Brittle with pain and the weight of time, he looked at her through drooping bloodhound eyes. Kate was shocked. She remembered a totally different man. He'd been larger than this. Handsome and full of life at the shows and church fundraisers. So much more outgoing than the other men in the district.

Before she could say hello, Nick walked in clutching a folder in his hands. Seeing him in his own home, in faded work jeans and a bright blue RM Williams heavy drill workshirt rolled up at the sleeves, took Kate's breath away. He nodded at her in greeting but his smile seemed forced.

'Now, Kate,' said Alice, pulling out a chair, 'you sit down next to Lance. He's been looking forward to this meeting, haven't you, dear?'

Kate glanced at Lance. It didn't seem as if he was looking forward to anything. She edged forward and offered her hand.

'Nice to meet you, Mr McDonnell.' The loudness in her voice covered her nervousness. Lance looked at her hand with a 'hmphh'.

It was normal for first-time consultations to have one or two reluctant participants in the family. Kate was used to it, but the atmosphere in the Rutherglen kitchen felt stormier than she'd ever experienced. She gathered her energy and turned on her brightest smile. She pulled her chair towards Lance. She knew he'd been a dog trialler before his accident. She decided to start on safe ground.

'I hope you don't mind, Mr McDonnell, but I brought a young dog along with me. She wasn't going to learn anything at home in the pens. Thought it'd do her good to be with me for the day. I've left her in the car, so she won't be any trouble. Cleared it with the boss first, mind you . . . putting a dog in a company rig.' She searched for a reaction from him, but Alice jumped in, filling the gap.

'Oh! You should tie her up in the garden and give her some water! Nick, why don't you go and do that for her?'

'No, no!' Kate said. 'She's fine, thanks. I gave her a run before we arrived and she's in season so she's best in the car. I've left the windows down a little and she's got a blanket to curl up on.' Kate glanced at Nick, her cheeks dusting pink. She felt frustration writhe in her. She wasn't used to feeling shy around men. She busied herself by unzipping her bag and pulling out her folder and pen.

'Working dog, is it?' came Lance's cracked voice.

'Yes,' Kate said.

'Kelpie?'

'Yes. My brother brought her from the mainland. Good bloodlines from O'Connell's Bagallah kelpies.'

'Ah! I'm impressed. She work all right?'

'She's showing some promise. The funny thing is . . .' Kate leaned towards Lance and went on in a half-whisper, 'Her name's *Bra*. Will called her that. You know, round 'em up and point 'em in the right direction. Bra.'

187

Lance pulled his mouth downwards and guffawed. Kate knew then she'd got him. He sat back in his chair, a twinkle in his eye for the first time.

'Nick's got a bloody good yard dog,' Lance said. 'Pandara bloodlines. You should think about joining them. Maybe get a good line of pups out of them.'

Kate raised her eyebrows, cleared her throat and looked down at her bookwork. She daren't look at Nick.

'Yes. Great idea.' Her voice quavered.

'What do you say, son?' Lance shot a glance towards Nick. 'You could let her out of the car, join 'em now.'

Nick nodded, looked at his feet and shoved his hands deep in his pockets. Kate was sure he was trying to stifle a smile.

'Yep. Good idea, Dad.' Then he looked at Kate and winked. Kate felt the buzz of electricity again. Focus, she told herself, focus.

Lance shifted in his seat a little and Kate saw him flinch in pain. He turned to take in Kate's profile.

'Now did I hear right? You're Henry Webster's daughter, from Bronty down the coast, right?'

'I am.'

'Well, I'll be. Haven't seen Henry in a good long while . . . used to run amok in the Young Farmers' dance days. Years ago. A bit like a B&S only a little more tame, from what I hear. Angus, our eldest, was right into B&Ss but Nick here doesn't go much on them. Do you, Nick?'

Nick shrugged, while Kate felt heat prickle in her cheeks. She couldn't believe she was making small talk with Nell's grandfather. It felt so strange. She nodded politely as she listened to Lance, outwardly calm. But panicking inside.

'I remember your mother at those dances,' Lance said. 'Lovely Irish look about her. Bit like yourself. I'm sorry she's not about anymore.' His voice trailed off. 'And your brother. I'm sorry about that, too.'

'Thanks.'

Feeling the conversation stretch to a place it shouldn't go, Alice stepped forward with a platter of sliced cake, biscuits and scones.

'Amazing how the sight of a pretty girl revives our Lance,' Alice said. 'Always has. Always will. Your mother cast the same spell on him. Cup of tea?'

Kate nodded. 'Yes, please.'

'You're not a dieter, are you?' Alice said, eyeing Kate's curvaceous figure. 'Take one of each if you like. Nick's Felicity is always watching her figure, though I don't know why, there's nothing of her. She's off doing a shift and you can bet your bottom dollar it'll be celery sticks for lunch.' She pushed a plate in Kate's direction.

'Thanks. Don't mind if I do.' Kate reached over and took up a scone and a slice of cake, while Alice placed a teapot on the table.

'That's more like it,' said Alice. 'It's nice to see a strong healthy girl enjoying my cooking.'

Nick glanced away, embarrassed by his mother.

Kate sucked in her stomach and sat up straighter. She felt mortified. To cover her discomfort she said with bravado, 'I'll be the size of a three-bay skillion shed by the time I've been with this company a few months.' She leant towards Lance. 'You know what these office types are like. My dad calls them scone-gobblers.'

She saw a light come into Lance's eyes again and he laughed. A soft chuckle. Meanwhile, Nick hovered in the doorway, frowning. Kate was confused. He'd been all smiles and flirtatiousness at the show, and he'd winked at her just before. Now he was being cagey again. She soldiered on. At this rate there'd be no chance to have a private conversation with him about Nell anyway. Relieved, she relaxed a little.

'Well,' she said, pushing the plate away for the moment and reaching for the folder, 'I don't want to take up your whole day. Let's get started, shall we?' She pulled out some pamphlets. If she just didn't look at Nick she'd be okay, she told herself. Throw yourself in and have a red-hot go. Professional, but passionate. She began to speak . . .

Two and a half hours later, Kate had transformed the energy in the room. Lance was slapping her on the shoulder and laughing; Alice was sitting close to her husband, leaning into him, her blue eyes alive with excitement. Nick sat at the other end of the table, a little removed from it all, but Kate could tell he'd been interested in what the service had to offer. As she began to pack up, she glanced at her watch.

'Have you got any more time?' Lance asked. 'You could try your bitch with that dog of Nick's. And Nick could take you out to where he reckons the dam should be.'

As Kate looked at Nick, panic resurfaced in her mind.

'Can't,' Nick said abruptly. 'I've had the excavator out. Redoing the pipes in the creek crossing while it's dry. Can't get a vehicle over.'

'You ride, don't you? If you're your mother's daughter you'll ride,' Lance said to Kate.

'Yes, but . . .'

'There's no point you going away to work on what we've discussed unless you've seen a bit of the place,' Lance insisted. 'Nick'll grab Felicity's horses. She won't mind. She's got a busy week and she'd be glad they've been worked.'

Nick went to protest, but Alice moved over to him.

'Go on,' she urged, not wanting to break the spell Kate had cast for her husband.

Nick glanced at his mother. A change had come over the room. It was as if they could suddenly see past the day-to-day drudgery of wound dressings, bag changes, drugs and pain. They could see a future. Nick looked at Kate, his eyes direct but soft as they questioned her.

'You up for it?'

How could she say no? She nodded. But the thought of being alone with Nick jangled Kate's nerves. She knew the time had come. Reluctantly she followed him as he led the way outside.

Twenty-one

The dogs bounded in circles ahead of Kate and Nick as they rode in silence away from the homestead over the green-drought paddocks. As she sat astride Felicity's towering ex-showjumper, Kate's mind tumbled with uncertainties. There was no getting out of it now. She would have to tell him. But how?

She watched as Tuff bounded up to Bra in full-on flirt mode, tail wagging, a hopeful expression on his face. Bra pulled him up short with a snap of her clacking crocodile-like teeth.

'Looks like she's giving him the cold shoulder,' Nick said.

Kate nodded, feeling painfully self-conscious. She squeezed her legs so her ambling horse would keep up with Nick's prancing young gelding. Kate was still settling into the feel of Felicity's tall stretch of a horse. She felt so high off the ground, compared to Matilda. As he'd saddled them, Nick had explained that the horse Kate was to ride was called Prince. He was well into his twenties and was, as Nick put it, 'Felicity's first love'. Kate looked away, embarrassed, the night of the B&S was still so vivid in her mind. Nick didn't seem to notice his poor choice of phrase, but then, Kate thought, his poker face gave little away when he chose to use it.

Forcing herself to concentrate on her job, Kate looked down

past the shoulder of her horse to inspect the pasture. She noticed how damaged it was. She knew that beneath the barren surface the white tangle of roots of clover and grass had been gnawed away by grubs.

'You know you've got a really bad cockchafer problem.'

There was a pause. God, Kate thought, flinching, I could've phrased that better!

'Cockchafers?' Nick said, amusement barely disguised on his face. 'I know – my cockchafer problem is a big one.'

'I can help you with it if you like,' said Kate, digging an even deeper hole for herself without meaning to.

'Really?' Nick was riding ahead of her again but she could tell he was smiling beneath his big black hat. 'Do you often ask blokes about their cockchafer problems straight up like that?' he called back over his shoulder. 'It's very forward of you.'

He was flirting again, Kate thought, stunned. She just couldn't figure this man out.

'Yes. I mean, no.' She kicked the old horse on so she was by Nick's side again. 'I mean, I was involved in red-headed cockchafer trials back in the department in New South Wales. Timing of the spray application was crucial . . . I can give you some good contacts. People who can help boost your results.' Her seriousness on the subject seemed to put a lid on his flirting.

'That'd be great,' Nick said. 'I'd like that.'

Kate nodded towards the expanse of paddock.

'When was it sown?'

Nick narrowed his eyes, thinking. His mouth twisted to one side, just the way Nell's did.

'Ah . . . summer over three years ago.'

Kate swallowed down her memories.

'Fertilised when?' she asked, trying to push the conversation on the pasture forward so she could shut out the loud voices in her head.

'Sorry?'

'When was it fertilised?'

'Um . . . not since.'

Kate took the information in.

'We might need to sit down with your dad and talk through the farm budgets about setting some money aside for fertiliser and grub control. We could do a few soil tests, see if it needs lime, or we could trial a bit of liquid humus . . . I hear they're having great results on a farm a bit further down the coast . . . even with the lack of rain.'

'Rain? What's that? Something Dad drones on about endlessly,' Nick said.

Kate realised she'd touched a nerve. Like Will, and so many other farmers' sons, Nick was constrained by his father and by the weather. Even though Lance was almost housebound, his word on what could happen on the farm was final. Poor seasons only compounded the problems and increased tensions. In all initial meetings with her clients, Kate gently tried to steer the talk away from the fathers and draw out the dreams of the younger generation.

'Nice toy you've got there,' she said, nodding at an excavator ahead of them. It sat idle like a sleeping yellow dinosaur, its giant bucket rested on the ground as if it had just consumed a bellyful of creekbed rocks and rubble and was slowly digesting its meal.

'It does the job,' Nick said, his horse shying from the sight of it. He urged the thoroughbred on, down through the steep gouge that the machine had left in the creekbed, the horse sliding a little on its haunches, dislodging tumbling rocks.

'You right?' he called back over his shoulder.

'Yep,' Kate said as Prince carefully picked his way down the slope.

'Then you're right to trot up this ridge here?'

'Yep,' Kate called again and soon they weren't just trotting side by side. The horses were loping together in an easy unified canter. Kate felt strange in the English saddle that seemed so open compared to her normal old stock saddle, but she relished the chance to ride out with this man.

She glanced over to Nick, who was watching her ride. He smiled. Pure white light. Kate felt goosebumps rush over her skin, despite the unseasonal warmth of the cloudy day. The smell of the bush engulfed her senses as the horses veered off the main track. Kate found herself travelling on a mottled path of silver-grey stones, frosted with pale green lichen. Serrated tussocks and thin spikes of silver grass covered the uneven ground. The dogs followed each other in the bush, leaping over logs and pricking their ears towards startled Forester kangaroos and Bennetts wallabies that crashed through the scrub ahead of them.

As the track narrowed and became almost enclosed by a soft green canopy of leafy wattles, the horses pulled up to a walk. Snorting, the geldings picked their way over fallen branches and through bracken ferns, disturbing the secret tunnels of wallabies and sending tiny insects scuttling. Above them, the finger-like branches of gum trees combed the low clouds. It felt like rain, but both Nick and Kate knew that it wouldn't rain today.

On top of the ridge, Nick pulled Calvin to a halt and slid from him. Kate followed suit. They stood looking out at a gully that was dotted with cattle and sheep. The paddocks were nestled between the clumps of thick bush that fringed the gully.

'I never knew you had all this country tucked behind here. It's beautiful.'

Nick nodded and extended his arm, his sleeve rolled to his elbow, and pointed. 'The boundary runs across that ridgeline and down to that creek. That's the corner of the place where Dad talked about building a dam.' Kate dragged her eyes away from his delicious muscled forearm and looked to where he indicated.

Nick continued. 'Because it's pretty remote from the homestead, Dad was looking at automatic pivot systems.'

Kate nodded. 'And? What had he got up to? Has he been through all the red tape and number crunching yet – environmental studies, Aboriginal studies, financing, cashflow of your enterprises, soil tests?'

Nick shrugged. 'Everything's been at a standstill since the accident.' He sat down on a fallen log. He plucked an old segment of bark from the log and began to run it between the tips of his callused fingers.

'He's lost interest in the farm,' he said. 'He's terrified of not leaving enough money for Mum, so he's stopped spending.' Kate felt the weight of emotion behind his words. Nick gestured to the hills. 'What's the point anyway? The neighbour's just sold out to trees. Anything we do crop now is just fodder for the wildlife.'

'Won't the company control the game populations?'

'You know the story,' Nick said. 'Five years' time, once the trees grow up, they stop all their "controls" – then the crops would be stuffed. I won't have poison, shooting's a lot of work and fencing – well, you know the cost, it makes the whole thing unviable. Bloody plantations. It'll bugger us.' He flicked the bark away and reached for another piece, peeling it from the tree.

'I've got to the point where I *want* him to sell it. So he and Mum can afford to buy a unit in town . . . and neither of them ever has to worry.' He glanced at Kate. Looking for something, someone to hear him. Kate wasn't expecting him to open up like this. She kept staring out across the gully as she sat beside him on the log. In his fingers, Nick kept snapping the bark into smaller and smaller pieces as he talked. He laughed sadly.

'Never thought I'd say that out loud to anyone. That I'd rather it was sold. But there you have it. Every other bastard round here's sold out to trees. What's the point of farming food when the government doesn't give a toss?'

Kate wanted to turn to him and put her arms around the large slab of his shoulders and pull him to her. But instead

196

she continued staring ahead at the beautiful stretch of gully below, the jagged line of the bush-filled hills, the crest of Freycinet Peninsula rising blue above it all in the distance. Nick kept on.

'But then *you* show up.' He glanced at her again and she felt the sting of his intensity. 'And blow me down if you don't bring the old man alive with ideas in just a few hours! Buggered if I've ever had that effect on him . . . And then you start to have an effect on *me*. I start believing that it can all work.'

'It's my job,' Kate said.

Nick shook his head. 'Is it just your job?' He turned to face her. 'Or is it who you are? The way you know so much about farming and the way you dag about with your dogs and don't give a damn.'

'Dag?' Kate said, devastated he'd chosen that word for her. She was supposed to be a professional. She turned to face him, thinking that the one man she really wanted in life was out of her league. He thought she was a *dag*. 'I suppose next to Felicity I would seem like a bit of a dag,' she said, looking down at her cracking Blundstone boots. Nick flicked more bark away and smiled his cute smile at her.

'I don't mean it as an insult. Christ! You don't even realise how pretty and clever you are, do you? You bowled Dad over back there and you didn't even notice it. And you don't notice the effect you've had on *me*.'

Kate glanced up into his blue, beautiful eyes, stunned. He was making a move on her, fiancée and all. He felt it too! That chemistry. The spark that was beyond all reason. But in that moment of delight, Kate also felt the weight of the past crushing her hopes with Nick. The truth had to come out. And then, like her college life, and her life at Bronty, it would be over before it had begun.

She heard Will's voice, like her conscience, urging her on. Nick was sitting closer to her now. Facing her. Leaning towards her, wanting to touch her hands.

'I know it's crazy, and there's Felicity to consider, but I can't stop thinking about you since I saw you again, rouse-abouting . . .' He broke off and looked away. 'Argh! Sorry,' he said, shutting his eyes and shaking his head. 'This is all coming out wrong.'

'It's okay,' Kate said. 'It's not coming out wrong. It sounds perfect to me, but . . .' She drew a breath and shook her head. Nick pushed his hat back and stared at her.

'I know,' he said. 'We hardly know each other, and your life isn't so simple – there's your daughter to think about. But it's there, isn't it, that feeling? It's not as if we're total strangers! God! That B&S! We parted as more than just friends, remember?' Nick laughed at the memory. 'I went back to boarding school the following week like I was King Kong. Man, I couldn't have asked for a better kick-start in growing up – my hormones went mad after you. You were every schoolboy's fantasy and there I was getting you for real. You were my Bundy goddess – I used to try and paint you in art class! – and I've never completely shaken you from my mind. And now you're back . . . You've made me see what I haven't got. You're amazing, Kate Webster. I want to get to know you all over again.'

As Nick laughed nervously, Kate felt tears rising. What she had longed for had at last come true. He *did* have feelings for her – but she knew that telling him about Nell would end every-thing. He leant forward on the log to peer behind the sheen of hair that she'd let fall from her ponytail to hide her face.

'*What*?' He frowned as Kate stood. She sucked the air in. She shut her eyes and pictured her mother and Will. Then she turned to Nick. She looked down at his handsome, hopeful face.

'You know Nell?' Kate began.

Nick's frown deepened.

'Yeeees,' he said slowly.

'Well . . . she . . . she's . . . That night when we . . . well, Nell is . . .'

Kate couldn't finish. She shut her mouth tightly and looked desperately at him. She saw Nick's mind working overtime, putting the pieces together. Adding up the years. Recalling the look of the little girl. She watched as he almost recoiled in horror.

'I'm sorry!' Kate blurted out. 'I'm sorry. I don't even know you.' Years of grief, loneliness and fear spilled out in the form of tears. There was no relief that it was out, only horror at what the news might do. Nick just stood shaking his head, his mouth open. Shocked.

He began to speak, but he had too many questions, too many words . . . a rush of thoughts.

'Why didn't you tell me?'

'Tell you? Why didn't I *tell* you?' Kate heard her voice rising. 'You were seventeen! What was I going to do? Ring you up and ask you to leave school and come and play happy families with me? I picked you out of a crowd, Nick. You were a dare! A stupid, *stupid* dare. That's all!' But as she spoke the words, Kate knew Nick was so much more than just a dare. He could just be the one . . . her soulmate.

'That's all? I've got a child walking around and you've never *told* me! Couldn't you have . . . ?' Nick was standing now, pacing. He flung his hat off and ran his fingers through his short sandy hair. Tears gathered in his eyes as he looked up to the sky. Tuff hovered, agitated by his master's distress.

'Couldn't you have . . . you know. Didn't you consider . . . ?' he began again.

'What? An abortion?' Kate said. 'Yes, I bloody well did consider it, but I didn't go through with it. That's my Nellie you're wishing dead right now. I didn't have an abortion, okay? I'd just lost my mother. I wasn't going to lose a chance at some other kind of life. And that's the end of it. I'm sorry if I made the wrong choice in your mind.'

'Sorry! *Sorry?*' Nick's voice cracked. 'What do I tell my parents? What do I tell Felicity?'

'They don't have to know. Only Will knew. And Janie and

199

Dave. They're the only living souls. And, besides, what do you care what Felicity might think? You were about to make a move on me behind her back! Why should Nell matter to her?'

'Oh my God.' Nick was incredulous. Anger creeping in. Visions of Nell in the shearing shed flashed in his head. He was her father. The phrase just kept turning over and over in his mind. He looked down at Kate, the anguished expression on her face.

'My mother had just died,' Kate almost begged. 'I was a mess.'

Nick knew he should understand the source of her pain, but couldn't help lashing out at her. He suddenly felt betrayed.

'And now you've made someone else's life a mess?'

'It doesn't have to make your life a mess. I'm not asking anything from you. You don't even have to acknowledge it. Her.'

Nick looked at her in disbelief. A coldness settled over his expression.

'You're supposed to fix up people's lives, Kate, not fuck them up.' Red-faced with anger and confusion, Nick backed away from Kate. He unhitched Calvin's reins and swung them over the horse's head. He lobbed up into the saddle. 'Find someone else to counsel,' he said bitterly. 'You know the way back.'

He kicked Calvin into a trot and started weaving his way back through the grey trunks of the peppermint gums.

Twenty-two

Felicity's yellow jellybean of a car scuttled along the driveway, trailing dust in its wake. Nick watched from the shadows of the machinery shed. Oil smudged his face where he'd rubbed his eyes with the backs of his hands. Kate's visit this afternoon sat like a stone in his heart.

When he shut his eyes he saw his father in the hospital. Lance's eyes closed in coma, not sleep. Brutally battered from his car accident, his wounds still fresh red, machines living for him, tubes sprouting from him. His own father, lying before him, broken. Then he saw Nell, her bright curly blonde hair. The way she, his daughter, clambered all over him in the wool bins, laughing and tugging wool over his face.

When Nick opened his eyes again, all he saw ahead of him was the thirsty landscape. An expanse of sickened, half-dead land. And the unsettling knowledge that it was his responsibility entirely. He cursed the farm. He cursed the hills on the horizon, ripped and ready for trees. He cursed his father. Then, he cursed Kate. And the news that he had a child. *He had a child.* He rolled the sentence around in his head. He felt the unspoken words swamp him. It wasn't supposed to be this way.

He was supposed to hold his new baby in the homestead nursery – the same nursery in which his mother had raised him and Angus. But that would be in a few years, with Felicity. Not now. Not right now.

Nick unleashed a punch. Crack. His fist met the unforgiving metal of the shed. His eyes shut again and an image of Kate's face was there. Looking at him with her dark eyes that pierced right through him. As Felicity's car neared, and the pain swam from his knuckles up his arm, he watched the horses prick their ears and whicker. She stopped the car near the feed shed and stepped out.

'Coming, boys,' Nick heard her call. Her voice a tinkling bell. It had begun to annoy him recently. She pulled a pale blue cardigan from the back seat and draped it over her slender shoulders, wrapping it around her crisp white nurse's uniform. She looked pretty and fragile in the afternoon light, with her hair pulled back neatly and her pale skin. His news might crush her.

But no. Nick knew Felicity's air of vulnerability was deceiving. His ice maiden had a touch so cold it warmed him. How would he tell her that he had fathered a child with someone else? A *child*. With Kate Webster.

Nick looked to the rafters of the shed. Their future together was supposed to be mapped out in the stars . . . marry, have kids, then farm the land. Be happy? He wasn't sure. Doubtful even. Be secure? Yes, if a dam was built and it rained and he was married, *then* he'd be secure. He'd be able to prop up his parents and mend their broken lives. But how could all that happen now that Kate was so inextricably linked to his life?

As Felicity lifted her head to search for him, Nick felt like he might throw up. He swallowed thickly. Surely, he reasoned, he didn't *have* to tell her? She didn't have to know. *Did she?* He could just continue on the way things were, before Kate Webster had walked back into his life. Before he knew that the cute little girl with the doll-like eyelashes and blonde curls was his.

He watched as Felicity mixed chaff, pellets and globs of

202

molasses, rinsing her hands medico-style under a tap. Once inside the gate, she stepped carefully around the horses' dung heaps in her white flat-soled shoes and set the feed tubs down. As the horses settled down to eat, Felicity pulled their rugs down from where they hung on the fence stays.

Nick sighed. He knew what was coming. He knew what she'd find. He deliberately hadn't hosed the horses down. It was as if he wanted it all to unravel. Whatever was between them, he wanted their relationship to be tested to the limits.

He watched as she began to swing the rug over Calvin, then stopped. She let the rug drop as her fingertips ran over the sweat-crusted girth mark that lay behind Calvin's front leg. She straightened, frowning. She ran her palm over the line on the horse's brow where the bridle had lain. Twisting her mouth, as if trying to solve a puzzle, she turned to inspect Prince. When she discovered a girth mark on Prince as well, Nick saw her stiffen with anger. Felicity spun round to scan the farmyard and the sheds. He turned his back to her and shut his eyes. But her voice reached out to him. It caught him lurking in the shadows like a naughty boy.

'Nick! Niiiiick?' she yelled as she walked. Before she entered the shed, Nick swung his leg over the farm bike. She was on her way to burn him, that much he knew. Her pretty mouth a thin red line. Her ice-blue eyes hot with anger. Nope, he thought clearly, as he watched her arriving like a blizzard, there's no way he could explain about Kate and the baby. There was no way she would understand or forgive.

'What have you been doing with my horses?' She put her hands on her slim hips and tilted her head to one side.

'Dad's idea,' Nick said, his face set.

'Brilliant. Who'd you go with?'

Nick clenched his jaw.

'The farm advisor.

'Who?' Felicity demanded.

'The rural advisor. She—'

'She? *She!*' Felicity stood before Nick. Her voice rose higher. Nick delivered the final blow.

'Kate Webster.'

'*How dare you*? How dare you take my show horses and that tart up the backblocks while I'm away at work!'

'It wasn't—'

'I don't give a toss what it was or wasn't! I don't want her anywhere near my horses. What were you thinking? You could've injured them! Don't you realise how valuable they are to me? And you didn't even have the brains to hose them down when you were done!'

'Sorry,' he said.

'Sorry? Is that all you're going to give me?'

'What more do you want?'

'What's that supposed to mean?' she said, glaring at him.

'You know.'

'No. I don't know. I think you ought to spell it out, Nick.'

'You and I both know you'd rather spend your time out here riding those bloody things round and round in circles than with me.'

'You poor, jealous little boy,' she said. 'I've tried to include you. Really I have.'

Nick knew it wasn't Felicity's fault, but he couldn't help resenting her. He'd seen the way Kate worked harder than a man in the sheds. The way she rode so confidently, without fuss or pride. The way they had shared so many easy conversations, the sort of conversations he would never have with his future wife. He wanted to hurt Felicity. The same way Kate had hurt him.

'Include me?' he shot at her sarcastically. 'Yeah? As a bloody strapper at your horse shows? Hanging about all day when you know there's a truckload of work to be done here. How often have you offered to take the bloody things bush with me to help with the stock? Once. *Once.* And you cracked it with me for riding them over a friggin' twig. I'd ride with you every bloody weekend if you wanted to do a bit of stock work or try a bit of polocrosse with me . . . but no! You're off at a show any chance you get. It's nothing to do with me. Ever. It's all about *you*.'

'Really? Is that so? I'm such a selfish person that I just think about me and the horses? Is that what you reckon?'

Nick looked down at the handlebars of the bike guiltily, knowing he was wrong.

'How much time have I given to your father in there, nursing him through? Propping up your poor mother when she needed it. Huh? It's had to come from me, because you're not capable of doing it. It's not all one-sided, Nick, and you know it.'

Shame flashed on Nick's face as he sat upright on the bike. He put his foot on the starter peg and turned the ignition switch to 'on'. He looked at Felicity coldly. 'You don't think much of me, do you? It's all horses and homesteads with you, isn't it? I could've been any bloke, really. So long as I had a horse paddock. Why do you need me to have brains and emotions as well? Haven't you got what you want?' Angrily, Nick jerked his foot downwards, the bike roared to life. He glanced at her stricken face, knowing the words he spoke held only fragments of truth. That he was being harsh and cruel. It made him all the more angry.

At the sound of the bike, Felicity's horses shied, Calvin clipping the edge of his feed bin with splayed legs. Nick deliberately spun the rear wheel, spraying dust and tiny stones towards the horse yard. He rode flat-knacker out of the gateway and on towards the creek. He was going back up to the ridgeline. Back to the fallen log where he and Kate had been. To sit. And to think.

That night, Kate lifted Nell from the bath and wrapped her up in a soft lilac towel. As she dried bath water and dwindling blobs of bubbles from her, Kate took in her daughter's perfect skin and the way it covered her strong, growing bones. A miniature version of Nick. Kate breathed in Nell's scent of talcum powder and apple shampoo and felt love surge through her. A mother's love. More powerful than the moon tugging the tide. She tried to block the image of Nick's shocked face from her mind and sang to Nell in her best Kasey Chambers twang.

Pulling the towel from Nell's body, Kate helped guide her little legs into her night nappy, then into her pyjamas. As she did up Nell's buttons and brushed down her hair, she could almost touch the golden glow of life and happiness radiating from her daughter's being. Nell, all warm and clean, hugged her mother around the neck and pressed her cheek against Kate's. Untainted perfection, Kate thought incredulously, despite all the mistakes Kate had made in raising this child. She hugged Nell and kissed her over and over. Tears surprised her.

'There you are, all ready for bed, Missy,' she said, swiping them away before Nell could see. 'Come on, let's get Mr Bunny so he can snuggle in with you.' She listened to the little thuds of Nell's footsteps as she followed Kate down the hallway to her bedroom.

Soft blue curtains with yellow stars, made by Janie, covered the window. Nell's night-light sent out a comforting glow in the room, as though Tinkerbell herself was sitting in the corner. With the toys packed away in baskets and her little patchwork quilt pulled back, Nell's room was so welcoming Kate wanted to curl up in the bed with her. Sheila ambled in and parked herself at Kate's feet as Nell scrambled into bed. She lay with a smile on her face, waiting for Kate to pull the quilt over her. Kate tucked the gangly, grubby bunny down beside her and picked up a selection of books to read.

'Wombats, elephants or the one about the smelly trousers?'

'Wombats!' Nell said, her excitement radiating out to her jiggling limbs. As Kate began to read, her mind wandered to Nick. She'd dwelt so long on actually telling him about Nell that she'd never given a thought to what might happen from that point. Now, with a rush, the questions came.

How would he feel when he'd had time for the news to settle? Would he want to be part of Nell's life? Would Nell want him near? Would he threaten to take her from her? She'd not been a good mother. Could he do that? Would he? Kate felt confusion and fear swell and swirl again, like eddies in a stream. Calm down, she told herself sternly.

She stroked Nell's silky cheek.

'Nell, sweetie,' she said.

'Read, Mummy. Please.'

'Yes, I'll read some more in a minute . . . but you know how you sometimes ask me why you don't have a daddy?'

Nell shrugged. 'Some people just don't have daddies. Ryan doesn't.'

Kate looked at Nell, surprised. She couldn't believe Nell remembered the little boy from playgroup in Orange, another kid with a single mum. Kate traced small circles on Nell's arm.

'Would you like a daddy? One day, maybe?'

Nell shrugged.

'Don't care.'

'Don't you?' Kate shifted a little on the bed to get a better look at Nell's face.

'Dave can be my daddy.'

'Yes, Nell.' Kate smiled. 'I suppose Dave could for now. I'm sure Brendan and Jasmine won't mind sharing him with you.'

Nell frowned and pushed the book back towards her.

'Now read, Mummy. P-lease.'

And Kate picked up the book and began to read again. But the feeling, like an invisible thread, still tugged at her. Now Nick knew, everything seemed to have shifted. She felt somehow connected to him, now more than ever before. His part in all this, this 'mistake' of her becoming a mother, was now so real. He was now too real.

Once Nell was asleep, Kate went back out into the lounge room. She threw herself into the chair by the phone and dialled

Janie's number. As she waited for her to pick up, she flicked through her mail. Bills, newsletters, catalogues, packages from head office. And then a yellow envelope. Tucking the phone between her shoulder and her ear, Kate tore at the paper. It was an invitation. To the Rouseabout B&S ball. Kate shut her eyes and a world from the past rose before her. Janie must've put her name down on the invitation list. There was no way she was going. No way in the world. She tossed the paper in the woodbin beside the fireplace. At that moment she heard Janie's voice saying hello.

'I've told him,' Kate said.

'And?'

'Not good,' Kate said. 'Not a good reaction at all. She's all over red rover, I reckon.'

Twenty-three

The afternoon sun set the tin on the roof cracking as the day cooled. Blowflies buzzed noisily about the office, bashing their large black bodies against the glass. Kate sat staring out the window, watching Matilda and Paterson dozing with their hindquarters to the warm northerly, the movement of their wind-captured tails echoed the dancing branches of the leafy fruit trees. Dust blasted from the sun-baked paddocks and whipped away in a haze to the fencelines. The sun was sinking but the heat of the day remained. Kate sighed tiredly as she tidied her desk. Her working week was over and it was almost time to pick up Nell from Dave's mum.

Her thoughts were interrupted when she heard a loud knock on the door, then stomping boots and clacking heels along the hallway. In the doorway stood Dave and Janie, Dave with a six-pack of rum under his arm. Janie was in a sexy black dress that showed off her 'yummy mummy' curves and highlighted her blonde hair. Dave was wearing the same suit he'd met Janie in, looking like a cross between a homeless man and James Bond after a fight.

Kate recalled the yellow invitation thrown in the woodbin a couple of months back. The bloody Rouseabout Ball! They'd all agreed that they were over B&S balls and they weren't going. Kate rolled her eyes.

'You're joking,' she said to them.

Janie's face was alight with glee.

'No joke, but it'll certainly be a laugh. I sent our money in ages ago. For all of us.'

'No. No. No. *No*. NO!'

'It's all arranged. Dave's mum's still got the kids. Nell just wants to see you dolled up, then you're outta here. You can't hide away from the world forever.'

'I'm not! I've been out just about every day working.'

'But you spend no time playing. It's unhealthy.'

'I don't want to go! I can't.'

'Think of it as getting back on the horse that bucked you off,' Dave said. 'We'll look after you. We won't let you get too drunk.'

'No!'

Dave glanced at his watch.

'We've already been here fifteen minutes – that's $2.50 I've wasted on the babysitter.'

'You're not paying your mum to have the kids, Dave, so don't put that one on me. I'll go over and help her with them after you've gone.'

'Kate . . . please. Come.'

Kate looked up at her friends and sighed.

'But what if *he's* there?'

Kate thought back over the months since she'd told Nick about Nell. In that time, there'd been only one phone message from him.

'Sorry for the things I said,' he had mumbled on the answering machine. 'Your news was a big shock. I just need some time to get over it.' He cleared his throat. 'Let me know about those pups when they come. I can help you sell them.'

The reserved matter-of-factness of his voice stung Kate. She played the message over and over, trying to extract any forgiveness from his tone, desperately wanting to call him back but not wanting to crowd him. Instead, she'd phoned her boss, Lisa, and asked her to take over on the McDonnell consultancy job. She couldn't face going out to Rutherglen again.

'I have a conflict of interest there,' Kate had told Lisa. Lisa hadn't pried.

'No worries,' she'd said brightly. 'Email me the details and I'll contact them.'

As the weeks rolled on and spring failed to deliver enough rains for a good flush of growth, Kate found herself swamped by the needs of her other clients. She was grateful to be busy. It distracted her from the continuous loop of questions that remained about Nick.

Now, in the summery little cottage, she looked up at Dave and Janie, fearful and exhilarated at the possibility of seeing Nick at the B&S.

'Nick won't be going,' Janie said emphatically. 'He's too boring to do anything like that these days.'

'How do I know he won't be there?'

Dave shook his head. 'He won't be. Trust me. I saw him in at Elders today and he said he wasn't going. He said it's for young people.'

Kate looked at Dave through narrowed eyes. 'What's he on about? He *is* young.'

'No, he's not. He's turned into a boring old bugger like you. He's not going.'

'Why do you need to avoid him anyway?' Janie asked. 'You've come clean with him about Nell. Now you can move on. It's time you got a life, Kate.'

Dave cracked open a can of Bundy and handed it to her.

'You've clocked off from work. We've got you a babysitter all weekend. Now get your gear on, woman. We have a B&S ball to go to!'

'But I don't have anything to wear.'

'That's what you think,' Janie said excitedly as she clacked from the room in her blocky black shoes. She was back in a flash and with a flourish she pulled from a plastic bag the most beautiful pale blue dress.

'Ta-da!' she said, trailing it before her from a wire coathanger. 'It was your bridesmaid material. Might as well use it now. It wasn't expensive. On special. And coz you had the kids the other weekend, I actually had time to start sewing something I enjoy! Girlie clothes!'

Kate gently rubbed the gorgeous fabric between her fingertips, overcome with the generosity and tenacity of her friends.

'Oh, Janie, it's beautiful.' She looked up at her. 'I'm sorry. I should've been a bridesmaid for you. I'm sorry.'

'Sorry, schmorry. You'll be sorry if you don't come with me tonight. Tonight you are my bridesmaid. Come on, get it on.'

The dress fitted perfectly. A straight sheath of blue fabric, it wrapped around her breasts and over her body, tight across her firm thighs, then flared out a touch at the bottom. Kate took in her image in the mirror and despite herself wished Nick was going to see her in the dress. She slipped some shoes on and walked out to the lounge room again.

'I'll have to walk like I've pooped myself,' Kate said, crossing one foot in front of the other as she tottered around the room. 'You don't think it's showing too much of my bingo wings?' She wiggled the flesh of her underarm.

'Don't be daft. You're too hard on yourself. You look fantastic. I was only guessing when I cut it. Think I got the size pretty right – it shows off your hot-mama assets very nicely.'

'It sure does,' said Dave appreciatively.

'Are you sure you couldn't run me up a quick Elvis suit instead? This is way too classy for me and too beautiful for a B&S,' Kate said.

Janie simply narrowed her eyes at her and folded her arms. 'So you're coming then?' she said.

'All right,' Kate said, holding up her hands in surrender. 'All right. But I'm not drinking to excess. You can hold me to that!'

Dave and Janie lifted their cans to the ceiling and cheered, then ducked for cover, screeching, when Dave's can connected with the lightglobe and glass, rum and sparks came showering down. In the dim room they fell about laughing.

At Rutherglen homestead Nick found his mother in the lounge room. She was staring vacantly at the television, exhaustion on her face.

'Dad still in bed?'

Alice looked up, startled. She smiled when she saw her handsome son in his dinner suit. She lifted her arm and waved her hand weakly. 'He's taken another turn. Pretty crook.'

'He'll get over it. Always does. He'll be right, Mum,' Nick said. He lingered, taking in her halo of blonde hair, the way her feet pointed into each other, like a little girl in a chair too big for her. The weariness of her. 'I'd take you with me to have a blinder at the B&S but I don't think Dad would approve.'

Alice smiled.

'You'll have Felicity with you. Make sure you take care of her tonight. She doesn't strike me as the B&S type.'

'I'm going to show her my wild side. She mightn't want me after that.'

There was an awkward pause as Nick's words were left hanging in the room. Alice sat up straighter, pressed the mute button on the remote so the television fell silent, and leant towards Nick.

'I hope you don't mind me asking but . . . are things okay between you two?'

Nick looked down at his black polished boots. In the past few weeks, Felicity had only come out briefly to Rutherglen to tend to her horses. She no longer stayed. She no longer bounced into the kitchen bossing Lance and cooing around Alice. His head still downcast, Nick angled his eyes up towards his mother. He cleared his throat.

'I told her some news she didn't want to hear,' he mumbled.

'Oh?' Alice's mind raced with questions. She turned her head to one side, imploring him with her eyes and her creased brow to talk more.

213

'I think she's come to terms with it,' Nick went on uncertainly.

'Is it anything I should know about?'

Nick shook his head, stepped towards his mother and knelt in front of her. His hands clasped before him, execution style.

'Oh, Mum,' he moaned. He'd been bottling it up now for weeks. Every day he'd thought about what Kate had told him, and that little child he'd played with in the Bronty shearing shed. Every day, Kate came to him in his mind's eye to frustrate him. At first, he'd tried to block her out by paying extra attention to Felicity. Tried to force their relationship to work. But as the days wore on, he felt more and more like a fraud.

He could feel tears springing to his eyes as he knelt before his mother. The worried look on her face made it worse. Then, he simply blurted it out.

'She had a baby. Kate Webster had a baby . . . and the baby is mine.'

Alice's eyes widened in shock. Her hand flew to her mouth. She absorbed the words. Then, as silence permeated the room, she settled her hands in her lap, trying to keep control. Willing herself to hide from her son just how shocked she was. She swallowed, trying desperately to recall if she'd seen the little child in the past. Picturing Kate, the bright, smart and pretty dark-haired girl in her kitchen as she walked them through their farm-business ideas. Alice felt herself shaking. Her son had a child in the world! He must've been so young. Kate's child was at least three, possibly even four, Alice surmised.

'I'm so sorry,' Nick said. 'I know it's a shock.' He rose and put his large arms around her, willing her to understand.

As Alice breathed in the fresh smell and warmth of him, she felt the words he had uttered settle in her. A child, she thought. A little child belonging to her son. She could choose the words to be welcome ones, if she willed it. She could choose them to be a blessing no matter what the situation. Alice felt calm returning. Her body relaxed. She could deal with this.

Nick eased back, hoping to find forgiveness on his mother's face. He searched her glistening eyes. She smiled gently.

'Is that all?' she said to Nick, taking up his hand and drawing it to her. 'It's not the end of the world, my boy.' She laid a palm on his face, and held back her tears.

A few moments later, when Nick stepped into his father's room, he felt like he was entering the den of a dying animal. The room had a rankness about it. His father lay hunched under the covers. Nick couldn't see if he was awake or not.

'Dad?' he said gingerly. He glanced back at his mother, who hovered in the hallway. She motioned him forward, still clutching a crumpled hanky. 'There's something I need to tell you,' Nick said. There was no reply. Nick licked his lips and shifted his weight from one foot to another. He put his hands in his pockets, then took them out, rubbed them palm to palm. They felt dry, yet clammy at the same time.

In the past weeks he'd had the words there, formed in his mouth. Almost spoken. But he hadn't uttered them. Not to his mother or his father, even though he was willing himself to tell them that he'd fathered a child. At night he imagined how the news of a grandchild could transform his father's life. Give him something to think about other than his pain. Would he be furious? Would he be joyful? Ashamed? Embarrassed? Nick didn't know. He had barely been able to make sense of the news himself.

'Dad?' He turned to Alice and mouthed the words, 'He's asleep.' Alice motioned for him to come out of the room.

'Sunday, then,' she said, straightening his bow tie, and brushing the shoulders of his jacket. 'When you come home on Sunday, you can tell him then.'

At the nurses' quarters in town, Nick watched Felicity striding like a catwalk model down the pathway towards his ute. Her dress was shimmering silver, like a fish in a stream, her shoes high and strappy. Afternoon sun picked up the reflections from her dress and cast tiny sparkles about the garden. Nick had to squint at her. Thin straps hugged her pale shoulders and her blonde hair was swept up dramatically. Diamantes glinted and dangled from her earlobes. She had a large black silk and silver sequined bag slung over her shoulder.

As he leant against the ute, his arms folded, his legs crossed at the ankles, Nick couldn't bring himself to say anything to her. He simply watched her move towards him, his face passive.

The past few weeks had been tense. Since the day Kate had come to Rutherglen Felicity had known something was wrong. She had made it her mission to prise the information from him. He had blurted it out and then was stunned by the tantrum that ensued. Now the fact of Nell lay like an open sore between them.

Nick pushed himself upright and walked towards her, put his hand in the small of her back and ushered her towards the ute. Neither of them smiled.

'Have you got a coat or something?' he said.

'Yes, thank you, Nick,' she said curtly. 'And thanks for saying how nice I look.'

'Sorry,' he said. 'It goes without saying. You're stunning. I'm just worried you'll freeze to death.'

'You farmers. You're all about practicality. There's no room for romance, is there?' She gave him a sideways glance, the sun picking up sparkles of light from powder and blush on her cheeks. Nick opened the door for her and overdid the gesture for her to get in.

'I've packed a bag with a jacket and a change of shoes.' She took the bag from her shoulder and thrust it at him. 'Give me a bit of credit.'

He watched as she pulled her perfectly waxed, moisturised and tanned legs into the ute. The spikes of her heels rested on the gravelly, dusty mat inside. He knew what she was thinking. He should've cleaned the ute for her.

Behind the wheel, Nick turned the key and as the engine revved to life, so too did the radio. 1620 AM Country Music

Tamworth, fuzzy but still audible as it was beamed through the ether from the mainland. Tania Kernaghan's latest song began to play.

'Yee ha, it's going to be a wild ride, Yee ha! That's how I wanna live our lives . . .'

Nick turned the volume up, feeling the giddy buzz he'd experienced years before, when he'd last headed to a B&S. He wondered if Kate Webster was going, and hoped she was. He needed to see her again. He reached beneath the seat and pulled out two cans of Bundy, offering one to Felicity. She shook her head. Her earrings jangled. Nick cracked the can open and swigged a mouthful of sweet black liquid, wishing bitterly that she'd have a drink with him once in a while.

Felicity turned the radio down. 'Can't we listen to something else?'

'Why? This is a good song.' He turned the radio back up and sang along. *'I love you just the way you are. Yee ha!'* Felicity sighed and looked out at the paddocks flashing past the window. After a few minutes of silence, she turned the music down again.

'This isn't working.'

'Yes it is. It's just the reception's not so good,' Nick said, turning the radio up again.

'Don't be a smartarse,' she said, turning it down. 'I don't mean the radio.'

Nick stared ahead at the road.

'Talk to me,' she said eventually.

'What about?'

'Anything. Us.'

'What do you suggest I say?'

'Anything.'

Nick paused. Frustration brimmed in him. 'Why just talk about us when we could talk about Dad being a cripple and Mum being a basketcase because of him. That's what we mostly talk about. Isn't it?'

Felicity shut her eyes in frustration, but she didn't bite back.

Nick wanted to yell at her that if she were Kate he could talk about real things that mattered to him. Like what to do with the breeding stock seeing that it still hadn't bloody rained. Or about the red-headed cockchafers in the top paddocks. Or, if Kate were there, he would just be allowed to be silent. Not under pressure to talk. Comfortable in his own thoughts, like she'd let him feel in the Bronty shed.

'Maybe you could pick your latest favourite topic,' he said. 'You know the one. About the fact that I've betrayed you. How about it? Even though, as I keep reminding you, I didn't even know you when I was with Kate.'

Felicity turned to him savagely. 'Do you have to be so angry?'

'*I'm not angry*,' he barked back. 'You're the one who's angry. I've never been yelled at over the phone so much in my life.'

'You might deserve it,' Felicity muttered, straightening her dress over her knees.

'What? For making a mistake?'

'Is that what you call it? A mistake? Maybe if you'd thought with this,' she tapped her head, 'instead of the thing in your pants you wouldn't have a mistake walking around in the shape of a three-year-old! If you could bring yourself to understand, Nick, it's not the best thing to find out about the person you're supposed to marry in a few months!'

'Well, maybe if you thought about what farming's really like instead of thinking about a big house and horses, you wouldn't even be wanting to marry me!'

'That's cruel, Nick, and you know it,' Felicity said, turning away from him. Reaching over, she turned the volume of the radio up so the cab was filled with the throb of country music. Conversation over. Nick set his eyes ahead on the road. Bugger her, he thought furiously. It was B&S time.

218

Twenty-four

Dusk at the Rouseabout B&S Ball carried with it a thousand promises. V8 engines throbbed as they wound their way towards the B&S entrance, and country music blared into the air, heralding the pledge of people intent on getting blind together on Bundy rum, and praying for a drought-busting rain.

It wasn't just the party that drew Kate's peers to the isolated spot in a barren, windswept valley in Tasmania's central highlands. It was something otherworldly. It was part of being. Here, beneath the shadows of long-dead great grey gums, it was something so specific as simply being country.

The B&S ball was an experience out of reach to most people. But Kate knew she was one of the lucky ones who belonged, who understood. She felt the contagious buzz of excitement rush through her. Goosebumps cloaked her skin. She loved the informality of country crowds. Rural youth, defiant and proud, who had turned their backs on the consumerism and political correctness that had infiltrated through Australia's cities. Kate hated the Americanisms that had spread like cancer to the suburbs and beyond, making every city look and sound the same. She loved country culture to the core.

Here, in this paddock on this weekend, there'd be no designer drugs. No doof-doof music. No baggy skate pants revealing bum-cracks. No Playstations. Instead, Kate knew there'd be booze and boots and 'bloody-oath, mates' and good, old-fashioned piss-wrecked fun. There'd be snags and chops wrapped in fluffy white bread with tomato sauce oozing through like a bullet wound. And the money raised by the B&S committee would be poured back into the community. Charity funds to help the local nursing home and health centre. Plus Kate knew that this weekend she'd see larks that would stay with her and make her smile years later, when she was old and grey. That was all part of it. Part of her world at the B&S ball.

Kate looked around . . . she was in the midst of a crowd of youth. Rural youth were deemed to be dying or at least dwindling, if the city media was to be believed. But here they were, vibrant and keen to be country. Big boys in big black suits wearing big black hats and big brown boots. And shirts that weren't so white. Girls who didn't give a damn. Stuff the fact they had a bit of a beer belly, tonight they would walk proud in their not-so-stylish dresses, with their not-so-flash hair. The rougher their ute, the sleeker their dogs, the tougher their hands, the more gorgeous they felt. Strong country girls, flexing muscles and flashing pretty smiles.

'We're from the country and we like it that way,' Kate sang to herself, wishing the big man himself, Lee Kernaghan, were here to sing it to her straight up. Wishing Will were here. From the window of Dave's ute, Kate looked ahead to the glinting snake of dust-smudged vehicles winding its way down into the B&S venue. She smelt rum and dust and pure, unbridled anticipation. They were about to be swallowed up for the weekend, swept back to their youth. The three of them, now young parents, all trying to forget that they were mums and dads for a night. Janie, Dave and Kate, revisiting the scene of their crimes. A chill ran down Kate's spine. Fear? Excitement? She wasn't sure. She leaned further out of the window and felt the breeze on her face, soaking it all in.

Ahead of them, the sound of slide guitars drawled from

giant boxy speakers set up in the back of some joker's ute. The golden globes of bull lights shone in rows from the roofs of utes, dispelling the half-light of the setting sun. Kate pointed out to Dave and Janie ute stickers like 'giddupindaback' and 'Help feed the world – F*** a Farmer.' A tailgate that read 'Glorious absence of sophistication' and 'Save a horse . . . ride a cowboy'. And they even watched in half-horror, half-hilarity as a taxidermied red heeler drove past, chained unnecessarily to the back of a Hilux. The stuffed dog sat, glassy-eyed in a frozen pose, next to his owner, who reclined with his arm about him.

A load of grinning boys drove by, jumping the queue. One of them pointed out Kate by raising his beer can in her direction. His mates whistled at the vision of the dark-haired girl in the soft blue dress, framed by the pink sky. She was half-hanging out of the ute to see how far she had come and how far she had to go. The lush curve of her bare shoulders. The fall of her glossy hair, lifted by the breeze. Unaware of how gorgeous she looked, Kate gave them the finger and the boys whooped and blew kisses before motoring away.

She sat back down on the bench seat, where Janie and Dave were playing lovers again. Dave's hand was wedged between Janie's thighs, while Janie strummed her imaginary guitar and leant her head on Dave's shoulder.

Beneath Kate's feet, empty rum cans rolled about with the lift and sway of the rough paddock under the tyres. Below her, far away in the valley, she could see the giant white rectangular shape of a marquee and the smaller blue oblong of a semi where the band would play. Portaloos flanked the site like Nell's plastic building blocks, rows of green and red cubes. And at the centre of the site stood an old corrugated-iron shearing shed, with a mix of wooden, W-strap and railway iron yards tapering out from the shed's base. In the shed paddock, dried wood was stacked high in places, like piles of grey fishbones, ready for a bonfire. And all around on the river flat, vehicles were filling up the paddocks in shiny rows. People, like ants, made tracks inward to the centre of the site and clustered at the marquee as if it were a slab of meringue. Kate smiled. She couldn't wait to be down there. In amongst it.

'Geez!' Dave said suddenly as he hit the brakes. The ute in front of them had stopped. The blast of an air horn made Kate jump. She glanced up just in time to see the blur of three boys in white shirts, black trousers and giant sombreros running towards them. Within seconds, the boys were on the bonnet of Dave's ute. Bare white backsides pressed to the windscreen. Too close to be pretty.

Janie screeched, Kate laughed and Dave turned on the windscreen washer, sending jets of water onto the boys' bums.

'Thanks for that, arse-wiper!' cried one of them before they danced away, trousers half-mast.

'They're those bloody serial B&Sers,' Dave said. 'You know, the ones that spend all their moolah going to most of the mainland B&S's and then they come over here – every year. Remember them? I can't believe they're still at it!'

'Yeah,' Kate said. 'I saw them at a few B&S's over there. Near Conargo and again around Dubbo. God. What are their names? That's the trouble with meeting people at a B&S. You're always too blind to remember. It was the Banditos, you know, Johnno, Simmo . . . and . . .'

'Blue,' Dave said.

'There *was* a redhead in them!' Janie said. 'That'd have to be Blue. I remember now. The one on the right. I suppose I shouldn't say he was a red-*head*. It wasn't his head I saw. More like a red-gluteus-maximus. But not maximus at all. In fact, really skinny . . . a skinny, red, hairy arse. A gluteus minimus. A Fanta-pants.'

'You didn't have to look *that* close!' Dave protested. 'You could've shut your eyes!'

'Oh, I could identikit the whole lot of them if asked. I'm very good on details. Very observant.'

'You must be desperate to have kept your eyes open with those posteriors shoved in your face,' Kate quipped.

'Desperate,' Janie said dryly, 'or a mother of twins.'

Silence settled on them as they all remembered their kids. They would be bathed and ready for bed by now. Nell in her bunny pyjamas, Jasmine in her Saddle Club nightie and Brendan wearing Thomas the Tank Engine. A whole world away from here. Kate shook her head.

'Why am I doing this?' she muttered under her breath. She was a mother now. And all of a sudden, she felt too much had changed.

Inside the shearing shed, next to the bar, boys in suits clustered together like penguins in a rookery. Girls in bright dresses pressed amongst them, bringing colour to the crush of black. Kate noticed two girls, side by side in white satin suits, Shania Twain-style. They were soaking up attention from the crowd and also soaking up a lot of liquid from the floor. Brown rum stains covered their jackets and the surface beneath their white boots had already turned to a soupy mix of mud, manure and beer. The shit-coloured liquid was beginning to creep up their flared trouser legs, like a tide mark at a sewage treatment plant. But they didn't care. The girls tossed back their glossy hair and laughed as the boys pranced around them. Kate recognised the shorter one as her boss Lisa.

Kate screeched a greeting and slung her arm about her. 'You look fantastic! And fucking funny!' she said.

Lisa, already drunk, 'oh, oh, oh'd' Shania-style and danced a few moves.

Simply wearing white to a B&S was funny in itself. That was the whole point. The grubbier, sillier, funnier the girls could get, the higher the kudos. The rougher and more tumbled they looked, the more approachable they were in the eyes of the country boys. And the Shanias were doing well.

'You'll be in for sure!' Kate said and Lisa's eyes gleamed.

'That's the plan, Stan! I'm going to trap one tonight!'

Kate looked down at her own pale blue dress. Too tame, she thought. But beautiful in itself – too beautiful for a B&S. Kate still wished Janie had made her an Elvis jumpsuit. That way she could hide behind sideburns and giant sunglasses. Instead, she felt like Barbie at a mud-wrestling match. Beautiful but out of place. She didn't mean to be ungrateful, it was just she wasn't used to wearing such stylish, tight-fitting clothes. But Janie had got it right – her curves did look good in the dress.

Kate saw Janie nod towards the bar and waved as Lisa and her friend danced away. It was time for a drink. But tonight, Kate vowed for the first time that she'd keep her senses. She'd prove to herself that she could still have fun without totalling herself.

Together, Dave, Janie and Kate pushed through the crowd. The bar staff, made up of locals in navy King Gee overalls, moved frantically back and forth trying to keep up with the push of people. Already, beer, rum and orange juice was awash on the trestle tables. As she leaned forward, Kate felt the liquid seep into the fabric of her dress, so it lay cold against her thighs and darkened the material in large patches. Oh well, she thought, bound to happen sooner or later.

Razor leant forward to serve them.

'Razor!' Kate said. 'Razor Sharp!'

'Miss Webster!' He beamed a smile, his bald head gleaming under the floodlights.

'How the flock are you?' Kate asked, taking in the way his overalls could barely be buttoned at the front over his stomach.

'Ram-bloody-unctuous! And ewe?'

'A bit sheepish in this frock, but fine,' she said, even though she felt far from fine. Though she belonged in this country crowd, she wondered if she still fitted into it, now she was a single mother. Could she ever feel that freedom at a B&S again, as she had in her life before Nell? She ran her hand self-consciously over the front of her dress, knowing that beneath the blue fabric her skin bore stretch marks from her pregnancy.

At first she'd been shocked every time she saw them, her tropical fish stripes, in the mirror. As the days and months passed after the birth, the glowing purple marks faded to faint brown. But still she felt branded by them. Forever changed in some way. When Razor passed her the drinks and took her grog tickets, he leant towards her.

'Don't be sheepish. You look lovely. Come back to my baa anytime.'

'Why thank you, kind sir.' Kate took a sip. 'Where's your off-sider, Jonesy? Surely he'd be up for a night out?'

'Got a shed up north. Otherwise he'd be here – looking all puppy-dog eyes at you, no doubt.'

'Nah,' she said dismissively, 'I don't reckon.' She raised her plastic rum-filled cups at him, before turning to pass them to Dave and Janie in the crush of bodies and the swirl and roar of animated conversation.

At the far end of the shed, on the grating, a PA system blurted out unintelligible words and another crowd was pushing together, four or five deep. Kate, Janie and Dave weaved their way through to see what was so interesting. There, on a particle-board floor with mats all around, rocked a mechanical bull. Kate was transported back in time as she watched a lean young jackaroo ride haphazardly. He flung one hand in the air, grimacing as he bumped his balls against the bull. Kate caught Janie looking at her.

'I dare you,' Janie said.

'Don't you start,' Kate said, pointing her finger at her. 'That's not funny.'

'No! I mean I dare you to have a ride of the bull!'

Kate looked at her friend, taking in the laughter in her eyes. They gathered each other up in a big buddy-hug, clanked plastic cups together and sculled.

'What are you girls toasting?' a voice asked. Kate spun around to see Aden. Although she hated to admit it, he looked clean-cut and very handsome in a metrosexual, Andrew Gee kind of way with his spiky, waxed, blond-tipped hair.

'Wouldn't you like to know,' Kate said.

'C'mon, Kate . . .' Aden said. 'I'm family. You can tell me.'

Kate couldn't help herself. She associated him so much with losing Will and Bronty. The gulf between her father and her. Annabelle's intrusion. It all came rushing back to her.

Janie saw the anger on Kate's face.

'Excuse me,' Janie said to Aden. 'I need my friend for a second. We'll see you later. Okay?' And she dragged Kate into the crowd, gathering her long dress up on the dance floor. Kate tried to banish the thoughts of Bronty that Aden had prompted in her. She shut her eyes and conjured the image of Will. It felt as if he were there, dancing with them. A smile radiated from her face. Suddenly Kate felt a rip. She looked down to see the seams of her dress parting like a zip towards her upper thigh.

'Great sewing,' she shouted to Janie above the music, indicating her bare leg. Janie cupped both hands over her mouth, her eyes wide.

'Oh my God!'

'Poor dress couldn't handle my thunder thighs!'

'Here, I'll fix it.' Janie stooped and reached for the other seam. *Riiiiiip. Two* slits in the front of Kate's dress now rose up from the floor.

'Oi! You scum-bucket!' Kate protested, looking down at her bare legs. Dave crossed his arms in front of his body and looked at Kate's two pale pins – so white compared to the sun-kissed skin of her shoulders. Her legs rose up out of thick explorer socks and Blundstone boots.

'Nice guideposts,' he said. 'No one will want to drive anything between those tonight, guaranteed.'

'Thanks,' Kate said flatly, but somehow she liked the dress better this way. Who gave a toss anyway? The one person she wanted to impress wasn't here tonight. She tipped back her rum and glanced at her watch. No more grog for another hour. She was pacing herself.

Turning, Kate saw Johnno, Simmo and Blue shuffling

towards them, their pants around their ankles. All three wore gaudy boxer shorts with cartoons of roosters on them. A tubby Johnno made a lunge for Kate, grabbing her from behind. He began to swing her around. Her feet flew outwards from the force, scattering people backwards. Simmo lifted Janie from the ground and swung her too. A puny Blue tried to reach around Dave's wide girth. But Blue only succeeded in pulling Dave off-balance. As Blue lay spread-eagled below Dave, like a beetle wearing a brick, the girls whirled round and round in their enforced dizzy whizzes. Kate screeched as Simmo gained momentum. Just when she thought she might throw up, she felt his arms give way. Next thing, she was flying through the crowd in an uncontrolled run. Laughter bubbled up from her. She was putting her arms out to break her fall when she collided with the rough lapel of somebody's jacket. She looked up, and her smile slipped away.

It was Nick. He looked down at her, his arms instinctively wrapping about her. His face so close to hers. The world still spun in dizzying circles around her and for a moment all she could focus on were his eyes. His wide, long-lashed, gorgeous blue eyes. Clasping his rock-hard upper arms, she found her balance again.

'Ooops,' she said, totally confused. Hadn't Dave said he wasn't coming? Lying bugger! 'Er, sorry, Nick,' she said shyly.

Before Nick could speak they were rushed again by the B&S Banditos, Johnno, Simmo and Blue, in a party-animal tackle. Kate was thrown against Nick's body again. She felt the shove and thrust of the boys' group hug at her back, pushing her into the hardness of Nick's wide chest. His firm arms were still around her. From where she stood, her cheek pressed against Nick's shirt, Kate could see Felicity through a gap in the huddle of bouncing boys. She was standing alone in a silver dress, her arms wrapped about her body. A sour look on her face, like she'd just smelt rotten meat. Not happy, Jan, Kate thought.

At last the boys broke away and Kate took a step back from

Nick, feeling Felicity's gaze settle on her like frost. But she could still breathe in Nick's lovely clean smell, and his touch was still fizzing through her senses, sending her brain into a spin.

'I didn't think you were coming,' she said breathlessly. He reached out and held her hand for a moment.

'I wasn't sure you were either. But I hoped you would.'

Kate took in his words, hardly daring to believe it. Those few words told her that he still felt the same way about her, despite the fact she'd told him about Nell. But then confusion swamped her. Felicity stood just metres away glaring at them. Was he stringing them both along? Playing games with them? But before she could say anything more, the B&S Banditos were back.

'Niiick!' Kate heard Simmo call in a blokey greeting.

'Niiick . . . maaaate!' echoed Johnno. Then Blue, who was puffing heavily after extracting himself from beneath Dave, called, 'Hey, Nick!'

'G'day,' he said. 'Been a while.'

'Yeah,' said Johnno. 'Last time we saw you was when they gave you a passport and sent you out of inbred-land to do that wool course with us. When was it? Coupla years back? Heard you were engaged.'

Simmo leered at Felicity, lifted her hand and peered through piggy eyes at the ring on her finger.

'Nice rock.' Simmo flicked the strap of Felicity's dress. It slipped down over her shoulder. 'Whoopsie daisie,' he said, eyeing her hungrily. The B&S Banditos gathered round. Girlie-girls in girlie dresses were always a target for boys like them, even ones engaged to mates.

'Come in behind, Simmo,' Nick growled, as if steadying a wayward sheepdog.

'Yes,' Felicity added. 'Settle, boys. Don't touch what you can't afford.'

'Doesn't look expensive,' Blue said. 'What's it made of? Your mum's Alfoil?' Felicity gave a snide smile but Kate noticed her flinch. 'Aren't you freezing your tits off in that?' Blue went on.

'I've got Nick here to keep me warm.' She slid her arm around him, delivering a gaze directly at Kate. Nick looked down at the floor.

'That's if she had any tits to freeze off,' Simmo quipped. 'Not like Pammy A and young Dolly P here . . .' Simmo slung his arms around Kate and Janie's necks and swung round to bury his nose in Kate's cleavage.

'Get your face out of my crevice,' Kate said, shoving him off.

'You sure your little lady hasn't got worms or something, Nicko mate? Coz it sure looks like she could do with a shot of Valbazen and a better paddock too, maybe.'

'Bugger off, Simmo,' Nick said, putting his arm protectively around Felicity's waist.

'Nice mates you've got, Nick,' Felicity said, frowning at them. The boys knew they'd got to her then. They pushed further. Simmo tugged up his shirt and began to rub his hairy beer-belly with the palm of his hand.

'Hey, Nick,' Johnno said, stooping and trying to look up Felicity's dress, 'you gotta check your stock for dags. Sure sign of worms.'

'Yeah,' Blue chipped in. 'And look out for them rubbing their bum against posts. You know, a bit of the itch . . .'

Blue began to rub his backside up against Felicity, until Nick grabbed him.

'Get your bum-cheeks off her,' Nick said. 'That's *enough*.' Nick's stern tone was enough to sober the boys momentarily.

'Yeah,' Kate added. 'Ease off, guys.' She turned to Felicity. 'Ignore them. They're just being pissed idiots. If you come to a B&S you kind of have to expect wallies like that.'

Felicity cast her an ice-cold look, tossed her head proudly and turned to Nick. 'I'm going back to the ute.'

'Ooooo!' chorused the Banditos.

Nick, cheeks flushed red, glanced up at Kate again. She

was trying to hide the mix of amusement and dismay on her face.

'I'll come with you,' Nick said.

'Don't bother,' Felicity snapped. 'Feel free to stick with your own kind.'

She gave them a frosty smile and then turned and stalked away.

'I . . .' Nick began, pointing after her. 'I'd better . . .' He cast another glance at Kate. 'Sorry,' he said, 'I'll catch up with you later.'

Kate watched his broad back disappear into the crowd. Joy, confusion, disappointment and jealousy swirled within her all at once. What was going on?

But she had no time to dwell on Nick as the band revved to life. The drummer thwacked his drumsticks together. One, two, three. He let loose on the drums. The crowd let out a cheer, just as the guitarist opened up on the amp, full throttle.

'Chisel! They're playing Chisel!' Simmo cried. 'Bandito Johnno! Bandito Blue! C'mon, amigos!' They were all swept up into the dance.

'I can't believe I used to think he was hot,' Janie said as she watched Johnno bouncing up and down to the music. 'Such dickheads.' She smiled at Dave. 'I sure made the right move that night!'

Dave collected Janie and Kate, one under each arm, and carried them into the heart and heat of the crowd, which was leaping, jumping and grooving to the music, so the whole shearing shed shook. As Kate danced she ran the words Nick had spoken through her head over and over. *I hoped you would be here.* Through the bobbing heads of dancers, she kept looking for him. But he was nowhere to be seen.

Twenty-five

When Kate saw Nick again, much later in the night, he was lying in the muck beneath the bar. His boots were long gone, and Simmo and Blue had hold of his ankles and were dragging him out from under the trestle tables. The crowd had thinned down to the diehard drunks, who watched as Johnno sat riding Nick's belly, rodeo-style. Nick's short sandy hair was black with grime and his shirt was mottled with food dye. His teeth shone out in a drunken grin from behind a mask of cracking mud. He and Johnno rolled and wrestled, trying to wrench small tubes of red food dye from each other's fists. When Nick succeeded in stealing Johnno's bottle, he put it to his lips, sucked it in, washed it round, then pursed his lips and sprayed Johnno full force in the face. Eyes scrunched, red liquid dripping, Johnno looked like a gunshot victim from a Quentin Tarantino film. He retaliated like a bad-tempered bull, roughly dragging Nick up in a head-lock. He grabbed a keg gun from the trestle table and squirted a jet of frothy beer into Nick's face. Felicity was nowhere in sight.

Kate watched, laughing at the boys' shenanigans. Blue was yapping at their ankles like a little dog trying to stir the big dogs into a fight as Nick and Johnno rolled and reefed each other about by their clothes, muscles straining. Two big country boys, drunk and playfighting. Young bulls going head to head.

When they accidentally kicked the leg out from under a trestle table and sent drinks flying, Razor at last stepped out from behind the bar. He put his big overalled body in between the boys and prised them apart.

'Outside,' Razor said sternly, spinning them round and giving them a good shove. Nick good-naturedly wavered his way towards the floodlit square of the shed's entrance, where moths danced on the hot surface of the lights. Kate fell in step with him as he staggered down the loading ramp.

Once clear of the shed, Nick bent over, puffing hard in the rocky sheep yards, his hands on his thighs.

'You right?' Kate said, standing a little way off.

'Shit-carted,' was all he could manage.

'Where's Felicity?'

Nick shrugged, too drunk to speak. Kate looked around. On the fringe of darkness, in the next yard, she could make out tufts of green grass rising up from the barren rubble of rocks and dust. There must be water over there, she thought. Scruffing Nick by the collar, she led him to the fence.

'Get over,' she commanded.

'Huh?'

She lifted his muddy foot onto the bottom rail. 'Over.'

Nick obediently began to climb. When he reached the top rail of the yards he mumbled something before toppling over the other side. He landed with a thud on his back. Small clouds of dust rose like smoke around his body and hovered above him in the light spilling from the shearing shed.

Kate grabbed him by the arm and pulled.

'C'mon, Nick. Just a little further.'

Once he was upright, he draped an arm over Kate's shoulder and hobbled in his socks towards a dark oblong water trough. When they reached the trough, Nick slumped down beside it.

'Stick your head in,' Kate commanded.

232

'Huh?'

'In the trough. Stick your head in.'

'Too bloody cold.'

Kate half lifted him. He splashed water onto his face.

'More than that,' she said, putting her hand on the back of his head and dunking him under. The first time he came up spluttering water and green weed. The second time he was swearing. The third, he was laughing.

'What are you doing? It's slimy in there!'

'You'll be right,' Kate said, feeling in his jacket pockets for something to wipe his face with. She pulled out a scrunched handkerchief, wet it and began to mop his face. He was so drunk his eyes were half-closed. She stared at the long wet lashes that feathered his strong cheekbones. His full mouth. A kissable mouth, now it was cleaner. She wet the cloth again and wiped more mud from his face and neck.

'Lucky you don't have those curls anymore,' she said. 'You'd never get this crud out of them.'

Nick didn't answer. His eyes were now almost completely closed. The band had stopped playing. Kate could hear the hiss of the trough's faulty float valve and the drip of water as it trickled from the trough. She was kneeling, the ground damp beneath her knees. Above them hung the moon, watching from over Nick's shoulder. A big moon, not yet quite full. Shining like an old silver coin on black velvet. A pesky moon that did nothing but prompt romance now they were alone.

'You trying to deflower me again,' Nick mumbled, his eyes suddenly open as he studied Kate's face.

'How can I ever do that again?'

'You could give it a go.' Nick reached out and clasped her arm. 'You're an amazing woman, Kate Webster. You're the mother of my child. Huh! 'Mazing.'

'You're drunk.'

Nick's head lolled forwards as if to confirm it.

'S'what if I am. You telling me you're sober?'

Kate smiled at him. Yes she was, actually. The first time ever and it felt good. Like she was in control. Her anger towards her father could not touch her tonight. Not with Nick near her. And the few rums she'd had were warming her soul, not removing it, as on other nights, where she'd lost herself for hours and woken up with a stranger in her bed. Here she was outside, alone with Nick. Trailing him. Thirsty for him. And sober.

'I just wanted to talk to you,' Kate said. She sat down next to him, trying to pull the shreds of her dress over her bare legs. Goosebumps rose over her skin as the dampness of the ground near the trough seeped through.

'I wanted to find out if you're okay. Okay about . . . Nell.'

Nick sighed. Kate watched a look of sobriety slide across his face for a moment.

'S'pose. I've been getting used to the idea. No choice.'

'And Felicity?'

'She knows.'

'She knows! What did she say about it?'

Nick waved the question away. 'Doesn't matter now.'

He pulled a ring from his pocket, waved it in front of Kate's face and tossed it. The ring caught the light, glimmered for a moment, then with a 'plop' it sank into the trough.

'Hey!' Kate said.

'Mutual separation. As of . . .' – Nick looked at his watch – 'two hours ago.' He began to slur his own version of his favourite Lee Kernaghan song, *'Baby don't lerve me, coz I'm country.'*

'Oh,' Kate said, feeling genuine sympathy for him, but also a rush of delight at the possibility of being with him.

'Had a D&M. Said I wasn't for her. You know the drum. Took my ute, she did. Vamoosed on me.'

'So you're a free man?'

'Me?' Nick said. 'A free man? You're joking. I've got a crook dad, a sad mum and a very recent daughter I never knew about, a buggered farm and a big bloody drought. Hardly

234

free! But there's one thing I could have that would set me free, baby,' he said, 'and that's you. You would be good. You would be nice. You would make me feel freeeee as a bird!' He wasn't looking at her, just mumbling drunk, his head downturned, his arms outstretched as if he had wings.

Kate laughed. 'You're pissed.' But as she took in his words, Kate felt the tug of the moon above them, watching them from on high. She felt the pull of Nell's heartbeat, asleep like an angel at home. She felt the surge of the seaswell that touched the shores of Bronty. And she felt Nick's presence . . . a pull so strong that it almost hurt. She turned to him and lifted his head so he would look at her. The expression on his face was one of sadness, but also of longing. He leant towards her.

'Can I kiss you?' he muttered. 'Like the last time?'

He gently traced his fingers over her cheeks. Then he rested the palm of his hand on the back of her head. His touch felt so right. He pulled her towards him. Kate breathed in his kiss. Laden sweet with alcohol and longing. She almost moaned at feeling him like this. She leaned closer, pressed her mouth to his. She felt his rough hands sliding over her skin, her bare shoulders, her neck. They kissed deeply. Hotly. Tongues slid together with want. Her hands slipped inside his wet shirt, needing to feel his skin. Her palms met with his torso as sleek and muscled as a bull. She heard his breathing, heavy with craving. She shut out the rest of the world. It was just her and Nick. And the moon and the night sky, silver on black. Her and Nick, kissing at the B&S. All over again.

Twenty-six

Kate shivered in the darkness. As she listened to Nick's steady gentle breathing she felt like pinching herself. Excitement and astonishment coursed through her. Here she was with *him*, in his swag. Even more unbelievable – they were both fully clothed. Kate wondered what had happened to the girl who would get naked with any man provided she was drunk enough. Here she was with a person she truly desired, whether she was drunk or sober. Yet she hadn't ripped his clothes off to claim him. Instead, she'd kissed him gently, stroked his hair and let him drift away into drunken sleep in her arms. Nick McDonnell. The love of her life.

She cast her eyes upwards to search the black sky. The moon had long since slid behind the hill and in the distance the bonfires were dying down into grey ash.

Kate nestled closer into Nick, tugging the damp doona up over her shoulders. She was searching for any part of him to warm her. She pressed her hands against his sides and tucked her bare feet between his legs. Although she couldn't see his face in the darkness, she sensed that her movement and her cold touch had woken him. When she felt his arms gathering her up and his body heat seeping through to her skin she almost purred.

'Hello, gorgeous girl,' he said, his voice cracked and rough from too much rum.

'Are you sure you know which girl you're holding? It's so dark.'

'Mmm.' Nick nestled his face into her neck. 'I'm holding the one in the red dress.'

'Red? She's the one in the *blue*. The girl in the red dress left years ago.'

'Oh, I think I found her again tonight.' Nick's hands slid up Kate's leg, beneath the torn fabric of her dress. 'Pity I passed out before she could take advantage of me again.' He began to nuzzle into Kate's shoulder.

Kate stopped his hand's languid journey up her thigh.

'You're sure you're not after the girl in the silver dress? Maybe you're supposed to be doing this to her, not me.'

Nick gently touched his finger to her lips.

'Shhh. Not anymore, I'm not.' He kissed her on her forehead.

They fell silent and just held each other. Gone now were the bright lights, the buzz of rum and the lure of music to hide the complexities. Reality was all they could find in the darkness. There was Nell to consider. A child. Nick and Kate's child. If they got together now, then what? Kate laid the palm of Nick's hand on her stomach.

'I never let blokes touch me here, you know,' she said, 'not since having the baby.' Nick began to move his palm in slow, warming circles on her tummy. She shut her eyes. Behind her eyelids, her world was even darker. She felt the comfort in Nick's touch.

'Was the birth scary?' he asked.

'Terrifying. I thought I'd die – it was bloody awful. But the bits before and after were pretty scary too.'

'I'm sorry for you.'

'Oh, don't get me wrong. There were good bits too. Unreal bits – like the first time I felt her move inside me. It was a flutter, like a butterfly.' Kate couldn't see Nick's face in the darkness, but she knew he was smiling.

'And the very first time I saw her face, lying there on my belly. She took my breath away. She was so beautiful.'

Nick stroked her hair. 'She still is beautiful.'

'Do you want to see her?' Kate felt Nick's hand stop moving. His palm lay heavy on her womb, heavy with heat.

'Yeah. I do, sure. But it's best if we take it slowly. Don't you think?'

Kate picked up his hand and held it. 'I'm not here to trap you with her,' she said. 'You know that, don't you? It's not what I'm about.'

'I know that,' Nick said.

'I'm not expecting you to just start playing happy families with us. Not now. Nellie and I are fine on our own. We started on our own. We'll finish on our own. You don't have to be part of it unless you want to.'

Nick shifted up onto his elbow.

'So what are you doing here with me?'

Kate considered her answer.

'Maybe I just wanted to try the grown version of Nick McDonnell tonight.' She ran her hand over his chest and let her fingertips slide over his jaw. Nick laughed softly. Almost sadly.

'Is that all?' he said.

'I think I'm too scared to admit it's anything more.'

Nick pulled her even closer.

'Don't be scared. Please.'

He began to cover her neck with soft kisses. His lips left a trail of goosebumps, like stars across her skin. They lit a pathway along her neck and up to the soft pale skin behind her ear. She moaned and shut her eyes, feeling him. His weight on top of her. His hands travelling up and over her breasts. She felt his desire build. His kisses became harder, his touch rougher. He tugged at the buttons of his suit pants, kissing her frantically. Wanting her. Kate, wanting him back.

'No,' Kate heard herself say. She caught her breath in surprise and pushed his hands away. 'Not now. I can't.'

She heard the frustration in his heavy sigh. 'Why not?'

'I don't know. Felicity maybe. It's just too soon.'

Nick was silent for a while. Then she felt him lie back next to her, his voice somehow changed. The intimacy gone. His control back in place.

'No. You're right. I understand.'

'Can't we just hold each other for now?'

'Of course we can. We can watch the sun come up together. As friends,' he said. Then he put his strong arms around her, and soon the blue glow of dawn began to filter through the blackness.

The smell of fat blistering from sausages on the barbecue and the crack of stockwhips began to stir the partygoers from their sleep. Boys crawled out from under ute tarps and, in full view, pulled off last night's trousers and heaved on shorts. They reached for eskies and cracked beer cans open, armed and ready for the B&S Recovery.

Kate heard the slamming of car doors and music beginning to blare from ute stereos. Engines revved, sending up fumes into the crystal-clear air. She sat up in the swag and tried to yank her fingers through her rum-matted hair. Yawning, she looked down at Nick, still sleeping. The fringe of his long eyelashes lay soft against his cheek. In the raw morning light he was still disturbingly handsome, even though stubble was pushing through on the strong angles of his jaw and his big farmer's hands were smeared with dirt. Kate wanted those hands to touch her all over. She wanted to kiss him and run her fingertips across the soft spikes of his short-cropped sandy hair. But she left him sleeping and reluctantly crawled from the swag. Better he woke alone, so he could slowly remember the events of last night. And not feel any pressure of having to be with her. A sober version of him might be very different, she concluded.

The sun on her skin and the cool pasture on her bare feet seemed to wake her senses. As she stooped to pull on her boots she felt the first realisation that she didn't have a hang-over. She was thirsty, and busting, but that was all. She walked past rows of cars with their windows fogged from boozed sleepers inside. Boys whistled at her from their utes and invited her into their swags. She smiled coyly at them, feeling exposed in her torn dress. Beyond the rows of utes a pair of boys were bent double, throwing up together on the fenceline.

'Nice work, guys,' she said to them. One of them gave her the thumbs up before retching again.

After a trip to a stinking portaloo, she was glad when she at last found Dave's old cruiser ute. Gently, Kate flipped back one corner of the tarp and reached in gingerly to find her bag.

'Who goes there?' came a croaky voice from beneath the tarp.

'Jane-ster, how are you?' Kate said.

'Crook as a dog.'

'And how's Dave?'

'So hungry I could eat the diff out of a shit truck,' came Dave's deep voice from beneath the tarp.

'Or eat the crotch from a low-flying duck,' Kate added.

'Or eat the arse of a nun through a cane chair,' Janie said.

'Lucky the barbie's going then,' Kate said. 'You'd better get up before the Banditos eat it all.'

'Eat it or wee on it,' Dave said dryly.

'How'd you go last night?' Janie asked.

'Yeah. Good.'

'Yeah? Good?' said Janie, peeling back the tarp and sitting upright. '*Yeah. Good.* What do you mean by that?'

'You know. Good,' said Kate, smiling at what she saw. Janie had mascara smudged beneath her eyes like a panda, her hair sticking up every which way.

From beneath the tarp Dave's voice grumbled up. 'Did someone park his big pink stationwagon in your garage?'

'Dave,' groaned Kate, 'shut up!'

'You have to tell me more than that, Kate. Who is he? Do we know him?'

'No time to talk,' Kate said, grabbing her bag. 'Think I might head back there in case he thinks I chewed my arm off to get away from him.'

'Kate!' Janie said. 'Name?'

'Starts with N,' Kate said, smiling, pulling her shorts and clean undies from her bag. 'And ends in "ick".'

'N? ick?' Janie's face opened up with surprise. 'Nick! No! *Nick*? It's not?'

'It is,' said Kate. She smiled as Janie squealed loudly and clapped her hands. Kate opened the ute door and quickly wiggled out of her knickers.

'Crikey! But what about Felicity? Tell me all about it! Tell me! Tell me!'

'Jeez, Janie! Let me get my clean grundies on first!'

Nick was propped up on one elbow, lying on top of his swag in the sun. He was smiling at Kate as she walked towards him. She felt more confident now she was back in Blunnie boots, shorts and her old favourite Dennie Ute Muster singlet. She had shoved her hair up under her old straw cowgirl hat and washed her face clean at a tap beside the shed. The hospital band around her wrist was still damp and felt cool against her skin in the morning air. She took in Nick's grin and realised there was nothing to doubt about him. He wasn't going anywhere . . . and he certainly wasn't going to chase after Felicity. She sat down cross-legged next to him and offered him a sausage in bread.

'Thought you'd done a runner on me.'

'Nah. Not me. Brought you breakfast,' she said.

Nick gently pushed the sausage away.

'Thanks, but I reckon I'll get to experience it twice if I eat that.'

'Bit seedy?' Kate asked, biting into the sausage.

'Never been sicker.'

Kate looked him over. His shirt had dried a caramel colour and stiffened like cardboard and his pants were ripped up the seam of one leg. His bare feet were black with dirt but Kate imagined washing them. Soaping them slowly. Rubbing her hands along his fine bones and sliding her fingers between his toes.

She tried not to desire him so much. Not yet. She looked out towards the cluster of early-morning drinkers having breakfast beers around the barbecue. She would focus on the Recovery . . . not on what might lie ahead for her and Nick. The bright light of morning had a clarity that the night lacked, and Kate decided to keep her distance from Nick – in a friendly way. After all, everyone knew Nick had been engaged to Felicity when he arrived at the B&S. Everyone knew something had gone on last night. She was about to start the conversation, this time sober, about what was going on between them, when she was distracted by shrieks. The crowd parted and a rumble of laughter erupted through it. Three naked boys, save for their boots, ran past the barbecue and up the hillside towards Kate and Nick. The boys' bodies – two tubby, one runt-skinny – were smeared with mud. As they ran, a stream of smoke seemed to follow each of them. As they bolted towards a concrete trough Kate saw the rolled-up tubes of newspaper protruding from their buttocks. The paper smouldered with licking orange flames. It was Simmo, Johnno and Blue.

'Flaming arseholes! Flaming arseholes!' yelled Blue as his small feet pounded the dirt past Nick and Kate. He followed the smoky trail of his friends until they were all diving bum-first into a paddock trough.

'Ah, jeez,' said Nick. 'Thanks for rescuing me from those guys when you did. If I'd have stuck with them all night that would've been me just then, naked, with my arse on fire.'

'I think you're the sensible type. You would've pulled up sooner than later.'

'Yeah, that's me, the sensible type. Everyone knows I'm such a boring bastard.'

'You mean you're not the sort of B&S legend who sticks a bit of roadkill on the barbie for a fry-up in the morning?'

242

'Nope . . . and I've never worn any gutted wallabies on my head either, like some I know.'

'Ah, Nick. You're not so straight. Not the Nick I know.'

'That's what I like about you, Kate Webster. You can see the wild man in me.'

He sat up and leant forward, about to kiss her, when Kate noticed Razor standing next to Dave down by the barbecue. Dave was pointing to them, an expression of concern on his face. Kate frowned. She knew something was wrong.

Nick noticed her freeze. He pulled away from his intended kiss and followed Kate's gaze. He watched Razor stride up the hill to them with a grim expression on his face. As he came towards them all the horrible possibilities flashed through Kate's mind. Was it Nell? Had something happened? Had Felicity done something? Kate steeled herself.

When Razor reached the swag he looked past Kate and said to Nick gently, 'Sorry, mate. It's your dad. He's in the hospital.'

'Hospital?'

Razor nodded.

'They took him in first thing this morning. We've had a radio call-in from the cops. Your mum wants you in there in case . . . Felicity's already there.'

Nick stared out ahead, not seeing anything.

'Thanks, Raze. Thanks.'

'Your mum said to not do anything silly like drive home or nothing. She knew you'd still be three-parts sprung. I'll give you a lift home for a shower – then I can run you to Hobart.' Razor placed a large hand on Nick's shoulder as Nick nodded absently. He turned to Kate, but she felt he wasn't really looking at her anymore.

'Better go,' he said.

'Do you want me to come with you?'

'Thanks, but better not. No need.'

'Sure?' Kate said. 'Is there anything I can do?'

'Maybe just roll my swag for me, okay? I'll pick it up later.'

And he stood and followed Razor back down the barren hillside.

Kate sat watching him go, thinking of Lance, the broken man in the big sad house. She wondered what had gone on? A cold wind blew up and Kate felt her skin prickle. The B&S revellers saluted the looming grey clouds with their raised beer cans. The golden light of morning turned suddenly drab and grey as clouds raced over the surrounding hills.

When giant drops, like liquid marbles, bounced on the ground a cheer went out. Excitement rumbled like thunder through the crowd as the smell of rain on dry dusty ground enveloped them.

'Rain, rain, rain,' the crowd chanted. And as if in answer, the cloud suddenly let it teem down. A summer storm rolled through, turning dust to mud within minutes. Steam hissed from the barbecue hotplate and people stood with their arms outstretched, faces upturned, mouths open. Cold drops landed on their tongues and trickled down their faces. Soon after its grand arrival the cloud moved away and the roaring rain eased. Now a blanket of still white cloud lay low over the landscape. A light warm mist draped quietly across the earth, a signal to the farmers that it was staying all day – or longer. People began to search out coats and hats from the backs of their cars and utes. Then they returned to the bonfires and barbecues to party on, singing in the rain. Drunker boys taking belly dives in the muddiest puddles. Everyone celebrated. Everyone except Kate, who hugged her knees to her chest beneath the dripping shelter of Nick's swag tarp. A tear slid down her cheek, as clear as a raindrop. Was her chance with Nick over before it began, like everything else in her life had been?

Twenty-seven

Kate's grubby clothes lay on the floor of the bathroom. The stench of sheep manure and stale alcohol rose from them and mingled with the steam in the tiny room. Inside the narrow shower bay, Kate poured a large silvery gob of shampoo into her palm and began to rub it through her hair, desperate to get clean and into her bed to sleep. She was exhausted by the emotions that piled themselves on top of one another inside her. A cluster of confusion and fear. There'd been no news at all from Nick. She'd been left hanging – not just about Lance McDonnell, but also about his son. Nick's muddy swag lay on the verandah, barely sheltered from the misty rain that seemed to be dampening everything. Kate wanted to take Nick's swag sheets and wash them for him. Dry them and fold them. Brush the mud from the stiff green canvas once it had dried. Air the mattress in the sun when it shone again. She couldn't wait to do that for him, as if touching his things would bring her closer to him.

As she stepped from the shower and pulled on her white bathrobe, she reached out and smeared a film of moisture across the bathroom window and peered out. She could see the dogs were bunkered down in their kennels, all except Bra, who was standing in the rain. Her coat bedraggled, like that of a wet cat, her pregnant belly drooping down towards the grating. Her eyes were bright with panic. She was panting hard and running in and out of her kennel, clawing at the wood. Turning in circles to snap at her belly.

Kate groaned. Bra was whelping! Now! She was long overdue – but why choose *now*, Kate lamented. She left the humid warmth of the bathroom and in her dressing-gown pulled gumboots on and stepped from the verandah out into the rain. She let Bra out of the pen and called her into the house, her paws leaving wet, muddy marks along the hallway. In the laundry next to her office Kate spread out newspapers and set up a cardboard box in the corner with bedding and a water dish. She called Bra in. The dog looked up at her and whined.

'I know what it's like,' Kate said. 'You poor girl. I'll come and check you soon.' She pulled the door shut, knowing it would be best to let her settle in alone.

She stood shivering in the cold lounge room and found herself wanting to cry. The imminent arrival of Bra's pups was another reminder of Nick. Just another connection to him, Kate thought. Another reason for her to call him and ask how he was. How his father was. She wanted the euphoria of new love to swamp her but that feeling wasn't there. She was just worried sick. About Nick, his dad, Nell, the future. Where did she stand with him? And where was Felicity in all of this? Was it really over between them?

Kate stacked away a few of Nell's toys and stooped to light the wood heater. The delicious smell of the freshly struck match rose up as she knelt on the rug in front of the fire, her hair wet, her face scrubbed clean and pink. She stared at the flames as they began to consume newspaper, twigs, pine cones, crumpled old tissues and long-dead blowflies. A summertime fire on a cold Tasmanian day. Kate was sorry Nell wasn't here to snuggle with her on the couch. But at the same time she felt absolute relief that she didn't have to take on her mothering duties again until tomorrow, apart from playing midwife to a kelpie. Janie's mum had offered to keep Nell for one more night. It would be good to go straight to bed now, Kate thought, instead of having to dish out steamed vegetables and fish fingers for Nell. Or organise bath, pyjamas, night nappy, bottle, teeth and bed.

There were messages on her answer machine. She could tell by the blinking light. There'd be some about work and there'd be one from her father. He'd left several messages over the past two weeks. But as soon as Kate heard his voice – that awkward clearing of his throat and the way he spoke her name as if it were a question – she'd delete the message. As if wiping his voice away would wipe out the hurt he had caused her.

Kate stoked the fire and loaded on more wood before shutting the heater's door. She looked in on Bra in the laundry, busy nesting but apparently more settled now, then she moved to her bedroom. She snuggled in under the doona and listened to the steady drumming of rain on the tin roof. She shut her eyes and conjured the image of Nick, asleep in his swag. And in the quiet of the grey afternoon, Kate drifted away to the place of her dreams.

Headlights swept across Kate's bedroom walls and the rumble of a diesel engine set the dogs barking. Kate, startled awake, sat up in bed. The glow from the clock told her it was after one in the morning. She pulled her robe about her and went to peer through the curtains. Through the rain she could just make out Nick's ute. She caught her breath. Him. Here. Now.

She watched as the dark figure got out of the ute and jogged to the cottage. He leapt over the small front gate just as Kate let the curtain fall back into place.

She opened the front door before he had the chance to knock. There he stood, distress on his face. Raindrops in his hair. She pulled him inside and hugged him close. He smelled of damp clothes and hospitals. Kate led him by the hand to the lounge room and sat with him on the couch. He stared at the glowing coals of the fire. Kate sat straight-backed, half-turned towards him, her hand resting gently on his back, her other hand clutching her robe closed at her chest. She could see the tension on Nick's face, his clenched jaw, the rise and fall of his Adam's apple. Gently she turned his face towards her and searched his eyes.

'Silly bastard,' he said at last. 'Took the wrong mix of his bloody pills.' His face twisted as he held in tears and covered his eyes with his forearm. Kate pulled him in closer. Was it deliberate, she wondered? Had Lance taken an overdose? It was likely. A family farm business undone by drought, the pain of his injuries, a mind closed to the possibilities of re-habilitation. An inability to accept that life had changed forever. A big man, shattered. Kate thought of the way he had come to life on the day she had visited. If only she and Lisa could've inspired him enough to see another choice for his life and for the farm. She waited for Nick to speak again. She watched the way he clasped his hands together and shook beneath her touch, from cold and from tiredness and shock.

'Mum said it rained all the way to town in the ambulance. But the silly old goat was out cold so he couldn't see it.'

'How is he now?'

Nick shrugged again. 'Still out of it. They won't know for a few days what damage it'll do to him.'

Kate began to rub Nick's back.

'Shouldn't you be in town with him? With your mum?'

Nick turned to face her, his eyes intense. His answer came in a kiss. Kate felt the passion surge through his touch. Soon he was pulling her robe from her body and his hands were running all over her. In the warm light from the glowing fire, Kate swung her leg over him and sat on his lap, facing him. She tugged at his shirt buttons, drawing back the fabric so she could feel her skin on his. Kissing, touching, sighing, wanting. Pressing her breasts against the warmth of his chest. Her hands reefed open his belt. Fingers popped the button of his jeans. Her grappling fingers slid his zip down. Eyes locked onto each other as he fumbled in his wallet for a condom.

Nick smiled and kissed her again as she lowered herself onto him. She moaned at the pleasure of him. She wanted to be as close to him as she could. As she pushed her weight onto him she felt the rhythm of their love, fast and frantic. Frustrations unleashed. Desire melding them as one.

As they both came in waves, the rain outside was picked up by a gust and hurled at the window. Kate laid her head on his shoulder as she breathed heavily. Nick pulled the robe up over her back. He held her there like that, kissing the crown of her head and stroking her long dark hair, as heavy rain tumbled down outside.

In Kate's rumpled bed in the hour before dawn they lay naked together. Drifting out of her sleep, Kate felt herself wrapped in a fog of joy – the joy of having Nick here with her. She could hear the rain still falling outside. Rolling over to face Nick, she drifted her fingers over the nape of his neck and kissed him lightly. Slowly, she began to work her way down with kisses to the soft stretch of skin over his hips. Kate felt him stir and heard him moan a little. His face warmed by a sleepy smile. He drew her near to kiss her and laid the weight of his body on top of her. Kate felt the luxury of skin on skin. Her back pressed to the sheets, she shut her eyes as they began to make slow love. And as Kate pulled him into her as deep as she could, she knew she had fallen in love with this man.

Afterwards, the rain was gone and the rising sun revealed a newly watered world. Kate lay looking out the window, Nick's arms wrapped around her. The paddocks glistened with wetness and the promise of new growth.

Kate rolled over to watch Nick as he propped himself up on his elbow. He smiled down at her and brushed the hair from her face.

'Good morning,' he said. 'How are you?'

'Happy, but sad. How are you?'

'About the same.' He kissed her gently. 'I'm sorry, but I'm going to have to go. Gotta get back to town. To the hospital.'

'I know. Can I do anything?'

Nick shook his head.

'Before you go, I've got a surprise for you,' Kate said.

'Have you now?' Nick said flirtily, his hand roving over her.

'No, not that kind of surprise. Go look in the laundry, next to my office.'

Earlier that morning, while Nick slept, Kate had already slipped out of his embrace to check once more on Bra. She discovered Bra busily licking five glossy black and tan pups. During the night she'd delivered them quickly, without a hitch, but she was proving to be a haphazard mother. She accidentally lay on the pups, making them squeal like baby birds. Kate could see the confusion on Bra's little red and tan face. Her eyes darted from her rear end to the pups and then up to Kate with a puzzled expression, her head tilted. She watched the pups squirm and wriggle at her teats, clearly surprised at what was happening.

Nick propped himself up on his elbow.

'The surprise wouldn't be pups, would it?'

Kate nodded.

'Last night when you were sleeping. Five of them, three dogs and two bitches.'

'Fantastic!' Nick took Kate's face in both hands and planted a kiss on her. 'Our first joint venture. Or would it be our second?' Kate smiled at his reference to Nell.

'How's Bra doing?' he asked. 'She's a bit young to be a mum.'

Kate laughed softly.

'She's fine. A bit of a numbskull but I can give her some tips.'

'You couldn't wish for a better cross,' he said with a wink.

'Yep, it's a damn fine cross,' Kate said.

Nick bent forward to kiss her again. This time tantalisingly.

'Would you like to have a shower with me?'

'Yes, but it's too small for two – so I'll wait.' She watched his lithe, perfect form as he got up from the bed and walked away from her. Before he walked through the door, he turned to catch her gaze.

'What are you looking at?' he said.

'A whole lot actually,' said Kate. 'You sure have grown.'

'Very funny,' he said, before disappearing into the hallway. Kate rolled over in bed, smiling as she listened to Nick talking gently to Bra. Then she heard the clunk of the old pipes and water spluttering from the decrepit showerhead. Though Nick hadn't mentioned anything, Kate knew Felicity would be there in town, pulling all her nurse's strings at the hospital to make Nick's dad more comfortable. She'd be propping Alice up, consoling Nick. Despite her happiness, Kate felt a stab of jealousy and mistrust. Should she say something to him? But she realised how selfish that would be. It was not the time or place to raise her insecurities. Kate rolled over again, drawing her knees to her chest. Hugging them to her.

It was then she noticed the time.

'Shit,' she said. It was eight o'clock! Janie's mum was dropping Nell back at the big house at seven-thirty. Kate jumped up and pulled on her robe. As she did she heard a knock on the door and Nell's small, tinkling voice.

Kate opened the door. There stood Janie, red-faced and rushed, on her way to town. She dumped Nell's bags and gently pushed Nell towards her mother.

'I'm really sorry, Janie,' Kate implored. Janie blew out a breath.

'No. Don't be. It was stupid of me to make an appointment on a Monday after a B&S.'

Kate felt Nell hugging her leg.

'Hello, chickpea,' she said to Nell, stooping to give her a quick kiss and hug. 'I missed you.' She ran her hands over the top of her head, smoothing down her flyaway hair. Kate noticed the twins bundled in the four-wheel drive, watching from their car seats. 'Gawd, Janie. I am so sorry. Have I made you really late?'

251

Janie waved it away. 'I'll get you back one day. After our blinder weekend, Dave and I are on a roll. We're in love all over again. It's the best! You can mind them when we go out for dinner next week.' She craned her head past Kate to see along the hall. 'Speaking of love, I see you've got a visitor.'

Kate couldn't stifle the beaming smile that involuntarily lit up her face. She wrangled her mouth under control.

'He just needed someone to talk to. About things. Got a lot on his mind lately.' Kate folded her arms about her body and frowned, trying to remain serious and sombre.

'How is his dad?'

'Not too sure. Still out to it. Stable I think.'

'And the bizzo with Felicity?' Janie whispered.

'Over, still. I think. I hope.'

Janie shot Kate a cautionary glance, then looked at her watch. 'Look, I've got to go. We'll never make it.'

'Sorry,' Kate said again as she watched Janie jog down the path and wave before she got in the 4WD and revved away. Kate turned to gather Nell up in a hug, but she'd already disappeared into the cottage, leaving a small trail of her coat, hat and gumboots along the hall.

Kate found them in the lounge room. Nick, freshly showered and dressed, was sitting next to Nell on the couch. She was snuggled close to him, showing him her favourite book, *Where Is the Green Sheep?* Kate watched as Nick looked down at Nell's face. There were tears in his eyes. He laid his hand on the crown of her head and nodded, listening attentively to her babble.

'Moon sheep. Star sheep,' Nell said.

He glanced up, saw Kate and gave her a solemn smile. For weeks he had tried to deny, then play down his connection with the two people who were with him in the room. But now, as he felt the warmth Nell radiated, he could no longer suppress the love he instantly felt for her. It shocked him. But at the same time it warmed him. He had a *daughter*. This was *his* daughter.

'Funny sheep,' he said, swaying towards her and nudging her a bit, delivering a warm smile. She nudged back, wrinkled her nose and turned the pages of her book. The days in the Bronty shed together, those long drawn-out rouseabouting days, had given them a special foundation. Now, Nick wanted more of the little girl. He was ready to accept this new and very strange situation that had seemed to just land in his life. He looked up at Kate again and winked. She almost melted from the intensity of the meaning behind the gesture.

'Stay for breakfast?' Kate asked.

Nick shook his head.

'Can't, *really* sorry. Got to get back. Mum'll be needing me.' He stood, explaining gently to Nell that he had to go, and that he'd be back soon to finish the book.

He came over and kissed Kate on the cheek, taking hold of both her hands, trying hard to keep a lid on his passion in front of Nell.

'Thanks,' he said. 'I'll see you in a few days.'

Kate nodded.

'Kiss me too!' Nell cried out.

Nick swept her up in a big hug and held her for a long time. When he kissed Nell's cheek and set her down again, Kate could see the emotion running fast beneath his serious face. He gave Kate another quick kiss, then he was gone.

Twenty-eight

For a week, while Kate waited for a call from Nick, she was plagued by dreams of Bronty. They were so vivid, she carried them with her all day, startled by flashes of them at any given moment. A constant in them all was the vision of the sea eroding the shore, taking great chunks of paddocks with it, swamping the house. An angry sea. A sea that rose so high it made it all the way up the dome-shaped hills and crashed against the gate where Will had died, ripping the wire fences away as if they were loose fishing lines, taking the gate and the mighty strainer posts with the waves.

This morning Kate had again woken breathless and panicky, wondering why the dreams just kept coming, as relentless as the waves themselves on the shore. Slow to get to work, delaying the moment she would take Nell up to Janie's for playgroup, Kate sat cuddling Nell on the couch.

The phone's shrill ring cut through the quiet of the cottage.

'Phone,' said Nell.

'Mummy will get it. You stay here. I won't be long.'

Kate pulled a rug up over Nell's knees and gave her a kiss, willing herself to not rush to the phone in the hope it was Nick, as she had been doing for the past week.

There'd been no news. She didn't have a mobile number for him and she couldn't ring the hospital. What if the nurse on the ward showed the message to Felicity? Maybe Janie would return from playgroup at lunchtime with some word – a shred of local gossip from the other mums about Nick and his dad. Anything.

She stared at the ringing phone. It could be her father again. He'd called three times in the past week. Two blunt messages on the machine for her to call him. The third time she'd answered, hoping it was Nick. When she heard Henry's voice, she told him she was busy with Nell and couldn't speak to him right now. She'd hung up on him, cutting his sentence in half and leaving her with a cloud of sadness. Now as she lifted the receiver she prayed with all her heart it was Nick.

'Hello?'

There was a pause. The rattle of coins dropped into a payphone. And then she heard his voice.

'Kate?'

'Nick?'

Another pause. Then his voice, broken and barely audible. 'We lost him, Kate.'

What? She heard the click and clunk of the payphone cord as Nick tried to hold himself together. Kate pictured him in the hospital foyer. He'd be wearing a tidy shirt, Wrangler jeans and his thick tan leather belt and boots, his broad shoulders stooped over. And somewhere in that big ugly hospital, his father would be on a steel trolley, being wheeled into the lift and taken down to the mortuary.

'Oh, God. I'm so sorry.' Kate hadn't anticipated this. She'd assumed Lance would be okay. She thought of him again, sitting at the kitchen table, like the captain of a grounded shipwreck. His sunken grey face. The lifelessness of his eyes. She felt anger rise up in her. He'd had a choice, not like her mother and brother. Life had been taken from them, whereas Lance had *chosen* to do this to his family. Kate felt the rush of fury. She wondered if he'd chosen to leave this life even with the knowledge that he now had a little granddaughter. She felt the words come, and before she could stop them she asked, 'Did he know he was a grandfather?'

'No,' Nick said. 'He never came round again. I did tell him but he couldn't hear me. He couldn't hear me.'

Kate knew Nick was crying now. She summoned up a strength in her voice.

'I'm sure he could, Nick. I'm certain he *could* hear you and he did,' Kate said. 'He died knowing.'

She wanted to say that Lance had loved him, but she couldn't bring the words out. How could he have loved his son if he'd chosen to leave him like that? She waited.

'It was my fault, you know,' Nick said eventually.

'No, it wasn't. How could it have been—'

'It was,' Nick cut in. 'He just mucked up his medication. It was too much for his already buggered system. Normally Felicity would've done it. She did all that. If I hadn't . . .' his voice trailed off. 'If she'd still been, you know, about, it wouldn't have happened.'

Kate knew he didn't mean to hurt her. He was in the shock of new grief. But she felt despair surface again at the impossibility of the situation. She felt like asking him what he really wanted. A nurse for his father or a partner for himself? But compassion rose again in her.

'It was no one's fault,' she said. There was silence on the line again, punctuated by loud clunks as he twisted the handpiece.

At last he said, 'I have to go now.'

'Okay,' Kate said in a small voice and then the line went dead. Kate wandered about the cottage like a ghost, drifting from room to room. Looking out the window to the brightness of the day. Last week's summer storm had prompted a vibrant flush across the pastures. Even the trees looked healthier in their cloak of summer green. Cottonball clouds puffed across a blue sky, leaving odd-shaped shadows on the landscape. But Kate didn't see the view. All she could think was, *dead*. Nick's father was dead. The words repeating in her mind. She knew so well the dark hole of grief that Nick was in. She knew he would be unreachable for a time. She understood his pain.

She thought of her own family. What was left of it. She had Nell here with her, and Auntie Maureen on the mainland. But it wasn't enough. Before Maureen and Nell, her parents and Will had been her whole world. Her father had once been part of that world. She had loved him, and she knew he had loved her. It was time to make amends.

Kate began to see her choices more clearly. She could keep cutting her father off and blaming Annabelle for the divide between them. Or she could choose to have a relationship with him, with both of them, before it was too late. Before death swallowed them all up into the earth.

Kate felt the thrill of possibility run through her. It would be a few hours before Nell got home. There was time to drive out to Bronty right now. She gathered up the whole farm plan for Bronty she'd been working on, grabbed her hat and headed to her ute. Before she left, she let Grumpy and Sheila from their pens, thinking she'd need them as allies. She let Bra out too, knowing a short time away from her pups and a burn down the highway would do her good. She was already getting fractious with them, reminding Kate of her own short-fuse as a first-time mother. She clipped all three dogs on the ute's tray before speeding off onto the highway. When Kate turned across the cattle grid at the entrance to Bronty, her heart leapt a beat. Panic filled her mind. Air was knocked from her lungs. There, freshly dug posts rose out of the earth and nailed to them was a sign. For Sale. *A once-in-a-lifetime coastal investment opportunity. 15 Waterfront Blocks, plus 3000 hectare farm with irrigation licence for 600 hectares, includes charming homestead. A further 3000 hectares of bushland, on three separate titles.* There was a diagram of the subdivision. Kate felt sick. She pressed the accelerator down and roared over the grid, up towards the house.

Slamming the ute door, Kate flung the garden gate open

and stormed up the path. She burst into the house, ready for a showdown. But she was met with silence, except for the lazy tick of the kitchen clock.

The room began to spin and as she swayed across it, clutching the chairs to keep herself upright, she began to call out, 'Mum?' Suddenly she was a barefoot child again, running along the hall, crying 'Mum? Mum!' She saw her hand reach out in front of her . . . but it wasn't her hand. It was a hand like Nell's. Small and chubby. Little fingers with dimples for knuckles. She felt herself push the door open.

'Will?' she heard a voice ask. It was her own, but it was as if she were outside herself. As if the house were fractured. Two times, two sets of families. The energies confused and swirling. When the door swung back on its hinges and Kate stepped inside the bedroom, there was nothing in there she could recognise as Will's. The room, freshly painted in an Annabelle blush of colour, was cluttered with Aden's things. There was no sense or feeling that Will had ever been. Kate felt herself hyperventilate. She needed to find something in this house that could connect her to the love she'd once felt here. She couldn't face losing this place.

She ran back along the hallway and reached out to pull down the rope to the attic stairs. The wedge of ceiling swung open from her rough tug and the wooden ladder unfolded itself to the floor. Kate stood looking up to the attic. The dim hole above her head. She began to climb the ladder.

The desk was still there. Beside it, newly packed boxes, stacked neatly, but looking ugly amongst the old timber seed cabinets. Kate walked towards the boxes, knowing what was in them. Will's things. Packed up and sealed with tape. His life, shoved out of the way in the attic. Anger surged through her. She looked through the thick old glass of the panelled windows to the sea. No sign of the island anymore. Just a wall of impossible clouds. She pictured the subdivision in front of her along the coast. The ribbon development of million-dollar mansions scarring the land. She turned her back.

Walking the length of the attic, she ran her fingers over the seed cabinets, hooking a finger into one of the drawer handles. She slid it open, taking in the packets stored and catalogued in neat rows. She ran her hand over her mother's writing. Tears streamed down her face and landed in drops on the wooden floor. She moved back to the desk, slumped in the office chair, her head in her hands. Her face scrunched with pain. *For sale?* How could he? She wanted her father to love her. She needed to feel her mother's love through him. She missed Will dreadfully. She cried silently, staring blankly at the surface of the wooden desk. How could he even dream of selling Bronty, Kate wondered? How could he wipe out this place? Her breath came in panting shudders. She felt her heart race.

After a long time, Kate swiped the back of her hand across her nose and sat up. She noticed a small stack of unopened letters. Absently she rifled through them; they were all addressed to her. Most of it was advertising mail – stuff her father had never bothered to send on. Horseland catalogues, Country Music Muster advertising, a newsletter from her old school. He'd probably thrown the letters there to give to her later, maybe, one day. He must've chosen the desk because it was the one space in this house that remained connected to her. As she flicked through the few letters, Kate noticed a white envelope with a serious looking logo on the top. Frowning, she opened the letter and began to scan it. The paper was thick with importance. The type neat and official, with an egotistical swirl of a signature in blue ink at the bottom. It was from an insurance company. And it referred to a Whole of Life Policy for Mr William Webster. It was asking for notification from Mr Webster's executor to make a claim for the insurance policy of $200,000 owing to the beneficiary, Ms Katherine Elaine Webster. Kate blinked. In her job she'd become used to wordy letters and the language of the business world, but in her present state it took her a while to take the information in. Will had insured himself for $200,000 and he was leaving the money to her? Kate felt a hollow sadness wash over her as she pictured her big, jovial brother. He'd been so overcautious since losing his mother, it didn't surprise Kate at all that he'd taken out life insurance. At just twenty-five, he'd been an old soul. Ever prepared. And now, this was his way of taking care of his little sister. Kate felt the tears rise in her again as she sat with the letter in her lap. Now what? What good was this now her father had Bronty on the market? What good was this now Annabelle was wiping out all their memories from this place? Now Kate had pushed her father away so often she hadn't given him the chance to grow love for her again.

She stuffed the letter in her back pocket. Anger fuelled her as she climbed down the stairs, marched along the hall, and went outside into the swirling weather, where rain and mist were claiming the once sunny day. She had to retaliate. Had to let them know she simply wouldn't let this thing happen. But how? She scanned the paddocks. There was a mob of sheep, about a hundred and fifty young wethers, not far away. She took all three dogs from the ute and jogged over to the gate. She cast Grumpy out and around while calling Bra and Sheila in behind her heels. Soon she had the sheep out in the farmyard, with all three dogs working the mob to her. She flung open the narrow garden gate and waited for the lead sheep to see the gap. Once in the garden, Kate shut the gate behind the sheep and watched as the hungry mob trampled flowerbeds and nibbled at the roses.

But it wasn't enough. Fuelled by anger, Kate opened the door to the house. The first few sheep had to be pushed inside. But with Grumpy leaping up on their backs, barking, and the other dogs holding them to the narrow funnel of the porch, soon the mob were tottering along the hallway and gingerly stepping over the soft cream carpet of Annabelle's lounge room. Figurines took a tumble and were trampled by sharp cloven hooves. The gold bauble clock landed, face first, into a fresh, slimy blob of sheep manure, and just before Kate shut the door she saw a sheep jump up onto the floral couch to peer through the window, looking for a way out. Urine trickled from its dangling pizzle onto an upturned floral cushion.

'Sorry to shut you in peachville, guys,' Kate said to the sheep through the window. 'You won't be in there long. I promise.' Satisfied, she clipped her dogs up in the ute again and headed down the drive towards the stretch of deep grey sea.

At the Bronty gateway, when Kate saw the imposing 'For Sale' sign again, any satisfaction she'd gained by trashing the house slid away from her. What good could come of her childish actions? She berated herself again for making yet another stupid decision. Feeling sorry for the sheep now but too hurt to go back. She drove the ute along the foreshore and pulled over in the dunes. She let the dogs off and picked out a track to the beach. Misty rain covered her face and slicked down her hair as she walked through the silver tussocks and boobyalla trees.

On the beach, her footsteps broke the wet grey crust to reveal dry white sand beneath. The dogs danced about, tongues hanging from their mouths, saltwater seeping into their coats as they loped in and out of the sea. Kate turned her back on the ocean and looked back over the fringe of tussocked sand dunes to Bronty.

What was the future for this land now? Once it was sold, Kate could see it all carved up into smaller titles along the foreshore. She knew the Tasmanian tradition of little old rundown beach shacks was dying out. It was being replaced with a mainland version of the beach house; yuppy dwellings, overdesigned by architects and plonked onto the vacant windswept coastlines by mainlanders with millions. Disconnected people searching for their seachange. Kate was standing on one of the last stretches of Australia's untouched eastern coastline, and it was about to be sold out and carved up. She could see her home, her farm and the animals that lived there replaced by chardonnay swillers and their sewage.

How could the local council allow it to happen, she wondered? How could her father do this?

She looked up to the bush-covered hills of Bronty. What fate lay ahead for Will's beloved valleys that were tucked between the coastal mountains? What would happen to the land the developers counted as worthless because it had no view of the sea? She imagined the dark shadow of a million plantation eucalypts rising up like a monster. Their roots grappling deep into the earth, turning the soil acidic. Their branches growing up so high as to blot out the sun and funnel the cold winds that hurtled over from the west.

She imagined thousands of wallabies and possums breeding up in the brooding cloisters of the plantations, only to be stung by 1080 and killed stone dead. And she saw planes sweeping in from the sea on still, fine days, pissing chemicals from their underbellies onto the dirt where young trees stood like foreign soldiers. Couldn't her father see what he was laying this land open to?

Kate thought of the whole farm plan document that lay on the front seat of her ute. She thought of Will and the dreams they had for the farm: the wildlife corridors and covenants; the historic vegetable seed-cropping venture. Seeds that preserved the past so they could grow a future. Seeds that could ensure Nell's grandchildren had healthy food to eat.

Henry's plan to cash in the land carelessly, as if it were a city apartment block, made Kate despair. This ancient place, bent by salt winds and weighted with memories and the spirits of the land's traditional owners, was more precious than anything. She knelt on the wet sand and felt hopelessness drowning her. Even the dogs, bounding towards her inviting play, couldn't coax a reaction from her. She felt powerless to defend the land. Who was she, anyway? A stupid, selfish girl, who had wound up a single mother. A girl who was so self-righteous she had thrown away her only chance of being here.

Twenty-nine

As Kate drove back into Dave and Janie's place and put the dogs back in the kennels, she noticed Janie in the chook house on the other side of the farmyard. Janie was cloaked in a grubby blue raincoat that hung down by the hood on her head. She looked weary as she stooped to check for eggs beneath a frumpy broody hen. Beside the shed, Janie's four-wheel drive had country music playing loudly from it.

Kate drove her ute across the yard and got out to look through the car windows. Nell was in the booster seat, asleep, her mouth slightly open. Beside her, the twins were grizzling. Snot ran in a silver drizzle down Brendan's nose to his top lip. When they saw Kate, they upped their grizzling to crying. She opened the door of the 4WD, passed them each a toy, wiped Brendan's nose and told them to wait just a minute longer.

'Mummy and I will be back really soon,' she said, before shutting the car door.

When Kate stooped into the chook pen the stench of damp chook poop rose up to meet her. Janie held an old saucepan with just one egg in it.

'I was trying to find something to give them for lunch. I've got bugger all at home. Not even a tin of beans. You haven't done a shop lately by any chance?'

263

Kate shook her head. Groceries were the last thing on her mind. Janie didn't look up from the intensity of her egg searching. Kate could tell she was rushed and stressed. If Janie had glanced at her, she would have seen that Kate's eyes were puffy and red-rimmed. Janie continued talking, her voice flat and cynical.

'Playgroup was a blast – we made paper plate pictures. Nell had a ball, if you're interested to know.' Then the tone of her voice softened. 'There was no news on Lance McDonnell though. No news at all. Just that he was still on life support.'

'He died,' Kate said. A shiver of rain settled on her skin and seeped coldness into her bones.

'Oh God,' Janie said. 'He died? No. When?' She looked at Kate and took in the devastation on her face. 'Oh, poor Nick.'

Kate held back tears as she tried to get out the words that added so much more to the hurt.

'And Bronty's . . . for sale.'

Janie shut her eyes and nodded.

'I know.'

'You *know*? How?'

'Playgroup . . .'

'And you weren't going to say anything?'

'I was . . . but after I'd got the kids in and settled.'

Kate felt another surge of anger. Didn't anyone understand?

'I know it wouldn't mean as much to you, but you didn't think to mention it first, ahead of paper plates?' she asked coldly.

'It does mean a lot to me!' Janie said, taken aback. 'Of course I know how hurt you must feel. But I was going to tell you once I'd got the kids fed and the twins down for their sleep. Then I thought we could sit down and figure out what to do about it. I know what you're going through, but at the moment the kids must come first.'

'Are you saying I'm a bad mother?' Kate accused.

'No! For once in your life, take a breath, calm down and put things in perspective. It's a shock, yes. It's important, yes.

264

ate shook her head. Groceries were the last thing on her
d. Janie didn't look up from the intensity of her egg
ching. Kate could tell she was rushed and stressed. If Janie
glanced at her, she would have seen that Kate's eyes were
y and red-rimmed. Janie continued talking, her voice flat
cynical.

Playgroup was a blast – we made paper plate pictures.
 had a ball, if you're interested to know.' Then the tone
er voice softened. 'There was no news on Lance McDonnell
igh. No news at all. Just that he was still on life support.'
He died,' Kate said. A shiver of rain settled on her skin
 seeped coldness into her bones.

Oh God,' Janie said. 'He died? No. When?' She looked at
e and took in the devastation on her face. 'Oh, poor Nick.'
ate held back tears as she tried to get out the words that
ed so much more to the hurt.

And Bronty's . . . for sale.'

anie shut her eyes and nodded.

 know.'

You *know*? How?'

Playgroup . . .'

And you weren't going to say anything?'

 was . . . but after I'd got the kids in and settled.'

ate felt another surge of anger. Didn't anyone understand?

 know it wouldn't mean as much to you, but you didn't
k to mention it first, ahead of paper plates?' she asked
lly.

It does mean a lot to me!' Janie said, taken aback. 'Of course
ow how hurt you must feel. But I was going to tell you
e I'd got the kids fed and the twins down for their sleep.
n I thought we could sit down and figure out what to do
ut it. I know what you're going through, but at the moment
kids must come first.'

Are you saying I'm a bad mother?' Kate accused.

No! For once in your life, take a breath, calm down and
things in perspective. It's a shock, yes. It's important, yes.

the door she saw a sheep jump up onto the floral couch to
peer through the window, looking for a way out. Urine trickled
from its dangling pizzle onto an upturned floral cushion.

'Sorry to shut you in peachville, guys,' Kate said to the
sheep through the window. 'You won't be in there long. I
promise.' Satisfied, she clipped her dogs up in the ute again
and headed down the drive towards the stretch of deep grey
sea.

At the Bronty gateway, when Kate saw the imposing 'For
Sale' sign again, any satisfaction she'd gained by trashing the
house slid away from her. What good could come of her
childish actions? She berated herself again for making yet
another stupid decision. Feeling sorry for the sheep now but
too hurt to go back. She drove the ute along the foreshore and
pulled over in the dunes. She let the dogs off and picked out
a track to the beach. Misty rain covered her face and slicked
down her hair as she walked through the silver tussocks and
boobyalla trees.

On the beach, her footsteps broke the wet grey crust to
reveal dry white sand beneath. The dogs danced about,
tongues hanging from their mouths, saltwater seeping into
their coats as they loped in and out of the sea. Kate turned
her back on the ocean and looked back over the fringe of
tussocked sand dunes to Bronty.

What was the future for this land now? Once it was sold,
Kate could see it all carved up into smaller titles along the
foreshore. She knew the Tasmanian tradition of little old
rundown beach shacks was dying out. It was being replaced
with a mainland version of the beach house; yuppy dwellings,
overdesigned by architects and plonked onto the vacant
windswept coastlines by mainlanders with millions. Disconnected people searching for their seachange. Kate was
standing on one of the last stretches of Australia's untouched
eastern coastline, and it was about to be sold out and carved
up. She could see her home, her farm and the animals that
lived there replaced by chardonnay swillers and their sewage.

How could the local council allow it to happen, she wondered? How could her father do this?

She looked up to the bush-covered hills of Bronty. What fate lay ahead for Will's beloved valleys that were tucked between the coastal mountains? What would happen to the land the developers counted as worthless because it had no view of the sea? She imagined the dark shadow of a million plantation eucalypts rising up like a monster. Their roots grappling deep into the earth, turning the soil acidic. Their branches growing up so high as to blot out the sun and funnel the cold winds that hurtled over from the west.

She imagined thousands of wallabies and possums breeding up in the brooding cloisters of the plantations, only to be stung by 1080 and killed stone dead. And she saw planes sweeping in from the sea on still, fine days, pissing chemicals from their underbellies onto the dirt where young trees stood like foreign soldiers. Couldn't her father see what he was laying this land open to?

Kate thought of the whole farm plan document that lay on the front seat of her ute. She thought of Will and the dreams they had for the farm: the wildlife corridors and covenants; the historic vegetable seed-cropping venture. Seeds that preserved the past so they could grow a future. Seeds that could ensure Nell's grandchildren had healthy food to eat.

Henry's plan to cash in the land carelessly, as if it were a city apartment block, made Kate despair. This ancient place, bent by salt winds and weighted with memories and the spirits of the land's traditional owners, was more precious than anything. She knelt on the wet sand and felt hopelessness drowning her. Even the dogs, bounding towards her inviting play, couldn't coax a reaction from her. She felt powerless to defend the land. Who was she, anyway? A stupid, selfish girl, who had wound up a single mother. A girl who was so self-righteous she had thrown away her only chance of being here.

Twenty-nine

As Kate drove back into Dave and Jani the dogs back in the kennels, she no chook house on the other side of the far cloaked in a grubby blue raincoat that hung on her head. She looked weary as she stoc eggs beneath a frumpy broody hen. Beside four-wheel drive had country music playin

Kate drove her ute across the yard and through the car windows. Nell was in the bo her mouth slightly open. Beside her, the twi Snot ran in a silver drizzle down Brendan' lip. When they saw Kate, they upped their g She opened the door of the 4WD, passed wiped Brendan's nose and told them to w longer.

'Mummy and I will be back really soon, shutting the car door.

When Kate stooped into the chook pen th chook poop rose up to meet her. Janie held with just one egg in it.

'I was trying to find something to give th got bugger all at home. Not even a tin of be done a shop lately by any chance?'

But there's no need to cause a scene in front of the kids, please. Farm or no farm, they need attention first.'

'This isn't about putting myself first, Janie. This is all about Nell . . . I'm doing this for her. She has a right to grow up on that property.'

'A right?' Janie's eyes narrowed in anger. 'Nothing comes to us in life unless we work for it, Kate. *Nothing*. If you want her to be on Bronty, you have to work for it.'

'I did work! I put myself through college and got a degree even though I'd just been to hell and back having a baby on my own. Now I've got a good job and all I bloody do is work! And I've spent hours drawing up new plans for the place.'

Janie shook her head. 'I don't just mean *work*, work and pieces of paper and your bloody clever brains and degrees. I mean you have to work at your relationships with people. Do you think I fitted in easily here on Dave's farm? Do you think Dave's dad is just handing it all to us? Do you think things are rosy between his mum and me with the kids every minute? No! We work at it – every day – by being forgiving, biting our tongues, being empathetic towards other people . . . not just being aggressive and reactive!'

'Oh, that's nice! My family farm is on the market, Nick's dad's just died and you're calling me aggressive and reactive! Giving me bloody holier-than-thou lectures! Just because you're Mrs Perfectly-organised-mother.'

'Kate,' said Janie in a tired voice, 'Dave and I have pulled out all the stops to help you, and you know it. Lots of people have because you're . . . well . . . you're you. Everyone knows how hard it must've been to lose your mother so young, but the trouble is, everyone's been tiptoeing round you ever since. If you can just recognise that no one is attacking you except yourself, you'll be a lot better off. Now, if we get the kids inside and settled, then we can talk about it. I'm just too bloody tired to be arguing with you.'

Kate closed her eyes. Janie's words cut deep.

'What am I supposed to do then?'

'You're the bloody farm counsellor . . . stop making it all about *you*. Try on someone else's shoes for a change . . . walk in your dad's shoes, even try on Annabelle's for a moment. She can't be all bad, just misdirected. And, for God's sake, *stop* getting pissed off with me for being a good mother. It's my job and it's a damn sight harder doing it full time than any degree or career anyone could have. So get over yourself, Webster.'

Kate sighed. 'You know, Janie, you're right. I'm sorry.'

Janie searched again in vain for another egg, her cheeks flushed. Kate hovered near her, pulling out the insurance company's letter from her back pocket.

She proffered it to Janie.

'What's that?' Janie said, annoyance in her voice as she tried to get past Kate and through the small chook-pen door.

'Read it.'

'I haven't got time now.' Janie pushed past and Kate followed her, paraphrasing the letter, emphasising the sum of two hundred thousand. At the 4WD, Janie looked up with wide blue eyes. 'Did you know about this?'

'Not until today. Will never said anything.'

Janie stood with her hand on the door handle ready to reef it open. 'You'll have to talk to your dad before you can get the money. He's the executor, isn't he?'

'Yep. He is. But I'll cross that bridge later. Once I did get the money we could use it as a deposit for Bronty.'

'Get real! Bronty would be worth millions!'

'Well, a piece of Bronty?'

'Aren't you jumping the gun a bit? Shouldn't you speak to your dad first? He mightn't want to sell once he's talked to you.'

'Why would he talk to me?'

Janie let out a half-strangled scream of frustration. Her cheeks red from stress as the twins cried more solidly in their car seats.

'He's been ringing you for the past three weeks, Kate, you

dip-shit!' she yelled. 'I can't believe how someone so smart can be so bloody thick! Don't you think you could be creating a lot of this crap between you and your dad?'

'It's not *my* crap! It's his.'

Janie looked at Kate in disbelief, then yanked open the door. 'Whatever you say, Kate,' she said wearily.

Kate watched as Janie got into the 4WD, the volume of the crying twins upped and spilling out into the rainy day.

'Would you and Dave be interested?' Kate said. 'We could go into a partnership and buy it.'

'We?' Janie said incredulously. She jabbed a finger at the dashboard and turned the radio off. The twins were still grizzling and now Nell was awake, looking sleepy and grumpy.

'You, me and Dave,' Kate said. 'You could expand. Take a step up from this place. It's just a thought. Just had it then!'

'Why would Dave and I want to do that?' Janie turned to face Kate, fury brimming over. 'We're perfectly happy here, we don't want to expand. We've got Dave's parents to consider and besides . . .' Janie let her words fall away. She started the 4WD with an angry twist of the key and glowered past Kate to the chook yard, where white hens scratched and strutted about in the shed.

'Besides, *what*?'

'Who can trust you? You're likely to leave town the next time the wind changes. I think sometimes even Nell senses that.'

Kate felt the sting of her words. She kicked at the ground with the toe of her boot. The rain began to fall heavier.

'You're not hearing me, are you?' Janie said. 'Kate. It's up to you to change in here . . .' – Janie tapped her fingertips on her heart-space – 'and here.' She tapped her index finger to her head. 'Then everything else will fall into place. Nick, Bronty, Nell. But it all starts with you giving up on this anger and talking to your dad.'

'Anger! What anger?' Kate spat.

'Kate,' soothed Janie, 'if you don't mind, I've got kids in

267

the car screaming . . . one of them happens to be yours, if you recall. It'd be nice if you could give me a hand. It's not easy with twins at the best of times. Let alone having a third to look after. I know you've had a hard time, Kate, but really, you should think of other people sometimes. See you back at the house.'

Janie slammed the door and drove away, leaving Kate to feel the full force of her words.

Thirty

The dart flew past Jonesy's ear and landed with a thwack, wedging itself in a stuffed trout mounted on the wall.

'Bloody hell, Webster,' Jonesy said, ducking his head, 'the bloody dartboard's over there, you crazy woman!' He turned his palms upwards towards the old ceiling of the pub. 'Can't an honest working man even have a quiet beer after he's bent over the stinking backsides of six hundred wethers all day?'

Kate poked out her tongue at him and sulked off, perching one buttock on the bar stool. She banged the bar, waiting for Jason or Bev to come and serve her.

All afternoon, Kate had tried to blot out Janie's words. She had almost followed Janie and the children to the house, but all the emotions boiling away inside her triggered her old instinct to run. She'd left in a white-hot fury. Mostly angry at herself. But at the time, she wanted to prove to them all that she *would* leave. Leave and never come back. Before she knew it, Kate had found herself in the ute, speeding down the highway. Chased by demons of guilt as she put more and more distance between herself and Nell. She kept having flashbacks of the miserable look on Nell's face, crumpled with tiredness, uncertainty in her eyes over her mother's mood.

Kate had had enough of herself. She wanted to lose herself again. She toyed with the vision of slamming the ute into a tree at a hundred clicks. To be finished with her life. But she knew she could never do that to Nell. She would never leave her. It made the act of driving away from her even worse.

At the pub Kate drowned her sad truths with defiance and drinking. To keep her mind off Nell, she steadily worked her way through songs she knew that contained drinks in the lyrics. She'd started off by sifting through the CDs on the jukebox, forcing a sense of fun upon her self-destructive binge. Her first song choice was 'Long Neck Bottle' by Garth Brooks.

As the pub's brightly lit CD machine came to life, she watched Jason, the halfwit, clink the metal top from a long neck of beer and push it her way. By the time the song had ended she'd nearly downed the entire contents of the tall brown glass bottle. Next, she ordered Jason to line up two pina coladas followed by a Captain Morgan as the crooning tones of another Garth Brooks song washed over the pub. Then she'd tackled Cold Chisel's 'Cheap Wine' and had worked her way through half a bottle of Passion Pop, until she could bear the sickly sweet liquid no more.

And now Jason was standing at the bar looking at Kate and the wall simultaneously with his wonky eyes as he asked, 'What is it this time?'

'One bourbon, one scotch and one beer,' Kate said, slurring her words a little.

'Ah! George Thoroughgood,' said Jason.

'Geez! You know your music. You should go on *Spicks & Specks*. You really are smarter than you look, eh?' she said, winking at him.

'Thanks,' he said, reaching up for the bourbon. 'Lots of people tell me that.'

Jonesy, with enough beers under his belt now for courage, sidled up to the bar and sat on the stool next to Kate. He leant on his elbows and looked at her with a cheeky, white-toothed grin. His sleeves were rolled up, he was freshly showered after his day in the shed, and the summer sun had turned the skin of his forearms a deep brown.

'Having a big one?'

'Are you offering a big one?' Kate said.

Jonesy sized her up. He could see she'd been here a while. That edge of wildness was there again . . . the edge she'd had, he recalled, when he'd seen her a few years back at the B&S. He turned to Jason and said, 'I'll have what she's having.'

An hour later Kate and Jonesy, rolling drunk from playing George Thoroughgood three times over, were keen for a round of pool. They spent several minutes fishing around in their pockets for coins.

'I know I've got a little gold bugger in here somewhere,' Kate said, jamming her hand into her pocket and grimacing.

'Here, I'll have a go,' Jonesy said. He tried to wedge his thick shearer's hand into her jeans. Kate spluttered with laughter when his hand got stuck. They swung about the room together.

'Stop trying to get into my pants, Jonesy!'

'You've been wanting me to get into your pants all night.'

'Bull! I have not! There's not enough room in there for you. Now git!' She hauled out his hand and at the same time a two-dollar coin came toppling out.

'Ah! There's the little bastard!'

Kate bent down to pick it up.

'Nice view,' Jonesy said, eyeing her backside appreciatively. Kate, too drunk to hear him, put the coins into the pool table slot. The balls clattered loudly as they fell out onto the tray.

'Your shot or mine?'

'Ladies first,' Jonesy said.

Kate set the white ball onto the dot on the table. She spread her fingertips on the green that lay like a miniature bowls lawn beneath the bright low-slung light. She unsteadily cracked the white with the cue so that it veered left, missing the clustered triangle of coloured balls. It sank with a plonk into the hole of the corner pocket.

'Bugger!'

271

'That's not how you hold a cue.' Jonesy stepped towards her. 'Didn't you learn anything at that fancy ag college? Here.' He took her hands and positioned them on the cue, then bent her over the table. Kate focused on the blue-chalked tip as Jonesy moved her hands.

'Stroke it nice and gentle,' he said, his warm breath in her ear.

'What? Are you talking about your balls? Or your big stick?' Kate spluttered.

'Concentrate or I'll bite you.' She felt his teeth wrap over her ear.

'Ouch!' Kate turned to face him and they began to wrestle. Jonesy had his arms around her and was now pretending to chew off her ear. Kate was screaming and laughing.

She was enjoying this. Bugger what Janie said about Nell and talking to her father about Bronty. Bugger Nick and Felicity. Bugger everything. Life felt fun again, for a change. Jonesy was a nice bloke, and if she shut her eyes while he wrestled her, she could pretend he was Will. The way they used to muck about when they were younger, before their mum died. She tried to get Jonesy in a headlock but he was too strong. He clasped her wrists and pinned her down to the table, her back pressed against the soft green cloth. When she stopped laughing, she looked up into his eyes. Her smile faded when she saw the desire on Jonesy's face. As he bent to kiss her, breathing heavily, she turned her head sharply away.

And found herself staring straight at Nick. He was standing tall and straight-backed at the bar, a newly poured beer in front of him, untouched. Kate watched as a look of recognition came to his face, then shocked hurt. By the time Kate pushed Jonesy off her and ran through the bar and out into the street, Nick was getting into his ute. He wouldn't look at her as he revved the engine.

'We were just having fun!' Kate shouted as she ran towards him. 'Nick?'

He looked up at her. Hurt on his face.

272

'We were just mucking around. It's nothing.'

'Didn't look like it,' Nick said.

Kate reached out and touched his arm. He jerked it away.

'I was on my way to Janie's to talk to you,' he said. 'But it's clearly not the time.'

'But, Nick . . .'

He dropped the clutch and revved away. Kate watched the red of his tail-lights flare as he slowed round the corner, then sped onto the highway and away into the night.

'Well, what about you?' she yelled after him. 'You and your bloody blonde nurse!' A solo barking dog was the only reply.

When she stepped back into the pub, Kate felt suddenly sober.

'Didn't touch his beer,' Jason said. 'You might as well have it, Kate.' He slid the drink towards her. 'Still, can't blame him. He's the fella whose old man just topped himself. Did you hear?'

Kate sat down on the edge of a table. Colour drained from her face. 'He didn't kill himself, all right?' she snapped. 'It was an accident.'

'C'mon,' Jonesy said. 'I'll take you home.'

'No, mate. You've done enough for me tonight. And you're too pissed.'

'Well, whose fault is that?' he asked, frustrated with her.

'Mine,' she said moodily. 'It's all my fault. Everything is always *my* bloody fault.'

The next morning Kate woke up with her skull feeling like it would split. She vowed to make it up to Janie and Nick . . . and especially to Nell. As she lay in bed, still in her rank-smelling T-shirt from the night before, she resolved to babysit the twins so Janie could rest. She'd even cook her a big batch of stew. Then, she'd ring Nick and ask him over, or offer to help him somehow on the farm.

She threw back the covers and staggered into the shower. Memories from the day before came flashing back. She cringed as she recalled the look of lust on Jonesy's face. The hurt on Nick's. She remembered getting a lift home in a stinking ute with one of the local possum and roo shooters, the alcohol and bitter smell of possum making her retch from his window. His gappy-toothed mate following behind in her ute, telling her when they arrived it needed a wheel alignment. Then with a jolt she remembered the phone call she'd made mid-afternoon from the pub.

'Cripes!' she said to herself as the fog of her hangover cleared momentarily. During her drunkenness she'd phoned a banking colleague in Hobart. She remembered talking to him animatedly on her mobile while kicking stones on the road outside the pub. She had raved on to him about her farm proposal and the sale of her family farm – how she needed advice on the purchase of it. Could she come and see him? Now she recalled, albeit foggily, she had an eleven o'clock appointment with him in Hobart – *today*.

Still dripping, wrapped in her bathrobe, Kate rushed to the office to see if her memory was correct. There, scattered on the floor, were the pages of her whole farm plan and farm budget. She'd fed the entire document through the fax at midnight last night. And what's more, scribbled a cover note: *Thanks Colin for dropping everything to talk to me. Here's my* WFP, *for your perusal before our meeting at eleven today, Kate.*

Phew, she thought, that wasn't too unprofessional. But as she picked up the last page, she grimaced. She'd drawn some hugs and kisses and a smiley face on the bottom, then written *Onya Col-baby!*

She glanced at the clock above her desk. She sighed, knowing she'd have to beg Janie to keep Nell a little longer at her house.

Kate picked up the phone. Her mouth went dry at the prospect of speaking to Janie, who had every right to be absolutely furious with her. She set the phone down again. As she did, she noticed the McDonnell file lying on her desktop. On the spur of the moment she dialled Nick's number, punching in the digits quickly, before she changed her mind. She bit her lip as it began to ring. But the phone clicked onto the machine and Kate heard Alice's crisp, light voice.

'Alice, Lance and Nick aren't available at present. You'll have to make do with a message . . .' Hearing Lance's name, Kate shut her eyes. Death was still so fresh. She hung up, not game to let her voice wander through the sadness of the huge empty old homestead.

Nausea swamping her, Kate picked up the phone again and quickly dialled Dave and Janie's number before she chickened out.

'Hello?' came Dave's voice. She could hear him still chewing as he scoffed down his breakfast cereal.

'It's only me.'

'Only you? Ah. Not *only you* to someone. You've got a little girl here who keeps asking when her mummy is coming back. What shall I tell her, Kate? Have you finished your bender? Because Janie and I assumed that's where you went. To the pub. That's your normal pattern, isn't it, Kate?'

She shut her eyes in shame.

'Can I speak to Janie please?' she asked quietly.

She heard Dave put down the phone. As she waited, she listened to the clattering of the family as they busied themselves with breakfast. The sound of the twins thumping their highchairs with cups was underscored by Nell's commands. Her little voice barking instructions to them.

'No, Brendan! Naughty! No. Put it down. No!'

God, Kate thought, horrified, hearing her own aggressive tone in Nell's voice. It was like gaining insight into her soul. Into her whole being.

'Jasmine. Stop it!' came Nell's bossing voice again.

'Hi,' said Janie above the din. 'You could come over and talk to me face to face, you know. We're only two hundred metres away.'

'I know. I'm gutless. I'm sorry.'

Kate felt a hollow silence on the line. She thought of her

275

little girl, abandoned. She couldn't leave her with Janie any longer. It wasn't fair on Nell. It wasn't fair on Janie. She'd totally overstepped the mark. Nell would just have to come too and Colin would have to cop it. She breathed in.

'I'm coming now,' Kate said. 'I'll pick her up.'

'Good,' said Janie, and hung up in her ear.

Thirty-one

Hobart sparkled with summer light as Kate and Nell drove in from the eastern shore. Yachts with white triangular sails flew along on the blue water of the Derwent. They clustered like flocks of seagulls and caught the eyes of motorists on the bridge. Kate slowed to merge into the traffic, pointing out glimpses of the landscape to Nell as she drove their dirty twin-cab towards Hobart's heart. The bush on the steep hillsides framed squat grey buildings on the river's edge. Above it all, Mount Wellington lay in the sunshine like a giant lion, dozing.

Kate remembered driving into the city with her mother and Will, to the Regatta or the Royal Hobart Show, or for Christmas shopping. She never remembered her father being with them on those trips. Kate had always assumed he hadn't wanted to come. But maybe it had been the pressures of running the farm – especially in the busy summer season – that had kept him at home. As Kate took in the beauty of the harbourside city, she wondered if he, like many farming men, found it hard to take the time off. But if he'd chosen to put the land ahead of his children, why was he now selling up that land? Kate suddenly felt a sadness for him for his loss of Laney. She now knew what it was like to love someone utterly. She felt Nick within her every minute, and the thought that she might never have a chance at a life with him left her feeling hollow. Starved.

Kate began to see now that Annabelle was not a replacement of Laney. Laney had been 'the one' for her father, his soulmate. Annabelle came nowhere near her. Although her father didn't know it, Kate could now see Annabelle was just a filler. A desperate grab for happiness. Her father wasn't putting Annabelle ahead of his own daughter, Kate suddenly realised. He was simply trying to survive a loss so great, it overshadowed everything in life. A loss that would consume him if he didn't make a decision to move on. Kate saw that both she and the farm itself were now excruciatingly painful reminders of everything he had lost. Without the family, the farm no longer meant a future to Henry Webster. It just pierced him with hurt from the bitter past. He had lost a wife, lost a son, and through a set of circumstances created mostly by Kate herself, he had lost a daughter. She remembered him laughing with Nell in the shearing shed. Because of her stubbornness, he'd lost a granddaughter too. She thought of him calling her over the past few weeks. The way she'd cut him off. She realised in horror how much her own actions had created this situation. The sale of the farm was simply a reaction by Henry. An act of devastation. An act of deep hurt.

Immersed in her thoughts, Kate drove on, past the leafy green gardens of Government House and the black and white heifers that grazed its paddocks on the fringes of the CBD. She glanced at her watch. She had ten minutes before the meeting with the banker. She put the indicator on, slipping beneath the green sign that read 'city'. She swore under her breath and quickly changed lanes. *What do I think I'm doing?* As if a banker would take her modest income and her two hundred thousand as a serious starter for a bid on Bronty. She berated herself for being such an idiot. She looked at Nell in the rear-vision mirror. She had been squinting out the window towards the Derwent, watching the yachts and boats dotting the water. Kate pulled over suddenly to the side of the road. She scrolled down the list on her phone and found the banker's number, then pressed dial.

'Colin?' she said when she had him on the line. 'Sorry to muck you about, but can we cancel our appointment?'

'Certainly,' he said, slightly bemused. 'You want to make another time?'

'No. I don't think that's necessary. Thank you all the same.'

The shop smelt musky and was noisy from cheeping birds that flittered about in cages at the back of the store. Goldfish swam about, orange and black blobs moving through clear water. Bubbles rose up from the helmets of tiny plastic divers and freshwater snails pressed their sluggy suctioned feet to the glass. Holding Nell's hand, Kate ushered her gently past colourful dog leads and brushes into the heart of the shop.

They stood before a cage in which a tumble of kittens frolicked about in shredded newspaper. A short-haired tabby with a cheeky white face. A ginger tom with attitude. Another tabby as drab as a winter's day, with a personality to match, and a tortoiseshell having a hissy spat with its similarly splodgy sibling.

'Which one would you like, Nell?' Kate said. Nell's eyes were bright with excitement as she watched the kittens. She jiggled on the spot. Her tongue protruded in concentration as she gazed through the glass.

'That one,' she said eventually, pointing.

'Which one?'

'The sleepy one.'

'Where?' Kate asked, peering at the commotion of cats.

'That border-collie one at the back.' Kate followed Nell's gaze. There, nestled deep within the newspaper shreds, was a black and white ball of fur, curled up so tight it looked like a pompom.

'It's not a border collie, Nell. It's a kitten.'

'It's a border-collie kitten,' she insisted.

'All right, Nell, we'll take it then.' Kate laughed, tears in her eyes. 'The border-collie kitten.'

Nell leapt up and down and flung her arms around Kate. 'Thank you, Mummy! Thank you! I love you!'

The worn, pockmarked faces of the sandstone buildings of Salamanca Place rose up beside Kate and Nell as they dodged their way through the lunchtime crowd. Kate took comfort in the feeling of Nell's small hand pressed warmly into her own. The kitten was now happily asleep in a new cat cage in the ute, the windows slightly open and the ute parked in the shade. Kate was now on a mission to find Nell the biggest ice-cream she could before taking a walk past the fishing boats that bobbed gently on their moorings at the docks.

They passed people clustered in the shade of umbrellas, fanning themselves with menus. Kate thought of her father, and of Nick. How would both of them be feeling at this moment? One grieving the loss of his father, the other grieving the loss of a son – and the anger of a daughter. If only she'd had enough faith in herself to know they both needed her in their lives. Nell, too. Kate vowed she'd get in touch with them both, to make a clearing for a fresh start, move on from the past and the mistakes she had made. But first, Kate was going to give Nell the best day of her life so far.

Kate led Nellie out of the clear light of the day into the darkness of an old warehouse café. People in fashionable town clothes sipped at lattes and read the mainland papers against the backdrop of hand-chipped convict stone. Kate looked around for a place to sit. The only empty seats were two metallic stools standing at the bench that ran the length of the front window and was stacked with glossy magazines. Kate heaved Nell up onto one stool, then clambered up on the other one herself, tugging down her skirt as she tried to extract her mobile from her bag. She looked at the phone's blank screen. No messages. If only she had a mobile number for Nick. He might even be in town right now, she thought, arranging his father's funeral. As she began to plug Rutherglen's number into the tiny grey screen, a lean, clean-cut waiter with a goatee brought a menu to her.

'Can I get you a drink to start?' he asked, taking in the pretty dark-haired girl in the short skirt and the funny little girl who was already fiddling with the long paper sachets of sugar.

'Just water, thanks, for me, and a lemonade for Nell here,' Kate said. 'And the biggest, fanciest ice-cream you have. No. Make that two big fancy ice-creams.'

Later, with the empty bowls before them, Nell and Kate took turns at sighing.

'Ah! Yum,' Kate sighed.

'Ah! Yum!' Nell mimicked.

Kate reached for her bag and shoved a twenty-dollar note under the bill. 'Do you want a drink of water before we get back to your border-collie kitten?' Nell nodded. 'Stay here for Mum, then,' Kate said as she slipped off the tall stool and headed to the water cooler.

Kate was about to fill two glasses when she stopped in amazement. There, stepping out of the glare of the summer's day, was Aden. He wore skate pants and runners and a trendy-again short-sleeved shirt. His hair was buzz-cut and gelled up. Beside him, looking like a nervous deer, stood Felicity. She was wearing a floaty white summer dress with thin straps tied in bows at the shoulders. Her long, bare limbs were bronzed and shining. Her blonde hair fell loose and straight over her shoulders.

Kate froze beside the water cooler, trying hopelessly to blend in with the art-house posters on the walls. She watched as Aden placed his hand in the small of Felicity's back and ushered her deeper into the long dark cave of the café. God! When had they hooked up? Questions flew in Kate's mind.

Then she remembered the Rouseabout. Aden looking so swish, Felicity so shiny. Her hasty departure. Kate smiled as it dawned on her that Aden must've 'rescued' Felicity that night. So, if Aden was taking Felicity out, then surely, she reasoned, surely things really were over between her and Nick? Kate didn't wait to see them settled at a table. She grabbed her bag, took hold of Nell, and dashed for the door. She had to find Nick. But first, she had to speak to her dad.

Squinting from the brightness of the day, Kate walked quickly in the direction of her ute, which was parked under the leafy elms flanking Parliament House. Nell toddled next to her, equally eager to get back to see her kitten. Kate's mind raced from the sight of Aden and Felicity together – and what their pairing might mean.

They were almost to the ute when a stand outside the newsagent's caught her eye. Stacked up in a white plastic-coated wire basket were the real-estate property guides. On the front cover was the sweeping crescent bay of Bronty. Inset was a picture of the low weatherboard homestead, half covered by the blooming white rose and framed with a lush garden. The headline read, '*Once in a lifetime coastal dreamscape.*'

Strong Tasmanian sunshine stung the back of Kate's neck. People moved past her in a blur. She stood. Staring. Her hand grasping Nell's. She couldn't bring herself to pick the paper up and open it.

Kate exhaled heavily. She had to talk to her father. She had to see him *now*.

The sea beyond Bronty had never looked so blue. Kate pulled her sunglasses down over her eyes as the dazzle of light played on the water. She could barely glance at the beach, it was such a pure white. Kate turned into the Bronty driveway and deliberately avoided looking at the large ugly 'For Sale' sign. She sped over the grid.

On the two and a half hour drive from Hobart she'd rehearsed her speech over and over in her mind, while Nell slept. She knew what she wanted to say to her father, yet still her thoughts swirled in her head. She checked Nell in the back. Still asleep. The kitten, too.

As she opened the door of the ute, the heat of the day swamped her. She was about to walk into the garden when she sensed movement in the sheds. She saw her father standing in the shadows, hands on hips, watching her through narrowed eyes. Was he scowling, or squinting at the sun? She couldn't tell. Kate reached into the ute, pulled her Bronty whole farm plan from the seat, wound the windows down for Nell and the kitten and walked over to him. She tried to carry her head high and look directly at him, but she felt like a little girl again.

When she stepped into the shade of the shed, she took in how handsome her father looked. Lean and strong.

'I'm here to see you about the farm,' she said.

'I've been trying to ring.' Her father's voice was tense.

'Yes. I've . . .' she began. 'Will and I . . . we . . .' Kate stopped and held out the folder towards him. 'We'd been working on a few ideas. It's all in here.'

Henry looked at the folder but didn't reach for it. 'Kate,' he said wearily. 'Annabelle and I have made up our minds.'

'About what?'

'You know. I've been trying to tell you in person. But you clearly don't want a bar of it. Of us.'

Kate stared at the ground.

'I know. I've messed up. I'm sorry. But I *do* want a bar of it. I do! It's just . . . I've been so . . . angry.' Her rehearsed talk forgotten, all Kate could feel was emotion. She stepped towards him. 'Just look at the plans, Dad. Please. I've figured it out, we can do this together. It's what Mum wanted to do all along.' At the mention of Laney, Kate saw Henry stiffen.

'Don't you think it's a little too late for this?' he asked bitterly. 'We've made up our minds.'

Kate felt panic rising in her. It came out as anger. 'Don't I get a say?'

'Kate, until now you've never *wanted* a say. You took off and left the farm to Will and me to run.'

'That's not true! You knew I was at Maureen's. You could've come.'

'You don't understand,' Henry bellowed. Then he lowered his tone, his voice choked. 'You've no idea what it was like to lose her.'

Kate caught a glimpse of her father's pain. The dark days after his wife died. She thought of Nick and her love for him. At last she had a sense of her father's loss.

'I've always wanted to be here on Bronty though, Dad,' she said. 'Always! I was just stupid and angry and young! And it's been impossible to accept that *she*'s part of your life . . .' She pointed in the direction of the house, indicating Annabelle. 'Well, I'm sorry, Dad, but I just can't stomach seeing her in Mum's place.'

'This isn't about Annabelle,' Henry said.

'But you're selling the farm because of her! How can you sell it when Will's and Mum's dreams are still here?'

'Kate, don't do this. It's my decision to sell. Not Annabelle's. There's nothing here for me now.'

'That's not true,' Kate said. She held out the plans again, beseeching him. 'Please, Dad. Just look at this. Please.' Her hands were shaking. She felt shame at the years of hurt she'd caused her father. And Will, too, knowing how he had constantly put out the spotfires she set alight in their family. 'I'm sorry. I'm really, really sorry,' Kate said again, her voice cracking.

Behind her, Nell woke and began to call out. Kate laid the folder at Henry's feet and backed away towards the ute. She took Nell into her arms and walked back to him, holding her. Kate felt years of remorse mount up within her. Janie's words had sunk in. Her father's too. And now, it was too late to change. She buried her face into Nell's neck and began to cry silently. All that was left was a deep sadness and a self-loathing, bitterness that it had taken so long for her to find the maturity to look at herself.

'Oh! Poor mummy,' comforted Nell. She stroked Kate's hair. 'Grandpa, Mummy is sad. Kiss for Mummy. Kiss better.'

Annabelle's voice cut through. She marched towards them, tanned from summer gardening, her blonde-grey hair swept up stylishly, looking every bit the glamorous farmer's wife.

'Don't think you can come back here and wave that child in front of him just to get your way,' she said, standing hands on hips. 'After what you did to our home, you're not welcome on this place anymore. I suppose you think it's funny putting sheep in a house. Well, it was our home, and you destroyed it. It's pushed us to this point! We're leaving because of the hurt you've caused everyone – including your father!'

'I'm sorry,' Kate said quietly.

'Pardon?'

Kate looked straight at Annabelle. There was a level of calmness in her voice now that came with complete defeat.

'I'm sorry. Really I am.'

'Mummy's sorry,' said Nell. Kate saw a flicker of emotion cross her father's stern face.

'Don't you use a child to emotionally blackmail us,' Annabelle said. 'Now leave, before I . . . I . . . call the police. We won't have vandals on this property.'

'Fine. I understand,' Kate said, her voice soft. Henry looked down at his boots to where the folder lay. Shaking, Kate lugged Nell to her ute and strapped her in, crying quietly as she did so.

Nell called out, 'Bye, Grandpa. Bye, An-bell.' Her little face solemn.

Shutting the ute door, Kate got in and drove quietly away, her vision of the sea ahead of her blurred by tears.

Thirty-two

Kate tried in vain to scrub the red food dye from her hands and fingers.

'Damn!' she said, glancing at the clock. She was going to be late for Lance McDonnell's funeral. She turned to Nell, who was happily seated at the kitchen table with the twins. They were engrossed in rolling the freshly made red play-dough and cutting it with thick plastic knives.

'Jeez, where are you, Janie?' Kate muttered, realising Janie must've felt this way about her own tardiness many times before. 'Come on, Nell. We have to get you dressed.' Nell took no notice. 'Up you get, please. Come and put a pretty dress on. We're going to church.'

'No! Want to play more with the playdo.'

'*Dough*. It's playdough, not play*do*.'

Ignoring her, Nell reached for a heart-shaped cutter. Kate took the cutter from her hand and picked her up, carting her, screaming, to the bedroom.

'What's got into you lately, Nell? You're being such a cranky-pants.' But Kate knew, as she tugged the dress over her sobbing child, that Nell was feeling insecure. How many times had Kate left her? How many times in the past few days had Nell seen her mother crying? She dragged the brush through Nell's hair and wiped her little nose.

'There,' she said with false brightness. 'All pretty. Take a look.'

Nell's face lit up when she saw herself in the mirror in her navy gingham dress done up with a pink bow. Standing behind her, Kate looked at her own image in the mirror. She wore a black dress that draped over her skin and accentuated her waist. The neckline was dotted with small stitches that formed tiny red flowers. Her black hair, clean and shining, fell across her olive-skinned shoulders. She looked down at the peaches-and-cream complexion of her fair little girl and sighed.

'Now, do you want to wear your sandals or your cowgirl boots?'

'Boots,' Nell said.

'I'm not sure that boots would be best,' Kate said, thinking of the stiff funeral crowd that would be gathering at the church, and the swelter of the day.

'Boots!' Nell said again and Kate reached into the cupboard to grab the miniature pink boots and a pair of odd socks.

'Just hurry, please,' Kate said, relieved to hear Janie's voice ring through the hall.

'Sorry I'm late!' Janie laughed when she saw Kate's hands. 'When you start using food dye to make playdough instead of spitting it on people at a B&S, you've definitely graduated as a mother. Welcome to the club,' she said, hoisting the twins onto her hips.

'Bugger,' said Janie as she gripped the steering wheel of the four-wheel drive and looked at a small party of family members, heads bowed at the graveside. Kate followed her gaze and had a sudden rush of memories of Will's burial. She glanced at the graveyard, where her mother and Will now lay.

'Looks like we missed the church service,' Janie went on. 'The rest of the mob must've gone on to Rutherglen.'

'Definitely family-only there,' said Kate, feeling conspicuous.

'I'm so sorry I was late,' Janie said. 'Dave and his bloody

sheep work. "It'll only take five minutes, darl",' she parodied. 'You know what sheep are like! Five minutes can mean five hours.'

Kate shrugged. 'Don't worry about it. Not your fault. I just can't seem to get my timing right for Nick, ever.'

'You got your timing right once though,' Janie said cheekily, flicking her head in Nell's direction.

'Ha. Bloody. Ha,' said Kate. She had tried to call Nick over the last few days. Even though she couldn't raise anyone, she noticed the message on the Rutherglen answering machine had changed. Despite hearing the new recording of Nick's voice, she still hadn't left a message. Where would she begin? Her thoughts were interrupted by Nell's small voice coming from the back seat.

'Mummy? Look!'

Kate swivelled round. 'Oh, no!' She took in the sight of Brendan and Jasmine. Nell had found her way into the lunch bag and had been spooning yoghurt to the twins from her car seat. Globs of strawberry yoghurt trailed over the seats and on the twins' faces. Nell licked her small fingers.

'Yum!'

'Great,' said Kate flatly.

'Don't worry, I'll fix 'em,' said Janie, reaching across Kate for a packet of moist wipes in the glovebox. Kate was about to suggest they go somewhere else to tidy the kids up. But Janie was already out of the car, turfing wipes and the yoghurt container into a plastic bag, and grabbing Jasmine's face between thumb and forefinger and wiping so hard Kate thought the child would lose her features.

Kate looked over to the hillock of the graveyard beside the church, where magpies dropped down from the gum trees and trawled for grubs amongst the bark scatterings. The service was clearly over. People were drawing each other into long embraces, and the minister was already tactfully trying to usher the family away, so he could go home and enjoy his afternoon.

Kate watched as the McDonnell family began to move towards them. As they got closer, Kate could make out Nick at Alice's side. A tall, bulky man held her other arm. Kate squinted.

'Is that Nick's brother?' she asked, swivelling round to Janie, wishing like hell she'd hurry up. One twin down. Another to wipe.

Janie looked up. 'Angus?'

'He's beefed up. Look at him! He was always big, but that is bloody huge!'

'That's what the high life will do to you. Too much champagne and caviar. Not enough post digging,' Janie said.

They watched as Nick and Angus ushered their mother towards a car parked not far from them. Alice looked so frail and thin, her blonde-grey hair whipped by the hot summer wind, her skirt blowing against her thin legs. Her nose was tinged pink from too many nose-blows and tissues. She reminded Kate of Nell after she'd been crying.

Kate looked back to the rest of the mourners, thinking that it was odd that some of them must be Nell's blood relatives, but one person in particular caught her eye. Felicity.

Kate felt a stab of jealousy followed by guilt. Of course Felicity would be there. She'd nursed Lance for a year or more. Kate told herself that Felicity's presence didn't mean anything with Nick.

'Can we go now?' she asked, feeling too gutless to step out of the car to offer her condolences.

Then she saw Nick watching them. His face looked so strained, it hurt her to see him that way. Suddenly she was out of the car, moving over to him. He had left his mother's side and was walking towards her.

They met in a quick embrace, rough and raw with emotion, but then Nick stepped back. He pulled away and stood before Kate. He looked so handsome in his suit and soft blue tie. The stress of the past few days was cast upon his lean face, but his tanned skin still glowed.

'I'm so sorry,' Kate said.

'So am I.'

'I'm *really* sorry. For everything.'

'I know,' he said. They held each other's gaze for a time. Then Nick spoke. 'Are you coming out to home?'

'Yes. If that's okay.'

Car doors slammed as Angus ushered Alice into a car and whistled sharply at Nick.

'Course it is. I'd better go. Thanks for coming,' Nick said abruptly.

He turned and was gone. Kate watched as he opened the front passenger door for Felicity. She cast Kate a glance before getting in. Nick lifted his hand in an uncertain wave and got in the back beside his mother.

At Rutherglen the mourners gathered on the deep verandah of the old homestead. A group of boys hung around the food table stuffing sandwiches in their mouths and holding stubbies in their blocky hands. Portly country ladies with large bosoms and pinafores bustled about, ferrying a seemingly endless supply of sausage rolls and butterfly cakes.

Despite the dressings of white linen and the fine crockery, the homestead looked shabby. The paint was peeling on the verandah uprights, and spiders had tangled webs behind the screens of the unused windows. It was such a huge, oppressive house, Kate wondered why girls like Felicity were drawn to them as objects of prestige. Then she realised how jealous she was of Felicity. That she was part of Nick's family, and Kate wasn't. Felicity had every right to be that involved, Kate told herself sternly. But it still left her doubting Nick. He'd seemed so distant at the churchyard. But what man wouldn't be removed after burying his own father?

Treading the verandah's worn timber boards, Kate picked up a plate of sandwiches and made her way back down the stone steps to the lawn. As she passed a group of older men and women chatting, she was shocked to see Annabelle and

Henry in the crowd. Then she recalled Lance's conversation, about knowing Henry in his younger days. Of course they'd be here too, Kate reasoned. Lance had been a well-respected farmer. Her father spotted her and raised his teacup in her direction. The fine floral cup looked small and awkward in his big hands. Beside him, Annabelle put a matching cup to her lips. Her eyes narrowed when she saw Kate, and she turned her back. Kate kept walking.

Back on the lawn, Kate looked out beyond the massive old evergreens to the sky. A change was rolling in. Giant grey tumbling clouds loomed a short distance away. The warm breeze was now starting to gust in cool tunnels of air and the day was darkening suddenly.

'Better eat up,' Kate said. 'Looks like there's a thunderstorm coming.' She handed the twins and Nell a sandwich. 'What do you say?'

'Sandwich!' said Nell.

'Yes . . . and what do you say?'

'Cheese!'

'Don't be a dag, Nell,' Kate said. 'You know you say "Thanks, lovely Mum", but you're just stirring me, aren't you?'

'Tanks, lubbly mum,' Nell said with a mouthful.

'Nice, but not with a mouthful, thanks, Nell,' Janie added as she unzipped a bag and brought out drink cups for Brendan and Jasmine. As Kate squatted down to help Janie, Nell trundled over and threw her arms around Kate's neck.

'Aw . . . cuddles! Thank you, Nellie.' She was kissing Nell and giving her a big hug when she saw Alice step onto the verandah. She seemed stronger and more composed in her own home, standing straight-backed and pretty in her delicate grey dress with a soft pink cardigan wrapped about her.

Alice looked up to the blustering sky and squinted from a sudden gust of wind. Then she looked down to Kate and Nell, cuddling on the lawn. A smile passed over her face and Kate was sure she detected a wistful look. Maybe she and Nell had prompted a memory from years before, when Alice and her own two boys had played outside on this very lawn. The memories of a mother. More precious than anything, Kate thought. More precious than any land or money. Kate pulled Nell to her, breathed in the scent of her freshly shampooed hair and shut her eyes. Remember that smell, she told herself. Remember this moment, where life and death are intertwined. Remember to love, no matter what.

'I love you,' she muttered, her lips brushing the soft skin of Nell's neck. When she opened her eyes, Nick was standing beside his mother on the verandah, looking at them. He leaned towards Alice and said something.

Kate realised he was about to come and talk to her. She sat upright on the lawn and smiled at him. Just as she did, Felicity hurried to his side. Thin in neat black pants and a pale green tailored shirt, she had swept her blonde-white hair up into a chignon.

'I'd better get back to town, Alice,' she said breathlessly. Kate watched as Felicity gathered Alice up in her arms. Then she reached for Nick's hand, squeezed it and pulled him into a quick hug. Kate looked away quickly. Then the three of them disappeared inside the house.

'Do you mind if Nell and I go for a walk?' Kate said quietly to Janie. She felt winded by seeing Felicity with Nick. Felicity had every right to be here, no matter what the situation was with Nick, Kate reminded herself for the umpteenth time. Still, her presence stung – even though she realised Felicity would be feeling the same discomfort seeing her and Nell here, whether she was in a new relationship with Aden or not. Janie nodded.

'We'll be here. Take your time. We'll see you later.'

Rutherglen's garden hadn't lost its grace despite the tangled, weedy beds and the long lawn studded with dandelions. Massive elm trees swung and moaned in the wind over the white gravel driveway as the green summer tendrils of giant willows were tugged violently about by the gusty blasts. Kate watched Nell running ahead in her gingham dress, laughing in the wind, tumbling over the lawn. Despite the joyful vision of her daughter, Kate felt heavy with sorrow.

Seeing Nick had filled Kate with longing and the same turmoil she'd carried with her for months. There was no man in this world she wanted more. But Kate knew she had to let go. Of Nick. Of Bronty. Of her anger at losing the people she loved. She had to let it go, or it would eat her up. Consume every cell of her. But there was one thing she knew she would never lose her connection with – and that was Nell. Nell was part of her. Her own flesh and blood. Growing into a life that held the possibility of being extraordinary.

Kate ran after her daughter and picked her up. She swung her around and around, letting the wind whip their hair about wildly. Nell's eyes scrunched up in joy, her pink lips stretched wide open in a white baby-tooth smile. Then, in giggling fits, they both collapsed on the lawn. Kate let the delicious weight of Nell lie across her puffing body. As their laughter died away to steady breathing, Kate heard a voice.

'Ah! I remember you now. It's come back to me at last.' She sat up. Blinded by a sudden flash of sun that had escaped from behind the wind-driven clouds, all she could make out was a large bulky silhouette of a man. Kate moved Nell off her, shielded her eyes and tilted her head to see who it was.

'Angus?'

'That's me. And you are . . . Catherine?'

'Kate.'

'Ah, yes. As in *Taming of the Shrew*, Kate. That's right. You're that wild bit of gear who cradle-snatched my baby brother at a B&S once, aren't you?'

Kate shrugged.

'This your kid?'

'Yep. Say hello to Angus, Nell.' *Uncle Angus*, Kate thought.

'Huwwo,' Nell said.

'Huwwo back,' said Angus. 'How old are you?'

'Free,' said Nell, holding up four fingers.

'Almost four,' Kate added.

After a pause, Angus nodded slowly, as if tallying the years. Trying to move the attention from Nell, Kate blurted out, 'I'm sorry about your father.'

Angus shrugged.

'He must've wanted to go. Shit happens. It's life.'

Kate could tell by the way he said it that his hurt was buried away somewhere deep, only to fester for years – a hurt like hers when she had lost her mother.

'They say animals can will themselves to die when they're injured. Reckon he did the same. It's not all bad. It frees Nick up,' he went on.

'What do you mean?'

'Means he can sell this tired old place and he's more likely to be able to buy me out of the farming inheritance. City types pay big bikkies for fancy-pants houses like that one. And the tree companies are sure to grab the land.' He indicated the homestead, where guests were moving the tables from the northern side of the house to the southern verandah, away from the wind. The women were all in a dither and reminded Kate of upset chooks with their bum feathers getting blasted about in the wind. The storm gathered momentum above them. The day was fast losing its heat.

'I've already got my OS contacts on the job of advertising it.'

Kate frowned, amazed at how different Nick was from this big brash man. Angus was more like Lance had been before his accident, she realised. She decided she'd be just as abrupt with him. She wasn't going to hold back over niceties if he wasn't.

'Talk of selling's a bit sudden, isn't it? What about your mum?'

'She's had it up to here with dusting and cleaning this big monster. She's had her eye on a small stone cottage down the coast.'

'And Nick?'

294

'He's got an eye on a place, too.' Angus folded his arms across his expansive chest. 'There's a property that's sub-divided off some cottages and farmland, on the coast. Whole lot's up for sale. Auction's on very soon, that's why we're moving fast . . . good investment for me and good ground for Nick. I believe you know it well.' Angus gave her a wink before turning and walking away. Just before he was out of earshot, he called out. 'Cute kid, by the way. Reminds me of someone I know.'

Kate watched him go, his words ringing in her ears. Not only did he seem to have sussed Nell was Nick's, he was also blatantly baiting her over buying Bronty. But why hadn't Nick told her they were interested in it? Did their time together mean nothing to him?

Instinctively, Kate reached around for Nell, who had been sitting beside her, plucking daisies from the lawn. But Nell wasn't there. Kate glanced about, but she couldn't see her anywhere on the lawn. Nor was she over at the house. She could see Janie and the twins, sheltering from the wind on the verandah with the other mourners, but no sign of Nell. Kate stood up and spun about.

With relief she saw Nell skipping into the dark shadows of the large trees that flanked the lawn. Kate began to jog towards the spot where Nell had disappeared amongst the giant old trees. As she did she felt a wind gust so strong that she was pushed forward by the force.

'Nell?' she called out, her voice stolen by the wind. It whirled the treetops about so violently that Kate was fright-ened. In that instant she heard the loud crack and a groan as a giant limb seemed to peel away from the canopy and began to fall.

'Nell!' Kate screamed. She was sprinting in an instant. Her legs pumping beneath her. Her footfalls eating up the distance. She saw heavy old limbs knocking each other down like domi-noes, and spear savagely into the ground. Soon she was in amongst the trees, scrabbling through a wall of freshly fallen limbs, crying and calling out Nell's name. And all about her surged the roaring wind.

People on the verandah heard the crash and watched the gnarled old boughs topple. They saw Kate running and knew something horrible had happened. A mother screaming. They were with her before she knew it. People clambering over branches in their suits and dresses, searching for a child in the dark knot of hundred-year-old trees.

'My little girl! She's in here. My little girl! Oh God! Nellie!' Kate screamed. 'Please don't take her too!' As the wind swirled about her she felt her heart breaking.

Kate sobbed as she grappled through branches, desperate to glimpse the blue gingham dress. Blood seeped from her hands from the scratch of rough boughs. When she stumbled and fell, gashing her knee, she felt two strong hands grip her. It was Nick, ashen-faced.

'They've found her, Kate.' He pulled her into his chest. 'It's okay. They've found her.' She clung to him. Shutting her eyes, trying not to scream. Wishing the wind would stop. She could hear voices all around her but she couldn't understand what they were saying. The clearest voice was Felicity's.

'She's gone into shock,' Kate heard her say. 'Here, give me your jacket.'

Kate felt someone drape a coat over her and her body shook uncontrollably. It took her a while to realise they were talking about her.

'Alice, you stay with her,' Felicity said. 'Nick. My car. First-aid kit. Run! Now!'

In a daze, Kate felt Alice's arms about her, gently guiding her to sit on the ground. Hands were stroking her hair. A mother's hands. Comforting and full of caring.

'Nellie, Nellie,' Kate cried, her fingers grappling at the grass and waste of fallen autumn leaves from long ago. 'Oh God, Nellie!'

'Shhh, shhh.' Alice pulled Kate's head onto her chest. 'She's all right, Kate. Your baby's all right. She's going to be fine.'

Kate heard Alice's words but nothing was making sense. Nell would die. Of that Kate was certain. That's how it was in her life. Anyone she loved was taken away from her.

'Where is she?' Kate tried to stand, looking over to a cluster of people amongst the branches. Kate saw Nick sprinting to deliver a box into Felicity's waiting hands.

'No,' moaned Kate. 'I don't want my baby to die.'

'Die?' Alice said, steadying Kate as they picked their way over the branches. 'She's not going to die, darling,' Alice soothed. 'You're in shock. Just let your mind settle. Your little girl's alive. She'll be okay. She's fine.'

Kate tried to focus on what was going on behind the cluster of people.

'Alive? She's *alive*?' Kate questioned desperately.

The people peeled back and Kate saw Nell lying on the grass, sobbing. Felicity was working quickly to stop the blood that gushed from a cut on Nell's head.

'Here,' Alice said, drawing her up. 'You can see her now.'

Kate dropped onto her knees beside Nell, kissing her and whimpering.

'Shhh, baby, shhh! Oh, Nell, it's going to be okay.' She looked up at Felicity, her eyes pleading for reassurance.

'Mummy's right, Nell,' Felicity said matter-of-factly. 'You'll be just fine. Now Mummy, you sit down over there, I'm going to clean Nell up before we all go back to the house.'

Felicity talked in hushed tones to Alice, and Kate felt Alice usher her over to a bare patch of ground. She sat her down and put her arms about her. Kate watched as Felicity checked Nell for breaks, peered into her pupils and felt her pulse. Nick was there too, gently brushing twigs and leaves from Nell's curls.

Kate turned back to Alice.

'She really is all right?'

Alice was crying now, but nodding and smiling too. Her curly blonde-grey hair had old brown leaves stuck in it. There was blood on her pale cardigan where Kate had kissed a bloodied Nell, then fallen into the support of Alice's shoulder.

'She's fine. Some cuts, that's all. And a bump to the head, but Felicity said she'll be fine. So she will be.'

Kate looked up. Her peripheral vision seemed to dance with a blend of white flashing lights and waving green leaves, but in the centre of the mottled frame was Nick. Clear as day. She squinted to see the person next to him and it was Henry, holding Nell's hand and stroking her blood-matted hair ever so gently. The wind whirled about, striking fear in Kate all over again.

'I have to go to her!' she said. A fresh wave of panic raced through her. What if they were lying? She tried to stand, but Alice gently pulled her down.

'Shhh! She's fine. Trust. Simply trust us, darling.' Alice stroked Kate's hair with a calm, soothing touch. Kate shut her eyes and tried to control her jagged breathing.

'I remember,' began Alice's dreamy voice, 'Nick cut his head once. When he was about Nell's age. Fell out of one of these trees, not far from here. In truth, I think Angus pushed him, but that's by the by. Anyway, his head bled like mad. When I came out of the house and saw him, I promptly fainted. When it's your own child you feel their pain too. Trust me. I could deal with all the blood and gore that the boys' friends inflicted on themselves when they were staying. And all the blood and gore of a farm. But I could never stand my own child's blood. Felicity is just cleaning her up and in a few moments you can give her a great big hug.'

'Are you sure?' Kate said, her voice quavering.

'I'm sure.' Alice sat up and looked into Kate's face. 'After all, she *is* my granddaughter. I should know if she's okay or not.'

Kate felt tears sting behind her eyes. She *knew*. Alice knew. Kate put her arms around Alice, holding her tightly. As tightly as she used to hold her own mother, when life was too scary for words.

* * *

Nick carried Nell, bundled in a tartan blanket, over to Kate and gently lowered her into Kate's arms.

'Oh, thank God! Thank God!' Kate buried her face in Nell's hair, which was washed pink with a mix of blood and water, her curls sticking to her scalp. Scratches and welts were beginning to pucker on her perfect little face. The beginnings of a puffy eye starting to swell. She felt Nick's hand on her back. Warm and firm. Kate looked beyond him and saw her father. He leant over and spoke gently to her.

'It's still not safe in here, Katie. You right to walk over to the house?'

As if to back his words, another burst of wind screamed over the lawn and hit the cluster of old trees. Limbs cracked overhead. Kate flinched and nodded. Nick gently lifted Nell from her arms. Kate looked into his eyes gratefully, before Henry and Alice helped her to stand. She felt her father's hands on her upper arm. He clasped her gently, steadying her, soothing her. She focused on walking, not taking her eyes off Nell and Nick's broad back as he walked ahead of them over the lawn.

Inside the quietness of the homestead, Felicity ordered Kate to sit on the couch.

'I'm all right, really,' Kate said, feeling woozy.

'Feet up,' Felicity said firmly. 'Here, Nick. Bring Nell over here and she can sit with her mummy for a bit.' Nick bent and placed Nell on the couch. She curled up in Kate's arms and began to cry silently. All Kate could do was hold her and cry too. People stood around looking down at them before Felicity bossed them away.

Alice, Nick, Felicity and Henry remained in the room. Annabelle stood hovering at the doorway, her mouth twisted with concern. They stood silently before Kate and Nell, not sure what to do or say. All except Felicity, who busied herself setting up a table with water and barley sugars for Kate.

Eventually, from beneath the blanket, a small voice said, 'Naughty trees!' Everyone laughed, their fractured relationships with one another momentarily mended. Kate sat up. She caught her father's eye, and his smile. There was a moment where love passed between them, she was sure. But as soon as it happened, Annabelle stepped in.

'Well, now we know everyone is safe and sound, we'd better be off, Henry darling. I've spoken to Janie, she'll drive you home, Kate.'

'Home,' echoed Kate absently, shock still muddling her mind. 'Thank you.'

Alice turned graciously towards Annabelle and laid her hand gently on Henry's upper arm.

'Thank you for your support. I really appreciate you coming. Lance spoke very fondly of you, Henry. But even more fondly of Laney. He thought she was truly beautiful,' Alice said with a twinkle in her eye. Kate felt a rush of warmth at hearing her mother's name spoken like that in front of everyone. Before Alice ushered Henry and Annabelle from the room, she spoke again – this time in a voice louder than usual.

'He would have loved to know we have a special family connection now. No doubt, because of it, we'll be seeing a bit more of the Websters, yes? Today is a sure sign from above that we're to take special care of our wonderful little grand-daughter.'

Henry and Annabelle looked at her blankly, then their expressions altered as they put two and two together, looking from Nick to Nell and back again. Oblivious to their stunned surprise, or choosing to ignore it, Alice continued.

'Now, with Lance gone, I can only see Nell as a blessing. She's a beautiful child. The Lord works in all sorts of ways to bring healing . . . and Nell is just that. Tonic for everyone. It's our job now to help her set sail in life. Wouldn't you agree?' Then, in her gentle but firm way, Alice escorted them along the hallway and out of the homestead.

In the silence that followed, Kate looked up awkwardly at Nick and Felicity. She waited for Felicity to explode. Instead, she just squatted down in front of Kate and said in her bossy voice, 'I'm certain there's no concussion but, just to be on the safe side, don't let her go to sleep for more than twenty minutes. I've told Janie what to look for. She won't need stitches either. Just keep the cuts clean and change the butterfly sutures in a few days' time. Take her into the nursing centre if you're at all concerned about them. And as for you, take it easy. Shock and stress can take their toll. I suggest resting for a day or so. Take a few days off work.'

'Thank you,' Kate said with genuine feeling.

Felicity shrugged. 'It's my job.' She smiled at Kate. 'People think I'm bossy, but I tend to click into autopilot in a crisis.'

Kate looked up at her gratefully.

'Felicity?'

Felicity held her head to one side, waiting to hear what Kate would say.

'I'm sorry for . . . for the trouble I've caused you,' Kate said, glancing upwards at Nick, then back to Felicity. 'You know. I'm really sorry.'

Felicity laid her cool thin hand on Kate's arm.

'It's been tough, hasn't it?' Her eyes glistened for a moment, then she gained control, lifting her chin up in a dignified way. 'But like Alice said, Nell might be a blessing in disguise. Nick and I have talked it through. We could've made a big mistake. We all know we weren't quite cut out for each other.' She looked up at Nick, sadly, then again steeled herself. 'Now I'll leave you to it.' She gave Nick a quick peck on the cheek and she was gone from the room.

When they were alone, Kate felt the shock rise in her again. A flash of the storming trees and the feeling of total panic. She began to cry, repeating over and over that she was sorry.

'Hey,' Nick soothed, wrapping his arms about her and pulling her head to his chest. He pulled Nell to him too and they sat there as a clock ticked loudly from the fireplace mantel.

'I'm sorry,' Kate said again.

'You've been saying that a bit lately.'

301

'You know I am. Sorry about your dad. About that night in the pub . . . I was . . . it was nothing.'

'Shhh. I know it was. Bloody Jonesy. I know he was the one doing the chasing. Not the other way round. Plus I know I left you high and dry after the Rouseabout. So let's start again, hey? From now. You, me and Nell?'

Kate felt his fingertips on her face as he drew her gently closer for what felt like their first kiss. As their lips touched, all the pain of their lives melted away and all they knew was each other. Each other and their little girl, snuggling in between them.

Thirty-three

Kate stretched, smiling sleepily. She lazily extended her hand towards the pillow next to her. With eyes shut, dark lashes fringing her cheeks, her fingers searched for Nick. For the past week it seemed she couldn't get enough of him; the warmth of his skin, the softness of his hair, the beautiful sound of his deep voice in the darkness. This morning, before she even opened her eyes, she felt confused. She greeted the day with the delicious knowledge that Nick was in her life. But she also had a sinking, sickly feeling because today was auction day. Today Bronty would be sold.

Before Kate opened her eyes, she wanted to feel Nick there with her. Her fingertips walked over the fabric of the sheets and at last met with the softest downy blush of hair on the pillow. Too soft for human hair! Her eyes flashed open. She saw a small ball of black and white fur that purred in the warm dint Nick's head had left behind in the feather-filled pillow.

'Bloody oath! Collie! You scared the bejesus out of me. Thought you were a rat! Get off the pillow!' Kate scooped the kitten up, and with her other hand she reached for her robe and manoeuvred it around her body. She stepped out of bed, almost treading on Sheila, who snored in old-dog style.

'Oh, you've snuck in too, have you, Sheils?' She plonked

the kitten down into the warm crevice created by Sheila's curled legs. 'Here, mind this.'

Sheila looked up at Kate through her foggy cataracts and licked her lips. She thumped her tail twice, sniffed at the kitten, sighed through her cracked leathery nose, then laid her head down and drifted back to sleep. The kitten sniffed at the dog, yawned, shook its head and recurled itself in Sheila's paws.

Wandering out in bare feet, Kate found Nick and Nell in the lounge room. Nick was on his knees, constructing a wooden train set for Nell. Nell, still in her pyjamas, had bird's-nest hair and Vegemite smeared from ear to ear on her bright morning face. Nick, delicious in just a pair of striped boxer shorts, looked up at Kate.

'Morning, lovely,' he said. 'I heard a critter rustling about in the house so I thought I'd get up to see what it was, and I found this.' He waved a red caboose in Nell's direction.

'Thanks,' said Kate. 'Well, I found several critters in my bedroom too, but not the critter I was after.' She knelt down between them.

'Morning, Nell,' she said, delivering her kiss just below the band-aid on Nell's forehead. 'And morning to you.' She turned to kiss Nick, looking up at him through her lashes, almost shy with him all over again. The rush of new love causing her insides to zing and do tumble-turns. He kissed her and held her face between his hands.

'You feeling okay?' he asked, referring to the Bronty sale.

Kate nodded.

'Toot, toot!' said Nell. Kate snuggled into Nick and they sat watching Nell push the train back and forth. She thought back over the blur of the past few days.

Nick had been busy with the farm and settling his father's estate, still saturated with confusion and grief, but at the same time buoyed by love. Kate, still shocked by Nell's accident, and worn down with the knowledge that Bronty would soon be lost forever, found herself in a bubble, shut off from the real world. She did her job but found no joy in it, living only

304

to see Nell and Nick at the end of the day. The only thing that brought freshness into her muffled, muted world was their presence in the cottage in the evenings. Nick came over each night, making the most of having Angus home to keep Alice company.

He ate dinner with Kate and Nell, absorbing himself in the novel routine of getting his young child to bed. Then, once Nell was asleep, he slowly and tantalisingly drew Kate back into their adult world. In the bedroom of the tiny cottage, they lost themselves in each other. Forgetting their grief and disappointments, they set about discovering new lands by exploring the geography of each other's bodies. The rise of a shoulder, the slope of a waist, the gentle curve of a hip, the cave of a navel and the valleys between toes. Falling in love deeper than the earth itself. Their souls entwining in the dead of night so that there were no boundaries between them. They looked at each other for minutes at a stretch, their eyes locked in wonder and love. New love that felt as old as time itself.

Also in those crazy evenings had come the loud, late-night knocks on the door that rattled windows and shook the walls and Nick's brother Angus would stomp into the tiny lounge with a bottle of the best scotch in his hands, crouching beneath the low ceilings.

'Blimey,' he'd said on his first visit, 'you could barely swing a cat in here.' Then he'd pointed to Nell's kitten. 'But we could have a go with that one. It's a tiddler. Remind me to look before I sit down. That thing's small enough to disappear up my bum forever.' Then he'd tipped his head back and hissed a laugh that sounded like steam being released. Kate was so relieved Nick was the complete opposite of his brother.

But when Angus turned up for the third evening in a row, this time with a bottle of Cointreau and a six-pack of boutique beer, Kate found herself getting used to him. A true 'bull artist', as Will would've described him. But smart as a fox. And a softy underneath. They sat with Bronty maps in front of them and copies of the whole farm plan printed from Kate's

305

computer. Nick with a pencil tucked behind his ear, Kate with a calculator and Angus with a fancy beer in hand hatching a plan to buy a portion of Bronty. The real-estate information lay before them. Lines covered the six-thousand-hectare property. There were subdivisions by the sea. And lines marking the rest in large squares.

Kate ran through the numbers she'd just crunched, explaining to Nick and Angus how much capital they'd need to buy the farming portion of Bronty. She pointed her finger to the areas that took in the homestead.

'I can only put two hundred thousand into the deal, even though it's a three-way partnership. But I'm willing to make up the shortfall by being a manager for the business in lieu of the extra capital.'

Angus looked over to Nick, approval in his wry smile.

'Good bird this one,' he said. He tapped his head with his finger. 'Smart. Nice upfront assets too.'

Kate ignored him and talked on.

'If we can put up a good argument that we've got enough base capital to secure this, then the banks will look at us for a loan that *might* compete with the timber giants and the mainland investors. But these other blocks' – she indicated the hillier portions on Bronty – 'we'll have to forget – that's basically all run country. The tree companies will oust us on that. We can't show the banks we'll make as much money on it when they compare us to the tree plantations and their outside investors and tax breaks propping them up.'

As they sat and pondered the maps, the phone rang. Kate rose and picked it up. She heard her father's voice on the line. Shocked into silence, she glanced from the plans of Bronty to Nick and pulled a puzzled face.

'Yes?' she said tentatively.

Henry cleared his throat and spoke matter-of-factly.

'I rang to see how Nell was getting on.'

'Yep,' Kate said tightly. 'She's fine. Her cuts are healing. No sign of concussion. Thanks.' A pause.

306

'Take care of her then.' Another pause.

'I will.'

'Good then. Okay. Goodnight, Kate.'

'Night,' she said. She put the phone down.

Nick looked at her, his face asking the question.

'It was Dad. Just calling to see how Nell was.'

Suddenly Kate was seeing elm trees again, and she could hear cracking branches and a roaring wind in her ears. Then she felt her father's touch soothing her as they walked back to the homestead. She recalled the moment when their eyes had met. She felt a tingle of lost love for him.

'Nice of him,' Angus said sarcastically. 'Didn't call to offer you a cut of the farm, eh?'

Kate shook her head sadly. It was too complicated to explain to anyone, let alone the blustery Angus. Hard as it was to cop, Kate now felt it was her father's right to sell the farm. She'd done nothing to work for it. To earn it. To keep his love.

'I'd prefer to try and buy a bit of it back, fair and square, with you boys. I like a challenge.' She narrowed her eyes at Angus. 'And you sure are a challenge!' Hands on her hips, she jokingly glowered at Angus.

'Not just smart,' Angus said to Nick, 'but a smartarse as well! I like the girl. You gonna marry this one too?'

Kate watched as colour flew to Nick's cheeks. He wouldn't look up at her, focusing squarely on the plans laid out before them.

'Nah!' Kate said, intervening for him. Smoothing it over. 'Get married? What for? We want to be partners, don't we, Nick? Business partners, farm partners, dog-breeding partners and, well, if he's up for it with me, *partner* partners. But there's a get-out clause on all of that. This marriage caper can wait, can't it? If at all.'

Nick looked up at her and smiled gratefully. Relieved? Kate wasn't sure, but she felt the moment move on. She wondered why she felt an ache in her heart. Maybe she really did want Nick to ask her. But she knew it was too soon. All this was gathering speed so fast. Days were tumbling and bumping into one another. As though the wasted years that Nick and Kate had been apart were at last colliding and pushing them forward. Their togetherness felt . . . fused. Not just in Nell, but in their rightness for each other. She could feel a new life forming with Nell and Nick so rapidly it was breathtaking. She'd gone from wondering about his feelings for her to forming a partnership with him to try to buy part of her family farm. It was a giddy rush and Kate was burning up with nervous energy. It was enough to be coping with the spinning feeling of blossoming love, tied in with all the other elements life had thrown at them lately: grief, discovery, fear, excitement and loss. Why throw marriage into the mix?

As she sat on the floor of the cottage in Nick's arms watching Nell play trains she remembered standing at the airport together, like a real family, seeing Angus off. Alice holding Nell's hand, Kate clutching Nick's hand and feeling like a lover, a mother, a daughter and sister-in-law all at once. Feeling grounded yet still strange in her instant family. Angus had lifted his reflector sunglasses and kissed his mother goodbye, shook Nick's hand and winked at Kate.

'Shame I can't stay for the bidding, but there's a yacht in the Caribbean waiting for me. And some luscious lady with a bottle of coconut oil, and a world out there with bigger fish to fry!'

'You tosser.' Kate laughed. 'Have a chuck over the side for me when it gets rough.'

He laughed back at her and bent to give her a kiss.

'Gotta watch this one,' he said to his mother. 'But she's more of a hoot than the last one.' And he beamed a smile at Kate. Nick frowned at him.

'Give me a call on the dog and bone on auction day.'

Kate pictured a well-oiled Angus, his back covered in hairs as curly as the poll of a big black bull, as he lay on the yacht shouting instruction down the phone to his little brother. And again, Kate was grateful the two boys weren't peas in a pod.

Kate was snapped back into the here and now by Nell's voice. Kate shifted in Nick's arms to look at her daughter.

'Mummy?' Nell looked up at her with her big blue eyes.

'Yes, Scary-hair?'

'Can Nick be my daddy?' She tilted her little head to one side.

Kate, stunned but brimming with a cautious joy, looked over to Nick. 'I don't know! Ask him!'

'Nick?' Nell said. 'You be my daddy? And Mummy can be my mummy?'

Kate saw tears in Nick's eyes. He was nodding.

'Sure,' he said, 'I'll be your daddy, Nell. Course I will.' Then he threw his head back and laughed, and it was a laugh that contained all the sadness and joy in the world. He looked down at his daughter. 'Nellie! I'm your man!'

Nell leapt up, jumped up and down on the spot, clapped her hands, then flung herself at him. He wrapped his arms about her in the biggest squeeze.

'I love you, Daddy!' Nell shrieked.

'And I love you too!' Nick said back, looking at Kate and smiling broadly.

Thirty-four

At Bronty, Nick helped Nell down from the back seat of the dual-cab ute and took her tiny hand in his. Kate took in the transformation of the Bronty garden. The auctioneer's marquee, facing strategically out to sea, took up most of the lawn. Kate felt sick just seeing the rows of white plastic chairs and the rostrum with the PA plugged in ready for the bidding. She reached for her cowgirl hat and jammed it on, feeling like she was going out to the main street for a gun fight. Nick put his arm around her shoulders.

'Ready?'

She nodded.

Walking over towards the house, Kate spotted Janie and Dave. She ran to them and hugged them both.

'You okay?' Janie asked.

All Kate could do was nod. Nick fidgeted with his phone, checking and rechecking that there was enough reception to get Angus on the line when the bidding began. They passed through the garden gate, which was propped open with an old-style tin of flowers. A nice touch, Kate thought bitterly. She glanced at the house, knowing Henry and Annabelle would be lurking somewhere in there, peering out at the prospective bidders. She clutched the sales brochure, taking in the printed glossy details.

The farmhouse and three-thousand-hectare allotment was to be sold first at noon. Then the ten waterfront coastal subdivisions. Finally the back country, conveniently divided up into portions large enough to satisfy the timber companies. Kate sighed. Nerves tangled in her gut. As they all took up seats at the back of the marquee, she felt people staring at her. Nick rechecked the bars on his phone, dialling out to Angus just to double-check the reception.

As Kate lifted Nell up onto her knee, she couldn't help looking at each and every person taking their places under the marquee. She knew most of them were local people coming to watch yet another historic agricultural property sold up. Most of the serious contenders would be in high-rise offices somewhere far away from the island, dialling up their agents, who were dotted through the crowd.

She looked at her watch. Time was moving towards noon. She imagined a bell tolling. A death knell. Nick slipped his hand into hers. He too could foresee what would happen once the land was sold. At Rutherglen, he'd experienced first hand what managed investment schemes meant for the land. His neighbours had been replaced by a company with only a phone number for a contact point. With the neighbours gone, there was no one to join forces with to fight weeds, re-strain boundary fences, plan for waterway rehabilitation. There was just the sudden arrival of professional game shooters in the middle of lambing, or the buzz of a plane overhead rudely announcing that chemicals would be sprayed today. The fear that a precious sheepdog might take a deadly 1080-poisoned carcass. The sense that no one in the cities or government believed farming mattered anymore.

Kate squeezed Nick's hand. They had talked late into the night about the injustice of government policies that allowed massive tax breaks to outside investors but not to farmers. They talked about succession planning and how, as each generation slowly moved on, they were confronted with questions

311

too hard for words. And together, Kate and Nick wondered what they had in their powers to do about it. Both of them were desperate to carve out a life for themselves on the land, but the odds were stacked against them.

Kate looked at the familiar faces of the farmers who sat looking to the front, beyond the podium, to the sea. Creased eyes, rolled-up sleeves, Blundstone boots crossed over at the ankles. Using the sale catalogues to fan air to their faces. None of them with the money to buy a property like Bronty. But all of them with a quiet unspoken anger over how the government was treating their industry.

Nell wiggled down from Kate's lap and began to leap along the tops of the straw bales that flanked the marquee. Kate rose wearily to retrieve her and tell her to settle down.

'Want to come and sit with me, Nell?' Janie asked.

Nell shook her head. 'Where's Grandpa?' she asked Kate. 'We find him?'

'No. I don't know. Come on. Sit down.'

As she swung Nell onto her hip, Kate looked across through the trees to the machinery shed where farmers were walking around, reviewing the equipment on hand. The land around the house was a walk-in-walk-out sale, but if the tree companies bought, there'd be a clearing sale and all the agricultural equipment would be up for grabs. Kate felt sorrow prickle in her when she noticed a cluster of men taking particular note of the tractor that had killed Will. She looked out towards the shining sea and tried to find the strength from Will and her mother out there.

When she turned around, there was Henry, already looking like a millionaire in a new, fashionable suit. Beside him stood Annabelle in white pants and a tangerine top, bright yellow beads slung about her neck, all ready for her new life in a Gold Coast penthouse. Henry glanced at his daughter but his eyes slid past her.

That was when Kate felt the old anger stir. She pressed her lips tightly together and let the feeling drift out to sea. She leaned her head on Nick's shoulder.

A moment later, the auctioneer, looking solid and wide in his navy jacket, barrelled past. He ushered Annabelle and Henry to the front seats, keen to get proceedings under way.

At the sight of the vendors, the crowd began to drift in beneath the shade of the marquee to find seats. As Kate tugged Nell and told her to sit down again, she accidentally caught Henry's eye. His face was blank and impassive, the emotion spent. For one long moment she looked back at him before lowering her head so he couldn't see the hurt on her face beneath the brim of her hat.

As the auctioneer switched on the microphone with a clunk, Kate put on her sunglasses with shaking hands.

'Ladies and gentlemen, welcome to Bronty,' the auctioneer said, 'and your chance of a lifetime to purchase a slice of Tasmanian paradise.' Kate felt sick. 'Just look at the splendour of that view!'

The auctioneer swung his gavel out behind him to where the sea glittered in the sunshine. A smoky summer haze lay over the crown of Schouten Island. It was as if the agents had paid for the day to be so glorious. A perfect Tasmanian summer day, the light so clear and the sea so blue that it dazzled. Kate felt every muscle in her body tense as the auctioneer rattled off Bronty's statistics. 'Seven kilometres of coastline, divided into ten seaside blocks. Plus the farm, including twelve kilometres of pristine river frontage with irrigation licence, two thousand, four hundred hectares of improved pasture with six hundred hectares of cropping ground. And a total of three thousand hectares of bushland and less improved pasture land.

'. . . and as you can see, a splendid garden and comfortable homestead, recently recarpeted and painted throughout.' Kate had a flash of memory. Of a sheep on a sofa. Of manure-coated hooves on cream carpet. She felt a rush of guilty amusement, then berated herself. But maybe it had been worth it?

'The sale will proceed in the following order. First, the farm and homestead will be . . .' The auctioneer's words faded from

313

Kate's hearing as her whole body began to shake. The reality of the sale was hitting home.

'Are we clear and ready to get under way?' the auctioneer asked, looking at each of his spotters and waiting for the final nod from Henry. Kate waited for Henry's nod but it didn't come. Instead, Annabelle sat forward and nodded for him.

Everything was swimming around her. All Kate knew was that Nick was beside her, dialling Angus. She heard the auctioneer read out the conditions of sale but she took in none of it. She heard Nick's voice as he talked to his brother.

'We're about to start, buddy,' he said. Kate sat upright as the auctioneer took the first bid at $350,000. She glanced round to see where the bids were coming from. An agent on a mobile, and another, and another, nodding as they spoke into their phones. She looked at Nick, his tanned arm bent at the elbow, holding the phone to his ear. His other hand was intertwined with Kate's. She felt him lift her hand up and at the same time nod his head, his big hat dipping with the movement. The spotter rang out 'Yes!', pointing at them. Kate felt a buzz run through her. They were bidding for Bronty! Together. She held on to hope.

But in an instant, the bid moved away. Then again she felt Nick lift her hand. Nod his head. 'Yes!' from the spotter, pointing at them again.

But when the bids climbed over the million-dollar mark, and the auctioneer sucked in a breath, Kate felt something within her die. It was over their price already. Nick shook his head. The electric touch that had run from his hand into hers had gone. She could hear Angus's voice over the line, consoling. Saying there were more fish in the sea. Kate looked out across the blue. But there was nowhere else in the world with sea and soil like this, Kate felt like saying to him. Nick hung up the phone and pulled her to him.

'We've missed it, babe,' he said sadly. Together they longed for a good life on a farm. The sort of life they wouldn't get if they stayed in the drier regions at Rutherglen, especially now it was completely surrounded by plantations. All of Angus's bluster and business savvy couldn't pull them through this one. Kate listened as the bids climbed and she jumped with nerves as the auctioneer's voice got louder and more hyped.

'What am I bid? Two million dollars! Two million dollars,' screamed the auctioneer in a frenzy. Quickly, he banged the hammer for a pause.

'We'll stop at this stage, ladies and gents, just before I let this magnificent property go.' The auctioneer had the crowd on the edge of their seats. 'I want you to consider what you're actually bidding for . . .'

Kate felt like she was dangling from a noose. She could hardly breathe. The tension in the crowd seemed to suck the oxygen from the air. Farmers were shaking their heads, watching another piece of land getting snapped up by big offshore business, the price resting between two absent phone bidders.

A well-dressed couple now opted out of the bidding and were whispering dejectedly to each other. The other farming interests had been left behind with Nick and Angus and Kate, long ago. Kate knew that in a few moments the gavel would fall and Bronty would be gone. Feeling emotion rise up and tears spill, she barely noticed Nell slip from her lap. Kate realised she couldn't face seeing the place sold. Hand covering her mouth, half-crouched over, she leaned into Nick, crying quietly for Will and for her mother.

'I tried to get it for us, Kate. I tried,' he said, rocking her back and forth gently. 'You know that, don't you?'

Kate, heartbroken, couldn't look at him. She knew what would happen next.

Within days, most of the animals would be sold to the slaughterhouse. Within months, the pastures would be ripped and put into rows of trees. Paddocks that weren't suited to gums would be left by the companies to run rank and grow weeds. The weeds would shed seeds that would be taken by the sea breeze and carried up to the bush-covered hills. And in a few short years, the fences and old bush yards and sheds out the back of the property would tumble down.

'I can move on from this, can't I, so long as I'm with you?' Kate said to Nick, taking in the kindness of his eyes, the strength of expression in his serious straight mouth.

'Yes. Of course you can,' he said. And he took her up in his arms and kissed her. There beneath the shelter of their two hats, Kate tasted the sea in his kiss. She felt the solidness of the hills in his embrace and she felt the beauty and strength of his soul in his love. He was her landscape. He was her everything. As they kissed, the world around them faded away. The loud, pushy voice of the auctioneer faded into the background. Kate was drifting away over the sea with her Nick. When they pulled apart, she looked into Nick's eyes and smiled.

'I never thought I could be so sad and so happy all at once.'

'Me too,' and he pulled her to his chest and hugged her again.

'Where's Nell?' Kate said suddenly, the familiar feeling of a mother's panic stirring in her.

They glanced up. The auctioneer's chants were reaching fever pitch.

'Three point two, three point two *million dollars*, all done and . . .' The auctioneer had his gavel raised, his voice left high in the air, like a sports commentator shouting for gold. The crowd was hushed with suspense. But just as the auctioneer was about to let the hammer fall, there was a loud clunk and his voice fell silent. And Henry was standing at the PA system with a cord in his hand. On his hip he held a little fair-haired girl. Nell. The crowd gasped. All eyes turned to Henry and Nell.

'Just a slight technical difficulty, ladies and gents,' the red-faced auctioneer called out, his hypnotic voice losing power off-mic. He set his gavel down on the rostrum. 'Got a problem, Henry?' he muttered through gritted teeth, walking over to him.

316

Kate found herself standing without even thinking about it and watched, amazed, as Henry laid his hand on the auctioneer's shoulder and spoke quietly to him. Then Henry stood aside, still holding Nell. The auctioneer plugged the PA in again and blew into the microphone.

'Ah . . . check, one, two. A-hem. Sorry about that, ladies and gentlemen.' Trying to seem unruffled, the auctioneer lowered his voice to a serious commanding tone. 'The vendor needs a little time. Please bear with us.'

An excited murmur rippled through the crowd.

'Just what do you think you're doing?' Annabelle hissed. Henry looked calmly at her.

'I'm sorry,' he said. 'I won't be long.'

Kate's eyes darted to Annabelle to see her reaction. She was trying to keep her façade of pleasant wife intact, shoving her shock and rage down inside her. But her smile was more of a grimace. She nodded curtly.

Henry, still carrying Nell, turned and walked over to Nick and Kate. He stood looking at them.

'Nick, would you mind looking after Nell for a moment?' he asked.

'Sure,' said Nick, receiving Nell into his open arms, a bemused look on his face.

'Kate? Could you come with me?' Henry asked softly.

'Sure,' Kate said, feeling all eyes on her. 'Sure.' She followed her father along the garden path and into the house.

In the cool dimness of the house, Kate watched as Henry hauled on the rope of the attic ladder. The ladder unfurled. Henry climbed. Kate watched the heels of his RM boots moving up the ladder. Barely believing what was happening, she climbed after him, puzzled, nervous and devastated all at once that their family had come to this day. And still, here she was on a cliff edge, not knowing what was going on.

In the attic, the air was summery-warm and the tin creaked noisily as if having its say about the invasion of people on the lawn.

Henry moved to the far side of the large desk and perched on it, looking out the window to sea. Kate followed his lead and sat beside him. Side by side. Father and daughter. Eyes squinted against the glory of the view. Below them, the white marquee was blinding in the sunshine. Cars and utes were parked in rows in the paddock, reminding Kate of a B&S. She took off her hat and sat it beside her on the desk.

'He's a nice bloke, that Nick,' Henry said suddenly. His voice so calm and slow it surprised Kate. 'You set on him?'

Kate smiled and nodded.

'Yes. He's the one.'

'Loves Nell, does he?'

'Absolutely.'

Henry pursed his lips and nodded. Then he sat in silence looking down at the crowd.

'There's a lot of people down there,' he said eventually.

Kate wondered if her father had gone mad. She nodded, leaving a gap of silence for him to explain himself. They sat for a time, surrounded by all the things from their past: the seed cabinets, Laney's diaries stacked in pigeonholes, Will's boxes of things, Kate's old wooden cot with her baby blanket and old stuffed toys.

'I want you to understand,' Henry said slowly. 'I really felt I had to sell this place. I just couldn't face it anymore. Not after all that's happened.' Kate nodded.

'I thought by marrying Annabelle I could forget the past. Change my life. But . . . then Will. Well, it went from bad to worse, didn't it? Things haven't worked out. And Annabelle is, well, she's Annabelle. But that's another story. One that's mine to deal with.' He shook his head. 'It's never been the same, since your mother. I'm sorry. And Will was the last straw.'

Kate looked at her father's profile, his head bowed, his hands clasped as if in prayer. He lifted one hand slowly to his face and covered his eyes in shame. She knew he was crying.

318

'If you could know the blackness that's come since she went. Since they both went.'

Her father's hands were shaking now, his forearm covering his eyes as he sobbed. He sucked in a breath that was like the wheeze of a dying man and then he composed himself. Reached for a handkerchief in his pocket, smeared it across his eyes.

'I know I haven't been the best dad,' he said in a broken voice.

'And I haven't been the best daughter either.' Kate reached for his hand. The weight of it, its bony strength, felt so alien to her. 'I'm sorry too, Dad. Really.'

'I know you are.' He squeezed her hand back and nudged her with his shoulder. Then he pulled her to him and put his arm around her. They looked out to the sparkling sea in silence. Soaking up the warmth of the attic and feeling the presence of the women who had worked and gossiped up there, sorting seeds, in the generations before them. They felt the nearness of Will, imagining him setting the desk in this very spot, in the hope of his sister returning. Kate felt the years peeling away to before Laney's death, when the future looked bright and her father was a man not lost to grief. When his love for her was as sure and firm as the Bronty ground.

'We've been through a lot,' he said. 'But not together. It's time to change that. I've decided I've made enough mistakes. I'm here for you, Katie.'

Kate nodded and leant her head on her father's shoulder. She watched the far-off seabirds surf the warm summer thermals, as if suspended on strings. She wondered about the people below and what they were thinking. Then she realised she didn't care anymore. She was just happy to be there with her dad. After a time, Henry spoke.

'I've read your plan. It's very good,' he said. 'You and Will could've really done something with the place.'

Kate felt her mouth tremble at the mention of Will.

'And then I saw you bidding with Nick. The two of you really want to be here, don't you?'

Kate was crying softly now, big tears sliding down her face and landing on her jeans.

'More than anything. Mostly for Nell. Mostly for her.'

'Well, will you take it on?' Henry asked.

Kate frowned, a puzzled expression on her face, wondering what he meant.

'If I hand Bronty over to you and Nell, what would you think?'

Kate's mouth fell open, hardly daring to believe.

'But . . .' she stammered, 'but what about all that?' She waved her hand towards the window, meaning the auction crowd below.

He shook his head again and laughed.

'Ignore that. That's the result of a desperate man, making another mistake.'

'So?' Kate asked. 'What's changed your mind?'

'Life,' he said. 'Life's changed. The future's out there in Nell. She's my future. She's *our* future.' Kate absorbed his words, questions milling around in her head, but only one word surfacing again and again.

'So, how about it? Are you up for running Bronty for me?'

'Yes,' Kate said emphatically. 'Yes!'

As Henry and Kate came out of the house, the crowd parted for them. Annabelle rushed forward, a mixture of concern, confusion and anger on her face.

'Henry?' she said.

'Come with me,' Henry said as he took her by the elbow and led her to the auctioneer, who still stood at the podium surrounded by his team. Nick, with Nell on his hip, came to stand by Kate and gave her a questioning glance.

Kate smiled at him and nodded towards the auctioneer, who switched on his mike.

'Ladies and gentlemen. It's been an interesting afternoon.

The most interesting afternoon of my career. Please be advised that the property, as of this moment, has been withdrawn from sale.'

Nick's mouth fell open as a collective gasp rose from the crowd and everyone started talking at once. The agents grabbed for their phones to call their clients. The journalists pushed forward with their notepads. Goosebumps rose on Kate's skin. She felt Nick's hand slide into hers. The auctioneer tried to quell the rumble that surged through the crowd. Annabelle stood beside Henry, mouth flapping open and shut, her cheeks flushed. Nell hugged Kate's leg and looked up at her, confused by all the commotion. Kate lifted her up and kissed her over and over, telling her everything was all right, better than all right. Kate, Nell and Nick moved over to stand beside Henry. The auctioneer banged his gavel repeatedly like a courtroom judge commanding order. He shouted into the mike.

'Under the terms the vendor has reserved the right to withdraw the property from sale at any time. Apologies to our losing bidders. Thank you.' And the auctioneer stepped from the rostrum. Henry looked at him apologetically.

'I'll be billing you for the advertising, Henry. You don't get out of it that easily.' But then his face opened up into a smile and he tweaked Nell's cheek.

'Bugger the tree companies, I say,' he said conspiratorially. 'Give this little girl a go at farming. Somebody's got to.'

Thirty-five

With a crack, the wave hit the horse and splashed Kate's bare tanned legs. She laughed from the shock of the cool water. She tasted salt on her lips and looked up to the bright blue sky. Sun lit up the droplets on Matilda's mane and warmed Kate's back. She sat astride her horse wearing red bathers and her big cowgirl hat. Her hair was loose under it, the strands whorled together like a horse's tail from the wind and saltwater. Kate wrapped her dirt-engrained fingers with their split and broken nails around the rope reins and half-turned the mare towards the shore. There she saw Nick in his boardshorts and hat, astride Will's big chestnut, Paterson. Nick was laughing at her, holding his horse still against the wash of frothy waves at the water's edge. Beside him stood Henry in his work shirt, King Gees rolled up over his calves as he stood in the cool water, his attention fully on Nell. Besotted.

He was holding a hot-pink lead rope. Attached to the rope with a big brass clip was a fat little roan pony with a mane as shaggy and coarse as a doormat. Nell sat on the pony in a miniature western saddle, wearing just her bright orange bathers and cowgirl boots. Her eyes were shaded by the brim of her too-big helmet, her smile as bright and white as the sand.

'Make him fast, Grandpa!' she squealed. 'Ask him, go fast!'

322

Kate smiled as she watched Henry galumph down the beach leading the pony in a juddery trot. Nell, in hysterics, jolted about in the saddle, her tiny hands gripping the pommel like mad and her hat wobbling.

Nick watched them too, laughing, before urging his horse into the water towards Kate.

'C'mon!' she called to him. She turned from him and squeezed her legs against Matilda's warm belly. The mare, ears pricked, waded deeper into the sea, beyond the break-line. Kate felt the cool water climb higher on her skin and the sudden lightness of her horse as the mare's strong legs began to strike out in front of her, swimming. Matilda's mane brushed delightfully against Kate's bare shoulders as she too began to swim, winding her fingers in the mare's mane. Matilda snorted rhythmically with each breath. As the water wrapped them both in a calm rich blue, Kate soaked up memories of the past few days.

The aches and pains of the afternoon's digging in the vegetable garden washed from her in the water. The weather was so glorious they had all downed tools and rushed to the beach with horses, towels and eskies in tow. Seawater stung Kate's blisters but she relished the feeling. The state of her hands symbolised her new life. The magic was coming back to Bronty's vegetable garden. Kate felt it pulsing up from the soil and rising beneath her skin. The garden's back fence was resurrected. Dave had come by and constructed a lopsided corrugated-iron cubby for Nell in the corner beneath the poplars. Beside the cubby stood Nell's mini red wheelbarrow, containing dried grassy balls of horse manure that she and the twins had collected. Collie, the kitten, rolled lazily in the newly crumbled soil and then skittered out of the way the moment the roaring rotary hoe was cranked to life. It had been Henry who'd suggested they all ride down to the beach.

As Nick drew near on his horse, a broad smile on his face, Kate glanced beyond him to the two squat stone cottages that peeked over the casuarinas at the far end of the bay.

There, Alice might be slowly stacking stones, rebuilding the old walls that framed the cottage garden leading right down to the sea. Or she might be inside, humming to herself and painting. Whitewashing walls. Creating a blank canvas on which to paint her life in new colours. Colours inspired by the sea. A widow, learning how to live again.

One paddock away, in the identical cottage, Henry had claimed his ground. He now lived alone – alone, but not lonely. In the three months since the auction, he'd set out plans for the renovation of the cottages. At first, Annabelle had tried to pretend she was excited by it, but as the days ground on she admitted she just couldn't live in the cottage as it was. Her resentment about the cancelled auction settled like toxic dust between them. With his blessing, Henry saw Annabelle resettled in Sydney for the time being. Both Aden and Amy lived there now. It was for the best.

Henry was taking his time with the stone cottage, knocking out walls here, letting light in there. He was working hard, but still taking whole days off at a stretch – just to be with Nell. He'd sit back in a chair on the Bronty verandah, watch her playing on her bike and sigh.

'Ah! It'll all happen,' he'd say to Kate and Nick. 'These projects take time. A lot of time. That's what I keep telling Annabelle. It could be years until it's finished. But the best thing is, she doesn't seem to mind. In fact, I think she's relieved.'

Nick and Kate swam side by side, clasping their horses' manes. Kate pulled one rein and Matilda turned to shore. Paterson followed. Soon the sand rose up beneath the horses' hooves and they emerged, dripping, from the sea.

'Shall we?' Kate dared Nick, nodding to the far stretch of shoreline. They kicked the horses into a canter and splashed through the shallows, whooping and laughing as they felt the rush of cool wind on their wet bodies. Riding bareback, side by side, racing towards the far end of the beach.

When they pulled up they were breathless. Laughing.

'Woo-hoo!' Nick said. 'I haven't ridden bareback since I was a little kid!' He looked at Kate, putting on the highest falsetto voice he could muster. 'I know why, too. I don't reckon Nell will ever get any brothers and sisters if I do that again!'

'Feeling two stone lighter?' Kate said in her own high-pitched voice.

'Maate!' Nick replied. Then the amused expression slid from his face and was replaced by one of love as he looked deeply into her eyes.

Kate took in his earnest expression. 'So you'd like more children?' she asked.

Nick reached out and touched her hand lightly, his strong bare chest rising and falling. Sand on his smooth skin. He dug a heel into his horse and manoeuvred Paterson right next to Matilda.

'Of course I want more kids with you,' he said. 'One day – when you feel ready.'

He leaned over and gave Kate a salty, lingering kiss. Again he looked deeply into her brown eyes.

'Marry me first, though,' he said.

A smile bloomed on Kate's face and she glanced up at the bright blue sky. There she saw two shimmering white seabirds hovering in the air above them.

'Yes!' she laughed. 'Yes!'

Acknowledgements

This novel began life as a screenplay in 2000. Thanks are due to Screen Tasmania, my screenwriting teacher, Ranald Allan, my fellow Cut & Polish course participants and screenplay editor, Megan Simpson Huberman.

The transition from screenplay to novel was made easier thanks to Joe Bugden and the Tasmanian Writers' Centre, which hosted the 'Write a Novel in a Year' course, led by Rosie Waitt. Thanks especially to Rosie and the people in my group, who helped guide me.

Thanks always to my writing inspirations: Liz Honey, Danielle Wood, Heather Rose, and Kathryn Lomer. And to all my girlfriends – sorry I buried myself in the office so much – hope to go for a gallop or share a road trip with you soon. A special thanks to the girls in the Saddle Bag Club for dropping in with Bundy at low points during the writing process. (Thanks to Damien for helping select the bottom for the cover design.) Thanks to Fenton, Darren and Lucy for inspiring me in the shearing shed. Thanks to the Woodsdale/Levendale community for being the best place on earth to be.

Thanks to the wonderful people at Penguin, who truly believed in this book, and special thanks to my friends and colleagues Ali Watts and Belinda Byrne.

For my agent, Margaret Connolly, I simply couldn't have

done this without you. Your wisdom and comfort came on lonely days when my writing was fighting a losing battle against the pressures of motherhood, farming and drought. Thanks for getting me moving!

This book wouldn't be here without the help of Maureen Williams. Thanks for loving and caring for our kids as much as your own. Thanks also to Tony, Grant, Jake and Brodie – we think the world of you. For the Rowlands family – thank you for making this farming life a joy. You are the best farm partners we could wish for. For Pete, Sally and Sam, thanks for being such wonderful neighbours. Thanks to my legendary webmaster, Allan Moult, for seeing the extra potential in me and creating my amazing website.

To Val, Jenny and the family – thanks for the food, veggie garden, child minding, firewood and love . . . and thanks for all the things that help give me more time to write.

To my in-laws (on the mainland) thanks for your ongoing love and support – we couldn't lead the rich and varied life we do without you.

To my animals – the dogs, ducks, chooks, horses and sheep – thanks for teaching me to listen and learn.

Most importantly – thanks to my children, Rosie and Charlie, who have graciously learned to share their mother with the demon who drives her to write. To the love of my life, John, these books exist because of you – they should have your name on the cover too. You are my inspiration in all that I do.

And lastly, thanks to God for giving me the gift of writing and for making it rain on Christmas Day! And thank God for farmers! We feed the world.

Now read the first chapter of Rachael Treasure's next novel

Timeless Land

Coming soon from Preface

One

Rosemary Highgrove-Jones focused on the dog through her camera's viewfinder. She chuckled, then pressed the shutter button down. Click. In the sweltering heat, amongst dozing red gums and drunken racegoers, she'd captured the image of a cocky little Jack Russell pissing on Prudence Beaton's chunky leg. Yellow urine seeped into Prue's beige pantyhose as she continued to sip, politely and obliviously, on equally yellow Chardonnay.

Satisfied, the Jack Russell snorted, pointed his stumpy tail to the sky and scuffed up dried grass and dust with rigid legs. He then turned his attention to Prue's Maltese Terrier. The two little dogs stood nose to tail, in a formation not unlike yin and yang, and began spinning slowly in a circle, oblivious to the throng of human activity above their heads. Rosemary had raised her camera again to capture the bum-sniffing on film, when she heard her mother's voice.

'Rosemary Highgrove-Jones! What in God's name are you doing?' Margaret hissed, firmly pushing the camera down. 'You're *supposed* to be working! Duncan's relying on you! You're not going to let him down again, are you?'

'Why do you think they do that, Mum?'

'Do what?' Margaret frowned, momentarily creasing her perfect foundation.

Rosemary nodded at the dogs. 'Sniff each other's bums like that.'

'Oh, Rosemary!' Margaret Highgrove-Jones took her daughter's elbow in a pincer-like grip and steered her towards the VIP tent. 'Now come on, I've got some people who are dying to get their faces in the social pages.'

Margaret, tall, slim and upright in her blocky heels, seemed to tower above her daughter. Rosemary squinted at the sun shimmering in her mother's rust-coloured organza dress and chanted to herself, 'I must not be antisocial when doing the social pages, I must not be antisocial when doing the social pages.'

'Let's huddle in close for a nice photograph for *The Chronicle*,' said Margaret as she gathered up a collection of old ladies sweating in race-day frocks.

Rosemary raised the camera, her eyes scanning the women. Her mother stood front and centre of the group, looking like a blonde version of Jackie Onassis. Click. Rosemary took up her pen and notebook and began to scribble down who was in the shot. No need to ask how to spell their names. They were her mother's regular rent-a-crowd of graziers' wives.

'Got time on your social rounds for a glass of shampoo?' Margaret asked, waving a champagne flute at her.

''Fraid I can't,' Rosemary said. 'Got to watch Sam in the next race.'

Rosemary walked through the crowd towards the racetrack. The men standing among the litter of betting slips glanced away from odds chalked up on the bookies' stands to watch the pretty girl pass. Some of them wore their dinner jackets with shorts and Blunnie boots. Others in proper suits had their shirtsleeves rolled and ties slackened about their necks. Beyond the fringe of bookies and punters, boys in jeans, blue singlets and big black hats slumped on a sagging couch on the back of a ute, drinking beer. They clutched cans in stubby holders while Lee Kernaghan's songs vibrated from the ute's stereo. When they saw Rosemary, one boy whistled.

Embarrassed, she looked away, but then stumbled as a green wheelie bin rolled past her. A tubby bloke stood tall in the wheelie bin, like Russell Crowe in a *Gladiator* chariot. He held his beer can high and roared 'Charge!' as his mate pushed him at high speed over the bumpy ground, scattering the crowd. Rosemary watched the boys until they were out of sight, then turned to see her father's serious face.

Gerald Highgrove-Jones was standing tall, like a slim grey gum, with other gentlemen of the 'tweed coat brigade'. These were the men of the district who never loosened their ties no matter how hot it was or how much alcohol they drank. Royal Show badges were pinned with pride to the thick woollen lapels of their jackets. Among them, his fine long legs clad in moleskin pants, was her brother Julian. As usual, he looked subdued and bored. Like Gerald he towered above the other men, but instead of standing upright he seemed to stoop, as if trying to hide.

Rosemary waved to him as she passed and Julian waved back, rolling his eyes to indicate boredom. At the racetrack rail she looked at the familiar faces in the crowd. Like Julian, she had tried so hard to fit in. Each year, she'd tried to get excited about the coming bush races. Weeks before, the volley of phone calls between the ladies in the district would begin. Who would do hors d'oeuvres? Salmon or shrimp in the vol-au-vents? Caramel slice or coconut ice? She tried to gush over the dresses in the latest catalogues from Maddison & Rose and be upbeat and bubbly about her mother's special trips to Laura Ashley and Country Road in Melbourne. Margaret was always striving for *Country Style* magazine perfection. But Rosemary and perfection just didn't fit.

She looked down at her now-creased white linen dress with its pattern of cornflowers and daisies. It had been ordered from Melbourne and had cost a bomb. But still, Sam had said she looked nice. She looked for him now in the area cordoned off for riders. Pretty girls in tight Wranglers, cowboy hats and singlets moved purposefully about their horses, carrying buckets, adjusting buckles, rubbing rough brushes over their mounts. They were girls her age. She'd known a couple of them at pony club, but her mother had refused to let her go on with her riding once she'd left the district for boarding school. In the years since she'd been home, the girls had barely spoken to her. Except when she was with Sam.

She saw him on the far side of the track. He was with a group of riders making their way to the starting line. Collected in on tight reins, the horses bowed their heads and swished their tails nervously. Sam's black gelding, Oakwood, loped in circles. Sam rode like a stockman, not a jockey, and he'd set his stirrups longer than the other riders as he always did at bush races. Rosemary eyed Sam's strong, tanned hands as he expertly gripped his reins. Beneath brown skin, the veins in his arms stood out. Oakwood, too, had rivers of veins running under his glossy coat. His Australian stockhorse freeze-brand gleamed against his dark coat. Rosemary felt a tingle run through her as she took in how magnificent Sam and Oakwood looked together. It was as if man and horse shared the same blood, veins pumping as one. As they came nearer she tottered closer to the rail in her high heels, waved and called out.

'Good luck, Sam!'

Sam and Oakwood spun in a circle and then leapt towards her.

'Make sure you get a winning photo of us, Pooky,' he called. His dark-brown eyes shone as he winked and smiled at her.

'I will!' She winked back. She hated it when he called her Pooky, but there he was. Gorgeous Sam. Handsome right down to his boxer shorts.

Behind him on the track rode Jillian Rogers, her long dark ponytail flying behind her. She thundered past on her leggy chestnut, yelling to Sam as she sped by, 'Are you coming to get your arse whipped or not?'

'You'll regret that, Rogers!' Sam called after her, laughing. 'See you soon, Pooks.'

Rosemary watched Oakwood's muscular hindquarters

bunch beneath him as Sam turned the gelding towards Jillian and cantered after her.

'Good luck,' she said again, but her voice was carried away on the wind.

Rosemary reached for the ring on her engagement finger and spun it around and around. As she touched the sapphire and smooth gold, she wondered again how it was that, of all the girls in the district, she was the one who was going to marry Sam Chillcott-Clark.

The voice of Rosemary's editor from *The Chronicle* crackled from the loudspeaker. Duncan Pellmet fancied himself as a race caller. He had a special nasal voice for the one day of the year that was marked for the Glenelg Bush Races.

'Well, ladies and gents, welcome back for the continuation of our Sunday bush racing program,' said Duncan. 'It's time for the feature event of the day – the Glenelg Stockman's Cup – sponsored by our very own local newspaper, *The Chronicle*. This event is open to all local stockmen and their horses. And these days, folks, "stock*men*" includes the ladies – that's right, fellas . . . look out! One little miss that'll be hard to beat this year is Jillian Rogers, riding her mare Victory. But she's up against three-time cup winner Sam Chillcott-Clark on his magnificent gelding Oakwood. Now, folks, Oakwood is no stranger to this track or the bush racing circuit. He's also a polocrosse champ, a second place-getter in the national Stockman's Challenge and gives a fair run at campdrafts all over the countryside. No surprises who the bookies' favourite is today . . .'

The public address system whined, as if complaining about Duncan's voice. But he was soon back on the airwaves talking to a crowd who had long since stopped listening.

'Er . . . now while the riders are getting ready for the start, some housekeeping . . . if anyone has seen my Jack Russell please show him to the secretary's office . . . thank you. He answers to Derek.'

The crowd hushed in anticipation as they waited for the mounted clerk of the course to drop the starter's flag. As the white flag fell, the line of horses leapt from their standing start on the far side of the track. Goosebumps rose on Rosemary's skin as Duncan Pellmet's excited commentary reverberated through her. She watched the horses bunch and gallop in the haze of summer heat, eating up dust, belting along as if they were one giant beast. As they came more clearly into view round the turn, the slower horses started falling away and from the pack emerged Oakwood and Victory, the chestnut and the black, doing battle neck and neck. Sam leant over his horse and hissed in his ear. Jillian, perched on short stirrups, called to her horse in a gutsy voice. Then with just a few lengths to go, Duncan's Jack Russell burst onto the track, yapping madly at the horses. Oakwood, a seasoned stockhorse, barely glanced at the little dog. But Jillian's thoroughbred mare, more used to showjumping than stockwork, threw her head and took a sidestep just on the line. Sam had won. The crowd erupted into cheers and the wheelie-bin boys ran onto the track to rugby-tackle the dog.

Rosemary made her way to the mounting yard where Sam, sweat trickling down his brown face, helmet under his arm, was holding onto the heaving Oakwood. He called out to Rosemary.

'Here! *Now* take your winning picture for the paper!'

She lined him up in the viewfinder. There he was, gorgeous Sam with dust sticking to the sweat on his face, a big white grin, and eyes that crinkled when he smiled. And his horse, head held high, nostrils flared and his ears thrust forward. Click.

Sam took a step towards Rosemary. 'Can you just hold him for a sec?' he asked.

Rosemary found herself juggling her handbag, camera and a set of sweat-covered reins. Oakwood swung his head around anxiously, knocking Rosemary's hat skew-whiff. He tossed his bit up and down so it clattered against his teeth. A long string of saliva trickled onto Rosemary's arm. His eyes rolled in his head and he danced on black hooves.

'Whoah, boy,' Rosemary said, stumbling as her heels sank deep into the turf. Then, as if he were telling her to shut up, Oakwood dropped his head low and rubbed his sweaty, dusty face all over her white dress. She glanced up, looking for Sam, and saw him in the corner of the mounting yard, his hand on Jillian's shoulder as she wiped away tears. She had her hat off and her dark hair had come loose, falling over her strong shoulders. Sam stooped a little to look into her eyes and smile gently at her. Then he glanced towards Rosemary, said something to Jillian and bounded back to her, the beaming smile again on his face. He grabbed the reins.

'Thanks.' He inclined his head towards Jillian. 'She's a sore loser, that one, but it wasn't entirely fair. Duncan's bloody dog. Anyway, better get this boy hosed down.' A quick kiss on her cheek and he began to lead his horse away.

'Where will we meet up?' Rosemary called out.

Sam spun around. 'Boys want to shout me a few winning beers. I won't be long. I promise. Just a couple at the pub.'

Rosemary's face fell. Sam came over and took her hands.

'Just *one* beer then,' he said.

'Let me come with you,' begged Rosemary. 'You *never* take me to the pub.'

'Your mum would tear strips off me if I took you there. You know she hates it. Besides, I heard your mum ask some of the girls back to your place for drinks. You can get on the Chards with my mum and talk weddings. Get some plans in place for when you move in.' He ran his hand over her slim waist. Rosemary wrinkled her nose.

'You're so cute when you're pooky, Pooky.' He tipped back her hat and kissed her on the brow. She looked down at her dusty Diana Ferrari slingbacks.

'All right. Piss off then,' she said sulkily.

'What?'

'I said piss off!'

'Oh! That's ladylike!' Sam said. 'I've just won the Stockman's Cup for you and you won't even let me go to the pub with my mates! Is this how it's going to be when we're married? I thought you'd *want* to go home with the girls. They're happy to do it. Isn't it good enough for you?'

'It's not that, Sam.'

'Well, what is it then?'

'I don't know.'

'You never know. That's your problem. That's why you need me!'

He pulled her to him and looked into her eyes.

'Just wait until we're married. When Mum and Dad move to the flat in South Yarra, you'll have the whole homestead to look after. You won't have time to "not know". It'll be perfect. You'll see. Okay?' Gently, he kissed her on the nose.

She nodded and smiled a little, but she still felt the frustration within her. She sighed. He could get any girl he wanted, that's what her mother said, and he had chosen her. She watched him saunter away in his tight denim jeans and his sweat-stained shirt.

Sitting in her dirty dress beside the Glenelg River, glad to be alone, Rosemary listened to the far-off sound of Duncan's droning commentary. Angrily, she swiped an unexpected tear from her cheek, then wondered why she was crying. All her mother's friends told her what a lucky girl she was, engaged to Sam. But so much seemed to be missing from her life. She wished she knew what it was like to thunder around the track on half a tonne of horse muscle, instead of just watching from the rail. She snapped a stick in half and threw it into the olive-green river. Why couldn't she be more like the other girls, the ones who'd be drinking in the pub with Sam tonight? she wondered. Why didn't he take her with him?

She turned her head towards the breeze. She wished it carried something with it, a whisper of things to come. As it lifted her straight blonde bob away from her sweating neck more tears fell from her eyes. Her mother would be looking for her. She covered her face with her hands and took some deep breaths. Suddenly she felt something warm and wet on her cheek.

Startled, she looked up. A red kelpie sat beside her, trying to lick away her tears.

'Rack off!' she said, gently pushing the dog away.

'He's just being friendly,' came a voice from behind her.

She turned and saw the silhouette of a man holding a horse. He stepped into the shadow of a red gum so she could see him clearly. It was Billy O'Rourke.

'Don't you like dogs?' he asked.

'No! Yes. I mean I do, but I . . .'

'You *should* like dogs.'

Rosie looked up at Billy's weather-beaten face. He was smiling at her kindly from beneath a broad-brimmed hat. He held his horse's reins lightly in his tanned fingers. She had seen Billy by the river often in Casterton as he schooled nervous, green-broke horses. And he sauntered into *The Chronicle*'s office each week to file his livestock sales reports.

'I do like dogs,' she said.

'That's good, because I've got a job for you. Are you in the office tomorrow?'

'Yes,' Rosemary nodded. Unfortunately, she thought to herself.

'Good. See you then.' And he began to lead his horse away.

'Hang on! What's the job?'

He turned and winked at her. 'You'll see.' Then he walked back towards the track, his legs slightly bowed and his shoulders rounded from all those years of bending over sheep in shearing sheds.

The red kelpie watched him leave but stayed sitting by Rosemary's side. He thrust his warm nose under her hand, begging for a pat. As Rosemary rubbed his velvety ears, he laid his chin on her knee, looked up at her with his chocolate-brown eyes and sighed.

'What do you want?' Rosemary asked.

Then Billy whistled and the dog was gone.

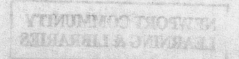

deep breaths. Suddenly she felt something warm and wet on her cheek.

Startled, she looked up. A red kelpie sat beside her, trying to lick away her tears.

'Rack off!' she said, gently pushing the dog away.

'He's just being friendly,' came a voice from behind her.

She turned and saw the silhouette of a man holding a horse. He stepped into the shadow of a red gum so she could see him clearly. It was Billy O'Rourke.

'Don't you like dogs?' he asked.

'No! Yes. I mean I do, but I . . .'

'You *should* like dogs.'

Rosie looked up at Billy's weather-beaten face. He was smiling at her kindly from beneath a broad-brimmed hat. He held his horse's reins lightly in his tanned fingers. She had seen Billy by the river often in Casterton as he schooled nervous, green-broke horses. And he sauntered into *The Chronicle*'s office each week to file his livestock sales reports.

'I do like dogs,' she said.

'That's good, because I've got a job for you. Are you in the office tomorrow?'

'Yes,' Rosemary nodded. Unfortunately, she thought to herself.

'Good. See you then.' And he began to lead his horse away.

'Hang on! What's the job?'

He turned and winked at her. 'You'll see.' Then he walked back towards the track, his legs slightly bowed and his shoulders rounded from all those years of bending over sheep in shearing sheds.

The red kelpie watched him leave but stayed sitting by Rosemary's side. He thrust his warm nose under her hand, begging for a pat. As Rosemary rubbed his velvety ears, he laid his chin on her knee, looked up at her with his chocolate-brown eyes and sighed.

'What do you want?' Rosemary asked.

Then Billy whistled and the dog was gone.

Also by Rachael Treasure

River Run Deep

Sometimes the hardest road is the one that leads home.

'From the road along the hillside, Rebecca couldn't bear to look at the sleepy green valley below. It tore her heart out to leave her river. Waters Meeting. Her place.'

But Rebecca's father has told her to get off the farm for ever, after she defied him once too often. In a family half-destroyed by anger and grief, Rebecca becomes an exile.

Heading north with her sheepdogs, she throws herself into a rollercoaster of work, parties and men – one of whom, the wildest and most handsome of them all, will capture her heart and turn her life upside down.

In this gripping story, set against the great open spaces of the Australian Outback, Rebecca Saunders faces a dreadful choice – follow the man of her heart to a place where she can never be happy, but where he must be, or return to the mountains to fight for the land and the river which runs through her soul. When finally tragedy strikes, she has to decide.

'Drama, fun, rocky romances and many adventures . . . By the end of this book, you yearn for a ute, a pair of boots, and the wide open spaces'

Australian Women's Weekly

Published by Preface   ISBN: 978 1 84809 085 9   £6.99

GZ 6/5/09
30/6/10 SK.